# BADGE OF GLORY

Douglas Reeman joined the Navy in 1941. He did convoy duty in the Atlantic, the Arctic, and the North Sea, and later served in motor torpedo boats.

As he says, 'I am always asked to account for the perennial appeal of the sea story, and its enduring interest for the people of so many nationalities and cultures. It would seem that the eternal and sometimes elusive triangle of man, ship and ocean, particularly under the stress of war, produces the best qualities of courage and compassion, irrespective of the rights and wrongs of conflict . . . The sea has no understanding of righteous or unjust causes. It is the common enemy, respected by all who serve on it, ignored at their peril.'

Apart from the many novels he has written under his own name, he has also written more than twenty historical novels featuring Richard Bolitho, under the pseudonym of Alexander Kent.

# BADGE OF GLORY

## Douglas Reeman

**arrow books**

First published by Arrow Books in 1983

19  20

Copyright © Highseas Authors ltd 1982

Douglas Reeman has asserted his right under the
Copyright, Designs and Patents Act, 1988 to be identified
as the author of this work

First published in the United Kingdom in 1982
by Hutchinson

Arrow Books
The Random House Group Limited
20 Vauxhall Bridge Road, London SW1V 2SA

Random House Australia (Pty) Limited
20 Alfred Street, Milsons Point, Sydney
New South Wales 2061, Australia

Random House New Zealand Limited
18 Poland Road, Glenfield
Auckland 10, New Zealand

Random House (Pty) Limited
Isle of Houghton, Corner of Boundary Road & Carse O'Gowrie,
Houghton 2198, South Africa

The Random House Group Limited Reg. No. 954009

www.randomhouse.co.uk

A CIP catalogue record for this book
is available from the British Library

The Random House Group Limited supports The Forest Stewardship
Council® (FSC®), the leading international forest-certification organisation.
Our books carrying the FSC label are printed on FSC®-certified paper.
FSC is the only forest-certification scheme supported by the leading
environmental organisations, including Greenpeace. Our
paper procurement policy can be found at
www.randomhouse.co.uk/environment

MIX
Paper from
responsible sources
FSC® C016897

ISBN 978 0 09 959405 5

Printed and bound in Great Britain by Clays Ltd, St Ives plc

For Winifred
with my love

## Acknowledgement

I wish to thank all the Royal Marines, past and present, who gave me their help and encouragement, and especially the Director and Staff of the Royal Marines Museum, Eastney and the RM Commando Training Centre at Lympstone.

# Contents

# Contents

# I

# *The Old Navy*

It was said that the August of 1850 was one of the hottest and finest anyone could remember. With only a few days left in the month it showed no sign of breaking, and on this particular evening the fleet anchored at Spithead breathed and quivered like molten gold. Only a certain mistiness around the Isle of Wight and longer shadows beneath the towering shapes of the assembled ships gave a hint that it was nearly sunset.

Between the land and the anchorage many smaller craft pulled busily back and forth, some connected with affairs of the fleet, and others, less expertly handled, to carry their untroubled passengers on sightseeing trips around the display of naval might.

One white-painted cutter thrust her way swiftly through the local traffic with what appeared to be casual ease. For she was one of the flagship's own boats, and woe betide anyone who was foolhardy enough to delay her passage.

In the sternsheets, his scarlet coatee making a bright contrast with the uniforms of the coxswain and the midshipman in charge, Captain Philip Blackwood looked around, surprised that he had almost reached the flagship and had barely noticed he had left the shore.

He searched his emotions for the hundredth time. Did he feel resignation or apathy, resentment or excitement? There seemed to be nothing at all. Like a clock which has stopped for no recognizable reason.

He glanced at the biggest vessel which was anchored at the

head of the line. Her Majesty's Ship *Audacious* of ninety guns, the squadron's flagship, and somehow a symbol of Britain's unchallenged sea power. She was not old, but had been laid down and built to a design which had barely altered since Trafalgar, nearly half a century ago. She seemed to grow and expand as the cutter glided closer, and Blackwood saw a levelled telescope at the entry port as his approach was watched and reported.

Everything appeared to be exactly the same as when he had left two weeks ago to spend his leave with his father in Hampshire. During those weeks he had made up his mind, or thought he had. He had sent his marine attendant on ahead to deliver a letter to his lieutenant, the only other marine officer in the ship, and to pack his personal belongings in readiness to leave for the barracks. Blackwood had broken his own journey to face the colonel commandant at Forton Barracks. It had not been an easy interview, and in his mind Blackwood could still feel the dry stillness of the room, hear the distorted cries of a drill sergeant on the square as new recruits pounded up and down under musket and full pack.

Colonel Menzies had said in his calm, unemotional tone, 'Resign the Corps? *Bloody rubbish*.' One eyebrow had risen slightly. 'What did you *expect* me to say, man?'

Everything Blackwood had prepared, each carefully thought out reason had seemed to wither away like dead leaves under the colonel's unhurried appraisal.

'I served with your father. I respect him. And what of your grandfather? Another fine marine. A great man.'

At any other time Blackwood might have smiled. The colonel commandant's admiration for the Blackwood family had stopped there. All the others had been soldiers.

Colonel Menzies had pressed his fingertips together and stared up from his desk.

'You are twenty-six years old, and already a captain. You have proved your worth on active service, so one will aid the other. In these days of peace it is not easy to gain advancement, especially in the Corps. But there is no reason why you should not be an asset to us, and a link in your family's tradition.'

Looking back over the last hours Blackwood could remember little of his own voice in that quiet room.

Menzies had finished the interview in an almost matter of fact fashion.

'In any case, it is out of the question, at present. I have been told that the squadron will proceed to sea within the week. To replace the flagship's senior marine officer at this stage . . .' Even his austere face had cracked slightly. '. . . Twenty-six years old or not, would be unthinkable. I am required to send additional marines to the squadron, many of whom will be new recruits. Officers and NCOs with combat experience will be like gold nuggets.'

'My request is dismissed then, Colonel?' They were the only words he could recall.

'What request, Blackwood?' It was over.

'*Boat ahoy!*' A challenge from the flagship's gangway brought him back to earth with a jerk.

The coxswain cupped his hands. '*Aye, aye!*'

Perhaps that was it, Blackwood thought. The tradition before all else. The gangway staff knew this was one of the *Audacious*'s boats, and the duty officer would already have been told that Captain Blackwood, Royal Marines, was returning on board. He sighed and grasped his sword scabbard firmly in his left hand.

The playful enmity between seamen and marines was still there, another tradition. He was not going to stoke anyone's fire by tripping over his sword under the eyes of the side-party or by falling headlong into the Solent.

He pulled himself swiftly up the tumblehome and onto the gangway, conscious that he was no longer breathless in doing so. Two weeks ashore after the close confines of a crowded ship had worked wonders for him. Long walks around the estate, riding every day with his half-sister Georgina. It was already like part of a dream, made more so as the ship opened out as if to swallow him.

Blackwood touched his shako to the quarterdeck and nod-ded to the side-party. To his surprise, his lieutenant, Dick Cleveland, was not there to greet him, and instead the towering figure of Colour-Sergeant M'Crystal waited with obvious impatience for him to speak with the officer-of-the-watch.

The latter said quickly, 'There's been a change, Major.' He sounded harassed, on edge.

Blackwood waited. Once again tradition had spoken. Always the captain of marines was referred to as major, but had anyone, he wondered, ever in the past confused him with a ship's commanding officer?

'The Flag has shifted.'

Blackwood felt a tinge of warning. Menzies had said nothing about that. A new admiral for the squadron. It should have been worth mentioning, surely.

'The captain left word for you to see him as soon as you came off shore, sir.'

'And what about my lieutenant?'

The officer-of-the-watch stared at him as if that was of no importance at all compared with the awesome responsibility of receiving a new admiral.

'Mr Cleveland's broken his leg.' He flushed. 'There was a party aboard *Swiftsure*.'

Blackwood controlled his features with an effort. The lieutenant need say no more. Parties in other ships were always Cleveland's true weakness. After a few glasses he seemed to go wild. Now a broken leg had taken him from *Audacious* when he was really needed.

Blackwood said curtly, 'I'll see the captain.'

He nodded to Colour-Sergeant M'Crystal. Thank God he at least was here. To some people M'Crystal appeared fright-ening. He was tall and solidly built yet without an ounce of spare flesh on his frame. His scarlet coatee matching his face which, in spite of long service ashore and afloat, refused to tan and remained brick-red. Blackwood had known him since he had been commissioned at the age of eighteeen. M'Crystal had not always been a sergeant, and his stripes had gone up and down with his misfortunes and his hasty temper. But Blackwood had seen the real worth of the man. In New Zealand, just four years back during the Maori War, he had watched M'Crystal rally a handful of marines when they had been outnumbered by ten to one.

'What is it, Colour-Sergeant?'

M'Crystal ran his eyes over the youthful captain as if to reassure himself about something. It felt like an inspection.

He said in his thick voice, 'You heard about Mr Cleveland, sir, in Haslar Hospital. Took a fall, he did.' Without any change of expression he hurried on, 'New admiral's coming aboard tomorrow forenoon, sir. Full guard and ceremonial required, o' course. Twenty new privates have joined today and Sarnt Quintin is settling 'em into the barracks right now. Private Doak is under arrest for drunkenness.'

'I see.' Blackwood waited. There was more to come. Anything short of mutiny would be accepted as normal routine by M'Crystal and his crony, Sergeant Quintin.

'You've not seen the orders yet, sir?' He did not wait. 'The flag-officer to command this squadron is Sir James Ashley-Chute.'

'Come aft to my quarters.'

Blackwood fell in step with the towering sergeant and together they ducked their heads beneath the poop and made for the companion ladder. It was strange he had just been remembering M'Crystal's courage in New Zealand just four years ago. Vice-Admiral Sir James Ashley-Chute's appointment to command the squadron would have roused a few memories for him also. No wonder Colonel Menzies had made no mention of it. To be in the same squadron was bad enough. In the same ship was far worse.

Blackwood could picture the ferocious fighting on North Island as if it had just happened. Blazing sun, choking clouds of dust and musket smoke as the army had fought to overthrow the well-defended Maori stronghold at Ruapekapeka. A contingent of seamen had been landed earlier to relieve pressure on the troops. Ashley-Chute had been in overall charge of the operation, and had seemed determined that no matter what the army attempted, his men could and would do better. Things went badly wrong from the outset. Unused to fighting ashore, the blue-jackets soon got themselves separated from the soldiers and were hemmed in by hundreds of the battle-crazed Maoris. Blackwood felt a chill at his spine as he relived the sights and the terrifying yells of the attacking Maoris.

M'Crystal had been a corporal at the time, having lost his sergeant's stripes after a brawl with a ship's cook.

The major in command of the marines had requested permission to attack and relieve the beleaguered seamen. Ashley-Chute had sent back a curt refusal. The major had snapped angrily, 'At least I *asked* him, dammit!' Then, drawing his sword, he had yelled above the din, 'Royal Marines will advance! *Fix bayonets!*'

There had been less than fifty marines, and twenty-five had fallen before the enemy had retreated and the stronghold had been taken. The naval commander had been grateful enough, but Ashley-Chute had sent an immediate summons for the major to report to him with an explanation for his actions.

Seeing Blackwood, then a lieutenant, he had snapped. 'I sent for your commanding officer! Has he not the courage to face me?'

Blackwood had been shaking with fatigue and the delayed shock of the short, savage fight. It had taken all his strength to place his list of casualties on the admiral's table.

'The major is among the dead, sir.'

There had been no sign of remorse or pity, not even the satisfaction of knowing that the marines' action had saved a terrible loss of life and almost certain defeat.

He had said coldly, 'Just as well for him.'

M'Crystal was watching him grimly. 'There was talk of you leaving the Corps, sir.'

Blackwood looked at him and smiled. There were no secrets in any ship or barracks.

'It was *just* talk.'

M'Crystal beamed. 'Good. I'll pass the word, sir.'

Blackwood thrust open the door of his cabin and stepped into its familiar surroundings. There was no sign of a chest or case, and he could see his uniforms hanging in their canvas wardrobe, swaying very slowly as the great ship tugged at her cable.

Smithett, his personal attendant for two years, seemed to dominate the small cabin. He was almost as tall as M'Crystal, but whereas the colour-sergeant was fierce or joyful as the mood took him, Smithett was always the same. He was a dour, dull-faced man, with all his lines turning down. His eyes, his mouth, even his chin, seemed to be set in permanent disapproval. Fortunately, Blackwood had grown to understand him and to appreciate his many skills. Servant, orderly, Smithett could turn his hand to various things which were never mentioned in regulations. He had volunteered for the work of marine officer's attendant, and when Blackwood had asked him why, Smithett had given as near as he dared to a shrug and had replied, 'Knew yer father, sir.' And that, apparently, was that.

Blackwood sat down on the edge of his cot.

'You didn't pack my gear then.'

Their eyes met.

Smithett said, 'No point, sir. We're sailin' next week.'

Blackwood could feel his earlier resolve fading away. M'Crystal's anxious scrutiny, Smithett's positive belief that he would not quit the Corps and all that it stood for had a lot to do with it.

When he had faced his father on the first day of his leave he had expected a rebuke, even a show of contempt. Lieutenant-Colonel Eugene Blackwood would still be on active service if he had his way. But promotion was restricted, and in peacetime any officer who wanted an appointment was considered fortunate to gain one.

But his father had said, 'I know you, Philip. You want action. You think that is all there is to being a marine. Action and glory. There are many like you, men who forget that it is continuity of service and training which count. A month of war requires years of experience and leadership.'

Blackwood had tried to describe his feelings when he had seen his own commanding officer fall in the Maori War. It had seemed senseless for a man like him to die out there in a place nobody had ever heard of.

But as he had tried to explain he had felt the same inner uncertainty as when he had faced the colonel commandant. Perhaps his father was right. Action and glory, was that what he really wanted for himself?

He thought suddenly of his grandfather. What had Menzies said of him? *A great man.* Curiously, Blackwood had always felt closer to his grandfather than his father. As a boy he had grown up with the old man's memories, had seen the pale eyes above the white whiskers light up from within as he had told and retold the stories of places and ships he had known. Names painted in history. The Nile. Copenhagen. Trafalgar. In memory it was always the same, with no gaps of fear or boredom in between. The old man had died in the same house where Blackwood had tried to persuade his father to see his point of view.

It might have been different if his mother was still alive, he thought. But she had died after a short fever, and Blackwood's father had remarried the following year to a girl twenty years younger than himself.

Perhaps his father had been too worried about his own news to care much for his son's uncertainty over his future.

He had eventually dropped his announcement with the forthrightness of a thirty-two-pound shot.

'We're selling Hawks Hill, Philip. Your mother, er, Claudia intends we should move to London. It's her sort of world, y'see.'

Blackwood frowned as he thought about it. He felt Smithett running a brush over his shoulders, patting his coatee into place. Routine and order.

It was unthinkable to be leaving Hawks Hill and the estate

in Hampshire. His father obviously hated the idea but, as usual, would do anything for his wife. The colonel's lady, as they called her in the village. They had never really accepted her, but then she had done little to encourage the 'local bumpkins', as she called them.

Blackwood said, 'I am going to see the captain. Tomorrow we shall have to do something about getting another lieutenant sent to us.'

It was always easy to say 'we' and 'us' to Smithett. Rather as you might to a faithful dog. He never answered back, but could make his displeasure known in other ways when he felt like it.

He picked up his shako and left the cabin. For a moment longer he paused and glanced aft towards the great cabin and private quarters where the admiral would hold court. It would be even worse for the ship's officers, he thought, unless they knew Ashley-Chute's little ways.

With a sigh Blackwood ran lightly up the companion ladder and turned towards the shadowy confines of the poop. In the short while he had been in his cabin it had grown dark. Around and beneath him the great ship of the line groaned and murmured, her massive timbers and towering masts and rigging keeping up their constant chorus as they had since the day she had first slid into salt water.

The smells too were like part of himself. Paint and tar, cordage and damp canvas. The old navy. Blackwood stopped short within view of the scarlet-coated sentry outside the stern cabin. That too might be a reason. He did not *want* to stay with a navy which seemed content to remain old and unchanged. Young officers were volunteering to serve in the discomfort and dirt of the new steam vessels simply because they *were* new, and young like themselves.

The marine sentry's heels came together with a snap, and the level stare beneath the man's shako fixed on a point above Blackwood's left epaulette.

Blackwood gave a grave smile. 'Good evening, Rocke.'

'Sar!' Rocke shot a quick grin.

Blackwood rapped on the screen door, wondering if he would ever discover a way of knowing which of the Rocke twins he was speaking to. Even standing together in the same squad they were completely alike. Sergeant Quintin knew they changed duties to suit themselves, but had never been able to prove it. The twins came from Somerset, and their father had been a marine too.

It was so often like that. As one sergeant had said, 'In the Corps we don't recruit marines. We breeds 'em!'

The door opened and the captain's clerk ushered Blackwood inside.

Blackwood walked aft and saw the glittering lights of the anchored ships through the great stern windows, distorted like fairy lanterns by the thick glass.

He was back. Whatever it was he had tried to fight was far stronger than he had imagined.

Captain John Ackworthy half rose from his chair and sank down again. He was a heavy man, with shaggy grey eyebrows and a face like tooled leather, criss-crossed with hundreds of tiny lines. Ackworthy was old for his rank, and had been at sea all his life from the age of twelve. *Audacious* would be his last command, and was certainly the biggest vessel he had ever served. With the previous admiral, who had been old like himself, he had felt content, and had accepted that he would never bridge the gulf to flag rank. When *Audacious* paid off, Captain Ackworthy would join all the other ancient mariners on the beach.

The swift change of events and the appointment of a new flag-officer in command had unsettled him considerably. There were four ships of the line in the squadron, and Ackworthy would willingly have taken command of the oldest and smallest to avoid having a vice-admiral's flag flying at the fore, especially one with a reputation like Ashley-Chute's.

He regarded the marine officer thoughtfully. Blackwood looked strained, and his jaw was set just a bit too tightly. Ackworthy had never really understood marines, but he had liked Blackwood from their first meeting. He had removed his shako and his brown hair was surprisingly tousled, so that he looked even younger. He had clean-cut features and level grey-blue eyes. A reliable English face, but one you might never know in a thousand years, Ackworthy decided.

'Sit you down, Major. I want to talk about tomorrow.' He glanced meaningly at the deckhead as if he could pierce it with a glance and already see the vice-admiral's flag breaking at the foremast truck.

Blackwood listened as Ackworthy rambled on about the admiral's time of arrival at Portsmouth Point, the requirements for guard and band, the need for a perfect turn-out from captain to ship's boy.

Did Captain Ackworthy know about Ashley-Chute's nickname, he wondered? *Monkey*. Very apt too. Perhaps he had changed after four years. It seemed unlikely.

Blackwood had often wondered if there had been any official enquiry or action taken by the Admiralty over Ashley-Chute's failure to recognize the danger to his landing parties at North Island on that terrible day. If so, it had been kept very quiet. But Ashley-Chute was still of the same rank, and for someone so ambitious it might be possible he had been quietly laid aside like Ackworthy. In which case he would be doubly determined to force his stamp on the squadron without delay.

Ackworthy ruffled through some papers on his table. 'Almost forgot. Guard-boat brought a message from Forton Barracks. A marine second lieutenant will be joining the ship tomorrow. Sounds as if he may be straight from training. Don't even know his name yet. But all the same . . .' He did not finish.

Blackwood gauged the moment. They were alone except for Ackworthy's cabin servant, who was probably waiting in his pantry for the call to bring in some of the captain's claret.

He said, 'May I ask what orders we are under, sir?'

Ackworthy pouted his lower lip. 'We are assuming the duties of the West African Squadron. For how long and to what purpose I cannot say at present.' He frowned so that his eyes almost vanished. 'I'd be obliged if you would not mention anything about it.'

Blackwood nodded. 'Of course, sir.' Poor old devil. You're scared of Monkey and he's not even here yet.

The servant entered quietly and placed a tray and glasses on the table, then withdrew just as softly.

Ackworthy picked up a decanter and held it to the deckhead lantern. In his great fist it looked like a flask.

'I understand you served with Sir James Ashley-Chute before?' He poured two glasses with elaborate care. 'That affair in New Zealand, wasn't it?'

Blackwood sipped the wine. 'Yes, sir. In forty-six.' He waited, the wine moistening his throat, calming him.

'I have a new third lieutenant since you went on leave.' Ackworthy poured himself another glass and some of the wine slopped across his papers. He did not seem to notice. 'Thought you should know. He's Sir James's son.' He moved violently away from the table and stared through the stern windows. 'As if I don't have enough trouble on my plate!' He seemed to realize he had exposed his feelings too much in front of a subordinate and added harshly, 'Just make certain your marines put on a good display tomorrow.' He turned away from the windows. 'I expect you've got things to do.'

Blackwood stood up. 'Yes, sir. And thank you.'

Ackworthy shrugged. 'Glad you're staying under my command, by the way.'

Blackwood left the cabin and walked slowly towards the quarterdeck. The West African Squadron. It was a long way to go. When he came home again there would be no house, no familiar places to walk and ride.

He thought then of his half-sister Georgina. She was sixteen, with the wild beauty of a young foal. She had kissed him goodbye this morning, was it only today? She had not acted like a sister, nor had he felt like a brother towards her as she had pressed against him. Perhaps West Africa was just about the right distance after all.

Colour-Sergeant M'Crystal and his friend Sergeant Quintin stood motionless in the shadows as Blackwood approached the glowing rectangle of the companionway.

M'Crystal said in a hoarse whisper, 'There he goes, Joe. Cool as steel. Nothing to worry about.'

Quintin grunted. 'We'll see about that, Hamish. You just get this bloody commission over an' done with, *an'* with yer stripes still on yer arm, *then* I'll believe yer!'

As the first pale stars glittered above the gently spiralling mastheads, the ship and the eight hundred and fifty souls who served her settled down to wait for the new day which might change things for all of them.

'Got a good day for it, sir.' Smithett flicked a piece of invisible dust from Blackwood's coatee and regarded him unsmilingly.

Blackwood was used to him and knew that he would never have to worry about taking a parade with some fault in his uniform or equipment. He glanced at himself in the mirror above his small writing table and grimaced. Perhaps he was making too much of Ashley-Chute's arrival. Maybe they all were. He sighed and said, 'Keep a weather-eye open for the new second lieutenant.'

He climbed up the companion ladder knowing that Smithett would vanish until the ceremonial was over.

On deck the sunlight was bright and the reflections across the Solent harsh to the eyes. Since the hands had been roused and then piped to breakfast after the decks had been washed down, a sort of expectancy had fallen over the whole ship.

Blackwood tugged on his white gloves and glanced quickly along the upper deck.

Every line and halliard neatly flaked or turned on its belaying pin, each strand of rigging taut and stiff like black glass. On either side of the deck, partly hidden by the two gangways which linked forecastle to quarterdeck, the upper batteries of twelve-pounders looked as if they had been positioned with the aid of a carpenter's rule.

He shifted his glance to the marine guard and the smaller figures of the boy fifers who were being lectured by Corporal Bly.

Across the poop there were further ranks of marines, and he guessed that Sergeant Quintin had had the good sense to place the new recruits as far aft as he could manage so that they would not disgrace him.

He walked slowly towards the guard, his eyes automatically picking out the familiar faces, the expressions which disguised their owners' backgrounds which were as varied as their names.

That was one of the main differences between a marine and a seaman, he thought. Sailors usually came from ports and harbours, or very close to the sea, whereas marines were often recruited miles inland, or joined to follow a family tradition. Marines were trained ashore, and seamen had to learn from the moment they stepped aboard their ship, from the deck up, and from the deck down.

The marines were standing in loose lines, their long muskets at their sides, their ranks rolling slightly to the ship's motion.

Colour-Sergeant M'Crystal tapped the deck gently with his half-pike. 'Marines . . .'

He did not shout or raise his voice. It was more like a deep rumble. But Blackwood saw the ranks of scarlet coatees and white trousers stiffen, as if an invisible force had thrust rods right through each line of men.

M'Crystal reported, 'Ready for inspection, *sir*.'

Blackwood walked slowly along each rank. He could feel the officers watching from the quarterdeck, the seamen who were working aloft in the shrouds or on the yards pausing in their search for last-minute faults to stare down as the marines went through their ritual.

Beneath the peak of each Albert shako he caught a brief glimpse of a blank, expressionless face. Like the white cross-belts and gleaming bayonets, it was part of the whole, but to Blackwood every one was different. Corporal Jones who fancied himself as a prize-fighter. Private Callow who had dived overboard to rescue a seaman who had fallen from the main-yard. Private Frazier who had been with him in New Zealand, a superb shot, but a man who shied away from promotion as if it was poison. The Rocke twins, like mirror images. M'Crystal had said that if one cut himself shaving the other would do the same to sustain the confusion. Private Bulford who had run away from home to enlist. Later they had discovered it was because his father was in jail for robbery.

It was a good turn-out, as he had expected. How they managed it in their quarters, called as always the barracks, he could barely imagine. Especially with the extra marines who had been sent across from the shore. And why did they need additional men anyway? There should be enough aboard the four ships of the line and their two frigates for any normal activity.

The midshipman-of-the-watch called in a shrill voice, 'Barge has left the sallyport, sir!'

The quarterdeck stirred into life immediately. As another midshipman ran to inform the captain, boatswain's mates stood at the entry port, moistening their silver calls on their lips in readiness to greet the new lord and master.

Seamen vanished from the yards, and those still on deck were dressed in their best uniforms, their horny feet confined uncomfortably in shoes.

Blackwood glanced at the quarterdeck where the lieutenants and senior warrant officers were lined up in sweating discomfort. It was unusual to see them all together except for special parades. Cocked hats and gold lace, swords and gloves. His glance settled on a short, pale-faced lieutenant in the front rank. That had to be Ashley-Chute's son. The same short legs which made his arms dangle at his sides as if they were too heavy for him. He felt a tinge of sympathy even though he did not know him. Blackwood had always managed to avoid serving under his own father, he had heard too many tales about the rift it could cause. Like the teacher whose son attends the same school and must therefore be the brightest pupil, no matter what.

Captain Ackworthy, even bulkier and more impressive in his full dress uniform, appeared on deck. He had probably been standing in his cabin listening and waiting, Blackwood thought.

Blackwood turned his head slightly and looked across the glistening water. There were plenty of local craft about again, and he could see the upturned faces and the bright colours of women's clothing as they bobbed around the anchored ships. The guard-boat pulled warily amongst them, just in case one might try to get too close on this special day.

Eight bells chimed out from the forecastle, and from the corner of his eye Blackwood saw *Audacious*'s dark green barge turning in a neat arc for the final approach to the main-chains. Through the arched backs of the bargemen he could see the cocked hat of the passenger. Behind him, one of the ship's lieutenants stood with the coxswain as if he was carved out of wood.

'Stand by on the quarterdeck!'

The marine fifers raised their instruments or adjusted their drums, and Blackwood drew his sword, recalling with sudden clarity that day he had faced Ashley-Chute across the table, the day the major had drawn his sword and had died leading his men.

Colour-Sergeant M'Crystal hissed in a fierce whisper, 'God Almighty, sir!'

It was so unlike M'Crystal to lose his self-control during a ceremonial parade that it was somehow worse than if he had shouted a terrible obscenity.

Blackwood saw another boat pulling purposefully towards the *Audacious*. It must have come around the stern when everyone was watching the opposite direction. It was a small boat, probably from Gosport, not that it mattered now. It had only one passenger, and Blackwood could well appreciate the strength of M'Crystal's feelings. There was no mistaking the uniform of a Royal Marines second lieutenant.

Captain Ackworthy opened and closed his mouth but no sound emerged.

It fell to Netten, *Audacious*'s first lieutenant, to yell, 'Stand away there!'

The guard-boat too had realized what was happening and increased speed to intercept the waterman. Unfortunately, one of her oarsmen lost the stroke and vanished into the bottom, legs kicking wildly, to the delight of the boy fifers. They were too young to realize the enormity of the disaster.

The barge hooked onto the chains, the oars rising like white bones as the side-boys steadied the gunwale against *Audacious*'s fat hull.

Then all was drowned by the shrill of calls, the stamp and crack of muskets being brought to the present and the fifers' rendering of 'Heart of Oak'.

Blackwood brought his sword down with a flourish and watched narrowly beneath the shadow of his peak as the cocked hat and epaulettes of Vice-Admiral Sir James Ashley-Chute, KCB, appeared at the top of the ladder.

He looked much the same, but older. He still wore his cocked hat at a rakish angle. If his subordinates had dared to wear their hats in anything but a fore and aft position they would have imagined the heavens had fallen on them.

A broad, puggy nose and large iron-grey sideburns, and the disdainful stare which Blackwood remembered so well. His mouth was set in a thin line, as if he had no lips at all. He was carrying a pair of white gloves and he flicked his hat with them, more like a dismissal than a salute.

As Ackworthy hurried to meet him he made the vice-admiral look even smaller. But only in stature, Blackwood thought. Somehow Ashley-Chute's tightly packed belligerence seemed to reduce the captain to shambling awkwardness.

'Welcome aboard, Sir James.'

The admiral's eyes moved across the guard of honour and rested just for a second on M'Crystal. They shifted to the ship, the neatly furled sails, the assembled lieutenants and the blue press of seamen on the upper deck.

'Quite so, Captain Ackworthy.' He slapped his palm with his gloves in time with his words. 'A fine looking ship.' Ackworthy's smile vanished as the little admiral added crisply, 'But then I have the right to insist on excellence, hmm?'

For the first time his eyes settled on Blackwood. 'You may fall out the guard. Very smart. As I would expect on such an occasion and with ample notice, hmm?'

'Would you care to meet the officers, sir?' Ackworthy sounded already lost.

'Later. I would like to see my quarters. My flag-lieutenant is arriving shortly with further stores for my use. You may however make a signal to the squadron for all captains to repair on board in two hours time.'

Ackworthy lowered his voice. 'I think Captain Boyd of the *Argyll* may be ashore, sir.'

Ashley-Chute glanced up at him curiously. 'I said *all* captains. Please see to it.'

He turned towards the poop and then hesitated. Without turning his head he said, 'There appeared to be a marine officer of sorts attempting to approach my flagship in a fashion more suited to a Spanish fisherman. See that he is disciplined. Or get rid of him, please attend to that also.'

As Ackworthy followed the admiral into the shadow of the poop the first lieutenant breathed out very slowly.

To Blackwood he said softly, 'Well, Major, a fine beginning, eh?'

The dismissed guard tramped past to make their way below, but M'Crystal waited behind, fuming as if he would burst into flames. Beneath his shako his ginger hair added to his appearance of barely controlled fury.

'I'll get that officer's name for you, sir!'

Blackwood eyed him gravely. 'No need, Colour-Sergeant. His name is the same as mine.'

As Lieutenant Netten had just remarked, it was a fine beginning.

# 2

# Of One Company

Philip Blackwood sat at his small writing table and glanced over the duty roster which M'Crystal and Quintin had prepared. He noticed that the new recruits had been carefully spread amongst the more experienced sections, and knew his NCOs would be quick to make further changes if the need arose.

He thought of the days since Vice-Admiral Sir James Ashley-Chute's flag had broken at the masthead. After the brisk scrutiny of the assembled officers and marine guard they had barely seen anything of him. Nothing had changed, Blackwood thought, not even that old idiosyncrasy which had stamped him like a hallmark. On the New Zealand station he had been notorious for his aloofness. He was rarely seen to speak to junior officers, let alone common seamen, but made his wrath felt through his captains. It was odd, but Blackwood could not recall Ashley-Chute ever being known for awarding a word of praise about anything.

The captains of the squadron had come aboard the flagship regularly each forenoon and had entered the admiral's quarters like men going to the scaffold. They had left in their various boats, with no word being exchanged but for the necessity of ceremony.

Blackwood leaned back in his chair and listened to the great ship around him. Ashley-Chute was like a force within the hull. The ship felt heavy with it.

He thought too of the army of carpenters and working parties which had converged on the admiral's quarters almost

within an hour of his arrival. Officers had been moved from
their cabins and made to share with others on the deck below.
Screens had been extended, fresh furniture brought from the
shore, and many of the guns withdrawn from the cabin ports
and replaced by cut down Quakers or wooden replicas to give
more space in Ashley-Chute's quarters. His flag-lieutenant, a
nervous, stiff-faced man named Pelham, was frequently seen
dashing ashore in the duty boat or rushing back again with
some important message for his master.

But apart from a rare glimpse of the great man on the poop
perhaps at sunset, or looking from the stern gallery of his
cabin, the admiral remained withdrawn from his ship and her
company.

Blackwood took up a pen and hesitated as he saw the name
of his junior officer at the top of the list. H. Blackwood,
RM2L.

As they had faced each other on the day of the admiral's
displeasure, Blackwood could remember his feelings of
annoyance, and something else perhaps, shame?

Harry Blackwood, his eighteen-year-old half-brother, was
too like Georgina for comfort. The same recklessness in the
eyes, the way of being serious and mocking at the same time.

It was not easy to be angry with him because of his
eagerness to join his first ship, even at the expense of infuriating the admiral and of course Colour-Sergeant M'Crystal.

Calls trilled overhead, and he heard the muffled cries of
boatswain's mates as they yelled at the working parties on
deck to stand easy and prepare for the midday meal.

It would be good to get away from England, Blackwood
thought suddenly. He was sick of all the uncertainties about
his father's proposed move to London, about his own feeble
attempts to resign his commission, about so many things.

He signed the list with an angry flourish and wished he
could go ashore for one last walk through the untroubled
crowds who were taking advantage of the late summer. But
he knew it would be too risky to leave his young second-in-
command to deal with the affairs of the flagship and a crowd

of new recruits as well. He must stay aboard and keep an eye on him without his knowing it.

But to face one more lunch in the wardroom with all the unspoken questions, the sense of uneasiness which pervaded it like an extension of the admiral's moods, was unbearable.

They had all received a surprise this morning, those who did not yet know of Ashley-Chute's habits. There was to be a 'grand reception' on board before sailing. In the afternoon there would be a squadron race for the fastest boat's crew. The ship's company would provide entertainment with hornpipes and other dances, and *then*, Vice-Admiral Ashley-Chute would entertain his own personal guests to dinner in his quarters.

A handful of the squadron's officers would also attend the dinner. The captains, the flag-lieutenant, Ashley-Chute's son and, to Blackwood's amazement, himself.

He walked to an open gunport and leaned out to look at the Solent. Calm and with barely a breeze to ruffle its surface. It was to be hoped it remained so until after the admiral's guests had come and gone.

There were plenty of boats still clustered along the ship's side. Food and stores, equipment and spare rigging, everything a ship-of-war might need on a passage to the shores of Africa.

Blackwood thought of his grandfather. It was as if he could still hear the old man's voice as he had retold the stories of great campaigns, the horror and comradeship of battles long past.

Now, when *Audacious* broke out her anchor and led the squadron away from her home port, she would meet nothing but servile foreign traders who would willingly dip their ensigns to Victoria's unchallenged might on the oceans. Routine, ceremonial, drills and more routine.

There was a tap at the door and he turned to see Second Lieutenant Harry Blackwood standing stiffly in the entrance.

'Come in.'

The youthful officer closed the screen door behind him and took up the same stance of eager attention.

Blackwood gestured to the other chair. 'Sit down, for God's sake, Harry.'

The lieutenant sat and crossed his legs, his eyes fixed on his half-brother with a mixture of innocence and amusement.

'I want you to go round the ship with one of the lieutenants and learn all you can while we've got the time.' Blackwood felt irritated with himself that he should sound on the defensive. He added shortly, 'Colour-Sergeant M'Crystal will put you right about the duties for our people. *Listen* to him, and do not try to be clever. He has little confidence in junior officers.' He smiled in spite of the tension between them. 'I certainly had to earn *my* spurs from him!'

Harry Blackwood asked quietly, 'We are to sail on the day after tomorrow, sir? To Africa.' His tongue lingered on the word like a caress. 'I am so *lucky* to be coming with you.'

Blackwood studied him warily. There was a certain softness to Harry's mouth. A gentleness, like his sister's.

He asked abruptly, 'How *did* you get a last moment transfer to *Audacious*, by the way? You were at Woolwich. I'd have thought a replacement could have been more easily sent from Portsmouth.' It came out like an accusation.

The lieutenant shrugged. 'It was mostly coincidence, sir. I had been told I was to join a Portsmouth ship very shortly, but when I heard about the squadron needing more marines, I made enquiries about vacancies for officers.' He dropped his eyes beneath Blackwood's gaze. 'Then, er, Mother spoke to someone and hastened things.'

Blackwood nodded slowly. 'Did she indeed?'

So there it was. Whether this squadron's duties were to be important or not was open to question, but in times of peace any activity outside ceremonial visits to foreign harbours was a rare opportunity for a young officer embarking on a new career, sailor or marine.

And the colonel's lady would be the first to recognize such a chance, he thought grimly.

He relented and said, 'You may not be as lucky as you

think, my lad. I am no favourite of the admiral's, but I expect you already know that?'

Harry Blackwood eyed him mildly. 'Really, sir?'

'So keep on your toes. For the sake of the men, if not for me. They're a reliable lot of fellows. Rough and ready, but they'll give as good as they get. So stand up for them. No matter what.'

Harry's eyes followed him across the small cabin. 'Even if they're in the wrong?'

Blackwood looked down at him. 'Yes, if need be. We'll deal with our own, in our own way, understood?'

He wondered why he was speaking like this. Did he resent sharing it with a member of his family? Or was he really so protective of something he had so recently tried to leave?

Harry Blackwood was at the door again, his shako balanced in the crook of his arm.

Blackwood waited. 'Well?'

'What's it like, sir?' He kept his gaze fixed on Blackwood's face. 'I've never really had the chance to know you in recent years. Either you've been at sea or I've been away somewhere.' He shrugged, the gesture making him look even younger and more vulnerable. 'But to *kill* someone. In battle. What is it really like?'

Blackwood turned away. The question had hit him like a fist. Maybe because at one time he had asked it so often himself.

'You don't think about it, Harry. You put your shoulder against that of a friend and you keep going. No matter what is happening or how bad it looks. Afterwards . . .' He glanced down at the deck. 'Well, maybe you remember pieces of the whole, I'm not sure even now.' He met his gaze steadily, knowing it was important. 'But to kill a man is just a part of it. Like loading and firing a gun. You do it right, or you go under.'

Corporal Bly hovered in the passageway, and as the lieutenant withdrew he reported, 'Gangway sentries ready for inspection, *sir*.'

The young lieutenant tugged the shako down across his forehead and followed Bly towards the companion ladder.

Blackwood saw Smithett waiting to tidy the cabin after he had gone to lunch. Nothing seemed to matter to the taciturn marine, Blackwood thought. If the squadron completed a full three year commission on that inhospitable African coast he would not care. But if they were away that long Blackwood would be nearly thirty when he returned, whereas Harry would still only be twenty-one with his whole life ahead of him.

'Damn and bloody hell!'

Smithett paused in brushing one of Blackwood's tunics. 'Sir?'

'Nothing.' He smiled ruefully. 'The usual feeling, I suppose.'

Smithett hung the jacket carefully on a rail. 'There's nothin' ashore for me, sir.' He glanced around the cabin as if it were his own. 'This is the life. In me ship. With me mates.'

It was the longest sentence Blackwood had ever heard him make, and he was strangely moved by his sincerity.

He left the cabin, still thinking about Smithett. Perhaps it was better to be like him. No thought for the impossible or the improbable. Just one day at a time. He chuckled to himself. 'With me mates.'

'By God, Captain Ackworthy, I do declare that *Audacious*'s cutter is in the lead!' Ashley-Chute moved his telescope slightly to watch the other boats in the race and added, 'Just as well, hmm?'

Ackworthy said nothing, and Blackwood, who was standing nearby on the quarterdeck, saw the captain's hands opening and closing as if to restrain his feelings. Only a week, and yet Ackworthy seemed to have aged even further.

And yet on the face of it everything was going well. The weather was clear and warm, although the evening would have a nip in it, and the snaking currents of the Solent looked harder and more silvery.

From the forenoon onwards the ship had steadily filled with visitors, some important, some less so. Local dignitaries and their wives, the port admiral and the senior captains from around the harbour. The marine fifers played lively jigs, and a small orchestra which had been brought specially from Southampton was ready to fill any gaps in the entertainment.

There was one very important visitor who was also a personal guest of the admiral. Sir Geoffrey Slade was known to be a top-ranking government adviser on overseas develop-ment, a man who was said to be equally at home in Court and in Parliament.

He seemed a quiet, unassuming man, quite at odds with his formidable reputation, and Blackwood wondered what he and Ashley-Chute could have in common.

But the eyes of everyone, from midshipman to first lieutenant, had been on the girl who had come aboard with Sir Geoffrey Slade. Young but sure of herself, Blackwood decided, with dark, almost black hair and a face which could make your head swim. She was Slade's niece, and that was all he knew about her. Yet.

There were plenty of other lady guests, and their presence swept aside the pre-sailing uncertainty and added a gaiety which the Navy always seemed to encourage.

Somewhere a cannon banged dully, and Ackworthy said, 'The races are finished, Sir James.'

'Good. Capital.' Ashley-Chute's puggy face surveyed the jostling visitors, the bright gowns and bare shoulders ming-ling amongst the epaulettes and gold lace. 'A keg of rum for the winners, hmm?'

It was incredible. Nobody who did not know Ashley-Chute would realize there was any other side to his nature. Short in stature he might be, but people seemed to look up to him as he swaggered amongst the guests and visitors, kissing a hand here, pinching a cheek there as he murmured some-thing under his breath which was guaranteed to bring out a blush of pleasure. Any other man taking similar liberties would probably have ended up with a bloody nose or worse.

Only twice did he show his other self, and Blackwood would have missed both had he not been watching.

To cope with the numbers of visitors, members of the ship's company, mostly seamen, had been pressed into service as mess servants and stewards. One man, overawed perhaps by so many women around him, dropped a full tray of glasses to the deck, splashing wine on a few gowns and the feet of several officers.

Ashley-Chute had frozen in the middle of a conversation and had given the man a glance which should have killed him stone dead.

Then an elderly captain from the dockyard had gestured towards Portsmouth Point. The sun was going down rapidly, and some of the ladies had sent for their shawls to protect their shoulders against the evening breeze. Etched against the fortifications and huddled dwellings around the Point was a long drifting smoke cloud. It was probably a paddle-wheeled tug, or one of the brand-new steam gunboats which had been vividly portrayed in the *Gazette* just a few weeks ago.

The old captain had said gruffly, 'Well, Sir James, what d'you think of the new Navy? I fear your squadron and its like may never be seen again.'

Ashley-Chute's eyes had fixed on him like needles.

*'Damn your impertinence!* You should stay ashore with the women, blast you!'

The captain had wilted. 'I beg of you sir – I – I did not infer that . . .'

Ashley-Chute had not even heard him. He had stared at the drifting cloud of black smoke with something like loathing.

'There is some small future for the steam vessel, but not in any true sense as a fighting ship. Beyond doubt, and entirely to my satisfaction, I believe that the fleet in being will remain under canvas and not be a victim of dirt and unreliability!'

He had turned on his heel and approached a young lieutenant who was holding hands with the mayor's daughter.

'Ah, my dear!' He had taken the girl's elbow and guided her aft towards the poop. 'Come and talk with me.' He had ignored the lieutenant completely.

Blackwood felt his half-brother move up beside him.

He asked, 'Is everything all right, Harry?'

'Yes, sir.' The lieutenant's eyes were searching among the crowd. 'Did you see that girl?'

'Which one?' Again Blackwood sensed his own stupid resentment. He knew well enough which one.

Harry Blackwood replied, 'The dark-haired beauty. Sir Geoffrey Slade's niece.' He rubbed his gloved hands together. 'She never smiles, but I'd lay odds I could make her.'

Blackwood saw Ackworthy beckoning to him. 'She'd have you for breakfast, you young ass!'

He heard Harry call after him, 'Her name's Davern Seymour, sir.' He could almost hear him stifling a laugh as he added, '*Miss*.'

Ackworthy said, 'The boats are leaving now, Major.' He glanced at the sky and at the dark tracery of rigging and spars overhead. 'Went well, I thought.'

It was a question, not a statement.

Blackwood watched the first of the visitors being assisted down into the various boats. There had been a plentiful supply of wine for everyone, and the *Audacious*'s own brand of punch had grown steadily stronger with each topping up by the admiral's steward. One or two of the guests looked as if they might have fallen into the sea and barely noticed it.

He said, 'They all enjoyed themselves, sir. By the time some of them sleep it off we'll be aweigh on the tide.'

He glanced across the nettings towards the other ships of the squadron. Their reflections glittered on the water as the sunlight faded, with coloured lights and the long lines of open gunports to make this last night a memorable one. Some would despair at seeing their husbands and sons depart on one more commission. Others would be secretly grateful and pray that the next reunion might be delayed. Grief, happiness, ambition and ignorance, none meant anything to the ships themselves.

Blackwood realized with a start that Ackworthy was speaking again.

'I never thought that I should be off on another campaign like this, Major.' He was talking almost to himself. 'I thought I should end up like the dockyard captain, the one who . . .' He did not finish it.

So Ackworthy had also seen the admiral vent his anger on the man.

He continued, 'But maybe when we get some sea-room things will seem different.'

Blackwood felt suddenly sorry for Ackworthy. Of all the officers in his ship he probably felt safe to speak his mind only with a marine who shared yet was quite apart from his chain of command.

Blackwood tried to draw him from his gloom. 'Sir Geoffrey Slade. Is he sailing with the squadron, sir?'

The captain shook his head, his mind already elsewhere. 'No, he's going ahead in a fast mail-packet. Don't like the smell of it. The Service and politics don't mix, not in my book.'

Some violins struck up, and the remaining guests moved aft towards the poop and the beckoning music.

Most of the screens in the admiral's quarters had either been removed or hoisted up to the deckhead to give as much space as possible. Tables of glasses and yet more punch to fill them lined the sides, and right aft in the great cabin itself Ashley-Chute's table had been fully extended to seat his guests in lavish comfort. Silver candlesticks were placed at measured intervals, and there was hardly an inch of its polished surface which was not filled with food, gleaming cutlery and flowers.

Ashley-Chute stood with his friend Slade and watched his guests' reactions with barely concealed satisfaction.

Pelham, the flag-lieutenant, glanced nervously around the

laughing, chattering throng and consulted his list of names and where each guest would be seated.

Blackwood took a glass from one of the temporary cabin servants and tried to remember how many drinks he had taken. This was no time to get drunk. The thought made him smile to himself. Ashley-Chute would probably put him ashore and Harry would be made to take over command of the marines in his place. 'Mother' would be pleased.

'Something amuses you, Captain Blackwood?'

He turned, startled, and saw her looking directly at him. She was even more striking close to, with the candlelight and deckhead lanterns making her dark ringlets shine against her bare shoulders.

'I – I'm sorry. Just something which might have spoiled an otherwise happy occasion.'

He watched for some break in her guard. Harry was right, she did not smile. But she had lovely skin, like cream in the reflected lights, and her eyes were dark, possibly violet, he thought.

He asked, 'How did you know my name?'

'Does it matter?'

Her directness took him off balance.

'Not really. I know yours, Miss Seymour.'

She looked away, but made no attempt to move. 'I hate these gatherings. So much talk. Too much.' She looked at him again. 'Actually, my uncle pointed you out to me. You were involved in the Maori War, I believe.'

Blackwood was getting out of his depth. There must be a great deal more to Slade than he had realized if he had kept note of the marines' part in the Maori War, especially that of a lowly lieutenant. Unless Ashley-Chute had said something. A warning clicked in his mind like a pistol hammer.

'I was there, yes.' When she said nothing he added, 'Straightforward landing operations. What we're trained for. It had to be done.'

'You don't sound so sure, Captain Blackwood.' She

watched him gravely, her gown rising and falling to her breathing.

Blackwood shrugged. 'I'm sure.' It was like listening to Harry all over again. *What is it really like?*

He looked down at her. God, she was lovely. He could smell her perfume. Like a part of her.

He added, 'We go where we're ordered, Miss Seymour. No country can survive without strength, but you must know that, surely?'

She shook her head, the dark ringlets barely touching her shoulder.

'I think it's wrong to oppress people. No matter who they are. Some folk seem to take a delight in power, at any cost. Greed and power usually go hand in hand.'

Blackwood retorted, 'I wouldn't know about that.' He had spoken sharply but could not help himself. She had got under his skin and he felt confused by her candour and her confidence. 'I do my — '

She nodded very slowly. 'Your duty, were you going to say?'

Lieutenant Pelham called in his reedy voice, 'Ladies and gentlemen! Dinner is about to be served!'

Blackwood found himself alone as the others moved eagerly to their allotted places. She had been laughing at him, had made him feel a fool, like a common foot soldier.

Pelham brushed his elbow. 'There, sir. Next to the lady mayoress.'

He was almost grateful to be submerged in a torrent of conversation and the din of eating and drinking.

The candles flickered across the bright gowns and the officers' epaulettes, and beneath the laden table Blackwood felt the ship stir as if made uneasy like himself.

The girl named Davern Seymour was seated at the head of the table with Ashley-Chute and her uncle. Occasionally he heard her laugh, but it was a controlled sound, and not once did she look in his direction.

The lady mayoress had had a great deal to drink and was leaning against him by the time the table was rearranged for a special pudding which had been prepared by the admiral's cook.

She said huskily, 'My father was a sailor, y'know.'

She had difficulty in focusing her eyes on Blackwood's face, but none at all in pressing her knee against his under the table.

Blackwood regarded her despairingly. She was sixty if she was a day. It would serve her right. He took another swallow of wine and dabbed his face with a napkin. What was the matter with him? Had that girl unsettled him so badly?

The lady mayoress seemed to take his silence for encouragement and he felt a hand on his thigh.

There was a sharp tap from the head of the table, and Blackwood thought for an instant that someone had seen what was happening.

Vice-Admiral Sir James Ashley-Chute rose to his feet and stared at the table until he had their full attention.

'Before the ladies retire, God bless 'em,' his eyes moved restlessly along their faces, 'I would like to say a few words on behalf of the squadron, *my* squadron, which is soon to quit these shores.' He tucked one hand inside his coat and continued, 'We are all living in stirring times. An age of discovery, the founding of trade and colonies the length and breadth of the globe. There will soon be no land worthwhile where the Union flag does not fly with authority. Our mother country will surely benefit and continue to do so.' Some of the gravity was thrust aside as he added, 'But I am a simple sailor. I leave such matters to others. Unlike some . . .' he paused and glanced coldly at Captain Boyd of the *Argyll* who was said to have a woman in Southsea, '. . . I am content to serve my country and take the ocean as *my* mistress.'

Somebody gave a nervous laugh.

The admiral stared into the distance, the lights shining on his iron-grey sideburns.

'We have a young queen on the throne, a fleet to be proud

of, and a future that holds no fears for those resourceful enough to *seek* and *win!*'

Captain Boyd of the *Argyll*, still flushed with anger at the admiral's pointed comment, muttered, 'God, you'd think we were going to fight a war!'

The lady mayoress slumped back, and Blackwood saw the girl watching him from the end of the table.

Ashley-Chute was saying, 'Loyalty and duty are the foundations of my faith.'

Blackwood watched the girl's mouth quiver very slightly. She was laughing at him. Goading him.

The admiral broke off and snapped, 'Well, what *is* it, Pelham?' He seemed irritated by his flag-lieutenant's sudden gestures. 'I am still *speaking*, man!'

But he listened none the less and then motioned for Pelham to relay his news to Captain Ackworthy.

Strangely ill at ease in his own ship, Ackworthy rose to his feet, his hair almost brushing the deckhead.

'I beg your pardon, ladies and gentlemen, but the master has sent his respects and apologies and insists that a squall is rising from the sou'-east. Under the circumstances, it might be in the interests of safety for visitors to return to the shore without delay.'

Ashley-Chute gave a fierce grin. 'Any lady still aboard will *remain* so, hmm?' He walked briskly to the cabin door to bid his guests farewell.

Blackwood said to the flag-lieutenant, 'A bit sudden, surely?'

The man shook his head wretchedly, probably visualizing all those hundreds of miles to Africa.

'Sir James is bored or tired, I'm never certain which. He *ordered* me to pass that message to him. There's no squall. It's an old trick of his.' He glanced at the long-armed lieutenant who was the admiral's son. 'I feel sorry for *him*. For all of us.'

'Come along, Pelham.' Ashley-Chute's voice was like a father speaking to a backward child. 'See that the ladies are escorted to the gangway.' He glanced at Blackwood and nodded curtly. 'So your brother is aboard, eh? A bit of string-pulling at the Admiralty, hmm?'

He turned aside to speak with his special guest.

The girl was waiting for him, her body concealed from her throat to her toes in a boat-cloak.

'Good night, Captain Blackwood.' She eyed him thoughtfully. 'I hope you are not *too* troubled by duty.' She did not offer her hand from the protection of her cloak.

Blackwood bowed from the waist. 'I look forward to our next meeting, Miss Seymour.'

She gave a brief smile. 'I fear that may be a long way off.'

She curtsied to the admiral, the movement taking her through the door and into the shadows like a trained dancer.

Blackwood walked out into the cool damp air and drew deeply on the tang of salt. Boats were already thrusting away from the ship's side, and he could hear laughter and muffled cheers as the occupants waved to the watching seamen on the gangway.

'How did you get on, sir?'

Blackwood swung on the scarlet blur of Harry's coatee in the gloom.

Then he shrugged. What had he expected anyway? That a girl like her would swoon into his arms merely because he was going overseas?

He said wearily, 'I survived, Harry.' He touched the lieutenant's sleeve, suddenly glad of his company. 'Come below and take a glass before you turn in.'

The admiral's quarters were already quiet, the screens replaced, a sentry planted beneath a lantern like a toy soldier.

Then, as Blackwood thrust open his cabin door they both heard Ashley-Chute's voice cutting through the screens and all else like a saw.

'What the *hell* were you thinking of, Ackworthy? Some of those servants were like ploughmen, more used to the dung in the fields than to civilized people!'

Ackworthy must have mumbled something and the admiral's voice rose even higher.

'It was a bloody shambles! I was humiliated by it! By God, Captain Ackworthy, you'll live to regret it if you repeat such incompetence!'

Harry Blackwood stared at his half-brother with astonishment.

'What was *that*?'

Blackwood glanced at the quiet cabin, the bottle and goblets where Smithett had placed them in readiness. He never needed to be told anything.

'I fear, Harry, that the party has just ended.'

# 3

# A Man of Authority

'Begin the salute.'

The crash of the first cannon shattered the afternoon silence and drove a cloud of gulls soaring into the sky in screaming protest.

Moving very slowly at the head of the squadron, the flagship *Audacious* headed purposefully towards the anchorage, beyond which the impressive slab of Gibraltar loomed up in the mist.

The sea was set in a flat calm, with only an occasional flurry of breeze to stir the ship's topsails and jib.

The squadron must make a fine if familiar picture from the shore, Blackwood thought. Like part of a great painting, or one of his grandfather's memories.

*Audacious* in the lead, with the three two-deckers, *Swiftsure*, *Valiant* and *Argyll* following obediently in her wake. Only the hulls were changed from those which had shaken to the roar of cannon fire at Trafalgar. White and black stripes instead of Nelson's black and buff. Otherwise there was little outward difference.

Gun for gun the salute to the governor on the Rock crashed out, to be returned with equal precision. Probably the only ones they would hear on this voyage, Blackwood thought.

He glanced forward from the quarterdeck at the assembled seamen who were waiting to wear ship in readiness to drop anchor. Others with their petty officers and lieutenants in their various parts of ship. To sway out the boats, to rig awnings and windsails, to man the side for visitors from the shore, and all within minutes of the great anchor splashing down.

The marines were paraded in three neat formations, Colour-Sergeant M'Crystal on the flank, Sergeant Quintin in the rear.

Second Lieutenant Harry Blackwood stood in front of the first platoon, his sword drawn and resting between his feet, his eyes slitted against the misty glare from the bay. Sea-haze mingled with the departing gunsmoke, and in the humid air the marines were getting the worst of it in their high-collared coatees.

'Ready, sir!'

Ackworthy nodded. 'Helm a'lee!'

Slowly and ponderously *Audacious* turned towards the wind. Sails flapped against the rigging in meek protest. There was barely enough air to carry her to the idling guard-boat with the bright pendant hoisted to mark where she should anchor.

Blackwood glanced across to the group by the quarterdeck rail. The misshapen figure of Ashley-Chute, his hands linked across his buttocks by a pair of white gloves which he had been tugging in time to the gun salute. Ackworthy and his first lieutenant, the signals midshipmen ready to make signals and acknowledge them, their assistants standing amongst the coloured bunting, very aware of the need for haste with their admiral barely yards away.

'Let go!'

As the anchor hurled spray high above the beakhead, the ship's sailing master glanced at his quartermaster and helmsman and gave a quick grimace. Blackwood could guess what he was thinking. It had taken fourteen of the longest days he could recall to reach Gibraltar from Spithead. With each dragging hour the ships of the squadron had gone through their paces in response to Ashley-Chute's endless procession of signals.

Three ships of the squadron had been spared. The little frigate *Peregrine* had been sent on ahead to Gibraltar, but even she had taken two days to draw away from her heavy consorts. The other frigate, the forty-four-gun *Laertes*, had held up to windward, a spectator as the ships of the line had formed up ahead or astern of their admiral, opened or closed distances as demanded, while the limp sails had been changed and reset until the various companies were worn out.

Only the squadron store-ship, *Amelia*, a very elderly vessel which had once been used for transporting convicts, had been allowed to make her own way south.

Even Biscay had been cruelly calm, with not the usual urgency of shortening sail and changing tack to keep the men's minds occupied. Around the north-west tip of Spain and still further south with the coast of Portugal just visible to the masthead lookouts.

Gun drill in blazing sunlight, the crews panting and cursing as they had hauled the great muzzles up to their ports, timed by the first lieutenant's watch, and with Ashley-Chute's small figure never far away from poop or quarterdeck.

Pelham stayed at his side like a lean shadow, a pad rarely absent from his hand, as the admiral's thin mouth opened occasionally to make a criticism or to ask who was responsible for a delay or a mistake.

It was a far, far cry from the eloquent host at the Spithead reception, the man who could describe the beauty of sail and dismiss the benefits of steam and leave no room for doubt among his listeners.

The slow passage had played its part. There had hardly been a day when the squadron had not been passed or, worse, overhauled by some packet or coaster.

In the Bay itself they had sighted a tell-tale plume of black smoke far astern, and Blackwood had heard the admiral say, 'Damn rattle-box! What did I tell you, Pelham? *Bloody useless!*'

But the little paddle-steamer had grown sharper in the telescope lens none the less, and when the hands had been piped to their midday meal she had been overtaking the squadron in fine style. Her master must have done it deliberately, for his after-deck was almost awash from the paddles' surging throw back. Smoke and sparks had belched from the spindly funnel, and the vessel had churned up a bow wave like a giant's moustache.

When the *Audacious*'s hands had been piped back to their various tasks once more the little paddle-steamer had been passing *Argyll*'s quarter at the rear of the line.

Ashley-Chute had snatched a telescope from a terrified midshipman and had shouted, 'Captain Boyd's people are *cheering* that filthy object!' He had hurled the glass at the midshipman. 'God damn it, Ackworthy, must I be served by fools?' He had swung away adding, 'Make a signal to the squadron. *Make more sail and close on the flagship.*'

Ackworthy had seen the protest in the sailing master's eyes and had pleaded, 'In these light airs, sir, it will do no use.'

Ashley-Chute had had to climb on to a bollard to seek out the paddle-steamer.

'Just do as I say! *More sail!*'

Like monkeys the seamen had swarmed up the ratlines in a living tide to set the topgallants and then the royals in an effort to draw ahead. It was pointless, and the great maincourse could barely lift its belly, so weak was the wind.

The other vessel had steamed past, dipping her ensign as she did so.

As the first lieutenant had said later, 'Not only that, but she was a bloody Frenchie!'

Harry Blackwood brought the hilt of his sword to his mouth with a flourish.

'Permission to fall out the marines, *sir!*'

From one corner of his eye Blackwood saw M'Crystal nod with approval. He did not know the half of it. Harry should have been an actor, not a marine.

He said calmly, 'Carry on, Mr Blackwood. Tell Sergeant Quintin to detail a shore picket, just in case our people are allowed off the ship.'

He shaded his eyes and looked up to watch the last of the

big sails being furled neatly to its yard. All down the squadron it would be the same. Another passage completed. A landfall made. At least they didn't have to put up with the admiral.

Blackwood walked on to the larboard gangway as the first of the boats was swayed up and over the side to a clatter of blocks and bellowed commands.

There were several steam vessels lying in the Rock's shadow. It must be marvellous to be able to manoeuvre at will and tell the wind to act as it pleased. To cut across an enemy's stern without the need to stand and receive a bellyful of iron because you have lost your sails in a broadside.

'Is this your first time here, Major?'

Blackwood turned and looked down at Ashley-Chute's son. He had barely spoken to the third lieutenant since he had joined the ship at Spithead. Their duties never seemed to meet, and he had thought him to be either aloof like his father or merely shy.

'No, I've been this way before.'

Blackwood watched him curiously. About his own age, and yet he seemed much older, or from another period altogether. He would not have looked out of place with Raleigh or Drake, he thought. He had deep lines at his mouth and nose, and his eyes were restless and heavy lidded. He gave the added impression of great physical strength, as if it was all gathered in his shoulders and long, ungainly arms.

Lieutenant Ashley-Chute pointed towards the shore. 'See that mast beyond the anchored store-ship?'

Blackwood shaded his eyes again. The lieutenant must have damn good vision as well.

Then he saw it. A raked mast, almost bare of spars and rigging, and a thin black funnel.

The young Ashley-Chute was saying, 'She's the *Satyr*. A new steam-frigate.' He could not contain the excitement he felt. It was like a secret pride. 'I was supposed to be joining her. I've completed the new gunnery course, everything.' His arms dropped to his sides as if they were too heavy. 'But I'm third lieutenant in *Audacious* instead.'

Blackwood did not need to ask why. 'Maybe you can transfer later on.'

'Later on?' He did not hide the bitterness in his voice. 'He'd never allow it. He wanted me here, to make certain I'd follow the "tradition".' He spat out each word. 'I love the Navy. I really do. And he's almost made me hate it!'

A petty officer hurried towards him and he thrust himself away from the side.

'Sorry about that, Major.'

Blackwood smiled. 'I think I understand how you feel.' He turned and stared again at the raked mast. Lithe, modern power; no wonder a young officer could dream of serving and maybe commanding such a vessel. 'Perhaps we could go over and look at her while we're here?' But when he twisted round Lieutenant Ashley-Chute had vanished.

The first lieutenant strolled across to join him. 'The captain wants a full quarter-guard mounted this evening, Major.' He removed his hat and wiped the inside rim with his handkerchief. 'More visitors to drink up our mess bills, I expect!'

But Netten, the first lieutenant, was wrong. The only important visitor to arrive aboard the flagship was Sir Geoffrey Slade, as neat and composed as ever, dressed all in white and removing his hat as he received full honours from the side-party.

Later, after dining with the admiral in his cabin, he came on deck where Blackwood was watching his marines mounting guard and listening to their night orders from Corporal Jones, the man who had wanted to be a prize-fighter.

He nodded companionably. 'Good to see you again, Blackwood.'

He seemed so relaxed and at ease that Blackwood asked, 'Are you remaining here at Gibraltar, Sir Geoffrey?'

Sir Geoffrey Slade shook his head and leaned out to watch some local trading boats idling as near as they dared to the ship's side. From the lower gunports there would be some brisk bartering between these boatmen and the sailors until the master-at-arms discovered what was happening.

'No. I shall continue in the mail-packet to Freetown and then, if everything is properly arranged, take a steam vessel on to Fernando Po. How the African coasts are opening up with these new craft, eh?' He gave an amused smile. 'I'm afraid I do not share Sir James's views on maritime progress!'

Blackwood hesitated. 'Er, your niece, sir . . .'

Slade regarded him calmly. 'She came with me, of course.' He saw Blackwood's surprise and added, 'But she's not here now. Left yesterday. Wouldn't wait, and I could not very well keep her company. My business here and in Africa is pressing.'

Blackwood had imagined the girl back in England. But she had been here and had already gone. It was making no sense.

Slade said, 'She wanted to join her father. She's a head-strong young woman. I've done all I can for her since her mother died. I can understand how she feels.' He waited and then said gently, 'You seem very interested in my niece.'

'I think she found me rather stupid, sir.' He shrugged. 'I thought she was fascinating, as it happens.'

'I see. Well, her father's a doctor. Could have been a great man in his profession, but he chose tropical medicine. It's what killed his wife, as a matter of fact. Now he's down there working his heart out in some wretched mission or other. I've sent word to our people in Freetown to help my niece as much as they can, but I'm not sure any more. The area where he was last known to be is in a state of turmoil. Which is why I am on my way there, and where you will eventually be required to make a show of strength, and I hope that is *all* that will be needed!'

He looked dreamily towards the Rock's great shadow. 'It's all there in Africa, y'know, Blackwood. The picklock of empire. People don't count for much when something's true value is realized.' He turned aft towards the poop. 'A game of

cards with Sir James before I go ashore, I think.' He gave a
casual wave. 'Remember what I said.'

Blackwood gripped the nettings with both hands and
stared at the glittering lights on the water.

She had known when she had spoken to him. *I think it's
wrong to oppress people.* Now she was on her way to Africa, to a
part which Slade had made clear was about to erupt for one of
a hundred reasons.

He walked quickly along the gangway, only partly aware
of the watching side-party and boatswain's mate, a marine
sentry who stiffened as he passed.

She might think differently of him if he could see her
again.

In his mind's eye he seemed to see Africa spreading like a
vast jungle, engulfing her and dragging her down into oblivion.

He thought of the screaming horde of Maoris as they had
charged towards the single line of marines, the jarring pain in
his arm as he had hacked one of them down, their faces almost
touching.

Blackwood stopped short at the forecastle. There was a
solitary marine sentry there on a little platform above the
beakhead. To watch over the cable, to ensure no unlawful
visitors used the great rope to pull themselves aboard. Like-
wise, he was useful to deter anyone from deserting.

The sentry stamped his heels to attention. Blackwood
peered through the gloom but could not put a name to the
stiff, youthful face.

'You're one of the new recruits?'

'*Sir!* Private Oldcastle, sixth company, sir!' He had a
Yorkshire dialect you could carry in a spoon.

'Have you settled in, Oldcastle?'

The sentry's eyes gleamed in the lantern light as they
moved across Blackwood's shoulder-belt and epaulettes.
*Something to tell the others later on.*

'Aye, sir.'

Blackwood nodded. 'How old are you?'

'Six . . .' He swallowed hard. 'I – I mean, seventeen, sir.'

Blackwood smiled gravely. He made him feel like an old man.

'Why did you enlist, Oldcastle?'

'My dad were a marine, sir. But 'e died last year, so I thought I'd take on like.'

Blackwood looked at him. 'Good. Learn all you can and do your . . .' he hesitated, remembering her eyes watching him along the table, '. . . er, duty.' He touched his shako and walked towards the stern again.

Suddenly things did not seem so ordinary after all.

The nightmare rose to a whirling climax, the carved Maori club, jagged and bloody, swinging overhead, ready to smash down. Somehow the image on the club had become alive, with staring eyes and tongue extended, like the warrior who held it.

Here it came. With a gasp Blackwood rolled on his side, his legs kicking at his sheet as he tried to escape the death blow.

He opened his eyes and raised himself on his elbows. The cabin was barely visible from a shuttered lantern, and he saw the startled eyes of a midshipman peering at him over the side of the cot.

Blackwood licked his lips. His body was wet with sweat and yet his throat was like a kiln. Reluctantly his memory came back. The talk with Slade, the mistake of pausing with the purser to have a few drinks before turning in. It had been the purser's birthday. It was always fatal to drink with a man who held the keys to a limitless supply of brandy.

'What is it?' It came out a croak.

The midshipman stammered, 'Beg pardon, sir, but the captain sends his compliments, and would you join him aft – ?'

Blackwood was out of his cot in a bound, his mind clearing as he peered at his watch on its stand. It was barely three in the morning.

'What the hell is happening?'

The midshipman's eyes followed Blackwood's nakedness around the cabin, his earlier nervousness giving way to curiosity.

'Don't know, sir. Guard-boat came off with the gentleman who was here earlier.'

'Slade?'

'I – I think so, sir.'

Blackwood tugged on his trousers and groped for a shirt. Folded and neat where Smithett had placed it.

'Rouse Mr Blackwood.' He snatched up a brush and glared at his dim reflection in the mirror. 'And don't take no for an answer.'

It was surprisingly cold on deck after the heat of the day. There were plenty of stars, with a black triangular gap in their array to betray the Rock's brooding presence.

The watch on deck shuffled their feet, and Blackwood heard the guard-boat squeaking alongside, the oarsmen murmuring together and clinking mugs of tea.

Ackworthy filled his stern cabin as he waited for Blackwood to sit down. Netten, the first lieutenant, was present, red-eyed and jaded, Pelham too, and in a chair by the stern windows Slade sat with one leg crossed negligently over the other, a cup and saucer balanced on his knee. He was still wearing the same white clothes, as if he had never left the ship.

Ackworthy said thickly, 'Courier-brig anchored two hours ago.' He did not seem to know how to continue.

There was a clink as Sir Geoffrey Slade handed his cup to the cabin servant.

'Despatches for me. Serious news, I'm afraid. There's been an uprising north of Freetown. Mdlaka, a local king I had hoped to meet, may have been butchered with many of his warriors. It could create a very dangerous situation to the trade missions, to the stability of the whole coast area – '

He paused as the door was flung open and Ashley-Chute, dressed in a full-length robe of plum-coloured silk, strode into the cabin, both hands crammed with papers which he slammed down on to Ackworthy's table.

'I read your despatches, Geoffrey, while I was being shaved.' He seemed to realize the presence of the others for the first time. 'Full muster of brains, hmm?'

Slade gave a faint smile. 'You agree it is serious?'

Ashley-Chute thrust his hands into his pockets. 'Serious? Of course. I've always maintained that damn coastline, all of it from Freetown to the Slave Coast, is a tinder-box. Slavery is forbidden, the great nations *agreed* upon that!' There was an edge to his tone as he added, 'After Britain had used a little "persuasion" on the more avaricious nations. And yet the traffic in African slaves seems as strong as ever. I have no personal objections to a settler or plantation owner using such labour. I expect that most of the so-called slaves are better off under ordered circumstances. But the law says otherwise, and I intend to enforce that law.' He calmed himself with an effort. 'When my squadron is on its proper station I shall be very firm in whatever methods I use.' He looked at Slade as if expecting him to argue.

Slade said quietly, 'The courier-brig made a record passage to reach me. Even so it took far too long. The whole situation may have worsened by now, lives lost, Her Majesty's subjects put in jeopardy.' He pressed his neat fingertips together and watched Ashley-Chute across the cabin. 'How *long* would it take you to reach the area?'

Ackworthy said bluntly, 'Month at least, sir. Even with favourable winds, I don't think — '

Ashley-Chute snapped, 'I will speak with you later, Captain Ackworthy!'

Slade persisted, 'This is very important. Her Majesty's Government has ordered me to investigate certain matters on the Slave Coast, which is why I am going to Fernando Po. Eventually.'

Ashley-Chute plucked at his sideburns and prowled about the cabin as if he were trapped.

Slade persisted, 'A month is too long.' He spoke gently, as

if he shared Ashley-Chute's inability to move his ships where they were most needed. At the same time he left no room for doubt as to his authority.

The deck moved very slightly as the ship swung to her cable. Hundreds of men slept throughout the squadron while a mere handful kept watch over them, all unaware of the tension here in this one cabin.

The first lieutenant broke the silence. 'I understand that there is a permanent patrol in the area you mention, sir.'

'Was.' Slade's eyes had not moved from the admiral. 'She is reported missing, and the remainder of our patrols are much further south.'

Ashley-Chute stopped his pacing. 'I don't see what I can be expected to do.'

It must have been what Slade was waiting for.

'There is a steam-frigate here at Gibraltar, Sir James.'

'What?' His eyes shone in the lantern light like stones. 'Yes, of course, I know. The *Satyr*. She is eventually to be with, if not *of*, my squadron.'

'I have spoken to the governor and will send word to London by the next packet. The *Satyr*, which I understand can reach the destination in fourteen days, perhaps less, is ready for sea. Every minute we wait here talking is a minute wasted.'

Blackwood watched, fascinated. There was nothing calm and gentle about Slade now. He was like steel, a rapier.

'I see.' Ashley-Chute walked to the windows and stooped down to peer at the sky. 'All decided, hmm?'

Slade did not reply but looked at Blackwood. '*Satyr* carries twenty marines. It may not be sufficient if the worst has happened. And there will be nobody to ask for aid.' He let his words sink in. 'I am certain that Sir James will be willing to transfer you to the *Satyr* with a force of your own men, to take overall command.' He gave a wry smile. 'Under *Satyr*'s captain, naturally.'

'Yes, sir.' Blackwood darted a quick glance at the admiral, waiting for the explosion.

Instead the little admiral appeared very calm and even. 'Of course. If you *insist* on this method, Geoffrey, then of course I shall do my utmost to support you. And if any marines must be sent, those from *my* flagship are the obvious choice.'

Slade kept his face immobile. Honour was satisfied. Almost.

Ashley-Chute could not resist adding, 'I have no doubt that *Satyr* will break down or run out of coal long before she reaches the Guinea Coast. I shall put to sea with the squadron tomorrow to provide the ultimate show of force.'

'I am grateful.' Slade stood up and straightened his coat. 'I suggest we leave at once.'

Blackwood asked, 'Are you sailing too, sir?'

'Yes. Parliament is always weeping and wailing about the costs of maintaining a powerful fleet. Perhaps this time they will be satisfied that some of the money at least is well spent!'

Blackwood left the cabin and walked out into the shadows. It was an effort to keep his mind steady on the details of the task in hand. In spite of his training and experience he could not control the surge of excitement, something he might have expected in a first-year recruit.

Colour-Sergeant M'Crystal loomed from the shadows. He was fully turned-out in uniform and equipment, ready for anything. The old sweat.

'I want thirty men, Colour-Sergeant. Full equipment and ammunition for work afloat or ashore.' He forced a smile. 'Not all the experienced men. Mix a few of the newcomers into the pudding.'

M'Crystal cleared his throat noisily. 'Right away, sir.' He bellowed, 'Corporal Bly! First sections as ordered! Ten minutes, not a second more!'

As was often the case, Blackwood wanted to praise M'Crystal for his resourcefulness. A plan for everything. A man for each task. But he knew M'Crystal would be embarrassed, even hurt, to think his efficiency could not be taken for granted.

Harry Blackwood, yawning and rubbing his eyes, blundered against M'Crystal, who did not even quiver.

Blackwood said, 'You will remain here in charge, with Sergeant Quintin.'

The lieutenant nodded vaguely. 'Remain here? Sergeant Quintin? Why, what is happening?'

'No time now.'

He saw Smithett carrying his personal pack and weapons, supervising the lowering of his captain's kit into a boat alongside.

Smithett marched over to him and snapped, 'All done, sir. Put a couple of bottles in the bag too, might be a long job.'

Blackwood felt his attendant clipping his belt around his waist and adjusting his sword so that it hung directly in line with his hip. If he ordered Smithett to take on the king of the Zulus single-handed, he had no doubt he would be smartly turned-out for it.

His half-brother was pounding after him as he strode over to watch the first section of marines clambering down into the boats.

'Look, sir, can't I come too?' He was actually pleading.

'No.' Blackwood turned and looked at him. 'You are *in charge* here. Sergeant Quintin has years of service behind him, but he expects an officer to give him his orders. So do it.' He gripped his wrist impetuously. 'You asked what it was like. This is all part of it. They expect you to lead them, though God knows most of them could manage well enough if all their officers fell dead.' He shook him gently. 'I shall ask Sergeant Quintin how you managed when we meet up again.'

The lieutenant nodded, his face lost in the darkness. 'Take care, sir. Philip.'

'Ready in the boat, sir!'

It was time to go.

Blackwood glanced up at the tapering masts, the creepers of shrouds and rigging which seemed to climb to the stars. He might never see *Audacious* again.

He added, 'And keep out of the admiral's way.'

Then he was scrambling into the boat, while others, loaded down with marines and equipment, shoved away from the chains and began to pull towards the inner anchorage.

Colour-Sergeant M'Crystal sat very upright in the stern-sheets, the oilskin cover of his flag standing between his knees like an umbrella.

He said hoarsely, 'More like it, sir. Bit o' soldiering for a change!' He twisted round and sniffed the air. 'What's that, sir?'

Blackwood felt a shiver of excitement again. Coal and oil, smoke and damp iron.

'*That*, Colour-Sergeant, is a steam-frigate.'

M'Crystal considered it. 'Och, sir, the sooner we get there, the quicker we can stretch our legs.'

Blackwood watched the bowsprit of the anchored frigate rising like a lance above the boat. Like the warrior's club in the nightmare. He blinked. That had been just two hours ago.

He saw sparks drifting above where the funnel must be, the unfamiliar swish and creak of machinery, voices calling and the clatter of a chain cable. It was another world. He felt a complete amateur, like a sailor trying to ride bareback.

The bowman hooked on, and faces peered and bobbed along the *Satyr*'s black bulwark. Smithett stood ready to steady him if he lost his step, and then he was up and over the rail on to the frigate's deck. Strange shadows and shapes stood around him, and he had little sense of being in a ship at all.

A figure detached itself from the side-party and a voice said, 'Lieutenant Lascelles, sir!'

Blackwood took his hand. Lascelles was supposed to be the Royal Marines officer aboard, but he was dressed in blue like a member of the RMA.

He sensed Blackwood's curiosity and said apologetically, 'Sorry about my rig, sir. But the red coat doesn't take too kindly to the smut and sparks here!'

Blackwood smiled. 'I'll remember that.'

He heard Slade's voice in the distance, probably speaking with *Satyr*'s captain. It was all so different, so new.

Lascelles saw M'Crystal. 'My sergeant has arranged berths for your men in the barracks and on the orlop. Bit cramped, I'm afraid. But in this ship the engines come first.' He jumped as a siren shrieked wildly overhead, the echoes banging around the bay like an insane chorus.

'Captain Blackwood?'

A broad-shouldered, sturdy officer in a watch-coat came out of the darkness.

'Yes, sir.'

'I'm Tobin. I command here.' The handshake was firm and rough. 'I hope you'll be happy with us while you're in *Satyr*.' His voice was deep and resonant, and he made no attempt to conceal his pride for his command. As an afterthought he said, 'I'll probably see you at breakfast.' Then he too was swallowed up in the drifting vapours of steam and funnel smoke.

Blackwood allowed himself to be led rather than guided down a companion ladder and eventually to a square panelled cabin.

Lascelles said, 'It's yours, sir. I'm bunking in with the third lieutenant.' He picked up a bag from the deck. 'It's the next cabin, if you need me.' Then he stepped outside and closed the door.

Smithett had somehow been here already. Probably even forced Lascelles to vacate the cabin in his favour.

The stand was there, ready for his watch. A clean shirt nearby.

Blackwood sat down on the bunk and felt the hull shaking impatiently. What pleasure it must have given *Satyr*'s captain to shatter the night watches with his siren before he quit the harbour. It had been for Ashley-Chute's benefit.

He lay back and thrust his hands behind his head. *Monkey*.

He would not sleep, he was certain of it. The ship echoed and rattled all around him, and he heard a whirring sound like a fan. And she was not even moving yet.

Poor Harry. He would probably be on deck as they steamed past the anchored flagship. That was the last conscious thought of Captain Philip Blackwood. Even as the first iron link of *Satyr*'s cable clanked through the fair-leads he fell fast asleep.

# 4

## First to Land

Private Smithett wedged himself in one corner of the cabin and muttered between his teeth, 'Is it *always* like this, sir?'

Blackwood pressed his body against a locker and peered at his reflection in a mirror. Each time he brought the razor to his face he could sense Smithett's quick intake of breath, as if he expected to see him cut his throat. It was not surprising. When he had been awakened by the ship noises around him he had been unable to recall where he was. Then, as his memory had returned, he had been startled by the unfamiliar clatter and growl of engines, and when he had tried to leave his bunk he had been hurled across the cabin and almost knocked senseless.

He answered tightly, 'I expect so.'

He laid down the razor and dabbed his skin with a towel. His body felt clammy, and he knew he was near to being sick. Smithett had already told him that several of the marines were 'spewin' fit to bust', but even he had lost his usual relish for disaster.

Blackwood thought of breakfast and clung to a stanchion for support as the deck rocked violently and the whole hull seemed to try and shake itself apart. Down and down, and then he heard the thunder of water alongside and saw a wave crest lift casually above the cabin scuttle. Breakfast? Not yet anyway.

He allowed Smithett to assist him with his coat and then struggled out into the cabin passageway which was also trying to roll on to its side.

Blackwood had been at sea in every sort of vessel from a line of battle ship like *Audacious* to a tiny brig, and had seen storms which had almost torn the masts from the decks. But never could he recall anything like this.

Staggering and gasping, he reached the foot of a companion ladder and looked up with surprise at a blue rectangle of sky. He had imagined they were entering a storm. Taking his time he climbed to the upper deck and clung to a handrail to get his bearings before stepping out into the open.

The *Satyr* was bigger than he had imagined her to be and totally unlike any warship he had seen. She had two masts and what appeared to be a brigantine rig, although all her sails were neatly furled, and his attention was immediately taken by the two giant paddle-boxes, one on either side, which were linked together by an unprotected catwalk like a bridge. Abaft the two paddles was a tall funnel, the smoke streaming towards the quarter in an unbroken trail. Just forward of the mizzen mast was a big double-wheel, but to his surprise Blackwood saw there was only one helmsman. The officer of the watch, a quartermaster and a red-cheeked midshipman completed the group near the compass.

'Morning, Major.'

Blackwood released his grip and almost fell. Captain Tobin had appeared from aft and was watching his reactions with some amusement.

'Sleep well?'

'Aye, sir.' Blackwood looked around again, the captain's obvious pride in his ship was giving him a kind of strength. 'I thought we were in a gale.'

'I should have warned you.'

Tobin had his hands jammed deeply in his watch-coat, and his salt-stained sea-going cap was tugged tightly down level with his eyes. He was a sturdy, ruddy-faced man in his mid-thirties, Blackwood guessed. You would know him as a sailor no matter what he was wearing.

Tobin added, 'You're used to carrying a lot of canvas, the same as I was. Steadies the hull, no matter how steep the angle. Here,' he waved his fist before replacing it in his pocket, 'we ride the sea.'

He rocked back on his heels and waited for the hull to plunge down into a deep Atlantic trough. The starboard paddle lifted slightly and Blackwood felt the same vibration as the blades churned up to the surface. Tobin's resonant voice carried easily above the regular thump of machinery and he spoke for several minutes about his ship, what she could do, if given half a chance.

Without bitterness he said, 'We are the scavengers of the fleet. We take any mission, any job so as not to give their lordships the chance to get rid of us.' He gave a crooked smile. 'But Sir James Ashley-Chute will have drilled *that* into you, eh? No place for steam, the majesty of sail and all that rot?'

*Satyr* was two hundred and forty-nine feet from her graceful stem to her taffrail, and was of nearly two thousand tons burden.

Blackwood listened without interruption. He had rarely heard a ship's captain speak with such understanding of every aspect of his command and the individual tasks of her company. It was something akin to love.

Tobin said, 'It's a long haul to our rendezvous, so I'll try and make your stay a pleasant one.' He grinned. 'Might even convert you too.'

Blackwood had noticed the apparent lack of guns. In any other ship you were always aware of the vessel's main purpose for being. On every deck, be she frigate or first rate, the guns pointed towards each broadside port. The seamen lived, ate and slept between them in their tiny messes. The guns were there when they were piped on deck. They were waiting when they were piped below.

Tobin saw his uncertainty and gestured with his chin towards the midships deck.

'Up forrard I've got two rifled ten-inch chasers, and abaft the paddle-boxes there are four-inchers divided on either broadside.' He pivoted easily on the deck and looked at him searchingly. 'Just six guns, compared with your average frigate's forty or so! Yet with my armament I can outshoot and outmanoeuvre anything else afloat.' He nodded to the lieutenant by the wheel. 'I'm going down to breakfast, Mr Spalding.' He looked at Blackwood. 'Well?'

Blackwood took a deep breath. His lurking sea-sickness had vanished completely.

'Thank you, sir.'

The captain's quarters were right aft, following the usual custom. There was little other similarity.

The dining space was panelled and unmarred by gunports. There was a proper carpet on the deck instead of painted canvas, and the place had a feeling of privacy and comfort. The captain's sword rested in its rack on the bulkhead, and nearby Blackwood saw a painting of a woman and a little girl by a stream.

Tobin had handed his cap to the cabin steward and sat at the table where Sir Geoffrey Slade was reading a sheaf of papers and sipping coffee, apparently oblivious to the ship's irregular plunges.

Tobin got down to a large breakfast, and Blackwood lost himself in his own thoughts. Steam and sail had one thing in common. Officers never spoke at breakfast unless absolutely essential. The wardroom was only yards away, and that too was silent.

Slade got up suddenly. He looked less at ease in the reflected sunlight.

'Are we making good time, Captain?' He smiled despite his inner worries. 'I know we have only been at sea for a matter of hours, however . . .'

Tobin watched him calmly. 'My officers are well aware of the importance of this passage, Sir Geoffrey. The chief engineer is confident enough. We shall put into Tenerife for more coal, although I *can* manage without it. But we might hear something useful.'

Slade nodded slowly, his mind moving on again. 'I hope so.' He moved to the door. 'I shall go and discover if my

secretary has managed to overcome his nausea. He's here to
work, not lie abed!'

As the door closed Tobin gave a slow grin. 'He seems
worried. I'm damn grateful to him all the same. I'd still be
anchored at Gib but for his insistence.'

'Why do you think so many senior officers object to steam,
sir?'

Tobin gestured to the steward to refill his cup. 'They've
never learned to handle it, to understand it. Lines of ships,
thousands of men, those they do understand. But God help
us when we go to war again, unless we've a steam-minded
Nelson somewhere!'

Blackwood made to leave the table but Tobin waved him
down again.

'A moment, Major. I asked you to mess with me and Sir
Geoffrey and not join my wardroom officers, for several reasons.
I think we might learn from each other. In my heart I have little
doubt that we are set on something dangerous. Sir Geoffrey
would not be here otherwise. And neither would you.'

He stood up and walked to a scuttle, his broad shoulders
balanced to his ship's persistent motion.

Almost dreamily he said, 'I worked the West African coast
for five years. On anti-slavery patrols mostly. I once commanded a little sloop down in the Gulf of Guinea when I was
very young and raw. God, what days! Most of the slavers were
better armed than we were, and they could show us a clean
pair of heels if they got the chance. If I'd had *Satyr* then it
would have been a different story.'

Blackwood waited. He could feel the man's powerful
restlessness. Something like his own.

Tobin said, 'Ever seen a slave-ship?' He did not wait for an
answer. 'If there is really a hell that must be it. Men and
young girls, babies even, chained like animals to lie in their
own filth until they reach a suitable market. And it's still
going on, believe me, even though their lordships look the
other way when it suits 'em. But now it's something worse.
As our patrols draw the net tighter the rush for quick cargoes

of black ivory, as they call them, are amounting. The whole coast will be in flames unless we can do something. All the trading missions we used to protect will have to be withdrawn. It will turn the clock back fifty years.' He pounded his palms together forcefully. 'We must act now, or a lot of people are going to get massacred.'

Blackwood tried not to think of the girl's face, or picture her going to search for her father. Perhaps one of Slade's subordinates would prevent her, but in his heart he knew she would get her way.

He said, 'And you think this new uprising is a part of it?'

'I do. I used to know Mdlaka, the king Sir Geoffrey was speaking about when he came aboard. Bloody pirate, cannibal too, I've heard, but loyal to the Crown? *Bought* might be a better word.'

When Blackwood grinned he said, 'Testing you, Major. You're my sort of man, I think!'

Calls trilled overhead and Tobin made to leave.

'Both watches of the hands to exercise. I like them to know I'm about.' He hesitated by the door. 'What makes this ship special is that she is new, and I don't just mean in timber and iron. Here, everyone has to learn something extra. It gives him pride, in the ship and himself. The Navy's no longer a place for felons and pressed men. It's become something they *want* to join and to put their skills into.' He grinned. 'I'm just saying this before Mr Lascelles tells you, Major. Because when we get to Tenerife and coal ship, everyone turns to and lends a hand.' His grin broadened. 'Even the marines. Understood?'

Blackwood smiled. 'Officers included?'

'*Everyone*.' The door had almost closed as he added, 'Except the captain.'

Deacon, *Satyr*'s lean first lieutenant, handed his telescope to Blackwood as he joined him at the quarterdeck rail.

'There it is, Major. We made landfall at first light.' Like Tobin, he did not conceal his pride.

Blackwood levelled the glass and studied the great sprawl of coastline. Tobin had promised Slade a fourteen-day passage. They had stayed for one day in Tenerife and had thrust out of port with the decks covered in black dust. Despite that, Tobin had made his landfall in only thirteen days. What an unhappy-looking coast, he thought. Humps of clay-coloured rock and steep hills, with a hint of high ridges further inland. A shimmering mist and probably blown sand made the picture in the lens vague and without substance.

The steam frigate had reduced speed and her decks were crammed with seamen and a sprinkling of marines, the old hands telling the new ones what it was like. The stories never changed. Only the tellers.

The great twenty-six-foot paddles were thrashing almost quietly at the blue water, a far cry from the din and bedlam of the past days.

Blackwood glanced along the upper deck and picked out some of his own men among the rest. It was hard to believe that some two hundred men could vanish into so crowded a hull. Almost a third of the ship was taken up by engines and boilers, and the warrant officers and the bulk of the complement had to fit in as best they could forward of the paddles. Aft, in comparative comfort, the officers, and of course the captain, had greater space, while below them on the orlop the odds and ends of the ship's company lived like owls with never a glimpse of natural light.

And yet, in spite of the overcrowding, machinery and coal before human beings, there was a real sense of camaraderie which Blackwood knew he would be loath to lose. During the discomfort of coaling ship he had seen it at work. In blazing sunlight, choking in clouds of grit and dust, the men had toiled back and forth to the bunkers with baskets of coal until Hamilton, the chief engineer, was satisfied. There had not been a uniform to be seen, and the blackened, almost naked figures had bumped against one another with a total disregard for rank and authority.

Even at sea, with the decks once more washed clean and the brasswork on the narrow bridge all agleam, it felt different. Not a cocked hat or epaulette in sight, and with Tobin usually in view somewhere on deck, Blackwood had shared the sailors' respect for a true seaman.

Blackwood had seen little of Slade after leaving Tenerife. He had been ashore during their short stay and had returned grim and unsmiling.

There was still no news of the missing patrol vessel. She was an armed schooner named *Kingsmill* and commanded by a young lieutenant. His first commission on the Slave Coast, so almost anything might have happened.

The first lieutenant tensed slightly and Blackwood knew that Tobin had joined them. For such a powerful man he could move like a cat.

'Well, there it is, damn it. That round-shouldered hill is the headland. The river winds inland to the south'rd of it. At this time of year it's too risky to head far up-river. But I'll close the land and anchor as near as I can.' Without turning his head he said, 'Alter course four points, Mr Oliver. Steer east by south.'

Blackwood turned to watch the order relayed by voice-pipe to the engine-room, and as the helm went over he saw the sudden increase of power on the nearest paddle-wheel. It was hot on the open quarterdeck. What it must be like down there as coal was shovelled into the hungry furnaces was hard to imagine.

'South by east, sir!'

'Steady as she goes, Mr Oliver.'

Tobin rubbed his chin. 'I'll bet a million bloody eyes are watching us already.' He looked at Blackwood. 'Have you got it fixed in your mind?'

Blackwood thought of the many hours he had spent with Tobin in his cabin. The captain had taken him over charts and sketches, had read him scraps from some of his old

note-books until he felt he knew this place from memory.
During each forenoon before the sun had become too hot he
had exercised the marines again and again until they too
knew what was expected of them once they had left the safety
of *Satyr*'s hull.

'Aye, sir, thanks to you.'

Tobin regarded him gravely. 'I'll not risk lives for
nothing.' Again a brief command. 'Dead slow, Mr Oliver.'

Somewhere a gong jangled and the great paddles rose and
fell to a quieter beat.

Slade strode from the companion-way, his face shaded by a
straw hat.

'Anything?'

'No, Sir Geoffrey. Not even a local fisherman. Like the
grave.'

Slade looked past him, his eyes cold. 'Very apt, I shouldn't
wonder.'

Suddenly he drew Blackwood aside. 'I did not intend this
should happen. The fact is, I must know what is happening
here, as it could have a vital effect on what action we must
take later on. The only people who can help are at the
mission. They were under Mdlaka's protection and able to do
much as they pleased. However . . .' The word hung in the
air like a threat. 'But if this uprising is no accidental affair to
settle old scores, someone's behind it, fanning the flames.'
Impetuously he touched Blackwood's arm. 'I'm sorry to ask
you to do this. But I *must* know.'

Blackwood said, 'I'm ready, sir.' He forced a smile. 'Do
my men good to stretch their legs.'

Slade did not smile. 'As quickly as you can. In and out
before nightfall.' He fixed his eyes on Blackwood's features as
if to try and memorize them. 'Right?'

'Right, sir.' Blackwood walked to the rail. 'Be ready,
Colour-Sergeant! As soon as we anchor!'

Lascelles stood beside him. He had changed into his scarlet
coatee.

Blackwood said, 'We'll take two boats, Mr Lascelles, that

way we shall divide the target.' He saw the lieutenant's eyes widen as if he had only just realized what was happening. 'I think we are in for some trouble, so check their weapons, and make certain each man carries an extra pouch of ammunition.'

Along the frigate's main-deck the marines dashed back and forth to prepare their equipment and weapons for loading into the boats. No longer the passengers, they made the rest of the ship's company look like mere spectators.

Lascelles would be quite useless. It hit Blackwood like a fist. Outwardly a good officer and popular with his own men, he would crack wide open in a real battle. But it was too late now.

Blackwood clapped him on the shoulder and felt the stiffness beneath the scarlet cloth. There was no nice, easy way.

'You draw your pay, Mr Lascelles. Now bloody well earn it!'

He watched the lieutenant march away, his face tight with humiliation.

Then he said quietly, 'Go with Mr Lascelles, Colour-Sergeant.' He saw all the arguments building up on M'Crystal's red face. 'I shall take his sergeant with me.'

M'Crystal nodded. 'Aye, sir. I understand.'

Tobin came out of the companion-way and said, 'I heard most of that, Major. You've an old head for one so young. Try and keep it on its shoulders. I think we're going to need you again before long.'

Lascelles came aft again and touched his shako. 'Landing party ready for inspection.' He did not look directly at Blackwood's face.

'Very well.' What was it his grandfather had told him? In the Corps it was always the same. *The first to land. The last to leave.* He glanced towards the bare line of hills and fallen rocks. And that meant anywhere.

When he spoke he was surprised his voice sounded so flat and unemotional. 'Once round that first bend and we shall be on our own. So remember, see to the men, no matter what.'

Much as he had said to young Harry. He would have loved this, hazards and all.

He paused by the second marine in the front rank. It was the young recruit he had spoken to aboard *Audacious* at Gibraltar.

'Eager to go, Oldcastle?' It was so cruelly simple to win the youth's heart merely by remembering his name.

'Yessir.' He could barely stand still as M'Crystal checked his weapons, pouches, bayonet and all the rest. 'Wh-where are we, sir?'

Blackwood looked at M'Crystal who snorted indignantly. 'That doesn't matter, boy, not now anyway!'

Half an hour later *Satyr* dropped anchor and swung to the current from around the headland.

At the last moment Blackwood glanced aft and saw Tobin watching him. He did not take his hands from his pockets but gave a slight nod.

Blackwood climbed out and down into one of the frigate's boats. Deacon, the first lieutenant, was already in the boat, and the marines were packed among the oarsmen like hammocks in the nettings.

'Shove off forrard! Out oars!' The boats sidled clear of the ship's shadow. 'Give way together!'

Blackwood gripped his chin strap with his teeth and tried not to blink in the glare. It was so quiet after the ship. Just the steady creak of oars, the occasional boom of waves somewhere around another hump of land. The water was deep and sluggish, and he could smell the shore, just as he could feel the stillness and the air of menace.

Deacon said quietly, 'We're going to look bloody silly if everything's normal here!'

Blackwood saw the stroke oarsman's eyes moving slightly, and when he turned saw that the headland had crept out like a great door to shut off the anchored frigate. How fine she looked above her own reflection, her ensign barely moving in the offshore breeze. The boat turned into the first bend and *Satyr* was hidden from view.

Blackwood noticed that the stroke oarsman had shifted his eyes to him. What are my chances with you? they were asking. Will you be any good if hell breaks loose?

He shut the man from his thoughts and tried to concentrate on what Tobin had taught him.

The river would widen in a moment. The trading mission would be to starboard. What sort of madmen would want to work in a place like this? He gritted his teeth on the chin strap. Stop wandering. You are on your own. No brave but foolhardy major to lead you this time.

He said, 'Next bend. If it's coming, that's where it will be. Private Frazier!'

But the sharpshooter was already crouched in the bows beside two seamen with a swivel gun, his long musket poking over the gunwale like a feeler.

He glanced at the other boat and was sickened to see Lascelles staring at him instead of watching over his men.

Deacon was examining his pistol and remarked, 'And to think I had the chance to go ashore and take a safe appointment in the dockyard!'

He looked up at Blackwood and they smiled at each other like conspirators.

The man at the stroke oar heaved back on his loom and let his limbs relax. The officers wouldn't joke about it if there was any real danger.

Along either side of the river the vegetation was thick and tangled. Blackwood watched it as it glided past, his mind darting from one possible eventuality to the next.

A seaman in the bows called, 'Comin' up now, sir!' He hushed his voice, as if he too was conscious of the unnatural stillness. Not a bird, not even a breeze here to make the bushes come alive.

Corporal Jones exclaimed, 'Flash from the top o' the hill, sir! Larboard quarter!'

Lascelles' sergeant muttered, 'Silly bugger!'

But Blackwood said, 'What was it, Jones?' He gestured to the boat's coxswain, and as the oars stilled the silence crowded in like a living force.

Of all the men in the boat, Corporal Jones had probably seen the most action. He had originally been a soldier in a line regiment stationed in India. If only half his barrack-room yarns were true, he had tackled every kind of situation a soldier on the Indian frontier could expect.

Jones said without hesitation, 'Light from a mirror, sir. A signal of some kind. Bloody Afghans used to do it.'

Blackwood looked across at the other boat and motioned with his hand. He waited for Lascelles to tell his men what to expect and prayed he had not forgotten everything at the first scent of danger.

Smithett stirred uneasily on the thwart. ' 'Ere, sir.' He handed Blackwood a loaded pistol. 'The other one's ready when you needs it.'

Blackwood looked at Deacon. 'Let's get it over.' As the boat moved forward again he added, 'Still think we're going to look bloody silly?'

Deacon did not answer.

Blackwood rose to his feet and stared across the heads of the seamen and marines. It was hard to hold his concentration after what Jones had seen. He could feel a tingling sensation at the nape of his neck, as if it was already fixed in a sharpshooter's sights.

The boat swept round the next bend and the river opened out immediately to a width of about a quarter mile. To larboard it was still steep and rocky, but to starboard the land fell away to a long stony beach with a fragile looking pier or jetty giving the first hint of human life. A twisting swirl of current betrayed the presence of a sand-bar in the centre of the stream. No wonder Tobin was loath to venture this far.

Deacon whispered, 'There's the mission!'

It was more like a low fort. It was well sited at the far end of the beach, its stout walls built of stones and layers of sand pounded rock-hard inside outer palisades of timber. Ugly, but safe against anything but trained artillery.

Deacon stood up beside him and grimaced. 'No sign of life.' Some of his confidence returned. 'It was probably all a rumour.'

Blackwood ignored him and said to the *Satyr*'s sergeant, 'If you were putting men ashore. Where is the most dangerous place?'

The sergeant hesitated, unused to being asked for an opinion.

Blackwood felt the sweat trickling down his spine and soaking his shirt around his waist. The distance was falling away, but the sergeant had to understand. In minutes, seconds even, he might be in sole command.

'That pier thing, sir. No cover. Long run up the beach.'

Blackwood reached down and touched his shoulder but did not take his eyes from the land.

'Good man. I agree.'

He made himself fold his arms. Someone with a glass might be watching for a sign of alarm. On open water they would stand no chance, no matter what any marksmen ashore might believe.

'Steer for the pier, cox'n. Nice, easy stroke. No fuss.' He even forced a grin as he glanced above the crowded hull. 'But when I give the word pull like hell for the end of the beach. Get the boat ashore and use it for cover.'

His voice was hoarse yet he was afraid to clear his throat. Here and there a hand moved to loosen a bayonet in its scabbard or a finger beat a nervous tattoo on a musket stock.

Blackwood measured the distance. If they could reach the beach it was fifty yards to the nearest cover, some broken rocks below the mission. It would be up to Lascelles to give them covering fire. If he failed . . . he thought of M'Crystal's red face and took comfort. He at least would give the order.

Deacon said hoarsely, 'I wonder where the bloody door is on that place?'

Blackwood replied, 'Facing inland, I expect.'

He was speaking to hold his thoughts in check. There was no sign of movement. No smoke, not even a moored boat.

The pier glided towards them, the current gurgling gently through the rough piles. This was where the fort would receive its stores to trade with the local tribes, and from where their gains could be collected. Slade had described it as the 'picklock of empire'. It looked like a place of the dead.

Jones hissed, 'Saw something move, sir! Bushes to the right of the mission! By the split rock.'

Blackwood turned slightly and said, 'Easy, lads. Not long now.' My God, but for Corporal Jones they might all be dead on that pier.

He said, 'Stand by. Swivel gun at the first sign of attack. Have you got the bearing?'

The two seamen in the bows bobbed their heads like puppets.

'*Now!*'

It only needed one seaman to catch a crab with his oar like that day at Spithead and it would end in chaos. But to the manner born the boat's crew threw themselves back on their looms, and as the tiller bar went hard over the rickety pier seemed to fall away as they swept past, the blades churning like *Satyr*'s paddles.

For just a moment longer Blackwood imagined he had made a stupid mistake, and then as shadows moved beyond the line of thick scrub he heard the sharp crack of a musket. A seamen yelped in alarm as a bullet struck the gunwale and left a neat hole above his knee before striking the opposite side. A very powerful weapon, and certainly not handled by an ignorant savage.

'Pull, lads! *Faster!*'

Another shot cracked out and whined above the sweating oarsmen.

In the bows, Frazier, the expert marksman, took slow and deliberate aim and then squeezed the trigger. Even at that range, and firing from a moving boat, he did not miss. Blackwood had never known him to lose a target.

A figure burst from the scrub and staggered against the split rock before pitching headlong down the slope. It could be anyone, Blackwood thought. Dressed in robes, more like an Arab than a local tribesman.

He drew his sword and pointed at the shore. *'Fire!'*

The swivel, training hard round until it was pointing abeam, spat out a long orange tongue, the crash of the shot echoing around the river like a thunder-clap. The tightly packed charge of canister exploded amongst the bushes and coarse scrub barely feet from where the figure had fallen.

From this distance it was like seeing a freak wind hitting the side of the hill. Stones and branches were hurled in all directions, and Blackwood imagined he saw someone crawling into deeper cover, wounded perhaps from the murderous charge of the 'daisy-cutter' as it was termed.

There was no more time to wonder about that. The beach was suddenly right here, and as the oars stilled seamen and marines tumbled over the gunwales to wade alongside and guide the boat firmly ashore.

Blackwood did not even remember getting his feet wet. One second he was steadying himself against the grounding, the next he was on the hot beach, his eyes everywhere as the marines ran and staggered into two sections, their eyes slitted as they peered around for another sign of an enemy.

Blackwood looked across the slowly moving water. God in heaven, Lascelles was in direct line with this boat. He would be unable to offer covering fire without killing and wounding half of the landing party. He saw the oars come to life again and breathed out noisily. Either Lascelles or M'Crystal had seen the danger in time.

Blackwood shouted, 'Take cover in those rocks! First section, *go!*'

The marines and the sergeant trotted up the beach, while the others knelt down and aimed their muskets at the place where the swivel had carved its path.

Lieutenant Deacon called, 'Shall I call in the second boat, Major?'

'Not yet.'

Blackwood wiped his eyes quickly with the back of his sleeve. The first section was there. Like fallen red plums dotted among the rocks. He gritted his teeth. His fingers were so slippery he could barely grip his sword. Where was courage now? *What does it feel like?*

Corporal Jones peered up at him, his homely Welsh features anxious. 'Sir?'

It steadied Blackwood. *Sir*. He must have spoken aloud without knowing it.

He bared his teeth in a grin but his face felt frozen. 'Second section, *advance*!'

What must it look like, he wondered, had there been anyone to see? A line of marines walking up the beach towards the mission. He glanced quickly to left and right. A mere handful of men, faces grim beneath their black shakos, muskets held at the ready as they trudged across the open ground.

Doak, who had been under arrest for drunkenness when he had returned from leave. Frazier, who could shoot an acorn out of a tree but would do anything to avoid promotion. Oldcastle, not even seventeen and already facing possible death.

*To think I nearly left them and others like them.*

He could see the other section amongst the rocks watching their progress, ready to fire if there was any sort of challenge.

His heart was beating against his ribs loud enough for Jones or the others to hear. Soon now. The crashing impact. Hopefully quickly done. Not the agony of *Satyr*'s surgeon, the humiliation of returning home a cripple.

They reached the rough wall and halted. Blackwood looked up and listened. The enemy, whoever they were, would know that the only way into the compound was through the gate, which was on the other side where they would be unprotected and shot down before they could get inside.

Corporal Jones said, 'Grapnel, sir?'

Blackwood nodded. Suppose the first attack had been a ruse to get them this far? The real menace might be inside the wall, waiting for them to enter or attempt to climb over.

Private Doak slung his musket and stood back from the wall, a grapnel swinging gently from one hand. A solitary man, in spite of his calling, with a secret sorrow, Blackwood had decided. Whatever it was, he did his best to lose it with rum whenever he got the chance.

He made up his mind and unclipped his scabbard and handed it and his sword to Smithett. His shako too, while the nearest marines watched him with tense expectancy.

Corporal Jones said cautiously, 'Won't do at all, sir, begging your pardon. I'll go.'

Blackwood watched as the grapnel soared up to the parapet and caught fast. Then he took the line and tested it, his eyes on the rough horizon between wall and sky. 'If I fall, Corporal Jones, retreat back to the boat.' He took a firm grip on the line and hoped his palms would not slip. It would take too long to explain to Jones.

He leaned back and pressed his foot against the wall. What had his father said of him? *Honour and glory.* He cursed aloud and began to haul himself up the line. He had been ready enough to give Lascelles advice. Now it was his turn to earn his pay.

Once he paused to gather his strength, aware of the silence again, the upturned faces below him. By his hand he saw an ant probing into a hole in the crude stonework. How many people had died to build this place? he wondered.

With a start he realized his head was level with the top. Holding his breath he reached out for a fingerhold, his mind throbbing with strain and concentration.

As his eyes rose higher he saw a burned-out roof and some fallen timber on the far side of a mud compound. But the gates were there right enough, and heavily barred with a massive timber. His nostrils twitched and he felt his body contract with fear. Death. He knew the smell of that all right.

'Anything, sir?' Jones was getting worried again.

Blackwood did not answer but very gingerly hauled his body up and up until he was lying prone on the top of the wall. He heard a bang and flinched as a ball slammed into a piece of timber supporting an inner parapet. There was an instant rattle of musket fire, then the bang of a swivel as the challenge was met from the boats.

Blackwood threw himself over the wall and dropped on his knees. As he tugged the pistol from his belt he saw a face peering at him over the edge of the same parapet. Bearded and filthy, with eyes ablaze with despair and worse, the creature shouted, 'In God's name! *Who are you?*'

Blackwood moved towards him, knowing the next seconds were vital. The man was armed, although his weapon was hidden beneath the parapet's planking. He was also on the verge of madness. One false move and he would get a full charge straight in his belly.

He said slowly, 'The marines are here.' He deliberately thrust the pistol back into his belt as he watched the man's eyes trying to translate what they saw. Faded eyes like his grandfather's.

It was unbearable to see the ragged creature as he began to weep. There was no sound at all, which made it worse, and all the time those eyes stared at Blackwood as if unable to accept what was happening.

A white leg came over the parapet and Corporal Jones crouched beside him.

'Hell's teeth, sir!' He sniffed. 'Corpses too!'

Blackwood lowered himself on to the ladder and stared at the ragged defender.

'How many of you?'

'F-four, I think.' He shook his head dazedly. 'Bin here for days fighting them off.' He waved vaguely with his musket. 'The devils are out there still.' He reached out and felt Blackwood's tunic with a filthy hand. '*Marines*, y'say?' His eyes were pleading. 'Come to help *us?*'

Blackwood stood up slowly, his mind rebelling as he saw

the corpses littered by the gate and sprawled in careless attitudes where they had fallen. It must have been a pitched battle. He listened to the dull buzz of flies but heard only the screams and yells which must have filled this terrible place.

He saw Smithett clambering over the parapet, ducking without any change of expression as a ball shrieked over his head.

'I think we need one of those bottles, Smithett.' To Jones he said, 'Call up the others and get them in position.' He thought suddenly of the boy Oldcastle. What would he think of the horrors here? Black men and white, staring eyes and gaping wounds. 'When you've done that, signal the first section to join us at the double.'

He turned towards the old man with the musket. 'Yes, we are here to help you.' He made himself smile when he felt like weeping. 'But first I want you to help me.'

# 5

# Battle Fury

Captain George Tobin stood with his shoulders set against the stern windows of his day cabin, his face grim as he listened to the first lieutenant's report. It was early evening, and although the wind had completely died *Satyr* rolled continuously in an offshore swell.

Sir Geoffrey Slade was sitting in one of Tobin's leather chairs, and huddled in a corner as if to be invisible. Barrow, the private secretary, peered at his papers, his pen scribbling at irregular intervals.

Lieutenant Deacon looked exhausted and had one wrist tied in a crude bandage as he completed his description of what they had found at the trading mission.

He said, 'The old man, Thomas Fenwick by name, says there were thirty-two white men in the fort.' He dropped his eyes as he remembered the gaping corpses, the swarming flies. 'Another died shortly after we scaled the wall. I brought the remaining three aboard for the surgeon.' He shrugged heavily as if it was all beyond imagination. 'Old Thomas Fenwick refused to leave, sir.'

Slade gave a wry smile. 'He would. He's been trading these coasts for as long as anyone can remember.' He stood up and crossed to the table and peered over his secretary's shoulder. 'If it's all true, Captain Tobin, I was wrong about Mdlaka. We were all wrong. The old king was not overthrown, he obviously planned the massacre himself, with outside aid.' He glanced up sharply, 'Rifled weapons, you say?'

Deacon nodded. 'Yes, sir. Captain Blackwood told me to

be sure I reported that. Not many of them, maybe only three or four. One shot went clean through the boat's side. No ordinary smooth-bore did that.'

Slade rubbed his chin thoughtfully. 'You waited all day and nothing else happened. Interesting. Our unexpected arrival in *Satyr* upset their plans, no doubt. They intended to kill the last of the defenders and make it look like a raid by somebody else.'

Tobin said, 'Any small vessel would have entered the estuary and moored at the pier as usual. Those few muskets would have cut down any attempt to make sail and escape. You're right, Sir Geoffrey, they'd not be expecting a steam-frigate.' There was no pride in his voice this time, only disgust.

Slade said, 'Wait outside, Mr Deacon, if you please.' As soon as the door was closed he said crisply, 'I cannot order you about, Captain Tobin. I can only *advise*, there is a subtle difference.'

Tobin smiled. 'I know, sir. I've been in the Navy long enough to learn that. I am the senior officer present, and until we reach higher authority at Freetown I must act as I think proper.'

Slade added, 'What you mean is that if you act wisely others will receive the praise, but if you make a mistake you alone will carry the blame?'

'Something like that, sir.'

'Then let me *advise* you. Mdlaka is just one of many African kings or chiefs who have kept an uneasy peace at our bidding. They grew rich on slavery, and now on a growing export of palm oil. Although most European countries have done their best to restrain slavery, if only in words, there are individuals who still see it as rich profit. Cuba, Brazil, even in the Indies there are ready markets for those who will run the risk of seizure. To compensate slave-owners was not enough. The sources must be stamped out. If an old king like Mdlaka can be bought with a few modern guns and induced to commit mass murder, there is no saying what will happen further south in the Gulf.'

Tobin sat down. 'Funny thing, sir, I was recently telling Captain Blackwood about *my* days in the Gulf.' He looked up, his eyes direct and hard. 'You're going to leave him there, aren't you?'

'You like him?' Slade walked to a scuttle and studied the golden sunlight on the water. It would soon be dusk. 'Yes, I must. If the fort had been taken and everyone killed, the bodies and evidence burnt, I might have left it at that.' His voice was cold as he continued, 'But Mdlaka knows me and will realize that I understand what he has done. If we leave now, the word will spread like a forest fire. The white man has fled from Mdlaka. There would be a stampede to copy his example.'

'And your advice, sir?'

'As soon as it is dark send the remaining marines across, and any stores you think Captain Blackwood might need.'

Tobin remained expressionless. There was no point in telling Slade there were only six marines still aboard. He was a landsman, a man of politics.

Slade said, 'I must reach Freetown without delay. There I shall discover the latest and, I trust, more accurate intelligence about what is happening.' He eyed the captain sadly. 'Do not fret too much about young Blackwood. He takes after his father, though I doubt he would admit to it. He is as resourceful as he is brave.' He shrugged. 'And like you, he is the only one who is available.'

Tobin moved from the chair. 'I'll tell my first lieutenant. The boats can go in as soon as it's dark.' He watched the other man and added, 'With respect, sir, you should have been an admiral yourself.'

Slade watched the door close and said, 'Have you written all that down, Barrow? I want no misinterpretation later on because you've omitted something.'

He peered through the scuttle again. Some people were frightened of Africa merely because it looked vast on a map. It just needed courage, the urge to explore and create a new way of life here. Already there was a steady stream of missionaries, religious and medical, some in the most feared and previously hostile territories. They were the true vanguard, whether they knew it or not. His mouth tightened. Not a thousand Mdlakas were going to ruin a dream of empire, there was far too much at stake.

Tobin came back and said, 'I've passed the word, sir.' He shook his head. 'A rum lot, these marines. The last six I had on board began to cheer when Mr Deacon told them they were being sent over.'

Slade smiled. 'You worry too much, Captain. Who knows, together we may be making a small part of history?'

Tobin cocked his head to listen to a boat being pulled around the stern. Stuck out there in the middle of nowhere. He considered how he would have felt under the same circumstances. Without a ship. Helpless.

He said, 'I've told the Chief to get under way as soon as the boats return, sir.'

Anything but sit here with this composed, practical man who seemed to consider any sort of sentiment as weakness.

It was completely dark when the boats returned and were hoisted smartly inboard.

Tobin was waiting to meet his first lieutenant on the quarterdeck, his mind for once uninterested in the coursing rumble of the engines and the gushing plume of smoke.

Deacon looked around the bustling seamen and listened to the clank of the capstan as if it was beautiful and inspiring music.

'How was it?' Tobin asked.

Deacon licked his lips. 'Terrible, sir. The stench, everything.' He tried to smile. 'Captain Blackwood sent you his best wishes, by the way. Cool as an ice-floe, that one.'

Tobin looked away. Shadows hovered around him, waiting for orders, ready to move, to prove once more what they could do. Deacon was a good man, but he didn't understand half of it.

He said harshly, 'I'll send him a message too. From us. The ship.'

Moments later, as the anchor rose dripping to the cathead and the frigate turned in a welter of froth and spray, her siren rent the sky apart with its piercing squawk.

Tobin climbed on to his unprotected bridge and examined the extra compass there. Then he looked astern where only the frothing wake left by paddles and rudder broke the darkness.

He said, 'I'll be back. Be certain of it.'

Captain Philip Blackwood walked slowly along the parapet, his eyes straining through the darkness which reached out from the barred gates like a black wall.

The marines had been hard at work all day with barely a break for rations and a gulp of fresh water. It was a marvel that any of them could even contemplate food, Blackwood thought. As it was, several of the marines had staggered retching from the grisly work of hauling the corpses to the parapets to fling them clear of the fort. Although the stench still lingered over the compound, the sights of horror were gone. The dead white men had been buried on part of the compound, while the food and stores sent across from *Satyr* had been stacked inside the communal building at the seaward end of the fort. The whole place measured about eighty yards by fifty, and from the size of the store huts, now burned to the ground, it must have been a thriving post until disaster had struck.

Brogan, *Satyr*'s marine sergeant, seemed very competent, and was outside the fort at this moment with a patrol of five men to make sure there were none of the attackers still in the undergrowth.

Blackwood paused and looked over the wall as he thought of his long talk with the remaining trader, Tom Fenwick. He was like something from a boy's story-book. Fenwick had been everywhere in his search for a fortune, which so far had eluded him. He had been at the fort for two years and knew the local tribes better than most.

As Sergeant Brogan had prepared to lead his patrol clear of

the gates he had said in his quavery voice, 'No point in it, Captain. Them buggers 'as gone. They'll be dancin' and jiggin' to their 'eathen rites right now, an' after they've filled their bellies with drink they'll be samplin' the local girls to make 'em feel like warriors again!'

Blackwood stared at the darkness, recalling his feelings when the *Satyr*'s siren had echoed along the river to signal her departure. It was typical of Tobin, of the man behind the uniform and the authority. He had seen the effect it had made on the others. The younger ones had gazed at each other as if only just aware that they had been left to fend for themselves. The older men had gone about their various tasks in silence. They knew what to expect, or thought they did.

Blackwood heard footsteps moving cautiously along the parapet and saw Lascelles peering towards him.

'Sentries mounted, sir. The rest are settling down as ordered.'

It was strange, Blackwood thought, but the lieutenant seemed more at a loss even than the recruits. Too long with a small detachment of marines in a modern vessel like *Satyr*, perhaps that was it. It would become easy to be a passenger under those circumstances.

He wrenched his mind away from vague uncertainties and said, 'We've got food and water for three weeks.' He saw him flinch. 'If need be. The water must be rationed, for although there is a stream, old Fenwick thinks it might have been poisoned. I've warned the men, but keep at them.' He felt drained and unreasonably angry that Lascelles seemed able to let him make all the decisions and offer nothing. 'Marines are taught to be clean and tidy at all times from the moment they enlist. They must unlearn that lesson immediately. I want all uniforms stowed away, and each man to stain his shirt so that it will not make him a target. Colour-Sergeant M'Crystal is dealing with that. Under protest.'

He pictured M'Crystal's red face, the look of horror when he had ordered him to use tea or coffee for staining the men's shirts. It must have sounded like blasphemy to him.

Blackwood added, 'We are trained to fight, but not to deal with this kind of enemy. I'll not have our men marked down by some bloody sharpshooter just because of the drill book.'

Lascelles rested his palms on the rough wall. 'You believe they'll come back?'

'Yes.'

He thought of old Tom Fenwick, the way he had somehow gained in stature after being on the threshold of hell itself. He had said that the king, Mdlaka, must have promised someone a clear passage down-river with an important cargo. It had to make sense. With the armed schooner *Kingsmill* missing, probably wrecked, it was a chance in a thousand to run a shipment to the coast for collection. Only the trading post stood in the way, and Mdlaka had had no intention of allowing a single soul here to survive. He had even sent men to steal the fort's two boats before the real attack had been started.

Fenwick had described it with little emotion. As if he had been somewhere else, or a mere spectator.

They had rushed the gates when they had been open for any would-be barter from the nearest villages, and the battle had surged back and forth, hand to hand and without quarter. Somehow they had driven the first attack clear of the compound long enough to bar the gates. After that it had been a slower, more terrifying process. Burning wads had been thrown over the walls to set fire to the huts, and several of the defenders had been shot down by marksmen concealed on the hillsides.

Two of the traders had decided to leave the fort and look for one of the missing boats. The next morning one of them had been found outside the gates horribly mutilated and apparently skinned alive. The next day the second man had been sighted tied to a tree directly opposite the gates but too far away for rescue. Even Fenwick, who had seen what savage torture could do, had said he did not know what had made the man stay alive for a whole day. 'They must've give 'im to the women to do that to 'im,' he had said harshly.

Blackwood said, 'They may try a mock attack to test our strength. But it's those rifled muskets I'm worried about.'

Lascelles said vaguely, 'The Corps will be getting them next year, sir, like the army.'

'That won't help us!' He relented, knowing it was fatigue and strain which were giving his tongue an edge. 'Fenwick has drawn a map for me.' He pointed across the wall into the blackness. 'There's a shallow dip in the ground beyond the ridge, and then a pointed hill, like a loaf. Perfect place for a spotting post. We'll have it manned as soon as we know the enemy are keeping their distance.'

Lascelles nodded and swallowed hard. 'I see, sir.'

Blackwood said, 'I know it sounds bad, but it's all we have. Whoever the enemy is, they're going to fight in their own way, and that is what we must do. This fort is an important key and it must be held. Now go around the sentries and I'll relieve you in an hour.' He groped his way to a ladder and lowered himself to the compound.

A fire was burning cheerfully behind a wall, all that was left of a store-room. Several marines, unfamiliar without their red coats and cross-belts, crouched around it, and Blackwood waved them down as they made to stand in his presence. He noticed that their weapons were in easy reach, the pouches of ammunition and percussion caps ready to be snatched up in seconds.

'Carry on, Corporal Jones.'

He walked to the shadows again and tried not to think of the *Satyr* as she pounded her way further and further to the south.

He found a blanket and rolled greatcoat propped by another wall, and a metal cup of brandy covered with a piece of wood to keep out any insects. He sat down carefully and sipped at the brandy. Thank God for Smithett.

Blackwood tried to free his mind from tomorrow, of Fenwick's horrific description of the mutilated traders.

He wondered if his father had taken any further steps to sell the estate and move to London. Compared with his own predicament, his father had led a very full life. Two wives, an eventful career in the Corps, with sons to carry on the tradition.

A creature shrilled beyond the palisade, and Blackwood rolled on to his side and pressed his eyes tightly shut. Harry stood a good chance of being the only one left.

He tried to think of the dark-haired girl named Davern, but her picture was blurred and indistinct. It made him suddenly apprehensive and sick, and when Lieutenant Lascelles came to rouse him he found him still wide awake, his chin resting on his knees as he stared at the leaping shadows from the marines' fire.

It was nearly dawn by the time he felt he could sleep, and by then it was too late.

He watched the men stirring and finding their bearings, glancing at each other for reassurance, to convince themselves it was really happening.

Beyond the wall and vigilant sentries the land was coming to life. Unusual bird cries, unlike yesterday's eerie silence, and a glint of sunlight on the ridged hillside.

Sergeant Brogan had reported finding dried blood where the swivel gun had blasted through the undergrowth, but the corpse had been spirited away, or as Fenwick had commented curtly, 'Probably eaten by some poxy hyena.' It made your flesh creep.

Blackwood surveyed his temporary command without enthusiasm. It looked like a forgotten place. It had even changed the marines. In their shirts and white trousers, unwashed and unshaven, they already had the appearance of renegades. It was a far cry from drilling on the barrack square at Forton, the stamp and swagger which even the foot guards envied.

Lascelles watched him anxiously. 'Both watches have eaten, sir. Weapons inspected.'

Blackwood glanced at the marines' shirts. The staining had only partly worked, but would certainly help to break up a man's outline, especially at night.

Old Fenwick was at the far side of the compound, his jaw

working on a piece of dried beef as he stared moodily at the line of graves. How well had he known them? How much did he miss them? Or was it like soldiering, Blackwood wondered, where survival was the only real consideration?

Fenwick turned as if he had felt him watching, but said, 'They're comin'!'

Lascelles stared at him. 'How can you be – ?'

Blackwood snapped, '*Stand to!*'

In total silence the marines seized their muskets and pouches and ran to the ladders as if it was all part of a regular drill. But Blackwood could recognize a pattern even here. Friends of long standing kept together. An old hand cast a cautious glance at a younger companion as he stood up to the parapet, his face like a mask.

Blackwood climbed to the parapet above the gates. He could hear it now for himself. A throbbing murmur of sound, like a giant bird beating its wings.

Fenwick wheezed up to join him and remarked, 'Gettin' up their courage, blast 'em!'

Blackwood bit on his chin strap until the pain steadied his tumbling thoughts. A cloud of dust was spreading over the side of the hill and the din was growing every minute.

He darted a glance at the nearest marines. Shakos tilted to shield their eyes from the sun, muskets at their sides and shoulders back. They must have been the same sort of men at the Nile or Trafalgar. Except that this was no fleet action, no field of honour.

'Here they come!' Sergeant Brogan pointed over the wall.

Lascelles whispered, 'Oh, my God!'

It was impossible to estimate the numbers or how far the advancing army extended. The swirling cloud of dust could not hide the black bodies which shone with sweat or the precision of the drum-like beat as they pounded their shields with spear hafts. Just ahead of the packed ranks a few individuals stood out as they capered in complicated steps, striking at the air with stabbing spears as they led their cohorts into battle.

Blackwood said, 'Mark those men down.'

He heard Private Frazier mutter a reply. He had doubtless already selected his first target.

Fenwick said, 'Mdlaka must've called in reinforcements. 'E means business right enough, God rot 'im!'

Blackwood stared at the oncoming, bobbing tide until his eyes were raw. This was no North Island, he thought grimly. No ships behind you to carry you off if things went against you. No soldiers and blue-jackets to give support.

The wall seemed to shiver as a great roar of voices came down the hillside like a roll of thunder. There must be hundreds and hundreds of them.

Then they started to run. It was not a controlled movement like their slow advance, but a mad rush, as if it was a matter of honour to be the first one at the gates.

Spears flew towards the fort and were trampled underfoot by the charging mass of figures.

Blackwood yelled, 'Face your front! Take aim!'

Along the parapet the muskets lifted and settled as one.

Blackwood tried to swallow but it was no use. He felt as if his throat was choked with that dust.

'*Fire!*'

The volley crashed out along the parapet, and as the first line of marines fell back to reload the second line stepped forward to the parapet wall and took aim.

'Present! *Fire!*'

Surely every shot must have found its mark, they could not miss, but it had as much effect on the mass of charging bodies as a pike against an elephant.

The first of them hit the gates and the wall on either side like something solid, and above the bark of commands and the sporadic bang of muskets the yells and screams were joined in one terrible chorus.

Loading and reloading, the marines kept up a steady fire, and as Blackwood emptied his pistol into the attackers directly below the parapet he saw heavy logs being rushed through the throng to be used as battering-rams against the gates.

A marine beside him fell gasping with a short spear embedded in his shoulder. Another was holding his face, his fingers running with blood.

'Load . . . present . . . *fire!*'

Sergeant Brogan was beating out the time as the ramrods rose and fell and the men stepped up once more to the parapet wall.

Someone yelled, 'They're attacking from the river, sir!'

Blackwood swung round. 'Mr Lascelles, take a section to support them!' He saw him nod jerkily, his eyes glazed like glass in the sunlight.

A marine whirled round and fired his musket from the hip as a black, screaming face appeared above the wall. They were handling logs and branches with the same skill as grenadiers would use scaling ladders.

The savage's face exploded in a scarlet blur as he dropped out of sight.

Blackwood tugged out his sword, remembering the dead major as he shouted hoarsely, 'Marines! *Fix bayonets!*'

The hiss of steel ran along the parapet, and as more struggling figures tried to pull themselves over the wall the blades rose and fell with desperate precision.

One attacker, his powerful body naked but for a twist of feathers, threw his leg over the wall and smashed down a marine with a knob-headed club. It all happened in a second. Blackwood saw the young recruit, Oldcastle, staring at the savage, his bayonet shaking, his face transfixed with horror. Then he was almost knocked down by Private Bulford as he thrust his bayonet into the man's belly. As he wrenched it free he swung the butt of his musket into the contorted features and set him crashing to the ground below.

He stared at Oldcastle. 'Don't *play* with it, sonny! The bugger'll do for you else!'

Colour-Sergeant M'Crystal, massive even in his stained shirt, shouted, 'They're running, sir!'

'*Cease firing!*'

Sergeant Brogan had to forcibly pull a musket from one marine's grip as the attack turned just as swiftly into a retreat. Bodies lay everywhere, some still, others writhing and groaning where they had dropped.

Blackwood removed his shako and wiped his face with a rag. *A near thing*. His heart was pounding faster than he had ever known, and he felt as if his stomach was filling with bile. He tugged on his hat again and gritted his jaws together. *Must not show it*.

He heard some of the injured marines whimpering like sick animals as they were carried into the shelter of the remaining building.

He heard himself say, 'Check the ammunition, Sergeant. Corporal Jones, how many wounded?'

Colour-Sergeant M'Crystal was wiping his sword very carefully on some dried grass. The blood looked black in the sunlight.

Old Fenwick chewed on his meat. 'They'll come again. Mdlaka will be watchin', the cunnin' bastard, weighin' up your strength. 'E'll try to pare it away if 'e can.'

Jones reported, 'Seven men wounded, sir. Private Simcoe's pretty bad. Lung, I think, sir.'

'Thank you.'

Blackwood stared at the hillside. It must be important for Mdlaka to risk so many lives. If some traders could defend the fort, the marines were a much tougher proposition. And yet there had been a madness, a fervour in the attack which made a mockery of numbers and experience.

What was the choice? Stay behind the walls and lose men with each ferocious attack, or get out and fight them in the open? There seemed no choice at all.

He raised his small telescope and examined the bare hill beyond the ridge. From its summit you would be able to see for miles.

*Crack!* A piece of stonework flew from the parapet and fanned past his face.

He stepped behind one of the supporting timbers as

M'Crystal said angrily, 'One of those new guns, sir. Och, I'd like to get my hands on that bugger!'

Blackwood deliberately turned his back towards the unseen marksman and said, 'I think we'll issue a tot of rum per man, Colour-Sergeant. This is thirsty work, eh?'

He felt his shoulder-blades throbbing as he waited for the pain. He saw some of the smoke-grimed marines peering at him, even grinning at his apparent contempt for the danger. It was working. They could still respond to his stupid bravado.

Sergeant Brogan came back again and said, 'Most of the men used up their extra ammunition. But they've got sixty rounds each, and the others which *Satyr* sent over for us. Course, it all depends how long we're 'ere, sir.'

Blackwood nodded. *They want reassurance.* They needed to know that things would be all right, that somehow their officer would think of a plan.

'Here they come again!'

'*Stand to!* Controlled firing this time!'

Another shot from the concealed marksman ripped into the wall and flung fragments over their heads.

If the marines were prevented from manning the parapet while the attackers smashed through the gates, it would all be over in minutes. He stared at the drifting dust cloud and the tangled barricade of scrub until he was blinded by it.

'*Fire!*'

The flashes of muskets rippled along the parapet and several charging figures pitched among those killed previously.

The marksman must have fired at the same time, for Blackwood saw a marine fall from the parapet to the compound below.

Corporal Jones ran to help him but looked up and shook his head before hurrying back to his section.

Blackwood's eyes smarted with hatred and despair.

Their first death.

He pushed forward to the wall and fired at a man directly below him. Smithett thrust a loaded pistol into his hand and he fired again, seeing a man fall and be trampled down by the writhing press of shining bodies and shields.

M'Crystal had taken up a musket from a wounded marine and stood like a bear at bay as he fired and reloaded more with rage than accuracy.

'Come on then, you black bastards!' M'Crystal had always seen himself dying gloriously in battle like one of the paintings at the marine barracks; the red coats, the impassive stares of the tightly formed square as they confronted their country's enemies.

To die here in squalor was unthinkable, and his fury seemed to transmit itself to the men near him so that they yelled and cheered like lunatics as they fired, reloaded and fired again.

Blackwood stood back and lowered his arm as the attackers waned and then scattered away from the fort.

'Cease firing!'

How many wounded this time? Blackwood was almost fearful to ask. He saw the dead marine being carried towards the other graves. One of the recruits. He could not even remember his name, his brain was pounding so badly.

He looked at Fenwick. 'What do you think?'

The old man plucked at his beard. ' 'E knows 'ow many men you've got now. 'E'll keep tryin'. Otherwise 'e'll lose face, an' 'e's an old man.' He showed his few teeth in a grimace. 'They'd soon get rid of 'im.'

*Keep trying.* Blackwood peered down at the scattered corpses and the few which still twitched in agony.

Sergeant Brogan looked up from the compound. 'We got fifteen wounded all told, sir. Private Carson 'as been killed, an' Private Simcoe's sinking fast, if you ask me, sir.'

Blackwood nodded. He did not trust himself to speak. Sixteen killed and wounded altogether. It was a third of their total strength, and all in one day!

Lascelles joined him and after a moment said, 'About that spotting post on the hill, sir.' He looked tight-lipped and desperate. Like a stranger.

'Yes?'

'I could reach it. If you think it will help, sir.'

Blackwood studied him gravely. 'If they keep attacking, and Fenwick knows them better than we do, we'll be down to a dozen men in a week, probably less. Mdlaka is running out of time. He's trying to swamp our defences.' He saw Lascelles' eyes watching a wounded man being assisted into shelter, his face running with blood. 'Fenwick believes that slavers are behind it, that they've put pressure on Mdlaka to destroy the fort. It makes sense to me. The use of a mirror for signals, the accuracy of that rifled weapon tells me there's another brain behind Mdlaka.' He was speaking his thoughts aloud. 'Those marksmen, no matter how few, can shoot down our men with each frontal attack. We either die piecemeal or get butchered when the others force the gates.' He faced Lascelles again and said quietly, 'I won't order you to go to the hill. You know the odds against survival, what might happen if you get captured.'

Lascelles swallowed hard, his eyes very bright in the sunlight. 'I'll go. I *want* to.'

'Very well.' He looked away, unable to watch Lascelles' fear, his fight to overcome it. 'At dusk, take Corporal Jones and Frazier and all the rations you need and make for the hill. When they rush the fort tomorrow, try and discover the sharpshooters.' He thrust his small telescope into Lascelles' limp hand. 'Jones and Frazier will do the rest.'

'What will *you* do, sir?'

Blackwood smiled. 'I'm not waiting here to die.' He gripped his arm and felt the strain Lascelles was enduring. 'If we fail, try and work your way to the headland and wait for *Satyr*. Someone should tell them what happened.'

Colour-Sergeant M'Crystal marched over the dried mud compound and waited, breathing heavily.

'Orders, sir?'

'Mr Lascelles is taking out a patrol as soon as it's dark. See that he gets all he needs.'

Blackwood looked around at the marines along the parapets, leaning on their weapons or the rough palisades, their eyes dark from fatigue and the fury of battle. The spirit was going out of them. They were not to blame. Perhaps it had been decreed from the beginning.

He came to a decision and added abruptly, 'After that, I want every fit man paraded for inspection. I want them washed and shaved and turned out like marines.'

He could feel the sudden apprehension around him. They imagined he had gone raving mad.

'The wounded men will be moved to the parapets before dawn, and I want every spare musket and pistol ready to fire. There may be no time to reload.'

Sergeant Brogan asked warily 'We goin' to fight 'em in the open, sir?'

Blackwood saw Smithett unrolling his kit below the wall. He must have ears like a fox.

Then he turned and looked at Lascelles again. 'Let me know when you're ready and I'll tell you what I intend.'

To Brogan he added, 'You will command the fort. If we fail tomorrow, I shall expect you to fight to the finish and not leave the wounded to suffer at the hands of those savages.'

Brogan nodded, his face pale. Now he understood.

Blackwood walked towards the wall, hoping that his light-headedness would not make him stumble.

Right or wrong, he had made a decision. Tomorrow would show if it was the right one.

# 6

# *One of the Best*

'Everything quiet, Sergeant?' Blackwood peered over the parapet for what felt like the thousandth time.

'Aye, sir.' Brogan, still dressed in his filthy shirt, made a sharp contrast with Blackwood's coatee and white shoulder-belt.

*Three hours since they had left.*

When Lascelles' party had lowered themselves over the rear wall which faced the river, Blackwood had expected a challenge or some terrible cry to show they had been captured. But there had been no sound at all. That might mean nothing. Fenwick had described only too clearly how his two companions had vanished without even a whimper.

'You know what to do?'

Brogan bit his lip. 'I'd rather be with you, sir.'

Blackwood thought of the wounded marines who had said much the same as Brogan. It had not been a stupid gesture of loyalty or courage. They were used to being together. The thought of being separated now in the face of almost certain death was too much for them.

Twelve wounded men might be able to defend the front wall for a short while. It would be up to Sergeant Brogan and old Fenwick to make as much noise and to fire as many weapons as they could to support the deception.

He looked at the sky. They would need plenty of time to get into position. In spite of all that Fenwick had told him, there was still a possibility that a few of Mdlaka's men were watching the fort. But why should they? There was no way of escape without boats, and Mdlaka knew it. If they attempted to force their way inland they would be tracked down and killed like wild animals.

He said, 'I shall inspect the men.'

Down in the compound, lit only by a flickering fire, the marines were paraded in two ranks as if aboard ship.

Blackwood, followed by M'Crystal, moved slowly along each rank, conscious of the silence, the strange air of resignation which seemed to hang over them.

No packs or unnecessary equipment this time. Muskets, bayonets and ammunition pouches were all they carried. In the dancing reflections from the fire their cross-belts and red coats added a final unreality. Dressed to kill, or be killed.

'Stand easy.' Blackwood did not raise his voice. He did not have to. 'We shall be leaving the fort very soon. No sound, no talking. We must be on the hillside before first light.' He glanced down the front rank. 'Private Ackland, don't forget your bugle. Suck a pebble if you must, but I don't want your mouth too dry to blow when I give the order!'

Some of them actually chuckled as if it was all a great joke.

Blackwood continued, 'When they attack the gates they will see only what they expect to see, our men shooting down at them.' *Provided*, a nagging voice seemed to whisper, Lascelles is not already dead or screaming out his life under torture, and provided the marksmen were not there when he made his move. 'The last thing they will expect is to be attacked from the rear, and by marines in proper kit, unlike Sergeant Brogan's scarecrows!'

A few even laughed outright this time.

Blackwood waited until they had quietened again and said, 'We did not ask to be here, and this might be the last day for all of us.' He let his words sink in and there was absolute silence now. 'But we are Royal Marines, and we shall act as such.'

He turned away, unwilling to watch their faces. In the strange, shadowy light they already looked like spectres from a battlefield.

Colour-Sergeant M'Crystal joined him by the wall. 'That was well said, sir. They'll not let you down.' He jerked his belt into place. 'Wait till Sarnt Quintin hears about this. He'd not have missed it for anything.'

Blackwood froze as a chilling scream rent the night air.

But M'Crystal said, 'No, sir. That was only an animal of some sort.'

Blackwood breathed out slowly. He could not take much more of it. Concealing the fear was squeezing his insides like giant claws, and hiding the uncertainty made every thought distorted.

'I hope so.' He saw Smithett pouring brandy into a cup for him. It was almost time. 'I'm just sorry it had to be here, in this wretched place.'

M'Crystal showed his teeth in a grin. 'My dad died fighting two sailors in a street in Naples, sir. If I've a choice, I'll do it this way.'

M'Crystal moved away into the shadows. He would pour some of his rough confidence into the recruits, although after this nobody could be termed an amateur, Blackwood thought.

The brandy was hot and strong, and he handed the cup to Smithett, who had already packed up everything which was not immediately needed. The perfect attendant. Now Smithett was adjusting his belt and bayonet. Soon he would be an equally perfect marine.

Lascelles lay prone in a narrow depression at the top of the hill, his body aching from a dozen cuts and bruises, after finding this place in the darkness. He could hear Frazier nearby, moving some scrub to cover his position, his musket already trained and resting on some loose stones.

It had been the most terrible journey Lascelles could remember. Every sound had been like approaching death, and even the rustle of dry leaves had been an invisible army. He had seen himself captured before he could turn his pistol on his temple. Pleading and whimpering while they had tormented him before burning and cutting the life from his body.

Reaching the hill was only a postponement, it had to be. But it felt like a triumph all the same. He looked fearfully at the sky. Surely it was already brighter? He wondered where Corporal Jones was at this moment. A few yards further down the hill where he would be better placed to see the marksmen, if and when they appeared.

Lascelles felt his eyes sting at the thought of the shipboard life he had come to enjoy so much. The smell of the sea was keener on the hill and he imagined a dozen vessels out there in the darkness, sailing too far out to see or realize what was happening here.

He hissed, 'Can you see Corporal Jones?'

Frazier took his time answering. Jones was the old campaigner and knew what he was doing. The lieutenant just had to say something. He snorted. Bloody officers.

'Down an' to the left,' he hesitated, 'sir.'

'Yes. Yes, I see.'

Lascelles groped for his flask and sipped some water. It was warm and made him feel sick. God, the waiting. *Waiting*.

He thought of Blackwood, his calm assurance and quick flashes of impatience. A captain at twenty-six, a real-life hero by all accounts. Now he was there at that damnable fort waiting to lead his remaining men to oblivion. Lascelles rubbed his eyes with his knuckles. It was *unfair*, wrong that they should be here. He thought of his cabin aboard the *Satyr*, his books, the portrait of his mother, of his married sister in England, and how her children had admired his uniform on his last leave.

A cold shiver ran through him as Frazier whispered, 'Somebody's about already. I 'eard a cough.'

Lascelles could barely breathe. A cough. As close as that? He felt for his pistols, suddenly petrified. He blinked rapidly to clear his vision and saw the slope below him, and further still a small black square. That must be the fort. Beyond it the river, and beyond that the sea. Safety. If only . . .

Frazier had sensed his lieutenant's fear. He had once seen an officer stand as stiff as a ramrod as if on parade, too stricken to move, to avoid the blade which had hacked him down.

He said tersely, 'Easy, sir. We're safe enough for the moment.' He turned his head a few inches and added, 'Here comes the corporal.'

Lascelles made a great effort to control his shaking limbs. He had neither heard nor seen Jones' stealthy approach, and he was a large man.

Jones knelt beside the little hiding-place and plucked at his torn shirt. Without taking his eyes from the hillside he said softly, 'One of the buggers is right below us by the rocks. I heard him talking with his mate. Dagoes, by the sound of 'em. The other one's further to the right. Can't see him now.'

Lascelles peered up at him, searching for comfort in the corporal's words.

'Well? What will we do?'

Jones did not glance at him then. Blackwood, even the boozy lieutenant Cleveland would have told *him* what to do.

'The first one's easy, sir. I'll take him myself. The other bugger is too far away. Won't see him until he starts firing.' He looked at the shadows. 'Up to you, Frazier.'

Lascelles nodded jerkily. 'Yes. That's right.'

Jones laid his musket down very carefully and drew out a broad-bladed knife.

Lascelles stared, horrified. 'With that?'

Jones shrugged. 'Took it off a Dago. Might as well give it back, so to speak.' His gentle Welsh voice made the words all the more horrific.

Frazier moved again very slightly and gripped his musket. 'Here we are then.'

Lascelles saw the first light making a small shadow below his out-thrust arm. He turned to speak to Jones but he had vanished, as if he had never been.

*

Sergeant Brogan watched the sky brightening above the ridged hills and knew that the sun would be showing itself at any moment.

Someone called, 'Simcoe's dead, Sarnt!'

'Very well. Leave him an' take up your post.'

Another voice muttered, 'He's better off out of it, if you ask me!'

Brogan snapped, 'We're *not* asking, so shut it!'

He looked along the fort's puny defences and wondered why he felt no fear. Maybe it was what he had always expected since he had first seen his father in a marine's red coat. Unlike some of the others, Brogan had never had any doubts. He had been born within sight and sound of the barracks, had got to know the routines and drills before he could write his own name.

God, what a mess they all looked, he thought bitterly. Wounded men propped along the parapet at intervals like a line of cripples, their stained shirts and rough bandages adding the final touch to their suffering. One sat with his legs out-thrust, his back to the wall. His eyes were tightly shut against the pain of a deep wound in his chest, but he was surrounded by pouches of shot and percussion caps and gripped a ramrod in his fingers like a talisman.

Brogan eyed him grimly. He did not look as if he would last much longer. But even with his eyes closed he could still reload the spare muskets until his strength finally gave out. Brogan knew his men well. They could clean or load their weapons in pitch-darkness if need be.

He saw the old, long-bearded trader, Fenwick, at the far corner, a great musket cradled across his chest. It looked as if it could knock down six men at once. What sort of fools would want to stay in this hell? To trade with a bunch of treacherous natives? Fenwick's mates had paid dearly for it, others would soon follow.

The man nearest him asked, 'Do you think we can 'old them, Sergeant?'

Brogan shrugged. 'Can't say, Oastler.' He tried not to

think of Lieutenant Lascelles and what use he might be if Captain Blackwood fell. Brogan had carried the lieutenant during their time together in *Satyr*, and they both knew it. He added, 'If we get rushed and the gates bust open, we'll re-form at the river end, right?'

They both turned, their eyes gleaming in the first red glow of sunlight as it painted the top of the hill.

Private Oastler gritted his teeth against the pain in his leg and said, 'They're comin' already, the bastards!'

Brogan glanced at his handful of men and then at the loaded weapons by his side.

He heard Fenwick call in his shaky voice, 'They'll 'ave the sun behind 'em.'

Brogan gripped a musket and stared at the departing shadows with quiet desperation. Why didn't the old bugger shut up? Most of the men knew what was happening, and the others, well, they were better off in ignorance.

The dust looked thicker this time, but the swish and thud against the shields sounded the same.

'Stand to.' He did not raise his voice. They were all as ready as they could be.

The sun lifted more rapidly, and Brogan tried to shade his eyes as he peered at the distorted shapes of rocks and dark undergrowth. For the first time he felt his chest tighten with anxiety. They were coming. How long before it was over, and how would he behave when it happened? He glanced again at his men, at their tight faces and pain-filled eyes. He had seen some of them reeling drunk, or taking part in fleet regattas with the best of them. He had heard them cursing his name when he had turned them out on deck for a kit inspection or for drill. He had seen their comradeship grow with the rough but reliable humour of the lower deck.

Brogan thought suddenly of Blackwood when he had outlined his impossible plan. God Almighty, it had been only yesterday, just hours ago. But he remembered even more clearly what he had said. 'Fight to the finish.' It seemed to pull him together, as if he had just heard him speak.

'*Face your front!*'

He ran a musket through his hands and rested it on the wall. One of the hidden marksmen might already see him, but it was more important that his men should think he was unafraid.

The drumming beat was louder, and Brogan saw the glint of light on naked backs and brandished weapons. They were heading straight for the fort but more spread out than before, as if to divide the marines' fire.

'Ready!'

Brogan heard his men trying to shout, some with their voices so cracked with pain they sounded like pensioners. Even Fenwick was yelling unintelligible commands, anything which might make the attackers believe there was the same number of men behind the walls.

Brogan squinted along the barrel and moved it in time with one of the running figures. It wouldn't take them long to realize the truth after the first volley.

'*Take aim!*'

Something hit the wall by the gates, a spear or a rock, Brogan did not know.

He heard the marine named Oastler gasping as if in further pain, while the man with his eyes shut who gripped the ramrod so tightly called, 'What was that, Tom? Tell me, mate!'

But Oastler could barely speak. All he managed was, 'It's the lads.'

Brogan could understand his emotion. He was hard put not to show it himself. At first he had imagined his own resolve had cracked.

Then, as the shadows rolled back even further, he heard it again, the blaring call of a bugle, as clear and as firm as he had first heard it as a young boy.

The charging mass of figures seemed to lose direction and swung round in a haphazard confusion as they realized what was happening.

Brogan said tightly, 'If I live to be a hundred I'll not forget it.'

As if rising out of the ground itself the line of scarlet-coated marines marched unhurriedly down the slope towards the fort. Their bayonets shone and caught the sun's early redness like blood, their muskets at the high port across each man's body. In the centre and slightly ahead of the slow-moving line Brogan saw the slim figure of the captain, and at the rear the heavier bulk of the colour-sergeant, his sword already drawn across his shoulder.

Brogan had to wrench himself from his trance.

'*Ready! Fire!*'

He snatched up the next musket almost before the aimed volley had swept among the mass of figures below.

Everyone was yelling like a madman, and two of the marines were standing up on the wall itself, regardless of the risk, as they reloaded and fired again.

But some of the attackers were still coming on and Brogan yelled, 'Fix bayonets!'

The last time? He no longer cared.

'There's the fort, sir.' M'Crystal kept his voice low as he watched the early sunlight give an outline to the wall and parapet.

Blackwood nodded and examined the lay of the land. How different it all seemed in daylight and from this angle. He could see the charred beams of the burned-out store-house above the parapet, the litter of black shapes around the gates, like dead leaves until the sun uncovered them too.

He saw a glint of light from the left of the wall as the strengthening rays touched a marine's badge like a tiny mirror.

'Listen?' M'Crystal turned his head as if to smell out the danger. 'They're early, sir.'

Blackwood crawled away, his mind grappling with what might happen. The marines were in a long line, kneeling or sitting among the high dried grass which was thicker than he had imagined. He tried not to think about Lascelles, or if the marksmen had been taken. Once they began to move it would be too late, each white cross-belt would make a perfect target.

He wiped one hand on his sleeve and then pulled on his white gloves. At least he would be able to retain a grip on his weapons, he thought.

'Get ready!'

His words were repeated and whispered along the line of concealed figures. Blackwood bit tightly on his chin strap as he tried to shut out the mounting din from around the hill.

He leaned forward, his sword blade slithering through the grass as he craned up to watch the first running figures as they charged into view. Not so many this time. Perhaps Fenwick had been right and some of the warriors had already deserted Mdlaka?

He glanced along his own men, or what he could see of them. They were still outnumbered by at least four to one. He closed his mind against it and called, 'Ready, Ackland?'

The freckle-faced marine nodded and spat out a pebble before he moistened the bugle with his tongue.

Blackwood found that he was looking into the eyes of Private Oldcastle. Just a boy, who but for a twist of fate would be settling down to a routine life aboard the *Audacious*.

'Are you all right?'

The boy licked his lips, but his tongue seemed to stick to them.

'Y-yes, sir.'

'Good. Keep together, remember it.'

What was the point? The full mass of the charging mob was visible now, heading towards the gates in a human tide. There was no time to worry about anyone's feelings.

He stood up and pointed towards the fort. Without looking he could feel his men rising up on either side of him.

Blackwood walked through the rank, his arm brushing against Oldcastle's musket as he did so.

He looked at him again. Of *course* there was a point, and it *did* matter.

'Stay near me.' He saw him nod, then he strode forward and shouted, '*Sound the Advance*!'

The bugle echoed up the hillside and across the lower flat ground where they would confront their fate.

Lieutenant Lascelles lurched to his knees and pointed wildly. 'Look at them! Just *look* at them!'

He felt Corporal Jones grip his arm and drag him down without bothering about dignity as he exclaimed, 'Watch out, sir!'

Lascelles stared past him, his breathing wheezing like an old man's as he watched the red line of figures march out of cover and on to the flat ground which faced the fort.

He saw the ripple of stabbing flames as the men on the parapet fired into the attackers, and two marines who had climbed up in full view as they reloaded to fire again. It was an awful madness, and yet the most inspiring thing Lascelles had ever seen or heard. The bugle's strident call, the marines advancing as if they had all the time in the world.

Frazier ignored the lieutenant's excitement and pressed his cheek against his musket with deliberate care. He too had seen the two madmen on the wall, he had also seen Jones wipe his knife on some grass as he had emerged from his hiding-place. One dead, another to go.

He held his breath as a shot echoed from the hillside, magnified by the fallen slabs of rock where the other marksman had been concealed. Frazier did not watch as one of the small figures pitched from the wall where it was immediately engulfed by a hacking, stabbing mob. Frazier concentrated on the drifting feather of smoke from the rocks, his eyes unblinking as he waited.

A head rose very slightly, and Frazier imagined he could see the man reloading. He was wasting his time, he thought, and squeezed the trigger, letting out his breath as the marksman leapt into the air and then rolled down the slope like a bundle of rags.

Jones said harshly, 'That's it, sir. We can join the others now.'

He watched as Lascelles half rose to his feet, his face empty as the air crackled with shots and another blare on the bugle.

Frazier fired again and saw one of the running figures fall spread-eagled even as he waved to some of his warriors to change direction towards the marines.

Lascelles licked his lips. 'I – I'm not sure.'

Frazier stood up and snapped his bayonet on his musket. 'I am.' He started to lope down the slope without another glance.

Corporal Jones said, 'Come along, sir. Captain Blackwood may expect it. You've done what he asked.'

He watched the officer's emotions with angry resignation. *Me and Frazier did all the work*. He could still feel his arm around the marksman's neck, his terrible gurgle as he had thrust the blade up and through his ribs.

But above all else Jones was a trained marine, and would no more leave his officer than fly. Frazier would probably be disciplined if any of them survived, but he was used to that.

He persisted, 'Now, sir.'

Lascelles nodded and picked up his pistols. Then together they walked down the slope.


'Halt! Prepare to fire!'

Blackwood did not turn his head as the odd numbers in the single line stepped forward and knelt on one knee while the others remained standing.

He hardly dared to draw breath, and was certain that every muscle and limb in his body was shaking beyond control.

But in spite of everything *they had remembered*. In the face of death, even the most junior recruit among them had recalled the drills aboard *Satyr*.

Blackwood looked at the oncoming tide of painted shields and glittering spears. The first surprise was over and the bulk of the attackers were now heading for the motionless marines. Blackwood had seen the man fall from the wall and guessed he had been shot by one of the marksmen. There had been no further shots from the rear as far as he could tell. He flinched as another crack made his hope a lie, but instead of a marine, one of the leading savages was flung to the ground by the force of a ball.

'*Present!*'

Blackwood raised his sword, his eyes fixed on the leading runners. Thirty yards, twenty, now less . . . he felt a spear thud into the ground nearby.

'*Fire!*'

The fusilade of shots ploughed through the advancing crowd like an invisible scythe.

There was not time to reload or for anything else. They were out in the open. No way back, and no help other than they could give each other.

'*Again*, Ackland!'

How he could blow his bugle after all the din and frenzy which confronted him was a miracle.

The front rank rose together, and as the others moved up to re-form the line Blackwood shouted, 'At 'em, lads!'

Keeping together they charged headlong towards the nearest shields. Every man was shouting and cursing, and the pace seemed to quicken as the attackers wavered, those behind colliding with their companions in a momentary tangle of limbs and weapons.

The marines hit the front ranks like a battering-ram, the bayonets knocking aside spears and clubs alike as their despair gave way to a desperate ferocity.

Blackwood vaguely heard a ragged volley of shots from the fort as Brogan did what he could to cause confusion from another direction. He saw a pair of bulging eyes above the rim of a shield and fired his pistol through the painted hide, seeing the man collapse even as he jumped over him and slashed another across the chest with his sword. He could hear Smithett at his side, saw his bloodied bayonet stabbing forward like a tongue, his boot thrusting the corpse free as he guarded his face from a club.

From one corner of his eye Blackwood saw a red coat fall among the stamping feet and stabbing bayonets. Another marine pitched amongst his attackers, his screams cut short by a single blow from an axe.

Blackwood trampled on more sprawled bodies and realized, as if in a daze, that they were advancing, that the enemy was reeling back and causing panic in their rear.

'*Halt!*'

Breathless and lurching, their eyes wild, the marines heard and obeyed.

Blackwood watched, his heart pounding like a hammer as he waited for the attack to begin again. But the gap was widening and there were no longer any battle cries to urge them on.

'Reload!'

He saw a figure dart from the stamping, gesturing mob and run headlong for the marines. One of their leaders making a last challenge which could so easily end everything.

Blackwood heard a solitary shot and saw the running man fall. Frazier was back with his comrades.

'Ready, sir!'

Blackwood looked down and saw blood on his leg. Yet he had felt nothing until now.

'*Present!*'

The muskets lifted again. Not so steadily this time, some of the men were finding it hard to breathe after their short, crazy charge.

'*Fire!*'

They did not even try to run. The volley hit the packed bodies and hurled several to the ground. But the others stayed where they were. More like beasts at the slaughter than the warriors they had been.

Surely it was enough? It had to be. Blackwood felt sick of the sights and the stench of death, but knew it was not yet finished.

Very deliberately he walked towards Mdlaka's warriors, praying that his leg would not give way as the pain came up to his thigh like a hot iron.

At any second one of them might lunge forward. Not even Frazier could do anything to save him.

Just ten paces clear he sheathed his sword, feeling its resistance as the blood caught on its scabbard.

He could smell them, feel their strength, temporarily lost for the lack of a leader.

Then they parted to allow a small figure to approach. Tiny, wrinkled, he was more monkey than man. The thought almost unnerved Blackwood as he thought of Ashley-Chute safe in his flagship, in another world. *Monkey*.

The old man must have taken his silence for dissatisfaction, for with surprising dignity he waved his arm towards his men and without hesitation they dropped their weapons and shields beside the corpses.

Blackwood looked at him, his mind cringing from all the senseless, brutal slaughter this place had seen.

Slade had spoken of meeting this man, who was obviously Mdlaka. Two of a kind perhaps. Dedicated to conquest.

Blackwood shook himself angrily. What the hell did it matter? Any of it?

He snapped, 'You are under arrest.' He saw emotion for the first time in the reddened eyes. Fear or contempt, he was not certain. He thought of what would be happening here if his tactics had failed and added coldly, 'Tell your people to go home. *Now!*' He motioned to the line of marines behind him. '*Present!*'

It was only a gesture, for he knew the marines had not even reloaded. Every eye had been fixed on him as he had strode to meet the enemy. But it was enough. Slowly at first, backing away as if suspecting some further trap, the crowd of warriors broke into a stampede.

Colour-Sergeant M'Crystal marched through the corpses and said thickly, 'God in heaven, that was a wild thing to do, begging your pardon, sir.' He glared at the king. 'What'll I do with *him*?'

Blackwood looked back at the men who had followed him without question to attempt the impossible. Three were obviously dead, several others crouched or hobbled among the motionless line of fixed bayonets.

Smithett joined him and exclaimed, 'Gawd, yer leg's done in, sir!' It sounded like an accusation.

But Blackwood ignored him. He stared instead at one sprawled figure with out-thrust legs, a musket still gripped in his hands as he stared unseeingly at the sky.

A sixteen-year-old boy from Yorkshire who had signed on when his father had died.

He said quietly, 'Put the prisoner in irons and see he is guarded.'

He tore his eyes from the dead marine, the boy who had been so frightened but who had trusted him.

'I want Mdlaka to share the shame of what he has done.' He could barely keep his voice under control. 'And I want to see him hanged.'

He looked at M'Crystal. 'Return to the fort. You know what to do.'

M'Crystal nodded, his face troubled. 'Aye, sir. We'll not leave any of our own out here.' He followed Blackwood's glance towards Oldcastle's body. 'Especially him.'

Blackwood turned on his heel and limped towards the gates. As if in a misty dream he saw they were open, that the handful of defenders were waving and cheering.

He knew he would collapse. The pain was worse, but it acted like a spur to drive him on and through those gates.

Sergeant Brogan ran to assist him, but from somewhere in the blur Smithett said fiercely, 'I can deal with 'im, Sarnt!'

Brogan stood aside as M'Crystal and the first section of marines tramped wearily through the gates.

'Close thing, Colour-Sergeant.'

M'Crystal watched Blackwood being lowered to a blanket by the wall, his face stiff against the pain.

To nobody in particular he murmured, 'He'll do me, and that's a fact. One o' the best.'

# 7

# Pride

'Starboard your helm, *steady*, steer east-nor'-east.'

Captain George Tobin watched narrowly as the frigate's bows began to swing towards the headland and then settle in direct line with the swirling current.

'Ring down dead slow.'

He would have smiled but for the anxiety in his mind. The engine-room responded to the order instantly, as if Hamilton, the Chief, had been sweating it out as he waited for the signal on his telegraph. They had steamed along the coast from Freetown with all the power the engine could offer, and Tobin had been forced to overrule Hamilton on a dozen occasions when he had pleaded with him to reduce speed.

Deacon touched his cap. 'Cleared for action, sir.'

Tobin grunted and took a telescope from his signals midshipman. The same bleak coast, the rocks and shoals he remembered so vividly from his days on the anti-slavery patrols.

No sign of life anywhere. Just a pall of drifting smoke which they had sighted soon after dawn as the great paddles had driven *Satyr* towards the land like an avenging demon.

He looked along his command, the men at the guns, Spalding, the third lieutenant, up forward by the two ten-inchers, his arms folded and with one foot on a flaked rope as he watched the shore with the others.

Tobin swore beneath his breath. One of the most powerful, modern ships afloat, but what use were *Satyr*'s big rifled guns against spears and poisoned arrows?

'I am going under the headland, Mr Deacon.'

Tobin tried not to think of what they might discover and concentrated instead on his ship's safety.

'Put the best leadsmen in the chains. I don't trust the charts hereabouts. Sand-bars come and go like smoke in these rivers.'

'Starboard two points.'

The slow-moving paddles threshed noisily as the first of the inshore current surged around the hull.

Tobin added, 'Be ready to lower boats and take the landing party ashore.'

Deacon nodded, his eyes on the top of the headland searching for a possible lookout.

How trivial they had tried to make it sound in Freetown, Tobin thought savagely. They were all too busy with their trade and lofty ideas of expanding it along the African mainland to take Blackwood's position seriously.

The senior naval officer, a commodore, had snapped testily, 'It could happen to any of us. It's what we're here for, dammit!' Perhaps he had just been told that Ashley-Chute would be relieving him of his command and could think of nothing else.

Even Slade, who had dashed ashore with his secretary within minutes of mooring, had said, 'He'll know what to do. He'd better.'

Very gingerly, the helm moving this way and that to compensate for the current, *Satyr* nosed her way into the shallows, the leadsman's cry making the master and his assistants tense with apprehension.

Tobin levelled his glass as the fort's low outline moved into view. He heard the clank of metal as the starboard ten-inch gun moved slightly on its slide, the black snout already trained on the fort.

It was still early morning, and a mist hovered along the shore to merge with the smoke from inland.

Lieutenant Deacon watched him curiously. If the captain ran this ship aground it would be the finish of his career. He saw a muscle jerk at the side of Tobin's jaw as a whistle shrilled and the signals midshipman called, 'Chief engineer, sir!'

Tobin strode to the big bell-mouthed voice-pipe and barked, 'Don't bother me now, Chief! I don't care if your dog-clutch *has* burst apart!' He paused and then said, 'My apologies, Chief,' and replaced the whistle in the pipe.

Then he glanced at Deacon and grimaced. 'Just wanted me to know I can have all the steam I want! And I almost tore his head off!'

They forgot Hamilton and his crashing, roaring world below decks as a lookout yelled, 'The fort, sir!'

Tobin stared as something moved on the wall. It was occupied. By whom and with what intent he did not know.

'Stand by, all guns!' Tobin glared at the master. 'Be ready to come about and keep an eye open for that bloody sand-spit!'

Deacon was so overwhelmed he touched his captain's arm with excitement. 'They're running up the Colours, sir!'

Tobin trained his glass again and watched the familiar flag jerking up to a crude pole above the wall. He saw red coats too, and somebody waving his hat in the air, his shouts lost in distance but no less moving in the telescope's lens.

'Larboard helm! *Steady*, man! Stand by on the fo'c'sle, Mr Spalding! Look alive there!'

Men dashed forward with rope fenders while others climbed out on to the cathead in readiness to leap on to the rickety pier.

Tobin snapped, 'Stop engine. Take over, Mr Deacon. I'm going ashore myself.'

Tobin knew now that his earlier fears had been false. He had expected them all to have been killed, wiped away like some of the other outposts he had heard about at Freetown. Normally he would have waited for the engine's last dying quiver before he relaxed, and then only until the next demand of duty. He was like that, even though he believed he could hide it from his subordinates.

But the sight of that flag, the one which he knew M'Crystal had carried ashore with him, had driven all caution aside like steam in the wind.

Lines snaked across the pier, and as men leapt down to secure the bow and stern ropes, *Satyr* ground against the sagging piles and came to rest.

Tobin beckoned to his midshipman. 'Come with me, Mr Allison!' Ignoring the glances of the second lieutenant and his armed landing party who were already mustered amidships, Tobin clambered out and down by the great paddle-box, the midshipman hurrying behind him.

He was only halfway up the beach when he stopped and said quietly, 'We'll wait a while, Mr Allison. Just a moment longer.'

He watched the file of marines as they appeared around the side of the fort, their fixed bayonets shining brightly in the early sunlight.

'Marines halt! R-i-g-h-t turn!'

Tobin said softly, 'Watch this, Mr Allison, and mark it well.'

Colour-Sergeant M'Crystal marched down the slope and saluted stiffly. Only near to could you see the stains on his trousers and coatee, the stubble around his chin.

Tobin returned his salute and asked, 'Was it bad?'

M'Crystal stared past him at the ship. 'Seven dead all told, sir. Not too bad when you consider the odds. We've got fifteen wounded too.' Only then did his eyes return to Tobin. 'Including Captain Blackwood, sir.'

Tobin said, 'Fetch the surgeon, Mr Allison, and tell Mr Oliver to take his landing party to the fort, at the double.'

Tobin walked up the slope with M'Crystal at his side. It was all so clear, as if he had taken part in it himself. The piled-up earth and stones where the corpses had been buried, the thousands of footmarks where a savage army had attacked this place again and again. As he got closer to the fort he saw the scars on the wall, the dark bloodstains both at the top and at the foot of the rough palisades where men had died.

'Will they attack again?'

M'Crystal glanced at him, seemingly surprised at the question.

'We fought 'em in the open, sir. Up there, by those rocks. Blade to blade.'

Feet pounded up the beach and seamen bustled past towards the fort, but Tobin did not see them. He saw only the small detachment of marines, fighting in the open, the only way they knew.

M'Crystal added firmly, 'No, sir, them buggers won't try it again.'

'What is the smoke?'

'Captain Blackwood insisted we pushed inland, in spite of his wound, sir. The day after the battle he took half of us and marched round that hill. We found several barracoons and burned them, big enough for two hundred slaves apiece they were. Empty when we got there, o' course. Just a couple o' dead ones and some shackles.' He added bitterly, 'For souvenirs.'

So that was it. The slavers had brought their live cargoes here to be collected by a ship of some kind. The fort, and then a handful of marines, had stopped them. They were probably fleeing through the bush right now with the slaves' own people in hot pursuit.

'I must see Captain Blackwood at once. How badly is he hurt?'

But M'Crystal stood his ground. 'With respect, sir, we've been waiting here for two weeks. Captain Blackwood would not thank me if I did not have you inspect the guard.'

Tobin had seen many sights on his various commissions around the African shores, but to inspect a single squad of gaunt and shabby marines who stood like ramrods as he looked at each unshaven face was one he would put above most of them.

Godby, the frigate's surgeon, met him inside the gates. 'Bad gash in his left leg, sir. Poison of some kind. Maybe it was on the weapon which made the wound. Can't do much here.' He darted a glance as the marine guard marched back into the fort. 'He might lose the leg anyway.'

Tobin followed him to a screened-off corner of the fort. Blackwood lay propped on some rolled blankets, his eyes closed as Smithett lathered his face and prepared to shave him. He did not seem to notice as the surgeon lifted a blanket and the dressing he had just cut from the wound.

Godby said softly, 'I can't smell anything putrid in it. Not yet.'

Tobin saw Blackwood's eyes staring at him. They were very bright and feverish.

Blackwood said, 'Good to see you again, sir.' He winced as Godby lifted his out-thrust leg to examine it again. '*Bloody* good. Things were a bit difficult here.'

'I've heard. Don't wear yourself out. You worked miracles.'

Blackwood murmured, 'Lost some good men. A few others will never do a parade again either. And for what? Some greedy, murderous chief and a couple of dead slaves.' He gave a crooked grin. 'The rest of the slaves scattered, so we won't even get the bounty money!'

He was delirious from the pain and the poison in his leg.

Tobin glanced at M'Crystal and asked, 'Where is Lieutenant Lascelles? Is he . . . ?'

The colour-sergeant shook his head. 'No, he's alive, sir. Out at the village with a patrol and old Fenwick. Making certain those devils don't have any more weapons hidden away. He'll burn the place to the ground if he finds 'em.'

Tobin looked away. It did not sound like the amiable Lascelles he knew. Then he glanced down at Blackwood again and guessed what must have changed him.

'Have the wounded carried to the ship right away. Mr Lascelles will take command here with one squad of marines.' He looked meaningly at M'Crystal's red face. '*Volunteers*. I shall leave a landing party and two six-pounders to give them some more authority – ' He broke off as Blackwood struggled up on his elbows.

'They are *my* men, sir!'

Tobin smiled sadly. 'You rest and finish your shave. I'm taking you to Freetown. No arguments. Have no fear about this bloody fort. I've seen what you did. A steam gunboat will be here tonight. She couldn't keep up with *Satyr!*'

The surgeon was signalling to some men with a stretcher but made himself wait until Smithett had completed the shave to his own satisfaction. Then Smithett eased Blackwood's arms into his coatee and made an attempt to adjust his shirt for him.

It was then that Blackwood realized how weak he had become, that Lascelles and the others had somehow managed to hide it from him.

Feet pounded across the compound and Lascelles appeared, gasping for breath.

'Don't worry, sir. Everything will be all right.' Their eyes met and he added quietly, 'Now.'

Blackwood was lifted on to the stretcher and faces swam around him like balloons.

Here and there a hand reached out to touch his shoulder or just the stretcher as he was carried from the fort. Beneath the gate he saw the marks of battle, the stains where one marine had been hacked down. Now it was his turn. He felt his eyes smarting as he tried to hide his despair. He would lose a leg. It was better to die like Simcoe, Oldcastle and the others.

At the pier he was able to open his eyes as a shadow spread over him. It was M'Crystal, as he knew it would be.

'I shall stay with Mr Lascelles, sir. But he's thriving on it now.' He was too used to duty and the stern demands of discipline and was unable to say what he really felt. Instead he said, 'I'll see you again soon, sir. When they come back for us.' He managed a grin. 'Last to leave, that's us.'

Blackwood twisted his head to answer him but he had already gone.

'Worth fifty men, is M'Crystal.' He even sounded as if he was dying, and his voice lacked any message of hope.

Tobin watched him being carried carefully up the frigate's

side and said to himself, 'You're worth a few yourself, my
friend.'

Later, as he lay in the same cabin he had used after joining
the ship at Gibraltar, Blackwood felt the hull begin to shake
and quiver to the power of her engine. He peered up desperately at the scuttle and tried to picture the scene as *Satyr* cast
off and thrashed violently clear of the piles. The surgeon must
have given him something because he could feel no pain, and
for a terrifying instant he imagined his leg had already been
taken off.

The door opened and Smithett padded to the scuttle and
opened it slightly. He did not speak but turned to watch his
officer's reaction as the sound of distant cheering penetrated
the cabin.

Blackwood tried to move higher but his strength failed
him.

'What are they cheering? Tell me, *please*!'

Smithett winced as the ship's siren blasted raucously along
the shore and to the hidden village whose king was now a
prisoner on the orlop deck.

He closed the scuttle tightly and replied, 'Cheerin', sir?
It's fer you, that's wot.'

Smithett picked up Blackwood's coatee and curled his lip.
Take a week to get it back into shape. Work, work, bloody
work, there's no end to it.

He glanced at Blackwood and waited until he was back in a
drugged sleep then left the cabin.

A petty officer was coming along the passageway and
paused to say, 'Glad you got out of it in one piece! You
deserve a bloody medal, to all accounts!' He hurried away to
his allotted station.

Smithett stood quite still, the coatee dangling from his
hand, as the ship began to surge ahead.

It was then, and only then, that he understood the true
significance of the petty officer's words. *He had survived.*

\*

Tobin entered the cabin and studied Blackwood thought-fully. He was required everywhere. Move to another anchor-age. Take on more coal. Report to the senior officer at Freetown for orders. But this moment was important too.

'How are you feeling?'

Blackwood raised himself on his elbows and winced as the pain came back. As if it had been lurking there. Lulling his defences.

'What's going to happen now?'

He felt rotten and knew that Tobin had already read the surgeon's report so knew better than he did about his condi-tion. The wound had been deep and badly infected. But for his stubborn insistence on following up their victory with a march on Mdlaka's village, he might be on his feet right now.

Tobin shrugged. 'You are being taken ashore. A surgeon there will be better placed to help you. After that . . .' He shrugged again. 'Back to England probably.' He attempted to smile. 'I did hear a rumour that you wanted to resign from the Corps anyway?' But he regretted it instantly as Black-wood's expression changed to one of dismay and loss.

Two seamen were in the passageway with a stretcher, and Smithett had already packed up their gear. The cabin looked empty and alien. Waiting for Lascelles to reclaim it.

Blackwood said quietly, 'I'm all right. No worse than some of the others, and better than the dead ones!'

He beckoned to Smithett who was standing behind the seamen.

'Here, help me up!'

Smithett stood fast and said dourly, 'Don't seem right to me, sir.'

'Do as you're told, damn you.' Blackwood was almost sobbing with pain and humiliation. 'Fetch my coat!'

Tobin's midshipman hovered in the passageway until the captain saw him.

'Mr Deacon's respects, sir, and *Audacious* is approaching the anchorage.'

He was careful not to stare at Blackwood.

'Thank you, Mr Allison.' Tobin carefully closed the door and shut out the others. 'So he finally got here.'

But Blackwood scarcely heard him. All the while he had been in *Satyr*, then at the fort, Ashley-Chute's squadron had been sailing ponderously for this same destination. The terrible sights and sounds, the feel of a man's last breath as he had hacked him down on that stretch of hard-fought land had meant nothing to the squadron as they had gone about their daily affairs. Now Monkey was here. Ready to take over command of operations from a mere commodore. It was a strange sort of promotion, but at this moment it was all Blackwood could think about, all he had left. If he went ashore he would be put aboard a home-bound ship. Marine captains, young or otherwise, carried little weight, and he knew he would be discharged without room for argument.

He knew too that it was desperately important he should hold on, and the *Audacious*, slow and outdated as she might be, was his only chance.

'I'd like to return to my ship, sir.'

Tobin stared at him. 'The admiral may think otherwise.'

'Let me *try*, sir.' He was pleading.

Tobin listened to the dull thud of a gun salute as the squadron flagship tacked towards the anchorage.

With any luck *Satyr* might be ordered to sea again within a day or so. Reports and despatches took time to pass from hand to hand, especially here at the Freetown naval base. He was probably doing Blackwood no favour, and he might end up a cripple if he rejected proper care. But Tobin could not forget his own feelings when he had seen the mission fort, the flag, the ragged defiance of M'Crystal's guard of honour. Nor would he ever lose the picture of these same men as they had watched Blackwood carried down to the ship. If they had held on to their strength, then Blackwood had certainly given it to them, and it had shown on their faces.

He made up his mind. 'Call away my gig for Captain Blackwood!'

He did not open the door but feet hurried away to do his

bidding. He did not want his men to see Blackwood's face.

Blackwood held out his hand. 'Thank you, *very* much.'

'It's worth a try.' Tobin opened the door for Smithett. 'I'll be waiting to hear. Perhaps you'll come back to *Satyr* one day.'

Very carefully Blackwood lowered himself to the deck while Smithett encircled his waist with a grip of steel. He could smell the rum on the marine's breath and guessed that he too had been saying his farewells in his own way. He gasped as the pain came again. *To me mates.*

It seemed to take an hour to reach the quarterdeck where he was almost blinded by the sunlight. There seemed to be ships everywhere, every class of war vessel, colourful native craft with huge lateen sails, even a stately East Indiaman unloading cargo into a mass of bobbing lighters.

But Blackwood had eyes only for the slow-moving flagship, her black and white hull shining like glass on the clear water, the receding gun smoke still clinging to her rigging and yards like muslin.

It was like a pain in his heart, and he wanted to tell Tobin how he felt.

Tobin gave a slow smile. 'I wish you luck.' Then he stood aside and saluted as Blackwood was carried bodily down to the gig alongside.

The first lieutenant joined him by the rail, eager to get on with the day's work. They were short-handed without the landing party.

Tobin watched the gig until it was swallowed up amidst the bustle of local craft and bat-like sails.

'If he lives long enough, that young man will do great things.'

'About coaling ship, sir?'

Tobin glanced at him and they both smiled. Deacon was not that good at hiding his feelings. Yet. He had been there when the attack had been made on the boats. He had memories of his own now.

'Yes, Mr Deacon, now what *about* coaling ship?'

\*

The flagship's side and tumblehome looked like a great cliff from the gig. Blackwood gritted his teeth as the bowman hooked on to the main chains and faces lined the gangway to peer down at him.

God, he must look a mess. The other marines had already been sent across from *Satyr*, except the badly wounded ones, so the story would be all over the ship.

Smithett muttered, 'Don't like it at all, I don't, an' that's a fact, sir.' He squinted up at the thick stairs to the entry port and then to a ladder which dangled from the gangway itself. Either way was asking for a fall.

Blackwood got into a more comfortable position on one leg, his arm around Smithett's shoulders. The gig's crew sat at attention as they watched his every move, and the midshipman in charge seemed at a total loss as to what to do next.

If only the pain would stay away. Blackwood could barely see through the mist as he fought to contain the rising fire in his leg. At any moment the wound would burst open. Why had he imagined he could do the impossible?

Smithett was watching him worriedly. 'I'll 'ave a bosun's chair sent down, sir!'

Feet clattered on the steps and Blackwood looked up into the eyes of his half-brother.

'Come along, sir.' He reached down and slipped his hand through Blackwood's arm. 'Easy now. Together.'

A seaman had also climbed down, and as they waited for the boat to lift and then settle again, Blackwood took his first step on to the tumblehome.

He nodded and tried to speak but nothing came.

Harry guided him carefully so that he could make use of the handholds. Blackwood could feel the protective strength of his arm, the care he was taking to help him. It was as if the whole ship was holding her breath, urging him to make the climb without failing.

His whole body was running with sweat, and from the wetness on his leg he guessed that some of his dressing had come loose.

'Never mind, Harry!' He peered up at the outstretched hands and concerned faces. 'Never bloody well mind, eh?' He was half gasping and half laughing as the senses of shock and pain joined against him.

Harry whispered against his ear, 'Oh, Philip, you crazy, wonderful idiot!' He did not seem to care if Blackwood heard him or not. All that mattered was the entry port, the bright blue sky above.

Blackwood felt more hands gripping his arms to lift him to the quarterdeck.

The sight of the assembled side-party, the officer of the watch and all the rest of this ordered world was too much for him.

What chance had he now of staying aboard? He had been stupid, too full of his own pride to accept the inevitable.

As if through a mist he saw Captain Ackworthy's great bulk striding towards him, and Sergeant Quintin coming aft from the main-deck. What a sight he must make.

Everybody froze as if suddenly bewitched, even their expressions of anxiety, surprise or merely curiosity remained fixed and set.

Only one small figure moved at the poop rail, head jutting forward, his voice cutting through the shipboard noises like a saw.

'It would appear that my captain of marines has decided that a life in coal dust and filth is not for him! He has shown some sense. I shall see him aft when he has collected himself, hmm?' He vanished.

Blackwood looked around him. Monkey neither could nor would bid him welcome, it was not his style. But at this moment it was the closest thing to it Blackwood had ever heard.

Slowly and carefully he straighted his back and balanced himself on one foot while he gauged the ship's gentle motion.

Then he looked at Ackworthy's strained face and touched his hat.

'I am rejoining the ship, sir.'

Ackworthy glanced from Blackwood's pale features to the bright spot of blood which had fallen to the deck by his feet where it gleamed like a malevolent red eye.

He needed to find the right words to convey what he felt, but all he could feel was envy. Not that it mattered, for at that moment Blackwood fainted.

# 8

# *Temptation*

For two whole weeks after he had boarded *Audacious* in such an undignified fashion, Blackwood lived in a state of mounting frustration. His relief at being allowed to return soon gave way to a feeling of reprieve, a momentary delay after which he would be sent packing to England. He had plenty of visitors, but noticed they were wary about discussing the daily routine, as if that might only make it harder when the axe fell.

Dalrymple, the senior surgeon, was not very encouraging and almost as gloomy as Smithett. *Too early to say. Wait and see* seemed to be the corner-stone of his diagnosis.

Confined to his cabin, Blackwood was very aware of his isolation. When he was not in a drugged sleep he lay in his cot putting faces and names to the sounds above and around him. There were several receptions and parties given on board, apparently to mark Ashley-Chute's taking command of the West Coast Squadron. As the temperature in his cabin rose to stifling humidity, Blackwood was forced to listen to muffled music, the clink of glasses and the carefree comings and goings of boats alongside.

He thought a great deal about the fort, and especially of the men who had fallen there. Of Oldcastle with his fear and determination, and Lascelles who had been prepared to throw his life away rather than let him down. What would become of Old Fenwick? he wondered. Stay there until the next traders joined him at the mission fort, or try his luck elsewhere in his hunt for riches?

At night, when the ship was quiet, Harry would come to the cabin and sit with him until he dozed off in his cot. Blackwood had got to know his eighteen-year-old half-brother better than he had ever done before, and together they had spoken about their futures, what would become of Hawks Hill and the estate after it had all been auctioned.

Harry had been more than candid about his mother. 'Far too young for the gov'nor. Still, but for her I suppose the Corps would be missing the services of a *superb* second lieutenant!'

Ashley-Chute's son had also visited him on a couple of occasions, but mostly it seemed to speak about *Satyr* and her performance rather than what lay ahead.

One late afternoon as Blackwood climbed from his cot to stand naked before Dalrymple and his assistant surgeon, he somehow knew it was the moment of decision. For several days he had heard stores being hoisted inboard from lighters, the familiar squeak of tackles punctuated by the twitter of boatswain's calls. A ship preparing to leave port.

He fixed his eyes on the mirror above his table and made himself stand quite still as Dalrymple's hard fingers probed at his leg. In the mirror he looked older, with deep lines at his mouth to reveal the strain he had been under.

Dalrymple said casually, 'Your other marines returned aboard today. They were brought from that fort by a gunboat. Full of bounce, they are. Fighting seems to agree with 'em.'

The assistant surgeon chuckled and wrote in his notebook as Dalrymple murmured something to him as an aside.

Blackwood felt a bead of sweat run from his hairline and drop on to his bare shoulder. They were back, apart from the ones who would never return.

*Think of them and stop being so bloody selfish. You lived. They did not.*

He could stand it no longer. 'Can I stay?'

Dalrymple looked up and a basin of water appeared as if by magic as Smithett eased his way round the cabin.

'Of course I shall make a report to the captain.' The surgeon's eyes settled on Blackwood. 'What do *you* think? Could you do your work under the same circumstances which gave you this wound?'

Smithett's voice broke the sudden uncertainty. 'Cap'n's comin', sir.'

The cabin seemed to shrink as Ackworthy stepped inside, his head lowered still further beneath the deckhead beams. He looked at Blackwood for several seconds, his eyes even more troubled than usual.

Blackwood guessed that Ashley-Chute had driven them all very hard on the passage from Gibraltar. Ackworthy more than anyone.

Ackworthy said abruptly, 'The squadron will weigh tomorrow morning.' He could not resist adding, 'Wind or no wind, apparently. How do you feel?'

Blackwood was very aware of the watching eyes, the two surgeons, and Smithett trying to be invisible in the background. He was more conscious of Ackworthy's tone than he was of standing naked in front of them.

The surgeon murmured, 'In my opinion, sir – '

Blackwood replied, 'I'm all right, sir. Bit stiff.' He had meant it to come out like an adjutant's report on the barrack square. Brief and firm. Instead he had sounded like a guilty schoolboy.

'Can you get dressed?' Ackworthy glanced round the cabin, probably remembering other ships, other times.

When Blackwood nodded he added, 'We are proceeding to Fernando Po. Sir Geoffrey Slade has already taken passage there in *Satyr*. Left yesterday.' He glanced at Blackwood's pale face. 'He didn't come and see you, did he?'

Blackwood shook his head, surprised he could still feel hurt about it after he had invented so many excuses for Slade's behaviour.

'By the time we've picked up the right winds it'll be close on two thousand miles to Fernando Po.' Ackworthy let his words sink in. 'It's a foul coast down there, all the way from

Lagos to Benin there's nothing but fever and trouble. There are some powerful slavers pushing the local kings into using their territory for the trade. Your experience with Mdlaka was just a tip of the iceberg.' He mopped his jowls with a handkerchief. 'Hardly apt, eh?'

Blackwood understood well enough. 'Then I must decide now. After tomorrow there'll be no turning back.' His leg throbbed as if to mock him.

'Correct. I have spoken with the admiral. He wants a report.' He managed a smile. 'Which means an hour ago.'

'I *want* to remain in *Audacious*, sir.'

The surgeon made one last attempt. 'I've not really *decided* . . .'

Ackworthy said bluntly, 'I have. He stays.' He tugged out his watch and examined it. 'I'll expect you aft in an hour.' He studied him questioningly. 'Can you get there?'

Blackwood grinned, the years falling from his face in spite of the pain.

'If I have to crawl.'

As Ackworthy made to leave Blackwood asked, 'The king, Mdlaka, has he been taken to a prison sir?' He could picture him without difficulty, old maybe, but with all the cunning of his ancestors.

Captain Ackworthy did not turn. 'He's been sent back to his village where he will be under British protection. He needs it now to survive. Sir Geoffrey Slade wrote the order himself. Better the devil you know . . . that kind of thing. Now you understand why Sir Geoffrey chose not to visit you.' The door closed with a bang.

The surgeons picked up their bags and Dalrymple said severely, 'I think it's madness.' He sensed Blackwood's sudden anger and added, 'Don't expect miracles, that's all I ask.' Then like ghouls they both withdrew.

Blackwood slumped on the cot and stared fixedly at the bulkhead.

'Well, Smithett, what did you make of that?'

Smithett unfolded a clean shirt and shook it out. ' 'Ow d'yer mean, sir?'

'We lost some *good men*.' He thought of Oldcastle, the way his arms had hung out like broken wings as he had been carried up to the fort for burial. 'For bloody nothing! I wish I'd shot that little bastard while I had the chance!'

Smithett regarded him calmly. 'Might 'ave 'ad someone worse to take 'is place like? We did wot we was *sent* to do, sir. It's all there is to it.'

Blackwood ran his fingers through his hair. *All there is to it*.

'Come on then, help me get into that shirt.' There was no getting the better of Smithett.

Vice-Admiral Sir James Ashley-Chute crossed one leg over the other and regarded Blackwood unsmilingly.

'I understand you consider yourself fit for active duty?' His lipless mouth opened and closed to ration each word. 'Another day and I would have had to discharge you from my command. However . . .' his cold stare dropped to Blackwood's leg, 'that would have meant transferring an officer from *Valiant* or *Argyll*. Untidy, and in any case you have been in this ship long enough to know your men and what they can do.' He indicated a pile of papers on his table. 'Interesting reading. It seems you were very *active* in the defence of the fort.'

Blackwood could sense Ackworthy's sweating discomfort somewhere behind him, the pain in his leg and the fact Ashley-Chute had pointedly not asked him to sit down.

Blackwood replied, 'Had I known what was intended, sir, I would have acted differently.'

'Indeed?' Ashley-Chute plucked at one of his grey side-burns. 'I think not. But I have to confess I did feel some irritation at the way that damned native was allowed to go about his business.' His eyes hardened. 'I'd have had him dancing at the main-yard in double quick time, politicians or no damned politicians, hmm?'

*Audacious* swung slightly on her cable, and through the cabin windows Blackwood saw the misty panorama of lush green hills and clusters of pale buildings along the shore.

Ashley-Chute continued in a more relaxed tone, 'However, everything will be changed from now on, as I explained to the commodore before he *left*.'

Blackwood tried to concentrate and ignore the ache and its attendant nausea. Ashley-Chute was testing him with no less dedication than the surgeon. There was still ample time for him to be put ashore.

The vice-admiral said, 'For years now we have been contending with fleets of slavers who have grown rich on their profits. Our patrols have taken a prize here and there and the guilty shipmasters have been punished. But the trade goes on, and will continue to do so while we play games instead of destroying it at its roots. Britannia rules the waves, so they say. But it has its disadvantages. Other nations who are supposed to be allies in stamping out slavery are content to let us get on with it. France is less cautious than our government in colonizing parts of Africa, she is careful to avoid antagonizing the local chiefs and traders. America is too slow to support our patrols and has sometimes accused us of hitting too hard.' His eyes settled on Blackwood's again. 'We shall hit harder, believe me!'

Ackworthy said, 'I think Captain Blackwood should be seated, Sir James.'

'Oh, really?' Ashley-Chute gave a thin smile. 'A chair, Blackwood.'

Blackwood sat down, almost hating Ackworthy for his genuine concern.

'Well, we've nearly three weeks to prepare ourselves.' Ashley-Chute stood up and walked to the stern windows, his hands grasped tightly behind him. 'I was given this station to *put things right*. Had I been appointed a year ago . . .' He shrugged. 'But there's no point in fretting over spilt milk, hmm?'

Blackwood was more confused than before. Why had

Ashley-Chute sent for him? Of all his captains and advisers, why pick on a junior marine officer?

Ashley-Chute continued, 'I intend to attack the slave trade in its own territory. No more chasing ships around the ocean only to discover they have already dropped their victims overboard at the first sight of danger. You may think that your skirmish at the fort was a waste of time, Blackwood. By God, I wish there were more such opportunities to show them we mean what we say, dammit!' He changed tack in a second. 'Any suggestions, by the way?'

Blackwood said, 'We're using old methods, sir.' He saw the warning light in Ashley-Chute's eyes but persisted. 'My father spoke of the same tactics in his day.'

Ashley-Chute said dryly, 'You talk of him as if he were deceased.'

Blackwood flushed. 'I'm sorry, sir. It's not that. But in the big ships of the line we drill and exercise as we have always done. On land we march and fight like infantry, form squares, and die if so ordered.'

He expected to be cut short but the admiral remained silent, his eyes boring into him, while Ackworthy's breathing got steadily heavier by the second.

He added, 'This is a different enemy, sir. They can fall back and regroup, while we must hang on with minimum rations and await the next attack. They *know* their territory, we do not.'

'Good. Capital. What I hoped you would say.' Ashley-Chute's thin lips split into a wide smile. 'I wanted to hear it from you. Somebody who has seen these conditions at close quarters, not from some shoe-licking staff officer who will tell me anything to gain favour.' He glanced past him towards Ackworthy. '*Fighting* men, that's what I want!'

Blackwood forgot the pain and discomfort in his leg. Ashley-Chute spoke as if he was embarking on a personal vendetta which only he could inspire. Perhaps it was true about him, that after the confusion in New Zealand he had been quietly censured. What was this appointment to him?

A chance to redeem himself, or was he to be a scapegoat if everything failed? Slade had said he was genuinely concerned with the expansion of an empire. He had left little doubt that he would use anyone to achieve that end. Blackwood bit his lip. Even me.

Ashley-Chute cocked his head as the bell chimed out from the forecastle. It was the moment to leave. The audience was over.

Blackwood got to his feet and hesitated. 'I should like to say something, sir.'

There was a brief spark of irritation. 'Well?'

'The rivers are the main channels for the slave-ships, sir. It will take time to get our people into position even without opposition from the shore.'

Ashley-Chute sounded almost relieved. As if he had been expecting something different.

'You are about to suggest I demand more steam vessels for this operation, am I right?' He shook his head. 'I am disappointed, Blackwood, and must put it down to the strain you have been under. This will be a perfect example of seamanship and discipline ashore and afloat. We are fighting slavers, Spanish and Portuguese for the most part, and ignorant, bloody savages! What would the world think if I ordered a fleet to do what any well trained flotilla should be capable of achieving, hmm?'

Ackworthy mumbled, 'I, er, I think – '

'I am delighted to hear *that*!' Ashley-Chute glanced at the pantry door. It was time for his glass of claret.

'Steam-powered ships are a novelty, Captain Blackwood, but they are not yet reliable under testing conditions.' His smile was almost gentle. 'Do I make myself clear?'

Blackwood left the admiral's quarters and tried not to limp until he was well clear of those probing eyes.

Ackworthy said thickly, 'In *your* place, Major, I'd have gone home, and that's a fact.'

'I doubt that, sir.'

He saw the huge captain wince as a midshipman scuttled

into view and gasped, 'Flag-lieutenant's respects, sir, and would you rejoin the admiral.' He swallowed miserably. 'Immediately, sir.'

Ackworthy turned heavily, his hands opening and closing like that day at Spithead. 'He'll be the death of me, I'm certain of it.' He seemed to be speaking to his ship.

Blackwood continued towards the filtered sunlight and saw M'Crystal waiting by the companion ladder. It was the first time they had met since he had been carried from the fort.

'Good to see you again, Colour-sergeant.'

M'Crystal's eyes flicked over Blackwood's uniform and injured leg. The inspection completed he said, 'Not sorry to be back either, sir.' He gestured with his head. 'The lads are having a sale of goods in the barracks, sir. The kit of the ones who didn't come through.'

Blackwood thrust his hand into his pocket for some coins. The custom was probably older than the Corps itself. The money might be some comfort to the widows and sweethearts in England. Once again he thought of Oldcastle. His mother had nobody at all now.

M'Crystal put the money in a bag and shook it. 'Och, it's not much, sir, but . . .'

'I know.'

M'Crystal turned to go and then said cheerfully, 'We're going into action again then, sir?'

There were no secrets.

'How does it suit, Colour-Sergeant?'

M'Crystal put one big foot on the ladder and replied, 'It's what I do best, sir.'

For him the fears of death or mutilation were in the past. Already he was looking forward to the next challenge.

Blackwood smiled to himself. Perhaps it was the best way to be.

The next day the squadron weighed and put to sea. It was a

slow, demanding business to get the ships into line, and *Audacious*'s yards were alive with signals for several hours until Ashley-Chute's captains had satisfied his demands.

After a few days it was as if nothing had ever happened and nothing would ever change. The curiosity shown by the ship's company whenever Blackwood had appeared on deck soon gave way to routine acceptance. Even when the surgeon examined and dressed his wound Blackwood found it hard to hold things in the right perspective; the fury of the fighting, the wild need to kill rather than be cut down by the attackers.

It was even difficult to recall the noisy, bounding excitement of Tobin's *Satyr*. This was the other navy again, slow, majestic, monotonous.

The squadron eventually altered course towards the east to steer deeper and deeper into the Gulf of Benin, where the coast of Africa was occasionally in view of the masthead lookouts.

Some said that Ashley-Chute was keeping well to seaward to give secrecy to his movements. Others, less charitable, insisted it was because he was making sure he would not meet with any steam vessels which could cruise close inshore in comparative safety.

Ten days after leaving Freetown the morning watch was roused by the mutter of distant gunfire.

Men swarmed up the ratlines and on to the yards in hopes of sighting something, and when the general signal was hoisted to make more sail they went to work with a will. Anything to break the boredom.

Eventually the lookouts reported that a sail had been sighted, the squadron's own frigate *Peregrine* which had been cruising well ahead of her massive consorts. Now she was coming about, and just beyond her, partly concealed in the morning mist, was a brigantine.

Netten, the first lieutenant, closed his telescope with a click.

'A bloody slaver. *Peregrine* must have run right down on her, the lucky devils.'

Ackworthy stood at the quarterdeck rail, his cap tugged down over his eyes.

'Alter course two points to larboard, Mr Tompkins.' He did not sound enthusiastic about this unexpected encounter. 'My compliments to the flag-lieutenant, and – '

'No need, Captain!' Ashley-Chute had appeared on deck, his eyes everywhere as he strode with his loping gait to the rail. 'Signal the squadron to proceed. *We* shall close with *Peregrine* and investigate.' He saw Blackwood on the lee side. 'Ah, Blackwood, I shall want you to go across and see what you can discover.' His pale eyes flickered in the glare. 'Not squeamish, I trust?' Again the barb, never far away. 'Not like *some*, hmm?'

Netten whispered, 'There'll be murder done if he doesn't stop goading the captain.'

It took most of the forenoon to reach the two drifting vessels. Blackwood could not help wondering if the little admiral had considered how speedily *Satyr* or one of her class would have executed the task.

As they drew nearer Blackwood could sense the mood around him. Seamen who had been cheerfully making bets on prize-money had fallen silent as the brigantine rolled heavily in the swell, her filthy hull in stark contrast with the little twenty-six-gun frigate.

'Heave to! All hands wear ship!'

*Audacious* responded slowly, her canvas in disarray as she turned into the wind. It was if she too was reluctant to stand close to the slaver.

Ashley-Chute crossed the deck and snapped, 'Thorough search, Blackwood. Bring the master back with you.' He rubbed his palms together. 'Nice little surprise.'

Sergeant Quintin tramped aft and saluted. 'Boat's in the water, sir.'

Netten followed Blackwood to the entry port. 'Even a slaver will be a change from the flagship,' was his only comment as they both climbed down to the waiting launch.

Close to, the brigantine looked like a hard-worked vessel.

Blackwood saw several armed seamen from the frigate placed at intervals around the deck, and a young lieutenant gesturing to somebody by the wheel.

The launch hooked on and Blackwood hauled himself bodily up the side, his leg moving clear of any bolt or protruding timber. He was getting good at it.

The lieutenant approached them and asked, 'Can I help you?'

Netten replied bluntly, 'We are from the admiral.' It was all he needed to say.

The young lieutenant pointed along the dirty, littered deck. 'Most of the crew are negroes, would you believe, sir. The master's a Spaniard, and his mates are Dutch half-castes.'

Blackwood glanced at some swivel guns which were depressed towards the hold and hatch covers. It was unbelievable to accept that the hull was crammed with people. He could smell brandy. The brigantine's after-guard must have been celebrating their transactions. They had certainly not been alert enough to see the frigate running down on them.

Netten asked, 'Want a look? I've seen it before many times.'

Blackwood walked to the nearest hatchway with Quintin close on his heels.

'Open it.'

Two seamen hauled aside the heavy iron staples and together pulled the doors apart. Blackwood had often heard old sailors speak of the stench in a slave-ship but he was unprepared for it nonetheless. Even though the brigantine carried a fresh batch of slaves, he doubted if the vessel had been cleaned for years. Decay, misery and death were all combined into something inhuman.

A petty officer said, 'Watch out, sir. If you fall amongst that lot we'll never be able to get you free in time.'

Blackwood stared down for a long moment until he saw the heaving mass of black bodies beneath him. While the vessel rolled into the troughs as she lay hove to, the sunlight spilled down the hatchway, and Blackwood saw it playing across hundreds of upturned eyes. It was unnerving, perhaps because of the total silence. As if all the packed bodies had died and only the eyes held on to life.

'Open all the hatches.'

They could not escape or try their fury on the newcomers. Blackwood had no doubt they would, given the opportunity. British seamen, Spanish slavers, they all looked the same to them.

He saw the shackles, the cruel way that all the slaves were linked to longer chains which ran from forward to aft through each hold and cargo space.

There must be two or three hundred of them.

Netten said offhandedly, 'I want to know his destination and the last anchorage.'

The young lieutenant grimaced. 'He threw his charts overboard.'

'That's not what I asked. Tell him I want the truth, and quickly.'

The petty officer murmured, 'There's a whole bunch o' women up forrard, sir.'

Blackwood glanced at him. He could sense it in the man's voice. Slaves were one thing, girls were different.

The sailors removed the canvas from the forward hold and lifted a hatch for Blackwood and his sergeant.

This time there was no mute silence. They had probably been expecting some of the slaver's crew to drag them on deck for their sexual pleasures, and the sight of Blackwood's red tunic brought a chorus of terrified voices.

Blackwood found himself staring at them. Young, small-breasted bodies, white teeth and pleading eyes. He knew he should be disgusted. Instead he was reacting no better than the petty officer.

He strode aft again. 'Do the prisoners understand what you say?'

The lieutenant shrugged. 'I – I'm not certain.'

Blackwood looked at the three prisoners. The master was as thin as a stick, the two half-castes just the reverse in their filthy duck trousers and straw hats. There were enough weapons on the deck where they had been dropped to arm a vessel twice her size.

'Take them across to the flaghip. I'm going to look further.'

As he lowered himself through a small companion-way by the wheel, Netten said to the *Peregrine*'s boarding officer, 'Marines. What can you do with them, eh?'

The young lieutenant frowned. 'But isn't he the one who . . .'

Netten watched the prisoners being pushed down to the launch. 'Yes. He's the one. That's what a *hero* looks like.'

Blackwood groped his way to the master's cabin, his body bent in the low confines of the hull. A skylight was wide open and he heard Netten's words with some surprise. Blackwood had not realized that his exploits had created a barrier between them. He had always liked Netten, but now he had changed. Surely not envious of nearly being killed? He wished suddenly he had not heard him.

He forced the door open and then tensed as he saw a pair of eyes watching him from a low bunk.

Behind him he heard Quintin exclaim, 'Gawd, the pick o' the bunch!'

She was blacker than most of the others, but even here amidst the squalor she had an arrogance to match her primitive beauty. She was naked with a gold chain around her neck which betrayed her breathing as she watched his uncertainty.

As she moved closer her body rolled towards him and her eyes never left his face. She touched her lips with her tongue and ran it along her teeth. It was very pink, like a tempting serpent.

And what the hell would it matter? They had saved all these people from slavery, and worse. No one would care. Quintin would keep his mouth shut, and even if he didn't the marines would make a joke of it.

He gripped her shoulder and felt her thrust towards him,

her lips parted like a trap. He touched her breast and squeezed it, thinking of that last time so long ago.

It was like releasing a spring, and she pulled herself up against him, her hand tightening on his groin.

'Look under the bunk!' He had to shout for his own sake as well as Quintin's. '*Now!*'

The sergeant dropped to the deck and flailed about under the bunk with his hands although his eyes were still on the girl's out-thrust leg.

Quintin lurched to his feet and stared at Blackwood with astonishment. ' 'Ow did you *know*, sir?'

Blackwood pushed the girl down on the bunk and took the gleaming weapon from Quintin's grip. Like the ones which had been used against the fort. New, rifled, and deadly.

Almost to himself he said, 'She's the slaver's mistress. That gold chain is worth a few guineas, he'd not waste it on a slut. She's too at home here. I guessed there must be a reason.'

She seemed to understand what was happening and flung herself from the bunk like an enraged puma, screaming and slashing at him with her fingers.

Quintin twisted her arms until she became quiet again. It had been a close thing.

Blackwood said, 'Watch her. I'm taking this over to Monk . . . I mean the admiral.'

Quintin grinned. 'Right, sir.'

He watched Blackwood leave. She had really got the young captain going. He pressed the girl's shoulders down on the bunk. There was no time now. But it was still a long way to Fernando Po.

His grin widened. 'Now you be a good lass an' the nice sergeant will look after you!'

On deck Blackwood handed the rifle to Smithett.

Netten whistled softly. 'Well now, that's a find. How was it missed?'

Blackwood glanced at the *Peregrine*'s lieutenant who looked at the deck and blushed.

'Easily done.' He saw Netten's surprise and realized his

voice must have betrayed his feelings. 'A marine was killed by one of those rifles. He was a hero too.'

He could feel Netten staring after him as he climbed down into the boat which had returned from *Audacious*.

Was it really the first lieutenant who had inflamed his anger? Or the sensuous girl in the cabin?

She would have killed him if she had got the chance. But to take her by force if necessary, to sink into her and forget everything, would have been worth the risk. Sergeant Quintin was probably laughing his head off.

'Wind's gettin' up a bit, sir.'

Smithett had seen the gleam in Blackwood's eyes and felt relieved. Nothing was changed. The captain was just as moody as before the battle at the fort. A real fire-brand he had picked for his officer.

Blackwood nodded. 'Good. The sooner we get this over and done with the better for all of us.'

Smithett had no idea what he was talking about and did not much care. They were all back together again, and that was what counted.

Captain John Ackworthy trod heavily around his day cabin, his head moving from side to side as he listened to the occasional shouted commands from the quarterdeck.

As Smithett had observed an hour earlier, the wind was freshening, and *Audacious* lay over on the larboard tack, her spars and shrouds rejoicing to the unusual turn of speed.

Ackworthy touched his sword on its rack and glanced at the seated officers who waited like actors unsure of their lines.

Pelham, the flag-lieutenant, blank-faced but watchful, too afraid of his master to miss even a tit-bit of information. Netten, who lounged in a chair, his shoes still stained from the slaver's filth.

In a chair on the opposite side of the cabin Blackwood watched Netten and wondered why he had not noticed the flaw before. Casual and relaxed, always ready with a quip when things got heated. That was not him at all. He was tensed like a spring, expectant, wary.

Ackworthy said, 'With luck we shall lop off a few days to Fernando Po with this wind.' He looked at them gravely. 'As you know, we have a consul there who is solely responsible for the rights of all traders of any nationality in the Bights of Benin and Biafra. Sir Geoffrey Slade will be with him now, and upon their decision will rest our part in future operations. The capture of the brigantine by *Peregrine* was a piece of good fortune as it turned out.' His gaze paused on Blackwood. 'The slaves were taken from Dahomey and on passage to Brazil. It is proof, if it was needed, that the trade is still flourishing.'

Blackwood thought of the packed, shining bodies and wondered if many would have reached their final destination. Probably half would have died. It was cruel, inhuman madness to throw lives away.

Ackworthy said in the same heavy tone, 'The discovery of the rifle in the master's cabin was something I did not expect. A new French rifle, part payment, part bribe for these scum.'

Blackwood could recall without effort Lascelles blurting out about the new Delvigne-Minie rifle as he had fought to overcome his own fear. What the British army were already being issued with and the marines would be getting next year. Maybe. So if anyone with the right money could obtain them, they could not lay the blame of arms smuggling at the French door.

'I am instructed to tell you that a private despatch is being sent to each captain in the squadron. Sir James Ashley-Chute,' he all but spat out his name, and Blackwood saw the flag-lieutenant stiffen in his chair, 'intends that we should attack the main supply route from Lagos as soon as we get the affirmative.' He looked at their faces and added, 'You are here because you will be in the leading flotilla.' He looked at Blackwood. 'Your experience will be important, even though you will not be in overall command of the marines taking part.'

Blackwood had guessed that already. *Argyll*'s marine officer was senior to him in both age and service. A major named Fynmore, he was known to be something of a perfectionist. He saw Netten watching him, waiting for a reaction.

Blackwood said, 'I understand.'

Ackworthy moved on. 'Mr Netten, I am to inform you that as of tomorrow you will assume the rank of commander. It is the admiral's wish that the promotion be advanced.'

Netten compressed his lips and then said, 'I never expected *that*, sir.'

Ackworthy regarded him coldly. 'Really?'

Blackwood shifted in his chair as he weighed up the admiral's tactics. Any captain in the squadron could have been put in direct command of a landing operation. But no, it had to be under Ashley-Chute's own hand. A major would lead the marines, but Netten would be in overall charge.

Ackworthy turned towards the stern windows where *Valiant* followed obediently some two cables astern.

'I did suggest that we act independently.' He measured each word as if he already saw them on a brief at his own court martial. 'We have captured a slaver with a full cargo. The master confessed to everything once he was confronted with the rifle. Slavery is one thing, but when Sir James had done with him he was almost convicted for piracy! I advised the admiral,' he turned to look at Pelham, 'that we should send a force ashore without further delay.'

Pelham fiddled with some papers. 'It is necessary for the squadron to proceed to Fernando Po, sir.' He was like a boy repeating a lesson. 'Sir Geoffrey Slade's instruction was — '

Ackworthy waved him aside. 'I *know* all that, Flags.'

Blackwood knew that the captain had said as much as he dared. By the time the squadron reached Fernando Po the news would have spread up and down the coast like a brush fire. If they did attempt to land and seek out the slavers' main base they would have no surprise on their side and might find a hot reception.

No wonder Ackworthy was worried. He was a sailor to his finger-tips, one of the old school, but no match for his admiral. Surely Ashley-Chute did not want a bloody confrontation? Or was it Slade, moving his pawns with quiet dedication while he hoped for just that?

Old Fenwick had spoken of it at the fort one night when they had walked the parapet together, waiting for the dawn and dreading it.

He had explained in his quavery voice, 'They let some well-intentioned missionary chance his luck with the tribes. If 'e keeps 'is 'ead on 'is shoulders, they allows a few traders to set up a post, then mebbe a fort to exchange their wares for somethin' better. When they get attacked or murdered, the soldiers arrives to restore order.' He wagged his unlit pipe like a sage. 'The difference is, Cap'n, that even if the priests and the traders go away, the military don't.' He had given his eerie chuckle, delighted by Blackwood's doubt. 'That's wot they calls empire, y'see?'

Fenwick, Slade and Mdlaka knew the rules. It was to be hoped that Ashley-Chute did too and did not merely see the operation as another North Island affray.

'So, gentlemen, you may carry on to your duties. Perhaps when we anchor we will receive contrary orders.' He did not sound as if he believed it.

As they left the cabin Netten said, 'We'll get a chance to do something useful after all.' He glanced at Blackwood. 'You all right?'

'Thank you, sir, yes.'

Netten grinned uneasily. 'Come along now. Not so much of the sir. We're between decks, not at divisions!'

Blackwood saw Harry waiting by the poop ladder, his features carefully composed.

'Tell me, sir, have you ever taken part in an operation like the one our admiral has in mind?' He saw a momentary uncertainty and added, 'It's not like a Spithead regatta, with a keg of rum for the winner!'

Netten's jaw tightened. 'To tell you the truth, I'm just

about sick of having your name jammed down my throat! You did your job, nothing more, now I'll do mine!' He strode away and brushed past the marine lieutenant without seeing him.

Blackwood sighed. It was better out in the open no matter what consequences it might bring.

'Storm-clouds, sir?' His voice was innocent.

'Shut up, Harry, and come down for a drink. I've got some thinking to do.'

In his cabin again Blackwood threw his tunic on the cot and massaged his leg while Harry poured two generous glasses of brandy. It was strange, but this was the first day he had not thought about his wound. Not until now.

Harry said, 'I hear that Major Fynmore is taking charge of our little war?'

Blackwood grinned. It was refreshing to have Harry with him even though he had first reacted against it.

The youthful lieutenant held up his glass to the light. 'Everyone's talking about it.' He shot him a direct glance. 'You two don't exactly hit it off, do you?'

Blackwood let the brandy run over his tongue. He could still feel the smoothness of her body, the animal heat as she had thrust herself at him.

'No, Harry. We don't. His father served with *our* father and they heartily disliked each other.'

He tossed back the brandy and gasped. What with Netten and Fynmore things would get very lively before long.

Harry did not look at him as he poured two more drinks. Even his hand shook as he said quietly, '*I can't wait.* Thank *God* I was able to get this appointment before you weighed anchor.'

Blackwood said nothing. He was eight years older than Harry. It might have been a hundred. But he remembered when he had felt like him, had itched for the chance to serve and fight rather than inspect some barrack guard.

It made him feel both protective and uneasy, as he had

about Oldcastle when he had looked at him on that dreadful day when Ackland had sounded the Advance.

'God? I thought it was your mother?'

Harry laughed. 'Same thing!'

Suddenly the worst was over and it was so good to be alive.

# 9

## Officers and Men

It was no great distance from the waterfront to the low-roofed buildings of the British Consulate of Fernando Po, but by the time he had forced his way through an endless throng of people Blackwood had cause to remember Ackworthy's warning. The heat was unbearable, so that his face felt as if it had been in a desert sandstorm. Noise, colour and a variety of smells and stenches made Blackwood wish more than once that he had remained in the flagship.

M'Crystal marched at his side, like a massive plough as he forced a passage for his captain. Without him Blackwood doubted if he would have been able to leave the waterfront.

The squadron had anchored in the early morning before the sun had gained its true power. Now, shimmering above their separate images, the four ships of the line, the frigates and their captured brigantine made an impressive array. Blackwood had often wondered why Britain had chosen a Spanish island like Fernando Po to set up this consulate which in fact controlled all the traders in the Bights of Benin and Biafra, which in turn affected the coastal shipping throughout the whole Gulf. But if the Spanish flag flew above the citadel, the impressive might of Ashley-Chute's squadron left no doubt as to where the real power lay.

It would be impossible to keep Ashley-Chute's intentions secret for long, he thought. The waterfront and anchorage were packed with vessels of every kind and nationality. Arab dhows and local coasters, Spanish scooners and American brigs. Ashore and afloat the place was a melting-pot of humanity.

M'Crystal said wearily, 'Och, there's the gate, sir.' He pushed a jabbering street vendor aside and guided Blackwood through the consulate's entrance and past the two sweating British sentries.

The wall acted like a shutter, so that as the street noises faded Blackwood felt a tinge of uncertainty. Harry had hinted that he was wasting his time when he had told him he intended to see Slade. Ashley-Chute would tear him limb from limb if he upset his old friend.

A robed servant appeared at a doorway and bowed smoothly. 'This way, sir.'

M'Crystal grunted. 'I'll be waiting, sir. Just in case.'

Blackwood glanced at him. The colour-sergeant had obviously seen through him as well. That thought and the sweating discomfort of this place made him unreasonably angry, and without a word he followed the servant into the shady entrance, which compared with the street was almost cool.

The servant gestured politely for him to wait and disappeared into one of the many doors which opened off the entrance hall. It was a plain, spartan building, with little to show of its true purpose.

A few minutes later Barrow, Slade's private secretary, came from one of the rooms and regarded him warily. When told of Blackwood's wish to see his master, Barrow pursed his lips and said, 'Sir Geoffrey is with the consul. However . . .' He sighed. 'I'll see what I can do.'

Blackwood tried to relax. Barrow had put him in his place with no trouble at all. He would leave it a few more minutes and then reappear to say that Slade was engaged, and anyway . . .

The door opened and Barrow said in his dry voice, 'Sir Geoffrey will see you now.'

Blackwood licked his lips and followed the private secretary through the door. He noticed that poor Barrow was wearing a heavy frock-coat, no doubt very suitable for London but certainly not here. The realization made him start. It would be December in a few more days. Perhaps there might even be snow over Hawks Hill, thoughts of Christmas in the cottages, decorations at the little church.

Through another door and there was Slade, standing behind a great marble-topped table as if he had been expecting him. There were papers and despatches all over the table, and two empty glasses. The consul must have made a discreet departure by another door.

Slade eyed him calmly. 'Unexpected visit.' He studied him for several seconds. 'You look recovered. I'm pleased.' Surprisingly, he smiled. 'Well, Captain Blackwood, since you seem to have forgotten what you intended to say, may I suggest you be seated.' He did not wait for a reply but rang a small bell and when a servant appeared said, 'Some hock.'

Blackwood sat down. He was out of his depth. What had he really expected? He looked at the one picture on the wall behind Slade's table. A portrait of the Queen. It must have been done soon after her wedding to Albert when she was twenty-one. A face which was both strong and sensitive. Now she was ten years older, and Blackwood wondered how she saw her expanding empire.

He blurted out, 'I wanted to ask you about Mdlaka, sir.'

'I thought you might. Naturally I was kept informed about what you did, the men you lost. But you must see that you and those like you are small though vital parts of the whole. I do my work as best I can, but even I cannot know the complete pattern. In war it is the same. There are always the lonely men who are never heard. The one on the prongs of a charge, or the first up the scaling ladders, men with little hope of survival.' He shrugged as if remembering something or someone. 'And others who out of necessity must be left behind to cover the retreat of their comrades. Peace too has such men.' He waited for the servant to place the glasses on the table and added, 'Mdlaka was a fool, but his weakness increased our influence over him. Mdlaka, alive and back with his own people, is unpredictable. But Mdlaka dead or in chains would leave a dangerous space which would soon be filled.'

Blackwood raised the glass to his lips. The hock was perfect, and he marvelled that it was so cold.

He said quietly, 'I wanted to kill him and burn his village to the ground.' He looked up, his eyes steady. 'But for my injured leg . . .'

Slade smiled gently and refilled his glass. 'You might act because of different reasons, but for revenge? I think not.' He seemed amused at Blackwood's surprise. 'I told you weeks ago. I take an interest in your affairs. Without officers like you, where would Her Majesty's ministers turn for aid?'

'You are laughing at me, sir.' He made to rise but Slade waved him down.

Slade said gravely, 'No. After what you have done, the courage you inspired in your men, only a fool would laugh, and that I am not.'

Barrow's head poked round a door. 'It is nearly time, Sir Geoffrey.' He pointedly did not look at Blackwood.

Slade nodded. 'Very well.' Then he turned to Blackwood and said, 'Sir James Ashley-Chute intends to mount an attack on an area which is known to be a main artery for the slavers. You know about it, of course, so I will not interfere. I guide the Navy and the military, I try not to impose my will.' Again the briefest of smiles. 'Not too obviously anyway.' He became serious once more. 'I must confess that I do not fully understand the ways of the Navy, but Sir James commands the forces in this theatre. He is a man of experience, of considerable determination.'

Blackwood waited, his earlier confusion forgotten. Slade seemed to be ticking off certain points in his mind, as if he expected each one to be challenged.

'If he insists on his present strategy, I am not the one to disagree.'

He hesitated, and for a second Blackwood imagined he saw anxiety on his features.

Then he said, 'You once asked about my niece.'

He turned, his eyes suddenly cold and fixed on Blackwood's reaction.

'Yes, sir. Is something wrong?'

'I have found out where she is. It is a mission some ten miles inland from where you may have to land your men.' He did not hide his concern now. 'Ten miles? In Africa that can be like a hundred!'

'Is she safe, sir?'

'At present, I believe so. But if Sir James's first approach fails, she and every other mission in the area will be in mortal peril. I must try not to think too much about it. I have to be above personal involvement. Results are the same as intentions where I am concerned. He walked round the table and grasped Blackwood's hand. 'But if you can, *bring her out.*'

Blackwood's head was awhirl. An argument, an eventual reprimand and worse, these he might have expected. In a few words Slade had dropped his guard, had revealed the agony he was enduring because of his headstrong niece.

Blackwood returned his grasp. 'You may rely on it, sir.'

Barrow entered the room, a warning frown on his urbane features.

Blackwood watched the change as Slade stepped easily into his other role.

'Don't fuss, Barrow. The wine was too good to hurry, eh, Blackwood?'

Alone with the Queen's portrait, Blackwood considered his discovery. That Slade, the instrument of government and empire, was just a man after all.

Major Rupert Fynmore leaned his hands on the sill of Ackworthy's cabin windows and peered at the shimmering jumble of passing craft.

Blackwood waited, wondering why he disliked the lean, sunburned major.

Fynmore straightened his back and turned towards him. He was forty years old but took every care not to show it. His coatee fitted his erect figure without a crease. His boots were like black glass, and his neat sandy hair looked as if it had just been trimmed by the company barber.

'Captain Ackworthy is ashore. He has allowed me the use of his day cabin while I prepare my orders.' He had a way of smiling with one side of his mouth, as if the lips were being turned upwards from within. The smile never quite reached his eyes. 'I was expecting to see you somewhat earlier.'

Blackwood said, 'I'm sorry, sir. I was not told of your intended visit.'

Visit?' The mouth lifted again. 'Hardly that. I am taking charge of the landing operations, eventually.'

Blackwood said quietly, 'Under Commander Netten, I believe, sir.'

'True.' Fynmore regarded him calmly. 'Funny how things turn out, don't you think? Meeting again like this, I mean?'

Blackwood remained silent. Fynmore was enjoying his new command. There was no sense in putting men's lives at risk by creating a wider rift between them.

Fynmore was saying in a level, matter of fact tone, 'My father served under yours at Lake Erie and at Navarino. Bit of a hard man in those days, I understand.'

Blackwood said, 'He never discussed it, I'm afraid, sir.' It was a lie but he saw the major's eyes spark with anger.

Fynmore snapped, 'No matter. I just want to get things straight before we go to work. I know about you, your ideas, your death or glory escapades. Well, I'll have no blind heroics on this mission. The job will be done. My way. Understood?'

'I think so, sir.' He was surprised how calm he felt. *Death or glory.* His father would have approved of this Fynmore.

Fynmore said sharply, 'You were at the consulate.'

'Sir.'

'By whose orders?'

'It was a friendly visit, sir.'

The lip lifted slightly and hovered as if uncertain what to do.

'Sir Geoffrey Slade?'

'Yes, sir.'

'Oh well, in that case . . .'

Fynmore walked to Ackworthy's table and opened his despatch bag.

Blackwood had heard a great deal about Fynmore. He was old for his rank and would use anything which might boost him to lieutenant-colonel and higher. And why not? Why should he be so unlikeable, Blackwood wondered? His old commanding officer at North Island who had died leading his men had been wild to a point of madness if an occasion offered itself. He had been a Scot like M'Crystal, and had been known to play the bagpipes while marching on the table at the end of a mess dinner. But the men had worshipped him, and in the face of death had followed him without hesitation.

Fynmore dragged some papers on to the table. 'Straightforward, seems to me.' He tried to relax. 'Sit down, won't you?' He smiled. 'We'll be the only two officers with field experience, how about that, eh?'

He hurried on, 'Won't come to anything probably. Flags of truce, while Commander Netten speaks with the local king.' He squinted at the top page of his notes. 'King Zwide, by all accounts. He should be no trouble.'

Blackwood watched the major's hawklike profile with sudden apprehension. It must be another of Fynmore's vanities that he was pretending he could read without effort when in fact his sight was obviously failing. Things were getting worse by the minute.

'May I suggest something, sir?'

'Well?' Fynmore looked at him warily.

'As senior marine officer could you not advise the admiral that we make use of some, if not all, of the steam vessels here?'

Fynmore chuckled. 'Thought of that already. I saw the admiral myself about it. He's made his own plans, of course, but only the flagship and the frigate *Peregrine* will be taking part in the operation. He did agree to one small steam gunboat, the *Norseman*, coming with us, more for use as a tug than as a warship, I suspect.' His chest shook with laughter, but no sound emerged.

Blackwood nodded. The bulk of the squadron would stay at anchor. They could do nothing anyway against the maze of rivers used by the slavers. By remaining at Fernando Po they might also put any spies off the scent.

'One steam vessel is better than nothing, from my experience.'

Fynmore faced him and said, 'Of course, you were in the *Satyr*. So you know all about that kind of thing, eh?'

Blackwood asked, 'Is that what it sounded like, sir?'

'I'm afraid it did. You know what your trouble is, Blackwood?' He gave his quick smile. 'Pride, that's what. Except that in your case it changes too quickly to arrogance.'

Blackwood stood up slowly. *He wants to provoke me.*

He said, 'You have the advantage of me, sir.' He watched Fynmore's eagerness fade. 'In rank, that is.'

Fynmore glared at him. 'You are dismissed. I shall let you know when I need you.' As Blackwood turned to leave he asked, 'Is your brother still aboard?'

Blackwood felt his throat go dry. Like that night on the wall of the fort. Fear. But not for himself this time. Fynmore's casual question was a threat. He knew well enough the name and seniority of every marine officer in the squadron. Men like Fynmore, who hungered for promotion and dreaded the prospect of being discharged from the Corps, always knew such things.

'He is.'

'Good. We must see he is suitably employed, what?'

Blackwood left the cabin and banged the screen door behind him.

Private Callow, who had once rescued a man from drowning, was the cabin sentry, but Blackwood did not even notice him.

Too proud, arrogant, hungry for glory? Blackwood had had just about enough for one day.

He thought suddenly of the girl with violet eyes, Davern

Seymour. What would Major bloody Fynmore say about her when he discovered what Slade intended?

By the time he had reached the quarterdeck he had regained his composure, outwardly at least.

As he stood by the nettings and took full advantage of the spread awnings he saw a boat approaching the main chains, and a boatswain's chair being lowered towards it.

He noticed several of the seamen who were working on deck grinning and nudging each other, and when he looked into the boat he saw Harry sitting in the sternsheets beside an African woman who was swathed from chin to toe in a long green robe. Blackwood stared as two seamen steadied the chair for her to climb into while the youthful marine lieutenant took her hand to help her.

The last time he had seen her she had been naked, like a wild animal as she had pressed herself against him. He found himself bunching his fingers into a tight fist as he remembered the feel of her breast under his hand, the way she had looked at him.

As the bosun's chair squeaked up towards the gangway she sensed him watching her. She held her robe up around her mouth and nose so that only her eyes remained visible, and they never moved from his face until she was lowered again and lost from view.

Harry appeared by his side and touched his hat, some of his jauntiness fading as he saw his expression.

'What is *she* doing aboard?'

Harry eyed him curiously. 'Apparently she's a princess. Daughter of a king near Benin. I received an order to fetch her from the slaver.'

Blackwood looked away. Slade's hand was doubtless behind this too. A bargaining point, a hostage, or a viper in their midst. It was not difficult to imagine the black princess selling her own people into slavery.

A huge woman in a brightly striped gown was now being hoisted aboard to the accompaniment of yells of encouragement from the sailors.

Harry was still watching him. 'A servant and guardian for the princess. She'll probably need one in a ship full of lusting tars!'

Blackwood glanced at him and smiled. 'The other way round.'

There was a quick step on the deck and Major Fynmore snapped irritably, 'I cannot have my officers setting a bad example by idling and gossiping, eh? We have extra marines coming aboard from the squadron, and I shall want a *full* inspection this afternoon, orders in the first dog watch, right?' He gave Harry the benefit of his crooked smile. 'No passengers here, what?'

Harry said softly as Fynmore bustled away, 'I wonder if he knows about the princess?'

Captain Ackworthy lowered his telescope and growled, 'Bad stretch of coast.'

With all sails furled to her yards, *Audacious* swung heavily to her cable, oblivious to the activity on the upper deck as boats were swayed out from their tier and dropped alongside. Slightly closer to the lush green coastline the small frigate *Peregrine* had also anchored, and was no doubt awaiting the next signal from the Flag.

Ashley-Chute stood by the nettings, well apart from his officers, hands gripped across his buttocks as he stared fixedly at the land.

Blackwood watched him. It was hard to tell what the admiral was thinking. If he was impatient at the delay in leaving Fernando Po, at the further irritations of failing wind and a snail's-pace to reach this point on the chart, he did not show it. He had given vent to some feeling on the first day at sea when, after gushing dense smoke high into the air, the little gunboat *Norseman* signalled that she had broken down and was unable to proceed.

Ashley-Chute had almost crowed with delight. 'What did I say, eh, eh?' He had darted his piercing stare from one officer to the next. 'No damn use! Bundle of bloody iron scrap, that's what *that* is!'

The officer of the watch approached Ackworthy and touched his hat.

'All boats lowered, sir.'

'Very well.'

Once again Blackwood noticed Ackworthy's hesitation. As if he was unwilling or unable to make the next decision. Or as if he had not been allowed to share his admiral's plans.

In that he could sympathize with the massive captain. Since Major Fynmore had come aboard, he and Commander Netten had been as thick as thieves, and had told him little beyond the needs of routine and preparation.

Fynmore seemed to revel in his new command. For the three days it had taken to reach this place, some fifty miles to the north-west of the Niger Delta, Fynmore had behaved as if the marines were to be employed on ceremonial parades rather than possible action. Every day they had been kept busy polishing and cleaning, painting their packs until they gleamed like black leather. Several marines had been awarded punishment for allegedly having grit in their muskets, although Blackwood had the nagging feeling it was Fynmore's way of covering up his poor eyesight when he inspected the weapons.

He looked at the shore and restrained a shudder as he recalled the last time. No birds, no tell-tale smoke, but he sensed that the two ships had been watched since first light as they had completed their slow approach.

It was a pity about the *Norseman*, he thought. She would have made the crossing to the shore easier and safer. It was four cables, at a guess, to the nearest wedge of green land, a long pull for the oarsmen with boats loaded with men and weapons. The marine landing party would consist of ninety men, with three lieutenants selected from other ships in the squadron. Blackwood glanced down to the main-deck where Harry was speaking with M'Crystal. He was coming too, for liaison work, as Fynmore had vaguely described it.

Netten would have a party of armed seamen from *Audacious*, and each boat would be under the command of a lieutenant or midshipman.

Blackwood looked again towards the shore. It was like something impenetrable, the overlapping layers of thickly wooded slopes completely hiding the rivers which twisted inland. He gripped the nettings until the pain steadied his nerves. They must not be outfoxed a second time.

Then he saw Fynmore, who had been called across to speak with the admiral. How pleased he looked.

He thought of Slade, two hundred miles away at the consulate. He was probably regretting that he had not joined them in the flagship, no matter what he said to his subordinates about responsibility which excluded all else. Or perhaps he realized that Ashley-Chute might see his presence here as a lack of confidence. But he had sent one of his aides, a mild-looking man named Patterson, whose knowledge of Africa in general and the slave trade in particular had astounded the whole wardroom.

One night he had walked the deck with Blackwood and had told him how Slade had tried over the years to tempt the African kings and chiefs away from their wretched trade by offering the lure of other profits. The greatest of these had been palm oil, which was always in growing demand in Europe. But the more powerful kings, and Zwide was one of them, had burned thousands of new trees to the ground to force their people back on the cruellest but most rewarding trade of all.

Slade must think very highly of Patterson to send him on such an important mission.

The officer of the watch coughed politely. 'Would you join the admiral, sir?'

Blackwood walked across the quarterdeck which was already half in shadow as the boatswain's party set to work rigging awnings above it.

Ashley-Chute regarded the small group of officers, his face expressionless. Netten would be in overall charge, Fynmore would command the landing force, and his own son was apparently taking control of the boats.

His eyes settled on Blackwood. 'All present. Capital. The sooner we begin, the better.' He looked at his son without any hint of recognition. 'Pass the order to start loading the boats.' He turned away, dismissing him. 'Questions?'

Netten leaned forward. 'If the king's people have left the area, sir, what — '

Ashley-Chute's wide mouth snapped open and shut like a trap. He said scornfully, '*Left?* Why should they? It is their reason for being, man. But Mr Patterson intends to speak with this Zwide fellow. After that it's up to him. But no damned arguments, hmm? I cannot abide upstart natives, and never have.' His cold stare swivelled to Blackwood. 'That's right, isn't it?'

'Yes, sir.'

Blackwood saw Fynmore's resentment. Something from the past which he did not share. Perhaps the little admiral had said it deliberately.

In the distance he heard Sergeant Quintin's rough voice yell, 'First section! Into the boats! Lively there! Private Shadbolt, 'old yer 'ead up, yer like a bloody whore on the mornin' after!'

Blackwood could picture them all grinning as if he were down there with them. Quintin's comments were always coarse and usually repeated until his men knew them word-perfect.

Ackworthy, who was standing a little apart from the group, said, 'Lookout has just sighted smoke to the sou'-east, sir. Must be the *Norseman*.'

Ashley-Chute scowled at the interruption. 'I'm not waiting for that madman! He'll likely blow up anyway!'

Netten laughed but Fynmore fiddled with his belt. Even he obviously disliked the way the admiral treated his flag-captain.

Patterson appeared below the poop yawning hugely as if he had just risen from his cot. He smiled gently. 'I'm ready, Sir James.'

To everyone's surprise, Ashley-Chute clapped him on his shoulder and exclaimed, 'Very good! Now go and tell that savage about our Queen's displeasure, or whatever you do in these circumstances!'

Several people laughed. It was rare for Ashley-Chute to be in such high spirits.

Then he turned on his heel and with a curt nod added, 'Carry on, gentlemen.'

Blackwood paused by the starboard gangway and stared along the upper deck. How empty it seemed after the squads of scarlet coats and piled weapons. He touched his shako to the quarterdeck and then scrambled quickly down into the nearest boat. Smithett was already in the sternsheets with his bag, and doubtless a bottle of something.

As he got his bearings the heat covered the boat like a heavy blanket. The marines were pressed together anyway to allow the oarsmen some room, and it was just the same in all the other boats as they idled clear of the ship's side.

Familiar faces leapt out of the crowd as he ran his eyes over them. Half smiles or carefully blank, he knew them all, as they did him. Some, like those who had been at the fort, knew him even better now.

He saw Harry sitting with Major Fynmore and Netten in the big launch, ready to perform his liaison duties, no doubt. He thought of the black princess who had remained in a carefully guarded cabin on the orlop deck forward of the sick-bay. This would be her first time in the open since she had been transferred from the brigantine. Her name was Nandi. Harry had told him after inspecting the sentries who had been posted to prevent any amorous seaman or marine from intruding on her privacy. From what he had heard, she had more to fear from Sergeant Quintin, who had protested at being taken off guard duty for the first time in living memory.

He saw Smithett's eyes flicker, and when he looked up he saw a midshipman and the mild Mr Patterson assisting the princess down the tumblehome towards the cutter.

Colour-Sergeant M'Crystal watched Blackwood's expression and wondered. Quintin had told him some of it, but there was more to come by the look of things.

In the next boat, Corporal Jones, wedged against Frazier the expert marksman, watched the second lieutenant who was aft with Major Fynmore. He grinned to himself. Cocky young buck. He had seen Second Lieutenant Blackwood, cool as you please, talking with the black girl in her makeshift cabin. Bloody good luck to him.

Private Ackland sat hunched over his pack and weapons, his lips pursed in a silent whistle as he stared unseeingly towards the shore. He was one of six brothers, all of whom worked on the land. Like a lot of farm labourers, he was a bit slower than those who lived by their wits. It had taken the Corps and several sergeants to sharpen him up. How his brothers had laughed at him when he had enlisted. It had happened almost by accident on market day in Tavistock. A recruiting party had been returning to camp, weary after a fruitless day trying to obtain volunteers for the Colours. The sergeant in charge had paused in front of Ackland and had said, 'Join us, lad. You'll not regret it.'

Ackland was a simple soul and his eyes pricked with pride as he thought of the day Captain Blackwood had just stood there and looked at him. A whole screaming mob lusting for blood, and he had spoken to him as if they were doing rounds between decks. *Sound the Advance.* If only his stupid brothers could have seen *that*.

The Rocke twins sat side by side, like peas in a pod, as they watched Private Doak trying to conceal a bottle of rum in his folded blanket. Nearby Private Bulford eased his cross-belt and watched the girl being helped into the other boat. Try as he might, he could not help thinking about his father. Shut up in jail for the rest of his natural life, they said. Some said he was lucky not have hanged for killing a man in a brawl. Bulford looked at the clear blue sky and felt the comforting jostle of his companions around him and was grateful. Lucky? To be shut up like a beast? Not for him.

Patterson thumped into the boat and fanned his thin face
with his hat.

'*Exhausting*, Captain Blackwood!'

But Blackwood was looking at the princess.

She said suddenly, 'It is you.'

Her English was fractured but clear. In the reflected glare
she looked graceful despite the all-enveloping robe, with the
grace of a puma.

He said, 'We are taking you to your father.'

She spat out the words, '*The King*.'

Blackwood retorted sharply, 'Just sit down and behave
yourself.' He could feel the eyes and grins around him.

She sat down at once and folded her hands in her lap, her
eyes turned to the shore.

Blackwood nodded to the bowman. 'Cast off.'

He tried to fix the picture of the chart in his mind. The
river with the sharp bend like a dog's hind leg. But instead he
kept looking at the girl on the thwart, now so aloof and
demure, a princess. It was hard to think of her as the nude
savage in that filthy cabin.

The midshipman by the tiller waited for the other boats to
form into line and then directed the cutter astern of the
leading one with the White Ensign curling from the stern-
post.

Patterson touched his arm. 'Join me, Captain.'

Blackwood half turned and sat, seeing the eyes dropping or
looking away as the crowded occupants pretended they had
noticed nothing.

Patterson said quietly, 'Sir Geoffrey explained things to
you?'

Their eyes met.

'Yes.'

'Good. I spoke to your admiral. If it can be done, then it
will be up to you.' He hesitated. '*If*.'

Blackwood felt the pressure of the princess's hip against his
side as the cutter rolled in the first inshore swell.

What would his father have done? His grandfather would

have made the best of it, he decided. Even in his last year alive
at Hawks Hill his faded eyes could still twinkle as he had
retold stories of the women he had met and 'served', as he
always put it.

He shook himself angrily. He must be mad to let his
dreams run riot. He looked at the green barrier which tilted
across the bows like a curtain, and then astern towards the
horizon. There, far away, was the tell-tale smudge of smoke.
Monkey's pet hate. She was too late now.

When he looked again he saw the gleam of trapped water
around the nearest headland and knew it was the entrance to
the river. Zwide's kingdom, which lay across the slave trails
like a treacherous snare. He glanced at the girl's hands in her
lap, but they were relaxed, and he could feel no tension in her
hip against his side.

He saw Lieutenant Ashley-Chute climb up in the leading
boat and raise his speaking trumpet. How deformed he looked
as he stood framed against the lush green slope at his back.

'*Take station!*' His voice sounded hollow in the trumpet.

Obedient to the order the boats changed formation until
they were in two matching lines, which once inside the river
would move out to opposite banks.

Blackwood waited until the midshipman by the tiller had
increased the stroke to bring the cutter to the head of the
starboard line, directly abeam of Netten's big launch.

It was all too casual, too easy. He could feel the warning
ringing in his mind like a bell.

He stood up and looked along the boat. 'Ready, lads.'

It was all he said, and in the next boat astern he saw
M'Crystal gesturing to his own party. He did not need
telling, any more than when he had taken charge when
Lascelles had lost his grip. Here and there a musket moved
across a gunwale, or a man shaded his eyes to watch the land
as it opened up to swallow them.

Blackwood looked at the midshipman. He was a popular
youth and aged about sixteen. He looked as if he was enjoying
all this enormously. Like a boy in a toy-shop.

'Mr Ward.' He saw the midshipman start. 'Leave the tiller to the cox'n and come here.' He waited for the midshipman to join him and then lowered his voice. 'If we come under fire I want you to take hold of the princess and *put her* on the bottom boards, right?'

The youth nodded jerkily. 'I – I think so, sir.'

'Good. I'm placing you in charge of her safety.' He forced a grin. 'Not every day we mix with royalty.'

Smithett muttered, 'I wish that bloomin' gunboat was 'ere.'

Blackwood glanced over at Fynmore. He was sitting bolt upright as if he was riding down The Mall in a carriage.

He saw Harry look towards him, his quick wave as if to reassure him he would be all right.

He touched the girl's shoulder and waited for her eyes to lift towards him.

'Your father. The *King*. When will he come?'

She did not even blink. 'He will come.'

Blackwood saw her nostrils dilate, like someone watching a terrible ritual. Seeing them all killed perhaps?

He turned to Patterson. 'Are we in danger yet?'

Patterson shrugged. 'Little is known about this place. Zwide is well protected on two flanks by the river. There is a ridge on the right, very soon now. Once past there we should be better placed.'

'Did you tell Major Fynmore about it?' Somehow he already knew the answer.

Patterson gave his shy smile. 'I did. He said it was best to leave such matters to professionals.'

'He would.'

No wonder they had given him a separate boat, he thought bitterly.

Patterson was watching him, reading his thoughts.

'Which is why I chose to accompany *you*, Captain.'

'Thank you for that.'

Midshipman Ward called, 'They've put up the white flag, sir!'

Blackwood bit his lip as he watched Netten's launch thrusting ahead under its two flags. It was so quiet, the boats had no substance, no reality.

He ran his finger round his collar. His skin felt like fire.

The bowman stood up and pointed excitedly. *'Here they come!'*

# 10

# Sudden Death

Harry Blackwood plucked his clothes away from his body which was running with sweat. Protected from any sort of breeze by the river banks and rising slopes of thick vegetation, the inside of the launch was like a furnace. He could feel Lieutenant Ashley-Chute moving behind him, speaking with the coxswain as he directed the slow procession of boats. There were ten in all, and when he looked across at the cutter which led the other line he gave his half-brother a quick wave without really knowing why.

Perhaps because of Fynmore, he thought. He had heard him speaking with the commander and had realized they were talking about Philip.

Netten had said something about Mdlaka and the admiral's reaction to the report on what had happened.

'Captain Blackwood as good as told Sir James he thought our methods were out-of-date. The admiral actually *listened* to him to all accounts. Any other time he'd have exploded!'

Fynmore had replied, 'That young chap is too damned intolerant with authority in my book. Needs taking down.'

They had changed the subject at that point.

Harry thought about England. It would be his birthday soon. He had always hated having it so close to Christmas. As a child he had loved opening his presents, but as he grew older some people seemed to think one gift would suit for both celebrations. He had thought a good deal about Hawks Hill and what would happen there. He enjoyed going to London but, like his childhood presents, he wanted to hoard those visits for something special.

He had always been a bit in awe of the old house where he had been born. It had been built originally as a fortified Tudor farmhouse with a moat all around it. Down over the years the house had spread and been added to until it stood as it did today, a great rambling cavern of rooms, hallways and little doors which led to the roof or down to the depths of the cellars. As a boy Harry had pretended the latter were dungeons and had almost frightened himself to death when he had become locked in a cupboard there.

Now the moat had all but gone, with just one strip preserved for the benefit of visiting swans and geese.

Hawks Hill had been bought from one of the previous owners by his great-grandfather, Major-General Samuel Blackwood, who, if his portraits were to be believed, was always employed in one war or another. He had served with Wolfe at Quebec, and had fought his way right through the American Revolution, after which he had retired from the army to settle in Hampshire.

It was strange to think that he had been the last soldier in the Blackwood family, and Harry had often wondered what had made his grandfather begin the new tradition with the Regiment of the Sea.

He heard Lieutenant Ashley-Chute say, 'The first bend is about half a mile ahead, sir.'

Netten grunted and raised his telescope to examine the nearest bank. The current was quite strong and the oarsmen were showing the strain.

Harry Blackwood dabbed his face yet again. The handkerchief was little more than a wet rag. He longed for the cool of the evening or the chance of a swim. He grimaced. It was doubtful if it was safe to paddle here, let alone swim.

He shaded his eyes to look at the cutter, at the girl in the green robe who was sitting with, yet somehow quite apart from his brother.

It was really strange, he thought, that his half-brother never seemed to understand women or that he was attractive to them. He had seen that attraction several times with a mixture of amusement and envy. Philip had a stiffness about him, a hint of experience far greater than his years, and yet he was totally unaware of it.

Harry had never met a black girl before, let alone one like the Princess Nandi. Even as he had tried to talk with her on *Audacious*'s orlop he had felt an urge to touch her, to make her want him.

He thought suddenly of the cellar where he had accidentally locked himself in a cupboard. His dungeon. When he was sixteen he had enticed one of the housemaids down there with him. She had been older than he, a friendly, buxom girl with a ready giggle.

By the light of a candle he had told her she was his prisoner, that she would be put to the rack and torture if she did not submit.

Her response had been astounding and immediate.

She had taken his hands and pulled them to her bosom, her eyes shut as she had murmured, 'I *submit*, Master Harry. Take me.'

Afterwards, full of frightened excitement and guilt, he had tortured himself by remembering every breathless, tantalizing moment of their embraces. Things which he had never known and now would never forget.

Her tongue in his mouth, their skin chilled in the cellar's dampness rising to passionate heat as they had come together while she had instructed and guided him until they were both completely spent.

He dragged at his tunic again. He was feeling it now in this heat.

Fynmore snapped, '*There!* They've sighted something!'

Netten raised his hand to silence the chatter in the boat. 'About time.'

Harry Blackwood peered between his two superiors and saw a boat coming from around a bend in the river.

It was not a crude dug-out canoe, but another long-boat, larger if anything than this launch. The oarsmen were black, but in the stern he could see two, maybe three white faces.

Netten exclaimed angrily, 'Dammit, they've dropped a stream-anchor!'

Harry watched as the other boat's oars rose and halted like frayed wings while the current surged around the hull as if it was going astern.

Netten twisted round. 'Signal the boats to anchor!' He gestured towards the boat directly abeam, and after a moment's hesitation the cutter began to pull towards them.

Fynmore shifted on the thwart and asked, 'What do you intend to do?'

Netten was watching the anchored long-boat. 'Patterson will speak with them. He'll probably know the white men. Slavers perhaps, but it'll not be like dealing with bloody savages.'

Harry was only eighteen but he recognized alarm when he heard it.

The cutter closed to within a few yards and Patterson called, 'The king is not with them. One of those men is called Lessard. The last time we met was in Senegal.' There was nothing mild about him now.

He nodded to himself. 'I think we should stand off and let him make the first move.'

Netten exploded, 'I've run up the white flag, he must know we've come to parley.'

Patterson shrugged. 'If King Zwide was here we could let him see his daughter. Without him we cannot bargain. Lessard has little regard for life, other people's that is.'

Netten glared at him. 'I'm not here to *bargain*, as you put it. I have come in the Queen's name, and you would do well to remember it!'

Fynmore looked across at Blackwood. 'What are your views?'

Harry watched his half-brother, fascinated as he replied without hesitation, 'We should fall back and land our people on the right hand bank, sir. It looked safer there, easy to defend. The gunboat *Norseman* will come up in support before dusk. Once she's here, Lessard and his friends will not dare to move against us.'

Fynmore let him finish. 'Is that *all*, Captain Blackwood? No fire and blood? We just *retreat*, is that it?'

Blackwood replied flatly, 'There is a ridge over there, sir. Not more than a cable distant. If they have marksmen placed in cover they can fire down into the boats. The oarsmen are tired. It's not worth the risk.'

Fynmore swallowed hard. 'I shall speak with you later.' To Netten he said, 'I say we should call his bluff. Now.'

Netten nodded. 'I agree.'

Fynmore turned towards the cutter once more. 'You anchor and take charge of the flotilla, Captain Blackwood. *And* the women, of course.'

Harry watched his brother's features, sickened at Fynmore's jibe.

Netten looked aft. 'Give way together, Cox'n.' But his eyes lingered on the other boats which were dragging on their anchors or grapnels, the oarsmen drooping over their looms while they regained their breath.

As the launch started to move ahead Blackwood stood in the cutter, his heart pounding against his ribs as he tried to contain his anger. He did not even remember getting to his feet, but was aware of the watching eyes of his men. Indifferent, critical, hostile, they were all lost in a haze of disbelief.

Patterson said softly, 'You spoke correctly. I know that for a professional fighting man it must go against the grain. But even as a civilian I think you are right.' He peered after the launch. 'I know Lessard. He has estates in America, in Georgia. He has others in Brazil and Cuba, and has grown rich beyond measure from slavery. And never once have we been able to prove it.'

Blackwood tried not to look towards the launch which was now almost blocking the view of Lessard's boat.

'Why should this Lessard be here?'

'It will be important.' Patterson looked briefly at the black princess. 'Too important to be frightened off by a few redcoats.'

Midshipman Ward asked huskily, 'Shall I anchor, sir?'

Blackwood looked at him. The boy was ashamed, for him and of him. In his eyes he had failed, had chosen caution when he should not have hesitated.

'No, Mr Ward.' He heard an edge in his tone as he spoke over their heads. 'Be ready to pull with all your might. I don't give a damn if your arms come out of their sockets. Corporal Bly, get up forrard with two of the best marksmen.'

It was like a cold wind blowing through the boat. Hands jerked at weapons and pouches, others tugged down shakos as their owners responded to the hint of danger.

'Remain in midstream.'

Blackwood heard Smithett checking his pistols.

Midshipman Ward said suddenly, 'There must have been a waggon over there, sir!' He pointed abeam at the first slope of the ridge.

Patterson remarked, 'Unlikely.'

Blackwood leaned over the seated girl and felt her tense away from him.

'Waggon be damned! They're cannon tracks!' He straightened up and shouted, 'Pull, lads! *Together!*' He felt the bottom boards shiver beneath his feet as the oarsmen flung themselves back on the looms. 'Signal the next boat to – '

The rest of his words and thoughts were scattered by a shattering explosion which echoed above the river like a clap of thunder.

A tall waterspout shot up beside the launch, so close that several of the oars were flung into the river. As the current took control the launch began to swing round, the seamen in confusion as they struggled to back water with the remaining oars.

Blackwood saw a puff of smoke from the ridge and felt sick as another ball slammed through the forepart of the boat and something which a second earlier had been a sailor was flung over the side like a piece of meat.

Thank God Netten had not had time to anchor within speaking distance of the other boat. Now the launch was drifting with the current while somebody was frantically trying to bale out the inrush of water from that last shot.

'Stand by in the bows!' Blackwood saw Ward staring at him, his eyes wide with shock. '*Keep down*, the rest of you!'

He heard the familiar crackle of firing from the ridge, saw feather-like splashes as shots pattered around the other boat or smacked into her planking.

Blackwood bit on his chin strap. *Our turn next*. God Almighty. 'Keep pulling!'

Midshipman Ward gave a yelp as a shot whipped his cap away like an invisible hand.

Blackwood felt his mouth set in an insane grin. 'You are not doing your duty, Mr Ward!' He seized his shoulder. 'Join the princess!'

The midshipman lowered himself until his body all but covered the girl on the bottom boards.

Across the boy's shoulder she stared up at Blackwood with neither fear nor hatred.

Blackwood saw the bowman getting ready to hurl his grapnel into the drifting launch. He could see Harry trying to drag an injured seaman aft away from the incoming water, and Fynmore standing up in the sternsheets, pointing at something, while one of the few marines in the launch opened fire on the river bank.

Shots cracked against the cutter now, and others whimpered overhead. A seaman gasped and fell across his oar, blood pouring from his skull, and another was hugging his chest and sobbing with agony.

Down-river a bugle wailed mournfully, and Blackwood guessed that the other boats were heading towards the shore. With three lieutenants who had never been in action before, it might fall once again on M'Crystal to drag the hot coals out of the fire.

The cutter lurched against the other boat and there was a stampede to drag the injured into an already overcrowded hull.

Blackwood stood on a thwart and ignored the deadly whisper of shots as they passed dangerously close. The launch was obviously sinking fast. There was blood everywhere, even splashed up on to the pathetic flag of truce.

Fynmore stared at him, his eyes wild as he shouted, 'They've got artillery, for God's sake!'

As if to taunt him another bang echoed across the river and they fell back gasping and spluttering in a cascade of stinking water.

Blackwood grabbed a wounded seaman's arm and hauled him bodily over the gunwale and shut his ears to his screams.

'What are the orders now, sir?'

Fynmore lurched aside. 'No good asking him.'

Commander Netten was still seated aft, his telescope grasped in his hands like a baton.

His chin and most of his face had been shot away, and yet above the torn flesh his eyes remained staring ahead, frozen at the moment of impact.

With the launch drifting clear, its dead occupants lolling deeper and deeper in water, Blackwood's boat turned and thrust towards the lower bank.

A few more shots struck the side, and near the bows an unconscious seaman was hit again but died feeling nothing.

Blackwood felt for his shako, but, like Ward's cap, it had been knocked from his head and he had not noticed.

He looked at Harry, his throat raw from shouting.

'Close thing.' He wanted to smile for both their sakes but nothing came. He kept thinking of Netten, how they had avoided each other after that day aboard the brigantine.

Then he glanced down as someone touched his foot and saw the girl staring at him. He dropped on one knee as he saw blood on her face, but as he reached out she shook her head, and then with unexplained tenderness put her arms around Midshipman Ward.

She said, 'His blood, not mine.'

Very gently they lifted the midshipman from the girl's body. A shaft of sunlight shone on his tightly closed eyes. It came through a neat hole in the planking where the bullet had found its mark.

Harry bent over his shoulder. 'Is he dead?'

Blackwood covered the midshipman's face with some canvas. *The boy in the toy-shop.*

He could barely speak and was afraid his voice would betray him.

'Yes, Harry. He was obeying orders, you see. *Protecting the women.*' He looked at Fynmore's stricken face. 'So you command, sir.'

Fynmore seemed to jerk himself from his trance.

'Yes. Get the men ashore.' His eyes followed the sinking launch as it drifted past, the terrible figure sitting upright in the sternsheets as if to seek out his killer.

Of the long-boat and the mysterious Lessard there was no sign.

Smithett let out his breath very slowly. 'Now fer a spot o' soldierin', I suppose.'

Blackwood looked at the river, the marines tumbling ashore and forming into squads like parts of a machine.

It was the same nightmare about to begin all over again.

Dust and gunsmoke mingled in a low cloud above the ridge as the hidden cannon kept up a measured bombardment of the river.

Blackwood watched the marines fanning out on either flank, their movements jerky as they responded to a hundred drills ashore and afloat. No more men had fallen, and the boats were huddled together as if for comfort below the nearest bank.

'What sort of guns, d'you reckon, Colour-Sergeant?'

M'Crystal's eyes vanished in concentration. 'Big enough, sir. Twelve-pounders, is my guess. Two, mebbe three o' them.'

Major Fynmore marched down the slope, his attendant trotting behind him carrying his sword and pistol like a native bearer.

He snapped, 'Where's the bloody gunboat, eh?'

Blackwood glanced at the tall colour-sergeant and said, 'She's very small, sir. Only mounts a six-pounder and a couple of mortars.'

Fynmore's eyes swivelled on him hotly. 'Not like the *Satyr*, eh?'

Blackwood watched the puffs of smoke from the scrub as Quartermain, one of the lieutenants, put his marksmen to work. Fynmore was beginning to sound just like Netten.

He said evenly, 'I meant that if we can drive those sharp-shooters off the ridge, *Norseman* can get inshore and use her mortars to better effect. If the cannon straddle her before she can bring her weapons into action, she'll stand no chance at all.'

Fynmore massaged his chin vigorously. 'I was thinking much the same.' He gestured to the nearest lieutenant. 'Mr Heighway! First platoon, prepare to advance!' He watched the officer hurry away, his face pale but determined. 'Young idiot.' He beckoned to his runner. 'Pass the word to both flanks. Covering fire.'

Patterson winced as a stray bullet smacked among some rocks. 'I think you're taking one hell of a risk, Major.'

'You stay out of this!' Fynmore swung on him. 'Get back with the wounded. I'll need you in a minute when that bloody slaver sees sense!'

A bugle blared, and all firing ceased along the ridge as if the hidden enemy had stopped to listen.

Fynmore eyed the deployment of his men with obvious impatience.

Harry said quietly. 'There go the skirmishers, sir.'

Fynmore raised his small telescope and studied the centre platoon of marines as they formed into two long lines.

'God damn his eyes! What is that fool Quartermain doing?' He looked at Blackwood. 'Get up there. I want that ridge cleared before they can move those cannon and lay them on *us*!'

Blackwood drew his sword and saw Harry's eyes following the blade, mesmerized as he laid it across his right shoulder, the steel warm against his neck.

Then he strode quickly up the slope, his boots crunching on sand and stones, and he stared unwinkingly at the lines of marines as they began to move forward.

He barely knew the lieutenant in charge, but guessed he was probably too stunned by the swift change of fortunes to have much else in his head.

Blackwood shouted, 'From the centre, *extend*!'

He hurried past the rear line of marines and caught up with the lieutenant.

'Keep them well spread out!' He saw the lieutenant staring at him, his expression a mixture of gratitude and confusion. 'And fix bayonets, *now*!'

Quartermain's head bobbed. 'Platoon, fix – '

The order was drowned by the sporadic rattle of musket and rifle fire. Shots whipped past and through the slowly advancing lines, but by a miracle nobody fell. Most of the marines were too busy dragging out their bayonets and snapping them to their muskets and did not even falter.

Blackwood licked his lips. A long line of heads had risen above the ridge. Not some blood-maddened natives, but men in robes, and others dressed much like Patterson. There were hundreds of them. An army. The mysterious Lessard must have banked everything on driving any British expedition from his territory with enough force to discourage further interference.

'Halt! Ready!' Blackwood saw the bayoneted muskets rise in a wavering line. '*Fire*!'

The mass of figures along the ridge swayed back and then forward again like corn in the wind.

'*Retire*!'

Blackwood watched the front line of marines fall back through the second rank and begin to reload as a corporal barked out the time as if on a firing range.

'Ready!'

Before the marines could fire another volley of shots lashed down from the hill, and here and there a marine fell or rolled gasping down the slope.

Somewhere a bugle sounded the Advance, and Blackwood knew that Fynmore was rushing up support. If only they could top the ridge and find some cover.

'*Fire!*' Quartermain was waving his sword, his face split into a madman's grin, as fear drove away caution.

Blackwood darted a glance down the slope and saw Lieutenant Heighway's platoon charging after them, the front line already passing one of the men who had fallen to the second fusilade of bullets.

He also saw Smithett close on his heels, his musket across his body as he loped easily over the rough ground.

The marines' refusal to fall back had obviously caught the enemy off guard. Perhaps they had imagined the destruction of Netten's launch and the presence of their heavy guns would be enough.

Blackwood saw them darting about among the scrub which lined the ridge like the ruff on a wild boar's back. They were shooting and dropping into cover to reload with practised ease. As they must have done so often when they had surprised a sleeping village to kill the old and carry the young away as slaves.

More red coats lay on the ground. It was taking too long, and, like the oarsmen, the marines were getting worn out by the uphill attack and the relentless heat.

Blackwood yelled, 'At 'em, lads!' It was the same madness. '*Charge!*'

Shouting and cheering like demons, the marines pounded up the steeper ground of the ridge, some firing as they ran, others breaking from their ranks to overtake their exhausted companions.

Blackwood slithered and almost fell as his foot caught in some brush, and he realized they had almost reached the top. A figure rose from the ground just yards away, teeth bared as he threw up his rifle and aimed straight at him.

There was a slapping sound and the man fell back, a bayonet, complete with its musket, impaling him like a lance. The marine who had hurled it cheered and ran forward, jerked it free and dashed on after other figures who were breaking from cover, unable to face such a fierce attack.

'Extend from the centre! Right section, covering fire!'

Blackwood saw stones jumping around him as bullets hammered into the ground. Some marksmen were keeping their heads and had already marked him down as a leader.

His face felt like a mask of dust and sweat, and without his shako to protect his eyes from the glare he had to mop his face repeatedly with his sleeve.

'Cease firing!'

Blackwood peered round for a bugler but saw him lying face down, blood pouring from his neck.

'Sergeant!' He waited until the man reached him. He did not know his name. 'Send your skirmishers along the other side. No risks. See if you can find where they've gone.' He was shouting, and yet with all firing stopped by both sides it was as quiet as a grave.

The sergeant blinked the sweat from his eyes. '*Sah!*' Then he was off again, calling names, whipping up their energy like hounds who had lost the scent.

Blackwood dropped on one knee and dragged his telescope from his belt. Beyond the ridge there was another, and then another. Where were those guns?

He turned and looked towards the river as it swung away towards the sea and wondered if they had heard the shooting aboard *Audacious*.

A runner dropped panting beside him, his eyes fixed on the dead bugler.

'Sir! Major Fynmore's compliments and will you rejoin him?'

Blackwood touched the runner's arm. He was young but would learn quickly if he survived this.

'Steady down, my lad.' He made himself smile. 'Tell the major I'll be with him as soon as I have deployed the men here.'

He beckoned to Lieutenant Quartermain and together they watched the runner scamper down the slope, zigzagging amongst the dead and wounded as if he was afraid of them.

Quartermain was still grinning with disbelief. 'There were *hundreds* of 'em, sir! Thirty of us, and they *ran*!'

Blackwood listened to the cries of the skirmishers as they called to each other among the scrub. He hoped the sergeant would remember to collect the new rifles if any had been left behind.

'They'll be back.'

What was the matter with Fynmore? Why didn't he come up here and show some encouragement to his men? It was not fear in his case. Fynmore had walked through the whole affair from the firing of the first cannon without any change of demeanour at all.

Quartermain took his silence for interest and added, 'I've had a look at some of the men we shot. Every race under the sun, I'd say, but mostly Spaniards and Portuguese by the cut of them. Bunch of bloody pirates.'

Blackwood stood up and tensed as if expecting a shot. 'Take over here.' He saw Smithett waiting for him, his face as mournful as ever. 'You did well.'

Quartermain beamed. 'Thank you, sir.'

Blackwood walked swiftly down from the ridge, his mind grappling with what they should do. Without support from *Norseman* they could achieve very little.

He saw a marine on his knees beside another who had fallen earlier in the fierce exchange of shots. He was trying to shield his friend's face from the sun with his body, and turned as Blackwood approached, his voice desperate.

'It's me mate, sir! Can't leave 'im like this!'

Smithett hurried forward and stooped beside them, his water flask held to the wounded man's lips. As Blackwood's shadow joined with the other marine's Smithett glanced up and gave a brief shake of his head.

Blackwood looked at the wounded man. His face was like parchment and there were flecks of blood on his lips. He was dying while he watched him, shot once, possibly twice in the stomach. It was amazing he had lasted this long.

His friend said, 'He'll be all right if we can get 'im back aboard ship, sir!'

Blackwood watched the dying man. 'Did you hear that?'

He seemed to realize for the first time Blackwood was there and whispered hoarsely, 'It ain't true, sir. Them bastards 'ave done for me.' He reached out to hold his friend's arm to console him but he had no more strength and his hand fell in the coarse grass as if its life had already gone.

'You go with the officer, Tim. I'll be all right 'ere. You see.'

Smithett said roughly, 'Do as 'e says. I'll stay with 'im.'

Blackwood walked away, his mind holding the picture of the dying man and his friend like an engraving. Behind him he could hear the other marine's dragging steps as he repeatedly stopped to look back up the ridge where Smithett crouched like some ancient warrior. He would not have to wait long.

Fynmore greeted him testily. 'Took your time.'

Blackwood ran his fingers through his dishevelled hair. It was filled with sand.

'We've taken the ridge, sir. There's less chance of being outflanked now.'

'Outflanked? Oh yes, I see.' Fynmore's lips twitched in a smile. 'A touch of steel. That did the trick. Knew it would. Damned barbarians!'

Sergeant Quintin crunched over the loose stones. 'Casualties, sir. Ten killed, includin' Commander Netten and Mr Ward. Twelve wounded.'

Blackwood saw Smithett coming from the slope, his shadow lengthening as he approached.

'Make that eleven killed, Sergeant.' He turned to the major. 'Will you move the third platoon to the ridge, sir?'

Fynmore rubbed his chin busily. 'I think not. We're better off here. I've already sent one of the boats back to *Audacious* with the first group of wounded, and my report to the admiral. It'll be an hour or two before we get fresh instructions. I suspect that Sir James will order us to return on board.' When Blackwood said nothing he snapped, *'Well?'*

'I think we should hold the high ground, at least until the gunboat arrives.'

Patterson had materialized from out of the rocks. 'And there's the matter of the *mission*, Major.' His eyes were calm but his tone was like a knife.

Slade chose his aides with great care, Blackwood thought. He could almost feel sorry for Fynmore as Patterson dropped this extra complication into his lap.

Patterson looked at Blackwood. 'You'd better get started. If you're not there by dawn, my guess is that you'll be too late. If we're not already.'

Fynmore exclaimed, 'I'll trouble you to stop giving orders to my officers.'

Patterson was unrepentant. 'Only Captain Blackwood knows what Sir Geoffrey's niece looks like, Major. Apart from Mr Blackwood junior that is. Dead or alive, Sir Geoffrey will insist on knowing and expect an answer.' He let his words sink in. 'Or I could go, of course.'

Fynmore looked trapped. 'No. I shall need you here, in case Lessard sues for peace.'

The idea of offending Slade had changed everything.

Patterson said, 'Well, Captain Blackwood, I wish you luck. At least by your going inland there's no possibility of a complete retreat.'

Blackwood glanced at Fynmore but he had moved away and had not heard the bitterness in Patterson's voice.

He saw Harry waiting to speak. 'Yes?'

'I've just been speaking with the Princess Nandi, sir.' He flushed under their combined stares. 'She will agree to guide us to the mission by a quicker route.'

Patterson pouted. 'Makes sense. She would know all the tracks around here. She could also be used as a hostage if need arose.'

Blackwood thought of it warily. The black princess might betray them as soon as they were away from the river, although she had certainly shown some dismay when her father had failed to meet her under the flag of truce. It was only this morning. The two lines of boats, Netten's hideous injuries, Midshipman Ward and the marine who had died on the hillside, unwilling to embarrass his friend with his final suffering.

Fynmore returned, his back erect and showing no sign of fatigue.

'That's settled then. Take eight men and Second Lieutenant Blackwood and leave as soon as you can.'

They watched one another like adversaries. Blackwood had already selected the men he would take, as if this had been decreed for a long while. Perhaps this was how it would end?

Fynmore added, 'As soon as you've gone I shall withdraw the men from the ridge.' It sounded like some sort of triumph.

'I think you're wrong, sir.'

Fynmore gave his twisted smile. 'Your privilege.' He turned on his heel, already searching for his runner. 'And I'll see that you eat your words, believe me!'

Patterson smiled wryly. 'He's a strange one, but I'll not deny his courage.' He knew Blackwood wanted to go and thrust out his hand. 'Good luck. And watch the black princess night and day.'

Later, as Blackwood and his small party moved away from the river and the long ridge where men had died, he heard the mournful call of the bugle once more.

He thought of Quartermain and wondered how he would accept retreat after overcoming his fear to lead his men to victory.

He saw two marines moving away ahead, scouting for any kind of danger as the bush and scrub thickened around them. *Eight good men and true*.

Blackwood turned and saw Harry following up in the rear, the black princess moving with easy grace just ahead of him. Had she really suggested she should lead them, or had Harry dreamed up the idea as some extra excitement?

By afternoon the river, and even the smell of the sea, had left them to their own devices.

# II

# *A Bargain Kept*

Blackwood tensed and was instantly awake as he felt a gentle pressure on his shoulder. Thoughts crowded through his mind as the realization of where he was drove away all ideas of sleep.

Smithett whispered, 'All still quiet, sir.'

Blackwood sat up slowly and gingerly, his body aching from the forced march through the bush, his face and skin pricking from countless insect bites and stings.

He felt Smithett put a cup in his hand and heard him pouring water from a flask.

Smithett said, 'I can give yer somethin' stronger if you want, sir.'

Blackwood sipped the water, it was lukewarm. 'Save it for later.'

He thrust his hand through his open shirt and rubbed his skin to drive away the itches. How quiet it was. Not like the first part of their uncomfortable march or when dusk had fallen and the air had been rent apart by strange animal shrieks and barks, like an insane asylum.

Only the princess had made light of it. She had never faltered or complained, and her feet had found a path when others had stumbled or cursed their way through clinging thorns and creeper.

Around him patches of deeper shadow showed where his men were sleeping, their weapons in easy reach. Sergeant Quintin would be out there in the darkness, making sure their sentries stayed awake.

He thought of the princess, the way she had looked at Quintin, goading him.

Blackwood smiled in the darkness. *As she did me*. But there had been no sign that she had betrayed them . . . yet. He had seen several places where an ambush could have been easily sited.

The mission was not far away now. Two miles at the most. It would have been folly to continue in the dark, and the men needed to rest. It was hardly what they had enlisted for, to fight slavers who were obviously better armed and prepared than they were themselves.

He looked at the sky, held like a small blue lake in a circle of trees. It was already lighter and the few stars had lost their brilliance. The realization stirred him and made him uneasy.

With an effort he got to his feet and crossed the clearing where they had made camp and eaten their meagre rations. Once again the black princess had shown her strength, had refused to share their food and had sat apart from them, missing nothing.

He would give his final instructions to Harry. If something was about to go wrong it would be soon.

Blackwood stopped dead as he saw his half-brother's shape, pale in the darkness. For a moment he could not speak or breathe. Harry was sprawled across a blanket, one arm outflung, his face pressed into the ground. Of the girl there was no sign.

Blackwood threw himself down and grasped Harry's arm. He had been guarding her. Sharing the duty with Corporal Jones. She must have had a knife or some other weapon concealed in her robe and . . .

Harry rolled on to his back and peered at him. 'What is it?'

Blackwood stood up violently. 'You bloody young fool, she's got away!'

Harry scrambled to his feet and they faced each other like strangers.

'She gave her word — '

Blackwood exclaimed angrily, 'Is that *all* she gave you?'

'You thought she'd murdered me, that's right, isn't it?'

'What the hell does it matter what I think! She's gone, and is probably getting her father's warriors on their way here right now!'

'Look, sir.' Harry's sudden formality made it even more unreal. 'It wasn't like that. She said that if her people saw her as our captive they would kill us, we'd have no chance. But once freed she *promised* to help us.'

Blackwood saw Jones groping through the scrub and beckoned to him. 'Rouse the men.' To Harry he added fiercely, 'If we get out of this alive I'll see you court-martialled, damn you, family or not!'

Sergeant Quintin stood aside as Blackwood pushed past him. 'Trouble, sir?'

Harry tried to smile but nothing happened. 'I seem to have put my foot in it, Sergeant.'

Quintin was glad the second lieutenant could not see his face. It wasn't only his foot he had put in it. Quintin had paused in his patrol around the clearing and had heard them, had seen Mr Blackwood's buttocks framed by the girl's black thighs. Going at it like a fiddler's elbow, he was. Lucky young bugger.

He said as calmly as he could, 'I s'pect it'll be all right, sir. I probably know 'im better than you do, in a manner o' speakin'.'

Harry said quietly, 'You're fond of him, aren't you?'

'Fond, sir? That's too strong a word fer the likes o' me. But as an officer 'e's the best I've served with. That'll do.' He could not restrain a grin. 'But then, sir, I'm not *family*!'

A few moments later Blackwood gathered the others around him. Sergeant Quintin and Corporal Jones, while his half-brother tried to stay invisible between them. In the clearing the marines were buckling on their belts and pouches, taking a last look at their weapons. Nobody said a word about the black princess. Blackwood was beginning to suspect he had been the only one not to know what was happening.

He said, 'We'll leave now. According to Mr Patterson's map and instructions the mission is about two miles distant. A short climb and then downhill all the way to another river.' He glanced at the sky again. But for the princess's unerring sense of direction he doubted if they would even have got halfway, let alone by dawn as Patterson had suggested. 'If the worst has happened we'll make our way back to where we landed.' He glanced at each one in turn. 'Tell the men that.' He had known it happen in the past. Marines were half-sailors at heart, and if the mission had been destroyed and the occupants butchered they would very likely continue down to the next river. To seamen and marines alike, water was not an enemy or a barrier, but a way out. Not this time, he thought grimly. 'Questions?'

Quintin said, 'Them slavers wot fired on the boats will be too busy to come this way, won't they, sir?'

Blackwood had already considered it. Lessard and others who used the local tribal chiefs like a private army must have some method of maintaining contact along hundreds of miles of coastline. They had seemed to know what Ashley-Chute had in mind before he did.

'We can't take that for granted. We are passing through King Zwide's territory. He may have other ideas about our progress.' He saw them glance at Harry and added shortly, 'But what's done is done. We'll have to take the chance. Once we reach the river,' He looked at Harry, 'you'll go with Corporal Jones and Private Frazier to a point above the mission while the rest of us move in to investigate.'

Harry remarked as lightly as he could, 'Rather like being an umpire, sir!'

Blackwood eyed him calmly. 'You'll be the bloody burial party if you don't watch out!'

He turned away, angry with himself and with Harry's inability to take things seriously.

'Corporal Jones, lead off. If you see or hear *anything*, I want to know instantly.'

He could feel his heart beating faster. And they had not

even started yet. He wished suddenly he had accepted Smithett's offer of something stronger than water.

As the marines waded into the clinging grass and bush Harry said quietly, 'Take my shako, sir.' He held it out to him and added simply, 'It might give them a bit of confidence at the mission.'

Blackwood bit back an angry retort and jammed the shako on his head.

'Thanks.'

Then he swung on his heel and followed the others into the remaining shadows.

Harry Blackwood paused only to look at the small, flattened patch of grass where the blanket had been. His legs still felt like jelly, and he could feel the scent of her body like something physical.

He saw the Rocke twins trudge past, muskets at the ready as they watched the scrub on either side. He was getting to know all of them, their ways and their attitudes. He thought of the sergeant's comment. *Too strong a word.* Perhaps it was trust which Philip offered them and in return they gave him an instant loyalty.

He sighed and fell in behind the twins, his pistol drawn and resting in the crook of his arm.

His mother and father would be proud of him, but in his heart he knew that the one man he needed to share it with was up there in the lead, wearing *his* shako.

Harry smiled, the mood past. After today nothing might matter any more.

The last part of the journey took longer than expected, and by the time Blackwood was satisfied they were close enough, the sky seemed too bright for any hope of surprise. With Sergeant Quintin breathing heavily behind him, he crawled through the treacherous gorse and dried grass to make sure each of his men was in position.

'What d'you think, Sergeant?'

Quintin had already discarded his shako and leaned on his

elbows as he scanned the river below their hiding-place. In the weak daylight it looked dirty yellow, the sluggish current moving idly through long reeds and around sand-bars as it continued towards the sea. In the protective arm of a bend stood the mission. A collection of crude huts and one central building which was larger but no less spartan than the others.

Blackwood waited while Quintin, the old campaigner, took stock of the situation. There was no sign of movement, nor of smoke from cooking fires. He shivered and felt the hair rise on his neck. Maybe they had already been seen and were surrounded, and at any second a spear might plunge into his back. He recalled with stark clarity what old Tom Fenwick had told him about the mutilation which had been done to his companions and felt the bile rise in his throat.

Quintin said slowly, 'There should be some natives at the mission, sir. But there's nobody, as far as I can make out.'

Blackwood swallowed. 'Very well. Two men with me. You stay here with the others.' Their eyes met and he added, 'If it's a trap, get out while you can. Lieutenant Blackwood and his two marksmen will cover you.'

He looked at the tangle of trees and creeper. Harry would be up there by now. Did he realize he had been sent with Jones and Frazier to keep him safe if things went wrong? Safe? Even the word was a mockery here.

Blackwood listened to the disturbed squawking of birds, or were they humans signalling to one another, preparing an ambush.

He got to his knees and examined his pistol. Smithett was ready to go with him, his face grim and strained. Another private, named Bell, a man almost legendary for his skills in brawls and hand to hand fighting alike, was the second one.

Quintin whispered, 'Pass the word. Be ready to fire.'

Blackwood nodded to Bell. 'To your left.'

Then, very slowly, crouching and hopping like frogs, they moved down the slope towards the huts. As they drew closer Blackwood felt a sense of apprehension and dread. They were too late. It was a dead place.

Bell dropped on one knee and held up his hand while he gripped his musket and bayonet firmly with the other.

Blackwood wormed his way among the scrub, unaware of the scrapes and cuts on his hands and face.

Bell whispered, 'Here, sir.' He did not need to explain further.

A man sat propped against some kindling wood, a floppy straw hat over his forehead as if to protect his face from the sun. A musket lay across his legs, and there was a wine bottle at his side.

Bell grasped the man's head and levered it back so that Blackwood could see the terrible slash across his throat which ran almost from ear to ear. It must have been swift and instant, for the man's eyes were wide and bulging, brought from his doze to meet an agonizing death.

He had certainly not been a member of the mission. Doubtless one of Lessard's men. Blackwood wiped his mouth with the back of his hand. Whoever had done it had left the musket behind, something more precious in Africa than gold itself. Somebody? He thought of his brother's explanation and wondered. Maybe he had been right, and the black princess had kept her word and had helped in the only way she understood.

Bell hissed, 'Someone's about, sir!'

Blackwood cocked his pistol with great care. He had heard nothing.

Then feet scraped on sand and a figure emerged from the main hut, ducking through the low entrance and then stretching up his arms and emitting a huge yawn. The yawn and the stretch froze as he saw Blackwood and the others. It was a matter of seconds, and yet they all seemed to stand stock still like statues for an eternity.

Blackwood bounded forward and fired, seeing the ball smash through the man's forehead and hurl him against the hut. He was dead before he touched the ground.

He shouted, '*Now!*' and charged for the low entrance, tossing his empty pistol aside as he dragged out his sword and ducked under the crude thatch.

The world exploded in his face in a livid flash and he was momentarily blinded, but aware the shot had missed him and had hit Bell who was immediately behind him.

Vague shadows swayed about him and he felt the pain in his wrist and arm as his blade cut through muscle and bone and then slashed hard against another.

A figure blotted out the light from the entrance but fell back inside gasping, propelled by the thrust of Smithett's bayonet which had taken him in the stomach.

Smithett finished it with a second lunge and then loped across to join Blackwood in the centre of the mud floor.

Blackwood ignored the two men he had just cut down and hurried to the hut's one other occupant. The girl lay against some old bedding and broken cases, her hands and ankles pinioned, her mouth cruelly gagged with a neckerchief. Her clothing had been ripped open almost to the waist, so that her bared breasts shone in the filtered daylight, moving painfully as she stared up at him in a mixture of terror and shocked disbelief.

Blackwood dropped down beside her and pulled her torn dress together across her breasts, feeling her eyes watching his every move.

'Fetch Sergeant Quintin and help Bell.'

Smithett glanced at the two groaning figures by the wall. 'Bell's done for, sir.' Then he hurried away.

Blackwood removed the gag with great care and held her shoulders as she gasped and choked, ashamed in spite of her suffering that he should watch her vomit on to the floor.

He had to use a knife to cut her bonds, and he felt her cringe as he massaged the bruised skin where they had bitten into her. They must have made her suffer. It was a wonder she was not driven mad by what she had seen and endured here.

She fell, breathing fast, against him, her eyes hidden by the cascade of hair across her face.

Outside the hut there was the sound of order and discipline as Quintin and the others arrived. It would not last for long, but the moment was precious to Blackwood as he held her, saying nothing, while he waited for her breathing to recover.

Then she said in a small voice, 'I can't believe it. You of all people.'

One hand moved up to touch her throat and breast and she turned away as some terrible memory was reborn.

He said, 'We came as fast as we could.' He could feel her sobbing, each beat driving against him as if he was sharing her pain. 'Now we must leave.'

He glanced up as Quintin stooped through the door. 'Two natives dead round the back, sir. Nobody else except . . .' He looked at the girl.

She said huskily, 'They took my father. He's done so much for the people here.'

Blackwood said, 'Smithett, come here. Look after this lady.' He released her shoulders and saw the tears making lines on her dusty face. 'Don't leave her.'

Outside the sunlight was brighter but seemed without warmth.

Quintin said heavily, 'They'd pegged 'im out by the river while 'e was still alive. There must be crocodiles round 'ere. There ain't much of 'im to bury.'

Blackwood leaned on his sword and closed his eyes tightly for several seconds.

'Must have happened recently.'

Quintin nodded. 'They came by boat. I found marks on the sand. The people at the mission must 'ave known 'em, or seen no reason to be afraid. There's no sign of a fight. It must 'ave bin over in minutes.' He spat out the words, 'The murderin' bastards!'

'That girl is in no state to walk. Make a litter. We must get away from here before any of Zwide's people find us.'

He ducked into the hut and waited for Smithett to move away.

He said, 'It's time to go, Miss Seymour. We've a hard march to reach the others. Then you'll be safe.' He looked around the hut at the upended boxes and chests. 'Is there anything you need?'

She shook her head violently. 'Nothing. I don't want to

touch any of it, ever.' Then in an almost level voice she said, 'My father knew there was trouble. He'd been warned often enough. All his helpers had left. He said he had to stay, *had to*. It was his purpose for being, especially after Mother died. Then a ship came.' She glanced at the low door. She did not seem to see the corpse which had been forced back on Smithett's bayonet. It was as if she saw the ship in the river.

Blackwood held her tightly, knowing the sudden calm could not last.

'I can remember what Father said.' Her voice shook. ' "It's the Navy, Davern. That young lieutenant who is always coming here to warn me." ' She turned and looked at Blackwood, her eyes in deep shadow. 'But it was not the Navy. It was men like those over there, like the ones who killed the house-boys, and then . . .' She pressed her face into Blackwood's shoulder, '. . . they took my father away . . . I could hear what they were doing to him . . .'

Blackwood tightened his grip around her as the sobs returned until it felt as if her body would break.

The vessel must have been the missing armed schooner *Kingsmill* which Slade had spoken of a million years ago. A young lieutenant and probably a couple of master's mates. The crew would likely have been made up of recruited natives, a lot of local vessels used Kroo seamen, usually reliable, but no match for this kind of thing.

'Now I'm going to ask you to stand.' Blackwood got to his feet but kept a firm hold of her hand. She shook her head and tried to pull away but he insisted, 'Please. For me. Will you try?'

Very slowly and carefully Blackwood helped her to rise and then steadied her until she was able to face him again.

She said in a voice so small he could barely hear, 'The last time we met I was rude and hurtful to you.' Then she began to weep uncontrollably and did not resist as he held her against his body as if to shield her from her suffering.

Sergeant Quintin re-entered the hut and said, 'Ready, sir.'

Blackwood looked at him across the girl's head. Quintin was carrying a shovel.

'Very well, we're coming.'

Quintin glanced coldly at the two moaning figures. 'Shall I do for 'em, sir?' He might have been discussing chickens for the pot.

Blackwood felt the girl go rigid against him as some part of her listened to what was happening.

'No. Leave them. A doctor could have helped. They can think about that.'

He guided the girl out into the sunlight where the handful of marines waited and watched in silence. Blackwood noticed a mound of sand and rocks by some trees, a crude cross with Bell's shako on the top of it. Another familiar face and voice wiped away.

One of the Rocke twins helped to break the tension. 'Litter's roight 'ere, Missy.' Whichever twin it was, his round Somerset dialect seemed to help.

Smithett and Quintin lifted the girl on to the litter as if she was a piece of delicate porcelain, and as she tried to hold her torn dress together her eyes remained fixed on the pathetic mound they were leaving behind.

Quintin said roughly, 'I took care of yer dad meself, Miss. 'E's safe enough now.'

Blackwood accepted a reloaded pistol from Smithett and sheathed his sword.

*What a sight we must look.* Not a bit like the fierce-eyed veterans in his grandfather's paintings at Hawks Hill. The lines of scarlet coats, the streaming flags, and not even a whisker out of place.

'Ackland, take the point.'

In single file, with the litter in the middle of their little force, they trudged back into the cover of the bush. At the prescribed place, Harry, with Jones and Frazier, joined them, and together they continued towards the other river.

When they were well clear of the mission Harry dropped back to walk beside his half-brother. He had not asked about the doctor who had been left for the crocodiles, nor even about Private Bell. The faces of the others and the presence of the exhausted girl on the litter spoke more than words.

He said, 'You were being watched, sir, did you know that?'

Blackwood looked at him. *'Watched?'*

'A hundred or so warriors were on the next hill to ours. Armed to the teeth. But they did nothing. They just stood and waited.'

Blackwood removed his borrowed shako and returned it to Harry. 'It seems you were right about the princess and I was wrong. She kept to the bargain, otherwise we'd all be dead.'

Harry glanced back at the litter. 'I'm really glad about her.' He looked at his half-brother's strained profile. 'For your sake too.'

Blackwood quickened his pace. 'Don't talk such damned rubbish, and get up front with Ackland.'

But in his heart he was pleased. It was hopeless, just as it was dangerous to fantasize at moments like these. They were to all intents and purposes fighting a war. Small, local and unheard of in Britain, but just as deadly as the grander fields of battle.

He turned to look at the girl as if to reassure himself it was not a dream and saw her watching him as the litter swayed between the two tall brothers.

Could she ever forget what had happened to her? Would she find some small part in her life which he might somehow share?

He heard Quintin rasp, 'Watch where yer walkin', Private Frazier! Yer a *marine*, remember?'

Blackwood sighed. That just about summed it up.

# 12

# 'Up the Royals!'

Major Rupert Fynmore sat on an upturned ration box and nodded impatiently.

'What shape is Sir Geoffrey's niece in? Must have been a terrible ordeal for her.'

Blackwood wiped his face with a filthy handkerchief. After the return march through the bush and the constant threat of being attacked, even Fynmore's brusque manner seemed like a relief.

As his small, weary party had scrambled down to this same river-bank he had left just three days earlier he had seen their step smarten, the air of defiance and something akin to pride as they had carried the crude litter to the boats.

Nothing had changed as far as he could see. A few marines were scattered among the rocks and others sat or lay in the shelter of the bank while they waited for orders.

Some more seamen had joined the landing party, and he saw Lieutenant Ashley-Chute moving among them as they loaded their weapons under the watchful eyes of their petty officers.

Blackwood said, 'Miss Seymour was wonderful. I can't imagine what she's been through!'

Fynmore's sharp eyes watched him curiously. 'Raped, d'you suppose?'

Blackwood looked away, his thoughts laid bare by Fynmore's brutal reality.

'No. I think Lessard had given his men certain instructions.'

Fynmore's mind had already moved on. It was no longer his responsibility.

'And you believe the schooner *Kingsmill* was responsible. That, more to the point, she's up there round the bend in the river?'

'Yes, sir. I think she must have entered the river just ahead of us.'

He watched his words sink in, but he was thinking of the moment when Lessard's long-boat had rounded the bend and confronted Netten's launch bows on. King Zwide's territory had been Lessard's haven. Now it could be a trap, provided Fynmore acted without any more delay.

Blackwood asked, 'Is there any word from the admiral?'

Again he felt Fynmore's cool scrutiny. It made him feel unclean and dishevelled. In contrast, the neat, sandy-haired major could have just come from a parade-ground.

'He ordered me to wait your return, until tomorrow anyway.' He gave his lopsided smile. 'I sent word to *Audacious* as soon as our pickets reported your approach. We'll just have to be patient.' He flinched as a crack echoed across the hillside and a bullet kicked into hard ground. He said irritably, 'We've had a few casualties because of those bloody sharpshooters!'

Blackwood looked at the ridge where Quartermain's platoon had charged among the enemy, where one marine had told his friend to leave him before he had died. Fynmore had kept his word and had withdrawn all his men from the high ground. A good marksman like Frazier could mark down an army from there.

But now it did not seem to matter. He tried to put it down to exhaustion, to the relief of getting his men safely back here. But in his mind he could see the girl being carried swiftly to one of the boats with Slade's agent, Mr Patterson, watching over her like a guard dog.

She was probably already aboard the flagship and would remember little of their flight through the bush. She had been barely conscious for most of the time and seemingly unaware of what was happening.

Fynmore remarked, 'The gunboat is here, by the way.' He regarded Blackwood calmly. 'The admiral will send her up to us shortly.' He compressed his lips into a tight smile. 'Not much choice really. The wind has veered. Nothing else can stand inshore.' It seemed to amuse him greatly.

*Crack.* Another shot echoed among the rocks and a sailor shouted angrily at the invisible marksman.

Fynmore said, 'And that black woman, the er, princess, you believe she called off the hounds?'

'Yes. No doubt about it. We were tracked all the way. They could have swamped us any time had they wanted to.'

Fynmore looked up as one of the lieutenants hurried towards him.

'Well, Mr Shephard?'

The lieutenant swallowed hard. 'Mr Heighway's pickets have sighted the gunboat, sir.'

But Fynmore glanced at him accusingly. 'Do up that button, sir! You are supposed to set an example to the men!' He calmed himself with an effort. 'Send a runner to Mr Quartermain's section. He knows what to do.'

Blackwood saw the neat major in another light. He was about to mount an attack, the method and the outcome of which were doubtful to say the least. And yet he could still find strength from petty detail, if only to cover his poor eyesight.

A finely-pitched whistle floated up the river and several birds rose flapping and screeching from among some reeds. The gunboat's siren was no match for Tobin's *Satyr*.

Minutes dragged by and eventually the small, shallow-draft gunboat, gushing smoke from a stick-like funnel, nosed around the first bend where everything had first started to go wrong.

After *Satyr*'s impressive size and raked bow, the *Norseman* seemed little more than a platform suspended between two thrashing paddles. Blackwood watched her approach, thinking of her two mortars and solitary six-pounder, hardly a match for those well-sited cannon. Unless she could get into a suitable position before she was severely mauled.

Several of the marines raised an ironic cheer as the gunboat's anchor cable rattled into the swirling water and she came to rest beneath a cloud of dense black smoke.

Fynmore snapped, 'My compliments to *Norseman*'s commander, and would he join me with alacrity.'

As a runner scampered away he turned to Blackwood again.

'This is the plan. *Norseman* will proceed up river followed by six boats to carry *Audacious*'s landing party. Mr Ashley-Chute will command the boats. As soon as action is joined I want you to lead a platoon ashore from the gunboat to harass the enemy's rear. The enemy can do one of two things, fall back to avoid being cut off from Zwide's stronghold or try to come this way, in which case the remaining marines will advance on them from here.'

He tugged down his impeccable coatee but was obviously awaiting Blackwood's reaction.

Blackwood said slowly, 'Unless we can get them to withdraw and take their cannon with them we shall be in for a hard fight.'

What was the point of reminding this infuriating man that had he left Quartermain's men on the ridge they could have attacked the battery from both sides at once. If he did not realize the fact, he soon would.

Lieutenant Heighway came panting up the slope, his face wet from hurrying between the sections of hidden marines.

'Sir!' He halted, gasping for breath.

Shipboard life had taken a hard toll on one so young, Blackwood thought. Heighway was not much older than Harry.

Fynmore scowled, 'Yes?'

'The admiral is here, sir!'

'*What?*' Fynmore jerked to his feet and adjusted his chin strap carefully. 'In a *steam* vessel?'

Round the side of the hill, accompanied by a sunburned officer who was obviously the gunboat's commander, the familiar shape of Sir James Ashley-Chute marched towards

Fynmore's command post, his hands behind him, his hat tilted at a rakish angle. Following at a discreet distance was Pelham, his flag-lieutenant.

'God in heaven, Major, what is going on here, a damned blood-bath?' He glanced briefly at Blackwood. 'You are untidy, sir, a spectacle!'

Fynmore stammered, ' 'Pon my word, Sir James, I didn't expect you . . .'

'I don't want a guard of honour, or one of your damned ceremonials, Major, I want *action*! I'll not have my squadron made a laughing-stock, tied down by a handful of bandits!'

Blackwood watched him as he worked himself into a white-hot rage. It was an act, and Blackwood had seen it many times, but it was always impressive. This tiny, deformed figure, long-armed and fierce-eyed, seemed to have the power of ten men. As his bright epaulettes bounced up and down in time with his words Fynmore seemed to wilt under the admiral's wrath.

Ashley-Chute shouted, 'Otherwise d'you imagine for a single second that I'd have set foot on that scruffy, *miserable object*?'

The *Norseman*'s commander said, 'She's a fine little ship, sir.'

'Hold your impertinence, sir!' The admiral was enjoying his anger. 'Begin the attack at once!'

Fynmore looked uncomfortably at Blackwood. 'Carry on, if you please. Signal when you are ready.'

Blackwood turned away and then heard Ashley-Chute shriek, '*What* did you say, Major? The *Kingsmill*?'

Blackwood glanced at Colour-Sergeant M'Crystal who had appeared as if by magic. Like Fynmore, he seemed able to remain clean and smart no matter what was happening.

He grinned broadly, 'We were all right glad to see you safely back with the poor lass, sir. Do you have orders for me?'

Blackwood shaded his eyes to look at the ridge. It would all depend on the gunboat, and the admiral knew it even if he would never admit such a thing.

He turned as the sunburned officer strode after him and said, 'I'm told I am to take a platoon aboard.' He could not restrain himself. 'She's a *fine* ship. I had to tell him, blast his eyes!'

His hurt pride made Blackwood smile. 'I'm Blackwood.' He held out his hand. 'I'm coming with you.'

The lieutenant grinned ruefully, 'I'm Ridley, acting-commander.'

M'Crystal was back again, his red face calm and reassuring. 'All taken care of, sir.' He cast a quick glance as the marines tramped past towards the boats.

Blackwood said, 'But the men who went to the mission with me are among them, Colour-Sergeant, they must still be tired from two forced marches.'

M'Crystal's eyes did not even flicker. 'Exactly what I told Sergeant Quintin. He said, begging your pardon, sir, that if you could do it, so too would they.'

Ridley fell in step beside Blackwood and together they walked down to the water. There had been no more firing for some time, and Blackwood guessed that Lessard's men had observed the gunboat's arrival and were now waiting to see what they intended to do.

Ridley watched the marines scrambling into the boats. 'A lot of men could die if things go wrong.'

Blackwood wiped his eyes and throat. 'A lot have already. So let's get started, shall we?'

Smithett, who was close behind him, bared his teeth in a mournful grin. The captain had put *him* in his place and no mistake.

'Shove off forrard!' The boat's coxswain held up his fist. 'As you were! Belay that order!' He watched despairingly as the marine second lieutenant ran the last few feet and vaulted into the boat.

Blackwood regarded his half-brother and waited for an explanation.

Harry took a deep breath as the boat gathered way. 'Major Fynmore ordered me to liaise between both detachments once

we have landed, sir.' He beamed under Blackwood's gaze.
'And of course, sir, you may need the use of my hat again?'

Blackwood looked at the bustling activity in the other
boats as the blue-jackets swarmed aboard with their weapons
and prepared to follow astern. Each boat mounted a bow-
gun, and there was a lieutenant in command of each craft.
Both flagship and frigate must have been stripped of everyone except for midshipmen and ancient warrant officers, he
thought. As well they might. It was not merely impatience
which had brought Monkey ashore in a hated steam vessel.
He knew better than anyone that his reputation was at stake.
He wondered how Captain Ackworthy was feeling about it.
Sir Geoffrey's shocked and terrified niece in his care, the
flagship denuded of lieutenants and a large part of her complement, all might be compensated in his eyes just by getting
rid of his admiral for a few hours.

It was barely a few feet to climb aboard the gunboat and in
no time the restricted upper deck seemed filled with marines
and their weapons.

Blackwood joined the *Norseman*'s commander by the wheel
and then he turned to face his brother.

'Report to Mr Quartermain, he is second in command.
Then join M'Crystal down aft.'

Harry faced him stubbornly. 'Out of danger, you mean? Like
the hill at the mission. I'm not a child, Philip, not any more.'

Blackwood smiled grimly. 'Just do as I tell you.'

Harry touched his hat. 'Yes, *sir*.'

Clank . . . clank . . . clank . . . the anchor cable was
already hove short. Somewhere below his feet a bell clanged
and the two motionless paddles began to revolve, slowly at
first, and then as the anchor rose dripping from the river with
ever increasing power. Coal dust gritted between his teeth,
and he could feel the hot air from the boiler-room like wind
off a desert.

Commander Ridley was calling orders to his helmsmen
and quartermaster as the gunboat forged out into deeper
water, and Blackwood saw the two mortars were already

manned and pointing their fat snouts towards the shore. Quartermain seemed to have forgotten his first nervousness and with the prospect of more action was giving separate instructions to the sergeants and corporals who would lead the attack.

'Mr Pooley! Slow ahead, if you please, or we shall leave the boats too far astern!'

Blackwood watched the paddles thrashing at the water. They were not massively heavy like *Satyr*'s, but appeared to tread delicately on the surface like the legs of a gnat.

But to Ridley, her young commander, she was everything, greater possibly even than *Audacious* was to Ackworthy.

There was a new crispness in Ridley's tone as he called to his second in command, 'She moves well, Mr Pooley.' Their eyes met. 'Hoist battle ensigns, if you please.'

The gunboat's wash disturbed some thick reeds and Blackwood saw part of a shattered boat, mercifully capsized among them. Perhaps Netten and his terrible face was still trapped inside, or maybe, like the girl's dead father, had already been devoured by crocodiles.

He raised his eyes as the White Ensigns broke from *Norseman*'s two small masts, and tried to recognize his own feelings at this particular moment. Death or glory, Fynmore had said, too much pride.

He looked again at his men as they took their positions beneath the gunboat's bulwark.

*I am proud of them at least.*

Smithett leaned forward. 'Sir?'

'Nothing.' Blackwood smiled tightly. He had not realized he had spoken aloud.

Then he thought of the girl who was aboard the flagship, protected now and yet more vulnerable to the eyes and unspoken questions. She would soon forget him, perhaps she had erased him already from her tortured mind, if only to save her sanity. Sir Geoffrey Slade would do his best to shield her, she . . . his thoughts came to a dead stop as a seaman shouted, '*Hill*, starboard bow, sir! *Enemy in sight!*'

*

'Bring her round two points to starboard, Mr Pooley!' Ridley had to shout as two of the concealed cannon banged out from the far end of the ridge. 'Keep as close to the shore as you can.'

He turned, squinting in the noon sunlight as twin water-spouts shot skywards on the far bank. He knew the cannon had no chance of hitting the gunboat as yet. They were too high on the ridge and probably protected by earthworks to make them invisible.

Blackwood also watched the fall of shot. The river was deep and powerful for the most part with occasional sand-bars and swaying reeds to betray the other dangers. It must have taken hundreds of King Zwide's people to haul and man-handle those massive guns up to the ridge. Was he there too, watching the approaching gunboat perhaps, or with his daughter who had spared their lives, even traded her own for Davern Seymour's?

The gunners would know they could not depress their muzzles enough to straddle *Norseman*'s bustling approach. They were probably firing to build up their own morale and to warn off the attackers at the same time.

There was a solitary explosion and a great gout of flame and blasted bushes from the opposite bank. M'Crystal had been right the first time. Three large cannon backed up an army of killers who had nothing to lose but their lives. In battle or on Her Majesty's gibbets, it would make no odds to them.

He glanced along the crouching section of marines, their muskets protruding over the bulwarks and some makeshift sandbags like uneven teeth. Lieutenant Quartermain, his sword unsheathed, a bugler, a mere child, beside him. Sergeant Quintin, chewing on his chin strap as he watched his men and the nearest paddle as it thrashed up the spray like rain.

Blackwood said, 'That's where the launch was hit. Right on the bend.'

Ridley lowered his telescope and grunted. 'Mr Pooley, pass the word to engage the moment we are up to that cairn of rocks!' To Blackwood he added, 'I have two boats towing

astern for your men. I'll do what I can to give you covering
fire.'

Two more bangs heralded another fall of shot. Water rose
and fell languidly, clear of the other bank this time.

A midshipman wrote busily on a slate and hung it near the
wheel. Would anyone ever read what he had recorded,
Blackwood wondered? He thought of Midshipman Ward
who had died trying to protect the black princess, the way she
had held him with apparent tenderness as his blood had fallen
on her.

Ridley said abruptly, 'The other boats can act on their own
for a while. Mr Pooley, tell the Chief to give me full speed
ahead!'

The slender paddles churned at the river and a long wash
rolled away to rock the nearest boats and break across the
bank like a small wave.

It was a tense yet exciting moment, the low hull shaking as
if to fall apart, the officers and seamen standing about their
weapons more like spectators than people about to fight.

Blackwood heard a solitary bang and waited as the shot
fanned above the foremast and burst in the water well abeam.
He could picture the gunners on the ridge, working with
crude tackle and handspikes to train their weapons towards
the small, thrashing vessel below them.

Some of the seamen were waving their hats and cheering, it
was the madness which no one seemed able to control.

Both mortars were squatting on their mountings, and
Blackwood saw *Norseman*'s gunner gesturing to his men to
adjust their elevation so that they would not be caught out
when the order to fire was given.

Blackwood tried to ignore the preparations on the crowded
deck, and looked instead at the oncoming bend in the river
where Lessard's long-boat had dropped a stream-anchor.

Soon now. Very soon. He glanced astern and saw the
flotilla of boats pulling strongly up river, their work made
even harder by the armed blue-jackets who were packed in
the hulls like beans in a box.

*Bang!* Blackwood flinched as the sunlight shimmered in a haze of pale smoke and a massive shot ripped across the water like a sounding dolphin. They had the range, and their guns would bear.

Ridley snapped, 'Closer inshore, Quartermaster! Boatswain's mate! Put a leadsman in the chains immediately!' He blinked as two shots roared down from the ridge and hurled shredded water high over the forecastle.

A seaman with a lead and line scampered forward to begin sounding as *Norseman* edged even closer to the land. He ducked violently as another shot hammered into the river, the shock of the explosion hitting the hull like a muffled fist.

'Open fire with the mortars!'

The gunner must have been watching his captain like a hawk. Each heavy mortar fired separately, the deck jolting as smoke drifted aft from the black muzzles.

Blackwood thought he saw where the charges exploded, and counted seconds while he tried to gauge the effect of the shots. But the hidden battery crashed out again, the pair first, and moments later the third one. The latter was more to the left, he thought, directly above the bend where the river narrowed.

The gunboat's little six-pounder fired sharply, and some of the younger marines who were peering over their defences at the ridge gasped with alarm and probably imagined they had been hit. Several grinned sheepishly as M'Crystal bellowed, 'Och, who'd want to shoot at *you* then, Private Morrison!'

Around the bend it was another cable or so before the river divided into twin forks. In the centre of one fork Zwide's village was sited perfectly, with only the easterly approach undefended by water. Lessard had chosen well.

Suddenly Blackwood knew that the next shot was going to strike. Sixth sense, fear or instinct, he did not know or care. *'Keep down!'*

The crash when it came was violent and terrible and must have hit the hull just forward of the starboard paddle. Blackwood heard it smashing through the deck below as if it would never stop, the splintering destruction of wood and metal which would kill or maim anyone between decks. He realized with a start that he had not even heard the gun which had fired.

'Mortars, Mr Pooley! Mark that one down!'

The starboard mortar recoiled and belched fire like a crouching dragon, the shot tearing through a line of trees and flinging up fronds and stones as it exploded.

Ridley snapped, 'Report damage!'

From forward the leadsman yelled, 'By the mark *two*!'

'Starboard your helm, Quartermaster!' Ridley glanced at Blackwood, his eyes glazed with concentration. 'I know she's shallow, but I don't want her to drive aground!'

Blackwood saw reeds and sand spewing from the paddle nearest the land, and heard someone give a sigh as the gunboat moved out a few more yards.

'By the mark three!'

Blackwood wiped the dust from his eyes and studied the shore. Time to go soon.

He sought out the lieutenant and shouted, 'First section aft, Mr Quartermain!'

The marines hurried towards the quarterdeck, their bodies bent almost double as they made their way to the boats which were towing astern.

Ridley said between his teeth, 'That overhang will offer some cover. I'll reduce to dead slow.' He raised his telescope again as both mortars fired together. 'I wish you luck.'

Blackwood nodded to Sergeant Quintin and another section came pounding aft, eyes averted as a shot tore overhead and brought down some signal halliards like broken creeper.

'First boat loaded, sir!'

Blackwood turned and saw Harry staring at him through the drifting smoke. His eyes were wide with excitement and strain, but his voice was steady.

'Very well, I want – '

He cringed down, pulling Harry with him, as the deck bucked wildly and threw splintered planks and gratings like crude arrows.

As the smoke funnelled through a gaping hole in the deck Blackwood imagined he saw the glint of water, but his ears were still ringing from the explosion and he could barely think. Several men had fallen to the hail of deadly splinters, and only the quartermaster still clung to the gunboat's double-wheel, his chest heaving in and out as if he had just been saved from drowning. Pooley, the first lieutenant, sat drooping against the bulwarks, his bloodied fingers grasping a great jagged splinter in his chest, his eyes misting over as his life ran into the scuppers.

One of the mortars had been upended, pinning down one of its crew, and Blackwood saw a man's body picked up by the whirling paddle and then smashed down into the frothing water. Blackwood saw a line snaking after the crushed corpse and guessed it was the leadsman.

As his hearing came back he heard shouted commands, screams and pitiful whimpers as the wounded groped at the legs of Ridley's men as they ran to repair the damage.

The foremast had gone and trailed over the side like a sea-anchor until axes hacked it free.

Ridley rose from the deck and shook himself like an angry dog.

'Slow ahead, Mr Poo . . .' He saw his dead lieutenant and yelled, 'Mr Thomas, take charge there!'

The remaining mortar continued to fire, the gunner unaware that he was splashed with blood from the other crew.

The paddles slowed reluctantly and Blackwood said, 'Come on, Harry. Our turn.' He watched him searchingly. 'All right?'

The young second lieutenant stared past him at the carnage, the strange patterns of blood which seemed to writhe with a life of their own as the churning paddles carried the gunboat forward.

He nodded and said in a forced whisper, 'I – I never thought it would be like this!'

Blackwood gripped his arm. He understood exactly how Harry felt. But there was no more time.

He heard himself explain, 'You wanted to know what it was like! Now *get down aft* with the other boat!' He pushed him roughly. 'They'll be looking to you today!'

He tore his eyes away as Harry lurched after the other marines. He wanted to keep him at his side, to make him understand. The thoughts surged through his mind in distorted confusion.

It was no use. Blackwood looked at Ridley. 'We'll do our best!'

He remembered the burly able seaman grinning at him and shouting, *'Up the Royals!'* The next instant he was staring at the deck, his cheek bleeding on the planking where he had been hurled by an explosion he had not heard. Wreckage and splinters were falling across the deck and splashing outboard to add to the turmoil. There were more cries and yells, and the hull seemed to be tilting right over so that for a moment he imagined they were sinking. A crazy thought shone through his cringing mind so that he wanted to laugh. They would sink in the shallows anyway, the dead leadsman had proved as much. His body convulsed violently and he thought he was going to vomit. He could barely move, as if he was pinioned to the deck.

Slowly and fearfully he tested each limb in turn, but apart from the raw pain of his wounded leg he felt nothing. He tried to lever himself up, his lungs rebelling against the smoke and stench of burned powder.

'Damn you, Fynmore!' The words were torn from him. *'Damn you to bloody hell!'*

He felt someone gripping his shoulder and when he twisted his head saw that it was Harry.

'Help me, Harry!'

His half-brother tore at some smoking timber which had tumbled across the deck like a trap.

'I – I thought you were dead! When you fell, I . . .' He could not continue.

Blackwood staggered to his feet and together they swayed about like a pair of drunks returning to barracks.

The motion was far worse, and there was a grating sound and deep crashes in the hull. There seemed to be blood everywhere, and men and pieces of men were flung about the deck in grisly profusion.

But all Blackwood could think of was Harry's face, the pale lines of tears which were cutting through the grime, like the terrified girl at the mission. It did more to steady him than any other thing, and he knew it.

Smithett rose from the chaos and groped for his musket and his precious bag.

Ridley knelt near the wheel, hands clasped as if in prayer. Even as he saw him, *Norseman*'s commander fell forward on his face and lay still.

Blackwood gasped and retched, and then heard the sound of a pump. Someone was alive and working to save the ship. Blurred figures were groping through the dead and dying, and then Blackwood heard a youthful voice ask, 'What are your orders, sir?'

It was the midshipman who had written a part of history on a slate just before the game had become stark reality.

Blackwood saw the starboard paddle spinning wildly, most of it broken and useless, while the other wheel continued to drive the hull in a wild arc towards the shore.

Through the smoke he could see the boats, the blurred red coats of the landing party which he was supposed to be leading.

Smithett said helpfully, 'There are six of th' lads still aboard, sir.'

'Fetch them.'

He looked at the midshipman. Like Harry, he was near to breaking. *As I was.* 'Now, Mr?'

The youth said huskily, 'Sampson, sir.'

'Well, Mr Sampson, you are in command of this vessel now.' He saw the midshipman's eyes widen. 'Stop the engine, and do what you can to anchor. We shall be wrecked if we are not careful.'

Corporal Jones and the remaining marines pounded past to

help the seamen and a solitary petty officer who were trying to put out a blaze on the forecastle.

The gunfire had stopped as the cannon could no longer be depressed enough to hit them.

Blackwood stared at the destruction and the gruesome litter of death. Instead of success it would be a disaster. The survivors of the attack would be lucky to get back to the original landing-place.

The broken paddle jerked noisily and then fell still, and Blackwood felt the keel quiver as the hull lurched on to a sandy bottom.

Harry was tearing at his collar as if it was choking him.

Blackwood eyed him gravely. 'Ready?'

'For what?'

'Lessard, or whatever his bloody name is, will know by now that his guns have done for *Norseman*.' It was like talking to yourself. There was no understanding on Harry's features. 'If *Kingsmill* is up river, this is the moment she'll break out. She's an agile vessel and has the wind's favour, the same one which is keeping our admiral's ships useless and too far off shore to help.' *Why am I telling him this?* Maybe to convince myself it is worth dying for. 'The *Kingsmill* will carve through our boats and kill every man-jack aboard, unless we act now.'

Harry stared at him. 'What can *we* do?'

Blackwood brushed some splinters and dust from his jacket. He was thinking aloud as he said, 'We can wade ashore here. Fetch Corporal Jones and the others.'

He touched Harry's arm impetuously. 'Of course, you never knew your grandfather, I was forgetting.' He smiled at his incomprehension. 'I know what *he'd* have done. Finish what he had started.'

He gestured to the handful of marines as they mustered by the listing bulwark.

'So then, Master Harry, shall we.'

# 13

# *Remember This Day . . .*

'Come on, at the double!' M'Crystal's voice carried above the floundering marines better than any bugle. He seized a man who had sprawled headlong within feet of dry land and dragged him bodily from the water. 'Pick up your musket, you silly wee man!'

A few stray shots whined overhead and splashed into the river.

Lieutenant Quartermain dropped to one knee and tugged his telescope from his belt.

It was hard to believe that minutes earlier they had been on *Norseman*'s deck, that they were abandoned now to their own resources.

Blackwood watched the last of the platoon scrambling ashore. The enemy must be surprised at their own success, he thought bitterly. The smoke from the stranded gunboat was swirling across the water in a protective screen. But for it, the marksmen along the ridge would already be shooting down at his men.

'Spread out! Take cover!'

He saw sand spurt from the bank and guessed that someone was already in position and testing the range. He gritted his teeth. They would have to get much nearer to have any chance of success.

Quartermain called, 'There's a deep fold in the land to our left, sir.' He grimaced as a shot smacked down beside him as if to answer him back.

'I see it.'

Blackwood made himself stare up at the ridge as a solitary cannon fired. It was the one which had been sited above the bend. He saw a brief puff of smoke before it was quenched by the gun's crew and sponged out to hide their position.

'Did you mark that, Mr Quartermain?'

The lieutenant wriggled amongst the brush and scattered stones. 'Aye, sir.'

Blackwood lay on his side and peered around at his men. Colour-Sergeant M'Crystal on the flank. Quintin with the fifer, Doak, Frazier and all the rest of them, hunched like animals facing a trap. They would fight well enough, but pinned down and killed piecemeal they would soon lose the will to move forward.

'Stand to!' Blackwood got to his feet, his eyes like slits in the dusty glare. '*Advance!*' He waited for the scattered groups to hurry into some semblance of order. 'Third section, *fire!*'

The muskets crackled as the leading lines of marines charged forward.

Quartermain yelled, 'Second section . . . ! Prepare to fire!'

Blackwood shut the lieutenant from his mind as he ran up the steep incline, his heart pounding as if it would burst from his body.

Shots cracked and whimpered around him and he heard one smack into flesh and bone, a terrible gasp as a marine was hurled on to his back.

Another man, just to his left, spun round and dropped his musket, his hands tearing the air as if to seize the invisible attacker.

Blackwood saw the astonishment in the marine's eyes, as if he was incapable of accepting what was happening to him. He rolled out of sight, and the man nearest to him hesitated, his bayonet drooping as he stared after his dying companion.

'*Forward!* Get up there, damn you!' Blackwood shook his sword at him and the line lurched forward again.

The third section had reloaded, and with M'Crystal bellowing like an enraged bull, charged up the slope, yelling and cheering while they passed through the motionless marines who had just fired, their ramrods rising and falling. Routine, discipline, tradition.

Two more were hit, their cries lost in the crack and hiss of musket fire.

Blackwood blinked the sweat from his eyes. Merciful God, they had reached the fold in the ground. It was very shallow, but as they threw themselves along the far side it felt like a fortress.

'Take aim!'

Blackwood stared at the ridge and thought he saw a figure dart from cover to cover.

'Independent!'

He sensed the aim steadying as they regained their breath.

'*Fire!*'

The next section bounced into the depression in a flounder of weapons and limbs.

Quartermain darted him a glance and grinned fiercely. 'Bloody *hell*!'

Blackwood drew a pistol and got to his feet. 'Covering fire!' He gestured with the pistol. 'Second section! *Advance!*'

As they struggled up again a volley of shots raked over the depression and two men were hit simultaneously. The little fifer stared horrified at the nearest one, he had been hit in the face and was making terrible gurgling noises as he drowned in his own blood.

Blackwood shouted, 'Sound the *Charge*!' He punched the boy's arm. '*Now!*'

The bugle responded, and Blackwood marvelled that he had managed to make any sound at all.

Up and running again. Here and there a man fell or crouched down while the next section bounded up in support.

There were fewer shots from the ridge, and Blackwood guessed that Frazier and his companions were keeping the enemy's marksmen pinned down.

'Mr Quartermain's hit!'

Blackwood saw a shadow move from a clump of trees and felt a shot whip past his cheek as one of the marines knelt and fired. The shadow merged with the grass and lay still.

In those brief seconds Blackwood saw Quartermain lying on his back, his teeth bared in agony while he gripped his left shoulder, his clenched fingers the same colour as his uniform.

Harry was running with a mere handful of men on the flank, but they were not in any sort of panic. They wheeled and zigzagged, fired and ran on again, and if anyone was foolish enough to break cover to try and shoot them down he would expose himself to Frazier or one of the others.

They burst into scrub and among trees, the shadows blinding them after the relentless glare. More shots whined through the bars of smoky sunlight and ricocheted from the trees like hornets.

'Take cover!'

Blackwood threw himself down and stared at another darting shape beyond the trees. The pistol jerked in his grasp but the shot went wide.

He heard his men crashing down and reloading, while others attempted to drag their wounded companions into some kind of shelter, no matter how flimsy.

He heard M'Crystal's deep voice calling the roll of survivors and pictured the individual face of each man who answered.

A wounded marine gasped, 'For God's sake shut yer bloody mouth, can't yer?'

M'Crystal's voice found him too. 'I heard that, you miserable man!' He seemed to relent slightly. 'See to him, Corporal Bly!'

Then M'Crystal called, 'Nineteen men fit for duty, sir. I think we've lost six dead.'

Blackwood rolled over and crawled to join Harry who was helping Smithett to cut away the lieutenant's sleeve.

Smithett remarked gloomily, 'Lost a lot er blood, sir.'

Blackwood leaned across the lieutenant and looked at the wound. It had missed the bone, but he was in great pain.

'I – I'm all right, sir.' His eyes flickered and tried to focus on Blackwood's face. 'Not too bad at all really.'

He fainted away and Blackwood said, 'Put a dressing on it.'

He stared round. Already his men were quietening down. The worst sign of all. Accepting it. Waiting for the inevitable.

Quintin said, 'I reckon that cannon is less'n fifty yards over yonder, sir.' He tugged his shako over his eyes. 'Them buggers is waitin' for our boats to appear.'

Blackwood stared at him. Surely Ashley-Chute's son would not continue with the attack now that the gunboat was run ashore and unable to assist? The thought of the little admiral's rage answered the question for him. He would never dare to retreat and face Monkey, not after all this.

Harry said in a whisper, 'Where is the major?'

Blackwood glanced at him, but he was not speaking to anyone. It sounded more like a prayer.

'Makes sense, Sergeant.' He clapped him on the arm. 'A diversion is what we need.'

Quintin sucked at his chin strap. 'I'll go.'

M'Crystal growled, 'Like hell you will, *Sergeant*!'

Blackwood wriggled between them and peered through some entangled thorns. He had not realized they were so near to the end of the ridge. The river was now on his left, he could even see a spiral of smoke from the stranded gunboat below the overhang. *Norseman* with her child-captain was safe only until Lessard's men had driven the marines back to the water again.

He looked down at his hands, filthy and cut in a dozen places. A tiny insect, smaller than a pin's-head, crawled across his fingers and he winced. It had a sting like a wasp. It had been a fatal mistake to bring his men here with no hope of retreat. When the gunboat had been put out of action and her commander killed, he should have broken off the attack altogether. It had been his decision. Pride again? It had cost his men dearly and worse was to come.

He dug his fingers into the hot ground until they were like claws.

Quintin said, 'Funny thing, sir. Them blacks 'ave kept out of it. Far as I can fathom it's only the slavers.' He sucked his teeth as a single shot brought down some leaves from overhead. 'But they're more 'n enough.'

Blackwood stared at him. Trust Quintin to notice what should have been obvious. The bully sergeant, feared, admired and seldom loved, but a real campaigner. Not for Quintin the complications of blame or final responsibility. He was the true professional and thought only of winning if there was still a way out.

Harry whispered, 'It's true.'

Blackwood took his telescope out and thrust it between the thorns. King Zwide was far cleverer than Mdlaka, it seemed. He was determined to see who was going to win before he threw in his weight of warriors.

They must move soon, and before dusk. Fynmore was obviously waiting for more support from the ships anchored off shore. What did he feel at this moment? Despair, or shame for what he had begun without thought for the consequences?

He heard a marine yell at someone to keep his head down and saw a seaman crawling anxiously through the scrub, his head swivelling from left to right as he searched for an officer.

M'Crystal groaned. 'All we need is Jolly Jack, I don't think.'

The seaman fell panting between Blackwood and his half-brother. He gasped, 'I've been sent from the boats, sir. Lieutenant Ashley-Chute's respects, an' 'e intends to refloat *Noreseman* an' tow 'er clear.' He fell silent, his job done, the responsibility safely handed over.

Blackwood looked away to hide his concern. The misshapen lieutenant was already beneath the overhang. *Save the ship*, every sailor's unspoken prayer. The solitary cannon had not fired for some time. He felt the hair rise on his neck.

Lessard's men must already be moving it where it could depress directly on the boats and the stranded *Norseman*.

He looked at the seaman. A plain, homely face you might see any day in a man-of-war or a barracks. He had a round Yorkshire voice. Like Oldcastle.

'My compliments to Mr Ashley-Chute. Tell him he is likely to be attacked at any moment, from above and from upstream.' It would take too long to explain all the dangers, and it was important that this seaman should get it right.

The seaman nodded. 'An' what shall I tell 'im about you, sir?'

'Tell him we are going to attack.'

The seaman hesitated. 'Aye, sir. I'll do that.' He started to crawl away and added, 'Good luck, sir.'

Quintin murmured, 'We'll need all er that, matey!'

Blackwood beckoned to the others. 'We'll attack in two halves. We can't afford anything grander. But it's now or never. I think . . .' he forced out each word, '. . . they're moving the gun. God knows where the other two are, but my guess is they'll be kept in case Major Fynmore's contingent arrives.' He watched their mixed emotions. Quintin's doubt, M'Crystal's grim acceptance and Harry's too-steady stare. He undersood now what it all meant. 'Share out the ammunition between the men. Leave everything else here.'

There was no more time for any of them. And yet it was important they should not leave without a word more.

He said quietly, 'This is a bad place to die, if die we must. But there's more at stake than just us.'

M'Crystal sighed. 'Och, I'm no bothered, sir.' He glanced at his friend. 'Sarnt Quintin will look after me!'

They crawled away and Blackwood felt as if a line had been cut.

Harry asked, 'Ready?'

'Attack from the right when I give the signal. If we fail, you must press on with the attack.' He touched his arm, hating each word. '*Must!*'

Muffled by the overhang he heard the sullen bang of

*Norseman*'s remaining mortar. It could hit nothing from there, but Lieutenant Ashley-Chute was showing that he understood the gamble which the marines were about to take.

Harry was saying, 'Attack from the right.' It was as if he was afraid he might forget at the last moment.

Then he said, 'I'll go and prepare the others.' His voice was quite calm again. 'I shan't let you down, Philip.'

Blackwood smiled. 'Never imagined you would.'

Then he turned and crawled into the dense thicket where the wounded had been dragged for safety. *Safety?*

Blackwood saw the small fifer watching him fearfully and said, 'You'll remain here with the wounded. Private Ackland has a bugle.'

He watched the boy's desperation give way to pitiful relief.

He added, 'If we lose today, you must get back to Major Fynmore.' He stumbled deeper into the thicket, grateful to be spared the boy's gratitude.

A wounded marine peered up at him and tried to wriggle into a sitting position. Blackwood noticed his musket was beside him, his bullets and caps within easy reach.

'All right, Collins?'

The man tried again to sit up. He had been shot in the side, how badly nobody had found time to discover.

'Yew'm not leavin' us, sir?'

More time was running out like sand from a glass. Blackwood patted his arm.

'No. We're going in to the attack. You rest easy.'

The man fell back and stared at the sky through the overhanging trees.

'Wish I was with you . . .' He peered round wildly, all his pain and despair seemingly gone as he yelled, 'Come on, lads! *Load! Present! Fire!*' His voice trailed away as he sank again into unconsciousness.

Corporal Bly looked down at him. 'Beggin' yer pardon, sir, but we're ready to move off.' He bent over and felt the other marine's chest. 'God's teeth, another good one gone.'

He looked at Blackwood, his eyes bleak. 'We'll take a few of them buggers with us, eh, sir?'

Blackwood nodded. 'I'll just speak with Mr Quartermain.'

Bly stared at him. 'Didn't you know, sir? The lieutenant's already gone!'

'*Gone?*' The picture of Quartermain's agonized face, the jagged wound in his shoulder, put a new sharpness to his voice. 'What the hell d'you mean?'

Bly said, 'Clipped on 'is sword and marched out bright as paint, sir.'

Blackwood left the thicket and hurried to find the others.

M'Crystal watched him warily. 'Aye, we know, sir. The lieutenant's gone.'

Blackwood drew his sword and took a pistol from Smithett, glad he had something to grip and so stop his hands from shaking.

Quartermain, a man he barely knew. Driven almost mad by his wound, and yet like the marine who had just died had held on to that one final spark of determination and courage.

He crawled to the last barrier of thorns and rough scrub, his eyes stinging in the glare as he stared straight at the spot where he had seen that tell-tale puff of smoke. Quartermain had realized what they were doing and had offered his own life when he knew he was most needed.

'Frazier! Corporal Jones!'

But they were already kneeling in position, as if they too had known. Even through his reeling thoughts Blackwood realized that Frazier had taken one of the captured rifles and was stroking it as if to pacify it.

'*Gawd!*'

Quintin's sharp exclamation made Blackwood turn towards the far side of the ridge. It was like some terrible dream, a nightmare coming alive even in the brightness of day. Lieutenant Quartermain was marching very stiffly up the slope, his drawn sword in hand, while his other arm hung motionless at his side. The dressing had burst open so in the distance his bared arm matched his coatee as he headed purposefully towards the summit.

There was the sudden crack of a musket and Quartermain halted as if to listen before continuing on his way.

*'On your feet!'*

Blackwood kept his eyes on the erect lieutenant and knew the tension around him was stretched like a taut cable.

'Ready, sir!' That was M'Crystal. Even he sounded different.

*Crack!* The musket's sharp bark echoed over the ground, and Blackwood held his breath as he saw Quartermain stagger and almost drop his sword.

Frazier watched only the ridge where the scrub and trees ended, his eyes unblinking as he cradled the rifle against his cheek.

The lieutenant had been hit. He could not take another. And yet he was still marching up the slope, his mouth opening and shutting as if he was shouting orders to his own invisible platoon.

Frazier's finger tightened on the trigger. A man's head and shoulders had appeared over the ridge, and another, then two more. Frazier could barely stop himself from laughing. They had their bodies turned away from the marines and were all looking at the oncoming spectre with the glistening arm.

'Ready, Jonesy?'

Corporal Jones grunted and gripped his musket even tighter. He heard the crack of muskets on the ridge and saw Quartermain fall, only to struggle up again, his shako gone, his head thrown back in torment as he staggered up towards the group who had left cover to shoot at him. Jones was sickened by what he saw, the pathetic figure as it fell and this time did not rise. He hated Frazier in those brief seconds for his callous acceptance, his interest only in the target and his aim.

Blackwood heard the muskets fire together, the sharper crack of Frazier's rifle ringing in his ears as he yelled, *'Charge!'*

Then they were bounding up the slope, oblivious to everything but the figures silhouetted against the sky. Two had fallen dead, and Frazier was already reloading. One of the men was standing by Quartermain, his body twisted round as he realized too late what was happening. Blackwood saw Quartermain's sword strike out at the man, as if it alone was trying to defend its owner.

He forgot everything else as they reached the top of the ridge and he saw the great gun directly below him in a shallow pit. It was surrounded by a litter of tackles and handspikes and there were more figures running from cover as the marines hurled themselves over the top.

Beyond the gun was the fork in the river, and he thought he could see the pointed huts of Zwide's kingdom on the far bank. There were two vessels at anchor, one he guessed was the captured *Kingsmill*. But none of it mattered any more. Blackwood saw a man in ragged white clothing running at him, a pike levelled at his stomach. He stepped aside and parried the pike with his sword and waited for the man to stumble before slashing the blade hard across his neck.

There was no time to reload now, and hand to hand, blade to blade the marines lunged and hacked their way remorselessly to the other side of the ridge. Here and there a red coat was down, and as Blackwood fired his pistol into a man's chest and slashed out at another with his sword he knew it could not last much longer.

Corporal Bly had lost his bayonet and was using his musket like a club. He swung round on loose sand, his mouth wide in a silent scream as a blade darted at his stomach like a steel tongue. Another figure leapt forward and drove a cutlass into his body again and again, until Quintin fought his way through and cut him down beside the dying corporal.

A great blaring bellow echoed and resounded against the ridge and far beyond to Zwide's kingdom.

Tiny pictures flitted through Blackwood's mind as he crossed blades with a tall, swarthy slaver and rocked back on his heels from the man's thrust.

*Satyr was here.*

Tobin, calm-faced and proud of ship, had come for them.

There was another blare from *Satyr*'s siren, followed immediately by the crash of one of her geat guns.

Blackwood saw the expression on the slaver's face change to apprehension and then hatred as some of the men around him threw down their weapons, the fight already gone out of them like blood.

He parried his blade and their hilts locked. Blackwood gasped as his wounded leg seemed to buckle under him and he felt himself falling.

The siren blared again and the slaver yelled, 'Too late for *you*!'

Blackwood lay on his back and stared at the other man's blade. No matter what happened, they had won. He tensed his body and prayed it would be quick.

There was a single shot and the shadow above him was flung aside like a curtain.

Corporal Jones ran the last few yards and lowered his smoking musket until the point of his bayonet touched the wounded slaver's throat.

Blackwood felt himself being hauled to his feet, the searing pain of his wound making him cry out. *I am alive*.

The wounded slaver gasped, '*Quarter!* In th' name of God!'

Corporal Jones looked around the dazed and bleeding figures and then saw Corporal Bly. They had served together for a long time. Had been made up to corporal together. Had made *Audacious*'s contingent of marines something special.

Jones was a gentle man for the most part and popular with everyone, even Frazier.

He looked straight into the slaver's eyes. 'Quarter, you bastard?'

Blackwood called thickly, 'Stop him, Sergeant!'

Jones leaned on the bayonet and watched the light in the slaver's eyes snuff out, as Bly's must have done.

Quintin pulled him roughly aside and said, 'I didn't see nothin', sir.'

Blackwood looked away and allowed Harry to guide him to the overhang above the *Norseman*. All the seamen on her deck and in the boats which crowded around her were waving and cheering, at him, and then at the great thrashing paddles of Tobin's *Satyr* as she ploughed towards the bend of the river.

Through a vague mist he saw patches of scarlet on the frigate's deck and knew she had picked up Fynmore and his rear-guard on her way up stream.

He said abruptly, 'Take charge of the prisoners, Harry.' He no longer recognized his own voice. It was thick and ragged, like his emotions. To Smithett he added, 'Help me to the lieutenant.'

It was a hundred yards down the slope from the hidden gun to where Quartermain lay staring at the sky.

Blackwood broke away from Smithett's hands and stumbled the last few paces on his own. He did not care about his reopened wound and the pain which grew with each foot of the way. It was desperately important that Quartermain should be alive, should know that he alone had carried the day.

Quartermain's eyes flickered and looked up at him.

Blackwood said, 'Get some water, Smithett.' Then he knelt down and said, 'I just wanted you to know that we took the battery. All because of you.'

Quartermain was smiling, but Blackwood sensed that he could not see him.

'So, so glad . . .' He tried to find his sword which had fallen beside him. 'W – wanted my son to wear this one day – one day. Now I'll not have one.'

Smithett thrust his flask into Blackwood's hand. ' 'Ere, sir.'

'Would you send it to my mother? Tell her . . .'

Blackwood held the flask to his lips but saw the water trickle unheeded across the lieutenant's cheek.

Then he closed Quartermain's eyes and waited for Smithett to help him to his feet.

*I'll tell her, have no fear.*

He limped away, resting on Smithett, the lieutenant's sword under one arm.

Some armed blue-jackets had climbed up from the boats while they had been away and were already herding the prisoners into line and searching them for weapons.

M'Crystal was shouting at the dazed handful of marines as they stared at the chaos around them, as if they no longer understood where they were or what they had done.

'Who d'you think you are? You're more like a bunch of sea-cooks than Royal Marines! Smarten yourselves up, *d'you hear*!'

He realized that Blackwood had returned, and when he swung about to face him Blackwood was shocked to see the hurt and despair in his eyes. He did not recall ever before seeing M'Crystal's guard drop.

The towering colour-sergeant reported hoarsely, 'Ready to move off, *sir*!'

Blackwood released his hold on Smithett's arm. Just as he had needed to see Quartermain before he had died, it was suddenly necessary he should face his men, the survivors.

The fire in his leg was almost unbearable, but he made himself walk along the single rank of men, only vaguely aware of the watching sailors and prisoners, now silent without knowing why.

Blackwood paused at each familiar face. Here and there one tried to smile, others were too stunned to meet his gaze. Jones, Doak, Frazier, and even the Rocke twins were still together.

He saw Harry take half a pace forward and realized he had expected him to fall. Blackwood clenched his jaw. He would not faint. Not yet anyway.

'Stand them at ease, please.' It sounded so formal, so out of place in this arena of death and hate that he needed to blaspheme or weep.

'I just wanted you to know . . .' They were all watching him now, but nothing was coming out right. He tried again. 'There will be other days, some worse than this and for less reason.'

He rested on Quartermain's sword and recalled the man

Jones had killed. But for his swift action with the musket he would be lying dead like Quartermain.

Blackwood continued, 'When that happens, I want you to remember this day with pride, and the friends we left here.' He was getting confused and could not see their faces properly. 'I am proud of each and every one of you.'

M'Crystal hissed, 'The major's here, sir.'

Fynmore's neat figure appeared over the ridge and Blackwood turned in time to see his face stiffen in a mask of disbelief as he saw the corpses and the small group of victors.

Then he strode forward and snapped, 'Well done. I am sorry I did not get here earlier but—'

Harry Blackwood ran from the others and caught his half-brother before he hit the ground. Through his teeth he exclaimed, 'I am sure we all understand, *sir*!'

When he looked up he saw Fynmore's face had gone pale, as if he had just been struck. Without another word the major turned away and, followed by his attendant, vanished down the slope.

A lieutenant from one of the boats hurried across the scorched grass and said, 'I'll have my men do the burials.'

Harry shook his head. 'No. Just get Captain Blackwood to the surgeon, will you.' He picked up Quartermain's stained sword and handed it to the naval officer. 'Take this too.' He looked at M'Crystal's grim features. 'Burial party, if you please, Colour-Sergeant.'

He saw a brief flicker in M'Crystal's eyes. For once he had said the right thing. What Philip would have done. *We take care of our own.*


The pounding in his head was louder and more insistent, and Blackwood had to use something like physical strength to force his eyelids apart. There was a vile taste in his mouth and he guessed he had been sick. He felt sudden terror and groped frantically beneath the sheet for his leg. He sobbed aloud.

There was a cool dressing, not some obscene stump where a leg had once been.

As his senses returned he peered around fearfully as memory after memory flooded through his aching mind. He was in a ship. A steam vessel. Alone in a cabin, but it was too dark to recognize anything. He heard the rumble of machinery, the surge of water against the hull as it frothed astern from the paddles. He thought of the little *Norseman* stranded on the river-bank, men cheering, the cold claws of fear and the wildness of battle.

He tried to recall Fynmore's face, what he had intended to say to him before he had collapsed. But nothing came, and he wondered how long he had been unconscious.

He thought of the girl on the litter, the way she had looked at him, the feverish touch of her skin when he had tried to cover her breasts. He groaned. It was all behind, over.

The door opened and someone stepped carefully over the coaming. Blackwood knew it was Captain Tobin. How did he know?

Tobin said, 'How are you feeling?' He must have smiled in the darkness because his voice changed as he added, 'Yes, you're back in *Satyr*, the same cabin too.'

Blackwood stared at the man's sturdy shadow. 'How long?'

'A week or so. You gave my surgeon a few scares, but you're on the mend now. It will be up to more professional doctors to finish the job.'

'Where are we headed? Freetown?'

Tobin cocked his head as a voice-pipe shrilled in the depths of the hull.

'We're going home. England. You've more than earned it.'

The door closed just as silently as it had opened. Blackwood lay back and stared into the darkness. Home. Hawks Hill. A new beginning.

Once he was able to move about again he would write to Davern Seymour and tell her . . . He smiled ruefully. Tell her what?

He was still thinking of her when he fell into a deep sleep.

# 14

# The Colonel's Lady

Philip Blackwood sat listlessly in a high-backed cane chair and stared at the snow-edged window. It was cold in spite of the stout walls, even for late January, and to Blackwood it felt like the nearness of death.

Instead of showing a steady improvement, Blackwood knew his health and his memory were faulty. Days and places overlapped, and the slow passing of time meant nothing.

He glanced around the room, practical and spartan like the place. The Royal Naval Hospital at Haslar. At night, if he was allowed up, he could see the lights of ships in the outlet to Portsmouth Harbour, the one remaining link with a life which seemed to have passed him by.

The surgeons had explained that his wound had been badly infected, that he had been fortunate not to lose the leg. He had suffered some kind of fever too, which in turn had blunted his memory. When Tobin had told him that *Satyr* was on passage to England, he had failed to mention that Blackwood had been desperately ill and the ship had in fact already been at Freetown. And he could remember nothing about it. Blurred images, pain, gentle hands, parts of a dream rather than reality.

In his eagerness to get Blackwood back to England without further delay, Tobin had driven his ship hard. *Satyr* had paid for his haste and was now out there in the dockyard having her engine overhauled and put to rights.

But it had given Blackwood his other link with the outside world. Lieutenant Lascelles had visited him at the hospital whenever he had been spared from his duties. Lascelles had been bursting with news, about the capture of Lessard's base, of the marines' victory against odds which had been far better armed and prepared.

Lessard was dead and would never stand trial after all. Perhaps someone had suspected he would still use his influence and wealth to evade punishment and had carried out his own judgement and execution. It seemed that Lessard had been ready to leave Zwide's anchorage and escape in the larger of the two vessels there. He had probably calculated that the Navy would be more intent on retaking the *Kingsmill* than in capturing the second vessel. The latter had been crammed to the deck beams with slaves, one last profitable cargo before he turned his attention elsewhere, Blackwood thought.

But *Satyr*'s sudden arrival firing her massive guns had put paid to escape. Lieutenant Ashley-Chute had sent a cutting-out party to board both vessels and in minutes it had ended.

Blackwood could vividly recall how a petty officer had warned him not to stand too close to a hold aboard the first slaver, the glittering pattern of white eyes from that stinking prison-ship.

Even as the slavers had flung down their weapons in surrender to the jubilant boarders, Lessard was said to have lost his balance and had fallen headlong into one of the tightly packed holds. Lascelles had described how Lessard had literally been torn to shreds.

Blackwood had had other visitors. The colonel from Forton Barracks who had somehow refrained from reminding him of their last meeting when Blackwood had tried to resign. He was very likely thinking that he would no longer need to resign. In his poor health he would more likely be discharged from the Corps.

Even the port admiral had paid him a visit and had brought a case of wine to mark the occasion. The case had been swiftly removed by a doctor after the admiral's departure.

Blackwood wondered why his father had not come immediately to see him. He had been told there had been regular enquiries from Hawks Hill, but always by courier. Perhaps his father was ill or unable to travel. It was only twenty miles from Hawks Hill to Portsmouth, but the whole country was under a blanket of snow, the worst anyone could remember. There was one good thing, Blackwood thought, they had not sold the old place. Not yet anyway.

The window shivered in a fresh squall and Blackwood turned to look at the framed painting above the bed. It was the Royal Marines crest, the globe and the laurel, and the famous Corps motto, *Per Mare per Terram*, underneath. Painted by a previous inmate, no doubt. How many had this and places like it seen, he wondered? Crippled, diseased, broken survivors of war.

'If I stay here much longer . . .' He stood up violently and prepared to meet the pain. He was sick of his own self-pity and anxiety. He did not have to think back as far as the unknown painter to recall faces he would never see again.

There was a discreet tap at the door and Smithett peered in at him.

Blackwood tried to stand without revealing the discomfort of his wound. Even Smithett had come to say good-bye. Off to serve another officer, or to make his own way in the ranks. With his mates.

Smithett regarded him mournfully. 'Jus' come from the company tailor, sir. You've lost so much weight I've 'ad to get some of yer tunics taken in like.' He tried to grin but all the lines remained pointing down. 'Can't 'ave the other MOAs sayin' I don't take proper care of me captain, can I?'

'You're *staying* with me?'

Smithett laid a tunic across the bed with great care.

'Course, sir. ''O else would want me?' He turned and looked at Blackwood's strained features. ' 'Sides, you got a visitor. She's wiv the 'ead sawbones right now.'

Blackwood stared. 'Visitor? She . . .'

Smithett looked round for somewhere to hang the other items of clothing.

'Yeh. That's right, sir. Yer mother.'

Blackwood sat down and allowed Smithett to prepare him for his visitor.

*I am a bloody fool. Who had I expected?*

Smithett waited for him to stand again and waited while Blackwood stepped carefully into his trousers. Not near enough to make the officer think he couldn't manage on his own, it was not Smithett's style.

'There, sir.'

Smithett nodded with approval as the red coatee slipped into place. That wily tailor had done a fair job, he concluded. Worth the rum he had 'won' for him.

'I never really thanked you for all you did . . .'

Smithett shrugged to hide his discomfort. Intolerant, impatient, bad-tempered officers he could accept. Blackwood's distress was something else.

He said, 'Somethin'll work out, sir. There'll be another war somewhere an' the Royals will be expected to put things shipshape again, you see, sir.'

'You're probably right. I wish to God we were with young Harry right now. Today's his birthday.'

Smithett flicked a brush across his shoulders and gave a secret smile. If the captain knew just half of what that young bugger had been up to he'd soon be his old self again.

He was very tempted, but at that moment the door was thrust open and the senior surgeon and his assistant entered the room.

But for once Blackwood was not looking at their faces to try and discover what would happen to him. Framed between them, his stepmother seemed to make the room empty, to reduce the surgeons to nothing. She had always been a beautiful woman, even though he had been unprepared to accept it. Now, set against the drab and austere surroundings, she was elegant, even regal.

Her hair was like rich chestnut and piled on top of her head to set off her perfect oval face and slender neck. Her skin was white, like marble, and she was completely composed, like an actress about to mount the stage.

In those few seconds Blackwood felt her steady gaze as it moved over him, missing nothing. *The colonel's lady.* How well it fitted her.

'Well, Philip, and what have you been up to?'

Her voice was exactly as he remembered it. Level and cool, like the woman, without any outward warmth. He doubted if she had reached her fortieth birthday but could not be sure, and was suddenly angry that he had not learned more about her.

He said, 'Sorry, I'm a bit of a mess.'

It came out like a complaining child. She did that to you.

The senior surgeon said breezily, 'Out of danger now, Ma'am! Captain Blackwood has inspired all of us.'

Her eyes, which were tawny brown like Harry's, turned towards him.

'In my opinion he would be better served in more suitable surroundings. My carriage is here.' She held up one hand and added in the same confident tone, '*You* must be Smithett.'

Smithett bobbed. 'Aye, Ma'am, that I am.'

'Fetch my groom and see to things, Smithett.'

Then she moved across the room and laid a gloved hand on Blackwood's arm.

He could smell her perfume and wanted to hold her, to hide his face on her perfect neck and tell her everything. What it had been like. About Harry and the others.

She said quietly, 'Just in time, I think.'

Blackwood looked at her and tried to smile. 'I'm so sorry. I was thinking only of myself. How are you and . . .'

But she had turned away and was giving curt instructions to her groom, a man Blackwood had not seen before.

To the senior surgeon she said, 'I will send news to you of my own doctor's opinion.'

Blackwood expected the surgeon to explode but the magic had already taken effect.

'Of course, Ma'am. My pleasure, Ma'am.'

She slipped her hand through Blackwood's arm, and when a hospital orderly hurried forward with a walking stick she said in the same calm voice, 'Captain Blackwood is a gallant officer. He is *not* an invalid.' She gave the surgeon a cool stare. 'Any more.'

Through the same corridors which Blackwood had seen so often in what felt like a century, along which he had been wheeled for examination, where he had been probed and prodded, discussed as if he were already dead, this too was like a dream.

Once he staggered and winced as the pain returned and he felt her grasp tighten on his arm.

'Just a few more steps, Philip. I'll not have you fall to suit their tiny brains.'

Outside the main entrance it was like pure ice, and yet it seemed to revive Blackwood. The crisp snow, the grey stones, the bracing wind from the Solent. In a moment he would wake up. The same room. The picture above the bed.

She said, 'Get inside, Philip, out of this wind.'

Blackwood stood beside the coach. Despite the thick patterns of slush on its side and door he saw it was a very elegant vehicle, and, like the groom, new.

He said, 'After you. I'm not an invalid now. You said so back there.'

She raised the hem of her gown and put a hand on his shoulder to steady herself before climbing into the coach.

'Well now, I almost forgot.' She lowered her head and waited for him to kiss her cheek. 'You may call me Marguerite if you wish.'

Blackwood followed her, his pain forgotten. Her cheek had been like ice too.

She tapped the window. 'Drive on, Lloyd. I'm not paying for horses to waste time and eat their heads off!'

Smithett climbed up beside the coachman and pulled a blanket around his knees.

'So that's the colonel's lady, eh?'

The coachman flicked his whip. 'Come on, Wizard! *Easy,*

Comet!' As he hauled on the reins he murmured between his teeth, 'You mind your words, soldier, she could take on your lot single-'anded.'

Smithett settled down and braced his legs against the savage motion. He even found time to wave a casual salute to a shivering group of hospital porters.

He had no idea where Hawks Hill was, nor did he care. Private Jack Smithett, who had drawn his first breath in a London slum, had become *somebody*.

It was getting dark by the time the carriage eventually turned off the road and through the familiar snow-capped gates.

With a start Blackwood realized he must have dozed off several times during the journey, but the sight of the tall, weathered pillars, the gatehouse banked with driven snow, drove the clinging weariness away like a cold wind.

His stepmother had replaced her elegant hat which she had tossed on to the opposite seat and was tying a ribbon beneath her chin while she studied herself in the mirror of her travelling case. She showed no sign of strain or the discomfort of the journey from Haslar, and was examining herself more with satisfaction than anxiety.

She glanced at him and closed the case with a snap.

'Home, Philip.'

Blackwood nodded and wiped one of the carriage windows as the banks of snow and grotesque shapes of trees and bushes rolled past.

He said, 'I'm glad you've decided to stay here.'

'For the present anyway. I've made some changes.' She watched him calmly. 'But they need not concern you. You need rest. You are tired out.'

The carriage swung round in a wide curve and Blackwood saw the broad façade of the main building loom through the snow flurries like a cliff. There were lights in several of the windows which painted yellow reflections on the driveway and churned slush.

Blackwood turned as she put one hand on his sleeve.

'I did not mention it earlier, Philip, but your father has been ill.' She studied his reaction impassively. 'He is over the worst of it. But I wanted to warn you. He had a stroke. He had been fretting about things.'

Blackwood said, 'I guessed as much. He was worried about leaving Hawks Hill. He told me.'

She gave a brief smile. 'Quite.'

The carriage lurched to a halt, and as the snow-covered groom clambered down from the rear and the coachman applied the brake, Smithett jumped on to the driveway and stood stiffly to attention.

She said, 'Help them with the bags, Smithett. The house-keeper has arranged a room for you.' She watched the tall marine curiously. 'Your *quarters*, as you will doubtless call them.'

The double doors at the top of the steps were opened and more light spilled across the mud-stained coach and its steaming horses.

Blackwood watched, fascinated, as his stepmother mounted the steps, her head erect as she entered the stone archway and gave a curt nod to the waiting servants.

They had kept Hawks Hill, but on her terms, Blackwood thought.

There were several unknown faces, and a smell of newness and fresh paint. He glanced into the great hall, which had looked more like an armoury with its collection of ancient weapons and militaria. There were still a few items on display, but they were high up and arranged around the minstrels' gallery in decorative patterns. He could not imagine his father giving permission to do that.

He realized she was watching him as she allowed a maid to remove her travelling cloak and take her hat.

She asked, 'Do you approve?'

Blackwood smiled. She sounded as if she did not really care what he thought, yet somehow he knew it was important to her.

'It's fine. Rather grand.' The heat from one of the blazing fires was making him dizzy again. 'Really.'

She pursed her lips. 'There were times when you did not expect to see it again.' It was a statement. 'There will be a lot of changes in future.'

'I was wondering.' He hesitated as he saw the sudden caution in her eyes. 'About Georgie?'

'Indeed?' She turned aside and examined herself in one of the long mirrors near the entrance. 'Miss Georgina, the little madam, is in Paris. It was decided to send her there to finish her education.' She faced him, composed once more. 'Do her good.'

'So very glad to see you back again, Captain.'

Blackwood turned and tried to hide his dismay as he saw a face which should have been very familiar. Oates, his father's old attendant, orderly, valet and friend. So much had happened since he had last seen him and yet it was barely six months ago. In that time Oates had become an old man, had lost his marine's bearing and was now bent over, his hair almost white.

Blackwood held out his hand. 'I'm grateful to be here, believe me.'

Oates seemed to hesitate and glanced quickly at his colonel's lady before returning Blackwood's handshake. As if he was seeking permission to do so.

Oates studied Blackwood sadly. 'The colonel asked to see you immediately you arrived, sir.'

Blackwood looked at his stepmother. So she had already decided to remove him from Haslar before she had left the house. That must have been early in the day, and yet she looked as if she had just dressed for dinner. Only some drying mud on the hem of her gown gave a hint she had been all the way to Gosport and back.

She met his gaze without flinching. 'Go to him. But don't tire yourself. We've a lot to talk about.'

She turned on her heel, and Blackwood saw the assembled servants part before her as she headed towards the drawing room, her maid hurrying behind her.

Blackwood said, 'Take me to my father. How is he?' He

thought he saw the old man's guard fall into place and persisted, 'I want to know.'

Oates fiddled with his white gloves. 'He's been taken all aback by his illness, sir. He'd been hoping, you see, hoping they'd ask him to return to the Colours.' It was obvious the faithful Oates hated to share his secret, to him it was like a betrayal. 'Now he knows there's no chance. He's finished.'

Oates led the way along the first landing and through a gallery where some of the family portraits had been rehung since his last visit. He caught an impression of watching faces and proud stances. Clouds of battle, ships of the line and prancing horses.

Then Oates opened the doors of the bedroom and Blackwood hurried past him, his mouth suddenly dry as he saw his father sitting by one of the tall windows, a small table and a decanter within easy reach.

He did not turn, and Blackwood guessed he could not do so unassisted.

Blackwood moved around the chair and looked down at him.

'Hello, Father.'

Lieutenant-Colonel Eugene Blackwood, the man who had once commanded Fynmore's father, raised his eyes and withdrew one hand from beneath a blanket.

'You're too thin, boy. Must tell cook to prepare one of your favourites, eh?'

Blackwood sat on a small stool and watched his father's efforts to be as he wanted to be remembered. But it was heartbreaking to see the way his face was set and twisted on one side, to feel the feebleness of his handshake which had been like steel.

'I'm glad you stayed here, Father.'

'Pour some madeira, Philip. Can't reach the damn thing myself.'

Blackwood filled two glasses. Like his father, they had been waiting here.

'Been reading all about your escapades, every deuced

word.' He lifted the glass and examined the wine carefully. 'In a skirmish like that you've always got to think and act fast. You did damn well to all accounts.' He moved restlessly in his chair. 'Though from what I've read in the *Gazette* and *The Times* you'd imagine Ashley-Chute had done it all on his own, blast his eyes!' He sank back again, even that small outburst had weakened him.

Blackwood raised his glass. 'To us, Father.'

But his father looked past him at the snow-dappled window, his eyes sad as he said, 'To the Corps.'

Blackwood watched him and felt disturbed. At any other time it would have been almost amusing to hear the past months described as a 'skirmish'. His father saw everything but a full-scale war as a necessary backwater and nothing more.

His father added abruptly, 'The papers were full of it. If it wasn't Ashley-Chute it was that other bloody upstart. Fynmore this and Fynmore that; I think if I see that name again I'll – I'll . . .'

He broke off and for a few moments seemed barely able to breathe.

The reports were much as Lascelles had told him in the hospital, Blackwood thought. It had obviously not fooled his father.

'Anyway . . .'

His father sounded drowsy, and Blackwood could sense Oates hovering outside the door like a guardian.

'You've shown them, my boy. They'll never forget the name of Blackwood in the Corps. Never.' He reached out and took Blackwood's wrist in his hand. 'They don't need me any more, but you have a real future. There'll be no more of those damned "Blue Colonels" blocking promotion, thank God. There'll be nothing to stop you after this. How was young Harry?'

Blackwood replied gently, 'He was good, Father. We were brought close together by what happened.' He watched the strength going from his father, his head drooping.

'Nothing like a bit of campaigning to do that, boy.' He jerked upright in the chair again as Blackwood made to leave. 'I'll want to hear all about it, don't you forget now. Names, places, everything. It's something to look forward to.'

As he left the room Blackwood knew that his father slept here alone and wondered if it had always been so.

As he expected, Oates was by the door.

'You've taken good care of him, Oates. He's sleeping now.'

The man nodded, pleased and sad at the same time. Blackwood could feel him watching him until he had descended the stairs.

His stepmother was waiting for him by a fire in the elegant drawing room. He barely recognized it. The walls, the high ceiling, even the furniture was changed.

She watched him and said, 'Mostly from London. Paris too.'

Blackwood sat in a chair and massaged his leg.

She said, 'I'll have Doctor Sturges over to look at that after you've rested.' She changed tack without waiting for an answer and asked, 'What did you think of him?'

Blackwood looked at the fire, remembering his father as he had once been.

'Ill. Tired. Worse than I expected.'

'I suppose so. Well, the weather should improve soon. I'll have him taken to the coast. Somewhere he can see his marines marching up and down. He'll like that.'

Blackwood tried to accept what she was saying. She spoke of his father as if he were a child. The thought made him angry and bitter. Nothing was the same. Even Georgina had been sent away by this unreachable woman. No wonder Harry had made jokes about it, that she was a god in her own right.

She was still watching him. 'You can have a light supper in your room. I've spoken to cook about it. Nothing heavy just yet.'

Blackwood stood up carefully. 'That would never do, would it?'

She ignored his angry sarcasm, if she even noticed it. In a matter of fact tone she said, 'By the way, Philip, I had a letter from that girl.' She picked an invisible hair from her gown. 'What was she like, pretty?'

Blackwood stared at her with disbelief. 'D'you mean Miss Seymour?'

She gave him a gentle frown. 'Remember where you are, Philip, dear. This is not a man-of-war, there are servants about.'

Blackwood sat down again and tried to calm himself. She had actually written about him and his stepmother had not even thought it worth mentioning until now.

'Well, *was* she pretty?'

'Yes.' Without noticing he had clasped his fingers together. 'As a matter of fact she is.' He tried not to plead. 'What did she say? In her letter?'

She smiled. 'Just how brave you were. That you saved her life, and that she hoped you would soon be in good health again.'

She had known about his fever and his injuries. All the time he had been in *Satyr* and she had been carried to safety in some place selected by her uncle, she had remembered him.

'Is that all she wrote?'

'More praise, is that what you want?'

He stood up and crossed to her chair. 'Please. Tell me. Don't tease. It's important to me.'

She nodded gravely. 'I can see that. She merely wanted us to know.' She bit her lip in thought. 'And to wish you well.'

'I see.'

She looked up at him and took his hand playfully in hers. 'Don't look so tragic, Philip. She has her life now. You gave it back to her. She's luckier than some.'

Blackwood looked at her and wondered if she was holding something back.

'I'm glad she's all right. It was a terrible ordeal.'

'I'm sure it was. You must tell me about it one day. Now off you go to your room. I've told Oates to instruct your man in his duties here. A very *strange* fellow is your Smithett.'

Blackwood realized he was still holding her hand, and as he made to release his grip she said quietly, 'She said she was going to get married. I did not intend to tell you, but there, it's in the open now. Best forgotten.'

Blackwood moved away. *If only I had known before.*

It was absurd. What could he have done? He did not know where she was or anything about her. But she had cared enough to write.

'I shall come up later, Philip. Try and rest now.'

At the door he paused and looked back at her, but she was already leafing through some sort of diary. She had changed everything, had made it her world.

He found Smithett waiting for him, a bath filled and ready.

Poor old Smithett, it must be worse for him. He might even see himself ending up like Oates.

He forced a smile. 'All settled in, Smithett? If anyone starts to chase you about, let me know at once.'

Smithett stared at him in surprise. 'Nothin' like that, sir. Easy as fallin' off a log, so to speak. When I've given 'em a bit er Colour-Sarnt M'Crystal's spit an' polish they'll be ready to enlist theirselves!'

Blackwood allowed Smithett to help him out of his clothes, the steam from the bath making him suddenly weary.

Smithett watched him warily and got ready to hold the wounded leg clear of the water.

'Bad, was 'e, sir?'

Blackwood tried to see his father as he had been before.

'I hope I never get like that, Smithett. When nobody wants you. When it's all gone.'

Smithett sighed as he remembered his own father. Usually fighting drunk and bashing his old woman about. Six kids too, all living in a place half the size of this one room. Officers? They didn't know they were born, most of them.

He said, 'All seem better in the mornin', sir.'

During the night the snow fell more heavily, and in the small cottages the families were thankful for warm beds and ample food for the days to come.

In the big house the staircases and alcoves, portraits and weapons shone only slightly from the light of a few candles. All the fires had burned low, but before dawn the maids would be up and about, cleaning out grates and laying new logs from the barn ready for another day.

There were very few people still awake on the first night of Captain Blackwood's return, and none of them saw the colonel's lady as she walked slowly along a gallery, a single candlestick held before her slender figure.

She looked into her husband's room and heard his breathing, uneven and heavy, his occasional meaningless words lost in his pillow.

Then she went to her stepson's room and stood for several minutes looking down at him in the small, flickering light. In sleep his face had lost its strain and its hurt and displayed nothing but youth. She bent over and touched his bare shoulder and held her hand there until he stirred in his sleep. She withdrew quickly, her heart pounding, ashamed and disgusted by her own thoughts and longings.

She had tried to win, to break free from Hawks Hill and its influence. She paused and looked down at the hall from the minstrels' gallery. A thousand shadows danced there. A masked ball perhaps?

Her own shadow moved on and, like the others, was soon swallowed up by the house.

# 15

# Something Personal

The days and then the weeks of Philip Blackwood's convalescence seemed to get longer and longer. The weather had not improved, so that he was even denied the freedom of riding around the estate as he had once done with Georgina.

Whenever he ventured from the house he was made very aware of the bitter cold and what his fever had cost him.

He was back at Hawks Hill, and yet he felt it had rejected him in some way, as if he did not properly exist.

Servants came and went about their business, a table was always set for one, so that at each solitary meal Blackwood could sense their polite watchfulness and nothing more.

His stepmother, after arranging regular visits by her own doctor and making certain his comfort was carefully regulated, left for London. When he mentioned it to his father he merely commented, 'She's more in London than here most of the time.' Then his eyes came alive as he had said, 'Now, where did we get to? You were telling me about the steam gunboats, and what use you think they'll be in the future.' If he was vague about his wife's activities or chose not to discuss them, there was nothing wrong with his memory on naval and military matters.

Then one day a ruddy-faced man named John Rainbott came up to the house, and upon finding that Mrs Blackwood was away, introduced himself as the new steward of the estate. He seemed a bright and cheerful fellow, and spent over an hour discussing the affairs and the business of running the estate. A true countryman, he had come from a similar position in the county of Surrey, once the home of the late Lord Lapidge.

His lordship had died, with nobody left to succeed him, and had arranged for his estate to be sold. Rainbott apparently knew Blackwood's stepmother very well, so his transfer to Hawks Hill was no surprise, or so it seemed.

Later, as Blackwood sat alone in the library, he considered what the steward had told him, although he had been less than forthcoming when asked more direct questions. Rather like old Oates, he thought, but who were they protecting and of whom were they afraid?

One thing was clear. Marguerite Blackwood had not only changed her mind about selling Hawks Hill, she had also decided to take very firm grasp of the tiller. She sat at the meetings for farmers and tenants, discussed repairs to buildings, and the purchase of stock and machinery. She was not merely beautiful, she was also a very forceful lady when it came to management.

Blackwood knew she had plenty of money of her own, far more than his father, but he had never heard any mention before of the late Lord Lapidge.

Thinking about the various possibilities and relationships helped to pass the time, but not for long. Each day Blackwood read and reread the news reports of the West African campaign, and pictured all the familiar faces and wondered what they were doing. He yearned to be back with them, and would have accepted any appointment in Ashley-Chute's squadron rather than endure his isolation.

Encouraged by the successes against the slavers and their armed camps, the Royal Navy was increasing its activities and had several more steam vessels employed up and down that wretched coast. The campaign must soon come to a head, he thought, while he would still be sitting out the hours and waiting for a reprieve. Around the world the Navy was involved in actions against everything from Chinese pirates to the growing illegal traffic in Irish emigrants to the USA. It was part of the aftermath of the terrible potato famine which had raged throughout Ireland just a few years before.

Now, families desperate for a chance to find a new life in America were buying their passages to be smuggled illegally, sometimes in vessels which were little better than the hulks.

In addition, many of these same people had been robbed of all their possessions and property in the process.

Blackwood felt he was being left behind by the speed of events. His mother, for instance, had not gone to London by coach as was her custom, but by train, something which would have been impossible not so long ago.

Trains had caused a certain amount of trouble in the countryside, the noisy engines and belching smoke having much the same effect on the farmers' cows as *Satyr*'s siren on African warriors.

Then his stepmother returned from her visit to London, and Blackwood was grateful for her company.

She rarely showed excitement about anything, but even as her maid had gathered up her parcels which had been brought in by Lloyd, the coachman, she exclaimed, 'I took tea with an old friend of mine, Lady Ballison.' She walked quickly to one of the mirrors and patted her hair into place, although to Blackwood it looked perfect. 'She was full of news, but then things are *always* happening in London.'

Blackwood looked over her shoulder and saw the sparkle in her eyes.

'I don't think I know her.'

Her gaze shifted to his reflection. 'You are silly sometimes. She's a lady-in-waiting to Her Majesty.' She offered him her cheek for a formal kiss. 'You're looking much better. I hope you have been properly attended to.' She hurried on, 'It seems that our Queen has been taking quite an interest in the East African campaign.'

Blackwood sighed. '*West* African.'

She pivoted round and glared at him. 'Well anyway, she has.'

Blackwood watched her as she moved across the floor, her

eyes everywhere as if to detect any idleness during her absence.

She said, 'It will be in the *Gazette* tomorrow. Darling Harry has been *promoted* to first lieutenant for leading an attack by boat and routing a force twice the size of his own!' This time she could not hide her elation. 'Isn't that wonderful, Philip? I knew he would do well, I just *knew* it, and my friend will ensure that Her Majesty is informed!'

Blackwood smiled. 'I'm glad.'

He looked at the snowflakes which ran slowly down the windows like tears. Was he glad? Or was he jealous and stupidly hurt by the news of Harry's success?

He added, 'I just wish . . .'

She crossed the floor and touched his lips with her fingers.

'Don't say it. It will make it harder for you. You *know* these things happen. You are lucky to be alive.'

He looked down at her and wondered. 'You think I shall be discharged, don't you?' He saw her smile fade and was suddenly angry. 'Well, I'm not giving in so easily!'

She moved away to a mirror again. 'Of course not, dear. But you must allow yourself time. And . . .' she darted a glance at his reflection, '. . . if the worst should happen, you could soon learn to manage things here.' She did not flinch under his stare. 'And eventually settle down.' She waited just a few seconds and added, 'Your poor father is a burden and will become more so. I cannot do *everything* on my own.'

Blackwood stared into the fire. He was beaten before even a skirmish, but knowing it did nothing to help.

He heard himself retort, 'You seem to do quite well, according to your Mr Rainbott.'

He looked up and was astonished to see the shocked disbelief on her face.

'When was he here? What did he tell you?'

Blackwood walked across the thick rug and grasped her hands in his.

'Forgive me. He came to see you about a farm matter. That was all. He had been in Winchester and did not know you had gone to London. I – I suppose I was being stupid. I really am sorry.'

She regarded him thoughtfully for a long moment. 'I have already forgotten it.' She thrust her hand through his arm and swung him round. 'Now come and see what I bought for you.'

Her change of mood was unnerving. She had not once asked about her husband's health, or his either for that matter. The mention of the cheerful Mr Rainbott had been uppermost in her thoughts.

A maid stood hovering by the door, a silver tray in one hand.

Marguerite Blackwood asked, 'What is it, Horrocks?'

The maid held out the tray to Blackwood and blushed. 'Th' post-boy's just bin 'ere, Ma'am. 'Tis a letter for the captain.'

Blackwood felt the grip tighten on his arm.

'Apparently someone else knows you're back.'

But Blackwood was looking at the envelope, the neat, sloping handwriting. His stepmother had somehow mislaid the other letter from Davern Seymour, but in his heart he knew this one was from her too.

'Thank you.' He took the letter and stared at it.

'I think you'd better go and read it, Philip.' She released his arm and turned towards the drawing room. 'Then come and tell me all about it.'

In the privacy of his room Blackwood slit open the envelope and sat quite still for several seconds. In that short time he felt all the emotions of a fifteen-year-old youth and not in the least like a man who had just escaped death.

The beginning was almost painful. *Dear Mr Blackwood* . . .

But after the opening formality he became lost in her words, as if he was hearing her speak, feeling her near like that terrible day at the mission, the stench of death and fear.

She was in London but only waiting for her uncle's return to England. She did not say what she had been doing, or where she was living, and Blackwood imagined it had taken a long time and a great deal of restraint to write as she had. She had come home in a fast packet, and 'people had been very kind'. Blackwood got up and strode to the window and held the letter to the dull light.

She would never forget what he had done or the way his men had acted to make things better for her.

Blackwood folded the letter carefully and placed it in his pocket. The last sentence was burned on his mind like a brand.

*As you may know, I am getting married shortly. I shall think of you often.* It was signed with equal formality, *Davern Seymour.*

Blackwood paced about the room and tried to find a glimmer of hope when he knew there was none. She was thanking him, and would probably want to forget him altogether. Any memory of him would link her immediately with her father's horrific death and everything which she had seen and suffered.

Eventually he went down to the drawing room and was surprised to see that his stepmother had changed her clothes. It seemed only minutes since he had gone to his room, but the curtains and shutters were closed and the place bright with the glow of lamps.

She looked up from some papers and watched him curiously.

'Good news?' She patted the sofa beside her. 'Sit down and tell me about it.'

Blackwood sat and stretched his hands towards the fire. 'It was nothing. Much the same as the one she wrote to you.' She remained silent and he added, 'Getting married.'

'That sounds like *everything*, the way you say it.' She put down the papers. 'How old is she?'

He tore his mind away from the girl's voice, the one he had heard in her letter, and replied, 'Twenty-four, I believe.'

'At that age she *should* be married. Not bustling around the world.' She softened her tone as she saw his face. 'No parents either?'

'None. Sir Geoffrey Slade, her uncle, told me that — '

She grasped his wrist. 'Slade? The man everyone's talking about?'

She shook his wrist chidingly. 'I had no idea.'

Blackwood looked at her and smiled. 'Perhaps you don't listen.'

She tossed her head. 'I would have remembered that. I know Lady Slade well enough to speak with. A rather grand lady, but I believe *he* is a nice little man.'

Blackwood thought of Slade's torn emotions. The concern for his niece, the need to hide his feelings from his subordinates.

He said, 'He's like stone when he feels like it.'

'Perhaps.' She was already miles away, her mind busy. 'But it will not hurt to make his acquaintance.'

Oates shambled into the room and looked at them patiently.

Blackwood said, 'Would you care for a drink before dinner?' He suddenly needed one very badly.

'If you like. Some sherry, I think.'

Oates glanced at Blackwood. 'And a glass of brandy for you, sir?' He moved away without awaiting an answer.

She said softly, 'I think you're drinking too much. Brandy before dinner indeed. I don't know what the Corps is coming to.'

Blackwood lay back on the sofa and replied, 'I'm going to London tomorrow.'

She took a finely cut glass from Oates' tray and remarked, 'I don't know what Doctor Sturges will say about it.' Then she smiled. 'But it might do you good. I'll give you an address, somewhere suitable.'

He barely heard her. 'I'll probably stay at the club.'

She tossed her head again and said disdainfully, 'You should be at home there. More like a barracks than a civilized place.'

Blackwood was surprised she had not probed more deeply or tried to prevent him from going. Perhaps, like Major

Fynmore, she was too impressed by Slade's reputation to care for other matters.

It was madness of course and he knew that he would suffer for it. But he had to know. She might not even be there, or refuse to see him. All at once he could not bear the waiting.

She asked wryly, 'Another drink, Philip?'

He started. The glass was empty and he had not remembered drinking anything.

'Sorry.'

There was the sound of a trolley being wheeled into the dining room, hushed voices as the evening ritual was begun.

She said, 'Be careful. That is all I ask. You are quite a catch, you know, for any young lady.'

They stood up together and she patted his cheek as if to reassure herself.

'We'll go in to dinner, Philip. I feel so proud to have a fine young man to escort me.'

Blackwood glanced at her but her face gave nothing away.

He had sensed she had been in his room the night he had arrived home. That she had been standing by the bed. He had told himself it was a dream, but now he knew differently, and the realization disturbed him. He thought of the rebellious Georgina who had been sent away to be 'finished'. Like mother like daughter.

He stared at the soup which had appeared before him. Perhaps his wound and the bloody fighting he had survived had also unhinged him in some way. He looked up and saw her watching him from the far end of the table. No, he was not mistaken. He could see it in her eyes like hunger.

He thought of his father upstairs in the large, silent room and the picture helped to steady him. Until the next time.

'Good afternoon, sir.' The butler was tall and impressive, like the house. 'May I be of assistance?'

Blackwood looked beyond the butler to the quiet elegance of Sir Geoffrey Slade's town house. The square in which it stood was subdued and totally apart from the London which Blackwood had seen on his way here. The noise of wheels and clattering hoofs, the smell of horses and damp clothing, a bedlam of haphazard crowds, vehicles and tall buildings.

Now he had finally reached the house he was suddenly apprehensive and less certain he had done the right thing. Even the hansom cab which had carried him from the club in St James's still idled at one corner of the square as if the cabby thought a young marine officer was out of place here.

He said, 'I was wondering if Sir Geoffrey Slade is at home.'

The butler stood firm, like a sergeant of the foot guards.

'Even if he were here, sir, I doubt he'd be free to entertain you without an appointment.'

Blackwood saw the man's gloved hand move the door very gently towards him.

'I will, of course, take a message, sir.'

Blackwood shrugged. It was hopeless. Perhaps he was really glad, that it was all better forgotten. Even as he thought it, he knew it was a lie.

The butler said persuasively, 'If you would care to leave your card, sir?' He was an old hand at this kind of thing.

Blackwood turned to look for the hansom cab but it had gone. Worse still, he was feeling slightly sick and dizzy. The journey by train had been exciting but taxing on his strength, and all the din and bustle of the London streets had not helped.

'Is anything wrong, sir?'

Blackwood licked his lips. 'No. This is the first time I've been outdoors for some while.' Why had he bothered to tell him that? 'But thank you.'

The butler seemed to loom over him. 'Good heavens, sir! It's Captain Blackwood, isn't it?' He held open the door. 'Please come in and wait by a fire. Her ladyship will be back directly. I'm *certain* she will wish to see you.'

Blackwood walked into the house, dimly aware of two small maids who were watching open-mouthed from a dark hallway. They were probably more used to visiting diplomats and ministers than a lowly captain, he thought.

The butler led the way to a snug little room which over-looked the square. He was saying, 'You must forgive me for not realizing who you were, sir. Unpardonable!'

Blackwood allowed himself to be helped into a deep chair, and wondered how to escape, what he would say when that 'rather grand lady', as his stepmother had described her, returned.

He asked, 'Is Miss Seymour staying here?' He saw the man's shoulders stiffen. 'I hoped I might see her.'

The butler plucked at one glove. 'We have had to be so careful, sir. All the trouble she's had, the wedding coming along.' Then he smiled and looked less formidable. 'But in your case, of course, sir.'

He turned as a maid called softly, 'They're 'ere, Mr Tomkins.'

Blackwood stood up, alone and suddenly nervous, as the butler left the room in three great strides. He heard the jangle of harness, the murmur of voices, the formidable Mr Tomkins saying something in a stage-whisper.

Lady Slade swept into the room, magnificent in a broad feathered hat and a long military-style coat.

She proffered her hand and said, 'So charming of you to drop in, Captain Blackwood. Such a *surprise*.'

Blackwood took her hand and kissed it lightly. She was certainly grand and more beside. She must be a head taller than her husband. Her greeting was partly a rebuke for not announcing his visit, but he did not care. His eyes were on the girl who stood quite motionless in the doorway. She was dressed in dark clothes, Blackwood did not know what, for he saw only her violet eyes, her hands which had risen to her breast as if she was remembering, and hating him for his intrusion.

He said quietly, 'I – I just wanted to wish you well, Miss Seymour. I apologize for coming in this fashion.'

Lady Slade sat down gracefully and folded her hands in her lap.

'It is nothing unusual, Captain Blackwood. Young people

these days are always in too much of a hurry.' Her face softened slightly. 'Please be seated again. I was going to visit your, er, father after Sir Geoffrey returned home. But it was really you I wished to see, so all's well that ends well.' She settled back on the cushions and waited.

Blackwood held a chair so that the girl could sit near the fire. He could feel her warmth, the touch of her gown against his hand as she sat down, her eyes averted.

Then she said, 'I wrote to you . . .' She faltered. 'I don't know if you . . .'

'Yes. I got it yesterday. I came to London today, by train.'

She lifted her face and studied him, her eyes misty as she said, 'You look tired. I'm so sorry.' She moved her hand as if to touch his but withdrew it.

Lady Slade said, 'You came in some haste, Captain Blackwood.'

It sounded like an accusation, but when he looked at her, her eyes were warm and friendly.

She stood up before Blackwood could help and said, 'I must see to the arrangements for a reception. I shall not be long.' She looked at the girl and asked gently, 'Unless you wish me to stay, my dear?'

She shook her head, her eyes still on Blackwood.

'I shall be all right, Aunt Lydia.'

Lady Slade swept through the door but left it partly ajar, the requirements of etiquette satisfied.

He said, 'She's very nice.'

'Yes.' She watched him as if it was an effort not to flinch as he sat down beside her. 'How are you, *really*?'

'Well enough. My leg is a bit troublesome, but much better.' He smiled. 'But I am afraid I find the weather a bit demanding after Africa.'

She said, 'I read about your brother today. Your family must be pleased.' She looked at him imploringly. 'Why did you come? *Tell me!*'

He tried to take her hand but she pulled it away.

She recovered quickly and said, 'I'm so sorry. It's just that I can't . . . I don't know . . . I'm trying very hard. Please don't be offended.'

Blackwood let her talk, feeling her pain as the words tumbled out of her.

She said, 'I am going away. Start a new life. But I don't want to hurt you.' She looked at him, her gaze level. 'You of all people. After what you did. Everything.' Her hand hovered against her breast again and then fell to her lap like a dying bird.

'I had to come. Why must you leave again so soon? You need time. Most wounds heal when given the chance.'

She reached out and grasped his hand in both of her own.

Blackwood watched his hand imprisoned in her two small ones, felt the longing course through him as she traced invisible patterns on the palm. Perhaps she was remembering that same hand gripping the sword which had hacked down her captors. The one which had touched her naked breasts as he had tried to cover her.

She whispered, 'What are you saying?'

'I am saying that I want you for myself.'

The sudden desperation was making him awkward and clumsy, and he knew that at any second she would leave him or their stately chaperon would return. Either way it would be finished, once and for all.

'Forgive my blunt manners, Miss Seymour. I am too used to the ways of ships and men under arms. I am out of place in this kind of world.'

He tried again, his eyes fixed on her hands, the gentle movement of her fingers against his skin.

'When I first saw you aboard the flagship I knew then there could be nobody else. For me nothing has changed, you must believe that. Given time you could learn to like me, I would make you!'

More carriage wheels rattled to a halt outside the house and Blackwood heard voices again, the butler's resonant tones as he hurried to greet a visitor.

Blackwood persisted, 'Please say that you will consider it?'

He felt her bracing herself to leave and knew he had failed.

She said in a low voice, 'I shall never forget you. Perhaps it would have been better if you had not found my father's mission at all.' She stood up quickly and released his hand. 'Goodbye, Captain Blackwood. I do not think we shall meet again.'

Without another glance she almost ran from the room.

Blackwood stood by the fire, unable to move, unwilling to accept what had happened.

The door opened and Lady Slade stood watching him, her face sad.

'It was so good of you to call. My husband will be sorry to have missed you. He wrote to me of your valour. You are a very brave young man.' She watched his despair and said, 'Do not blame yourself. She imagines she is acting for the best.'

'May I ask, Lady Slade, what sort of man she is to marry?'

'A member of the medical profession, once a colleague of her late father. I barely know him, except by reputation. She intends to help him with his work, to cut free from society. But then I have said too much already. You will know that my husband is a man for offering advice. Then I shall do the same. Find a good, sensible girl and marry her. Someone who will complement your profession. Better still, marry one who can help you reach your goal in life. Otherwise, I warn you, you will end up with a broken heart.' She offered her hand and added gently, 'If at any time you feel my husband can help you, perhaps a transfer to London . . .' She smiled as he straightened up. 'No, I think not, Captain. You are too much the man of action. God bless you, and remember what I said.'

Blackwood found himself on the pavement again, the door closed behind him. It was all unreal, as if he had dreamt it.

He glanced at the house and thought he saw a curtain move slightly as someone looked down at him.

Then he turned on his heel and walked rapidly towards the park, oblivious to saluting guardsmen, nursemaids with their prams, even the fact that the snow had stopped and the trees were heavy with a thaw.

He reached the club, his leg throbbing from the exercise, his mind still going over what she had said, how she had held his hand.

It was almost obligatory for naval and military officers to be members of this respected club, but most of them used it as a refuge from the world outside, something more familiar, like wardroom or garrison.

Blackwood slumped down in a leather chair in the spacious smoking room and signalled to a waiter to bring him some brandy. His stepmother had been right. He was drinking too much, but unknown to her it had been going on for some time. A prop for courage, a shield against fear. He smiled at his own rambling thoughts.

He had seen a few left-over wrecks in various establishments and barracks. Put ashore to 'keep things going'; who drank their pay away until, like dead marines, they were quietly disposed of.

There were only two other people in the room and they were discussing the news.

One said irritably, 'Bloody country's going to the dogs. No spirit any more. This damn government is cutting down everything. They say that half of the fleet is laid up an' rottin' for the want of good hands. They should have been around when the press gangs were on the prowl, eh?' He gave a thick chuckle. 'Do some of today's youngsters a spot of good, what?'

Blackwood smiled wearily and signalled to the waiter for another drink. The anonymous member was like his father, he thought.

The second voice said, 'I was at Christie's the other day.'

'Oh yes? Didn't know you were interested in auctions, George.'

'I'm not really. But it was poor old Lord Lapidge's stuff. Furniture and that kind of thing. Went along out of curiosity, I suppose. Not nice to see such personal things under the hammer.'

Blackwood's glass froze in midair as the voice droned on.

'Thought of him when I read about the young marine who was mentioned in the *Gazette* today. His mother was the old boy's mistress, y'know.'

'You don't say! I didn't know that!'

The other man gave a fruity laugh. 'You're about the only one in London who didn't then!'

Blackwood left his drink and strode blindly from the room. No wonder she had changed her mind about leaving Hawks Hill and moving to London. Her mind had been changed for her. It was all horribly clear, the transformation of the house at any expense, the planned improvements to the estate, everything.

But when the source of her wealth had been revealed in Lord Lapidge's will the rest had followed swiftly.

Blackwood entered his small room and sat on the edge of the bed. He thought of his father, confined more than ever by his poor health, young Harry, now on the crest of a wave with his new-found fame. Georgina too would have to be protected, but how?

He stood up and began to pace about the room, his mind busy as he thought of how he would confront her. He would leave for Hawks Hill first thing in the morning and settle things once and for all.

Blackwood stared around the room and listened to the muffled murmur of carriage wheels beyond the heavy curtains. Coming to London had been a mistake. A double defeat which he had brought upon himself.

# 16

## Last Farewell

It was late afternoon when Blackwood arrived back at Hawks Hill. It had been a slow and frustrating journey, and the final part he had shared with a local carrier who had offered him a ride in his little cart from the railway station.

He could barely recall what the talkative carrier had said as they had trotted down familiar lanes until the tall gate pillars had come in sight.

In spite of the time it had taken to reach Hawks Hill he felt angrier rather than calmer. He had filled a flask with brandy at the club and yet he had not touched it. That in itself had surprised him.

Blackwood hurried up the stone steps and pushed open the doors. He saw Mrs Purvis, the housekeeper, staring at him as if she had just seen a ghost and said, 'I came back early.' Something touched his mind like a warning. 'What is it? Has something happened?'

She exclaimed, ' 'Tis the colonel, sir. He's been taken bad again. The doctor's just gone.'

Blackwood removed his gloves and handed his heavy coat to one of the maids. It gave him time to think. To settle his mind. Like a moment in battle when the obvious has changed to something entirely different.

The housekeeper was watching him anxiously. 'Master Harry's here, sir. Arrived first thing.' She sounded close to breaking down. 'He looks a fine sight, bless him.'

'I'll go up.'

Blackwood mounted the stairs slowly and deliberately. He

had pictured his half-brother in Africa or patrolling the coast with Ashley-Chute's squadron. The unexpected news of his return made him feel even more out of touch and vulnerable.

At the end of the passageway he saw Oates slumped in a chair outside the door. He looked like death but got to his feet as he heard Blackwood's footsteps.

He said huskily, 'We found him lying on the floor, sir.' He dropped his eyes, again ashamed of revealing something secret. 'He was trying to put on his dress-uniform when it happened.'

'Who else was there, Oates?' He thought he already knew.

'The colonel's lady, sir. She sent your man for the doctor. Must have flown like the devil.'

Blackwood looked away. Poor Smithett had ridden nothing but a mule in his whole life as far as he knew. He was a man of many surprises.

He gripped the handle and said, 'Try and rest.'

He pushed open the door and saw the table with the decanter and glasses near the window. As if his father had been waiting for another detailed account of his exploits in Africa.

His stepmother came from the shadows near the bed and reached out to take both of his hands.

'I'm so glad you came, Philip. It was as if you knew.'

Blackwood kissed her cheek, searching for a sign, some hint of what had happened here. He was conscious of her perfume, the cool smoothness of her skin, and the fact that in spite of everything she was beautifullly dressed in a dove-grey gown and her hair was set in a crown which left her ears bare.

He said, 'Tell me!'

She moved to the end of the bed and looked at her husband. Blackwood joined her and saw that his father was in a deep sleep, his eyes screwed up as if to protect them from danger.

She said quietly, 'I could not rest. The house seemed empty with you away.'

She touched his arm and he watched her fingers on his sleeve, fascinated even as he tried to hate her.

'I often feel like that, Philip. I was walking in the gallery, watching the shadows in the moonlight. Then I heard him cry out.' She turned away as if to dismiss it from her thoughts. 'He was wearing his uniform, or part of it. Doctor Sturges says he is over the worst.' Then she faced Blackwood and held his eyes with her own. 'But any bad shock might bring on another stroke, and that would kill him.'

Blackwood returned to the bed and saw the dress-coat lying on a chair. What had made his father do it, he wondered? Like that dying marine perhaps, who had found the strength to yell commands and encouragement to his invisible comrades.

'Harry's here, by the way.'

Without turning he could see her expression. It was as if she knew, had been prepared for something like this. He recalled with sudden clarity how she had lost her composure for a few revealing seconds when he had told her about Rainbott's visit. The late Lord Lapidge's steward.

'I heard.'

She came round and gripped his arm. 'Something's happened. Was it that girl?'

*That girl.* 'I saw her.'

He could not bear to speak about her here. He felt trapped, outmanoeuvred.

'Well, perhaps it's better this way.'

He swung round, his voice shaking in a harsh whisper. 'What do you know about her? How can you possibly understand?' He saw her step back as if he had tried to strike her.

The door opened and Harry strolled into the room, his eyes moving between them as he said, 'Hello, Philip, I feel better now that you're here.'

Blackwood looked at him and crossed the room in quick strides. His half-brother was wearing his uniform trousers and his shirt which was open to the waist. He looked tousled and tired, and somehow even younger than ever.

Blackwood clapped his hands on his shoulders.

'Sorry I missed your birthday, Harry.' He knew he was not

making any sense, just as he knew he was already beaten.

'Why don't you two go downstairs and get Mrs Purvis to fetch you something. I'll stay here for a while.'

Blackwood looked at her. She was watching him steadily, her hands relaxed by her sides. She knew too.

Blackwood left the room and together with his half-brother walked along the gallery which was dappled in weak sunlight.

Harry asked quietly, 'What do you think about the old man? Did he have a shock or something?'

Blackwood paused by a window and in his mind's eye saw his stepmother walking through the silent house in the darkness. Something she often did. He felt the same sensation of warning. Perhaps his father had also found out about Lord Lapidge? He gripped his hands together until the pain calmed him.

'What's *wrong*, Philip?'

Blackwood shrugged. 'I went to see Miss Seymour.'

'Yes, Mother said. Bad luck, but it happens.'

Blackwood studied him. *You sound just like her.*

He said, 'It's me, I expect.'

Harry looked different in some way. More confident, and yet with the same old touch of recklessness.

He said, 'Congratulations on your promotion, by the way.'

Harry grinned. 'Yes. I'm catching you up.' Then he said, 'Seriously, I think it's terrible you've had no recognition for what you did. But for you there would have been no "afterwards".'

Harry's mood changed again. 'Anyway, things will be different now. The squadron's being split up. Some of the older ships are being paid off, and others are being ordered to the Mediterranean. I came home in a steam-frigate.' He sliced his hands through the air. '*Whoosh!* Like a streak of lightning. Well . . . almost!'

'What did Doctor Sturges say?'

Harry grimaced. 'Nothing much. He's arranging for a senior physician to come down from London. But he said that

Father will be better off here than in some damned hospital, and I agree.'

Blackwood thought of his quiet room at Haslar, the painting of the crest above the bed. His father would go out of his mind there.

One of the maids bustled past, her arms laden with towels.

She saw them and blushed as Harry said, 'Why, Jenny, I do declare you're prettier than ever!' She tried to pass but he blocked her way and said, 'I shall have to do something about you one of these days, or nights, eh?'

Blackwood watched her as she fled down the passageway. Harry made him feel older than his years with his casual treatment of the local girls. Yet they seemed to love it.

He felt Harry watching him as he said, 'You had a bad time, Philip. After you'd been put aboard ship for passage home there were some who said you'd never recover.' He touched his arm with sudden affection. 'Not me though. I know you better than that. Now.'

Together they descended the stairs, and Blackwood asked, 'How were the others when you left?'

Harry toyed with the idea of teasing him and then blurted out, 'You'll see for yourself. They're all here, at Forton Barracks.' He watched the life returning to Blackwood's eyes. 'Two new companies are being formed. They need all the trained men they can get.'

Blackwood strode to a fire and held out his hands. 'When have things ever been otherwise?' He was strangely excited at the prospect of returning to duty, just as he was touched by Harry's genuine pleasure in seeing him.

Harry was saying dreamily, 'Someone in high places must have listened to your ideas about new methods of training for the Corps instead of the Waterloo mentality.'

Blackwood looked up quickly. 'How's Fynmore?' It was not difficult to recall his face that day when he had climbed up from the boats and had seen the carnage.

'Oh, didn't I say?' He was not that good an actor. 'He's *in command*. Been made up to half-colonel too for his brilliance!'

Blackwood smiled grimly. It was much as Lascelles had told him at the hospital. Fynmore had not allowed the grass to grow under his feet.

He asked, 'What about the new companies?'

Harry played with the front of his shirt. 'Ogilvie's got one, and a Major Brabazon's been given the other. He's also second in command.'

Blackwood nodded. He had no right to feel disappointed, but he did. He was lucky to be alive, and that had to be enough. But to think of Fynmore being given overall command of some crack contingent was laughable.

Harry changed the subject. 'Mother's a marvel, don't you think? All this worry and responsibility, yet she seems to ride right over it.'

Blackwood walked to a window, afraid Harry would see his expression. *She's a whore with no thought for anyone but herself and her greed.*

He said, 'I can see where *you* get it from.' But the joke went flat.

Smithett appeared silently and said, 'They're bringin' yer 'orse, sir.'

Harry nodded and began to fasten his shirt. 'Thanks.'

He sauntered away to dress himself, and Blackwood said, 'You remain at Hawks Hill, Smithett. I'm going to Forton to report for duty.'

Smithett watched him passively. 'Somethin' wrong, sir?'

'Probably not. But I'd like you here, just in case. Poor old Oates is getting shaky. It would please my father no end if there was a *real* marine nearby when he feels better.'

'I dunno about that, sir.' But Smithett was obviously pleased with the compliment.

Half an hour later they were both ready to leave.

Harry clasped his mother to his chest and hugged her. Blackwood saw that she was watching him instead of listening to her son, her eyes level and challenging.

He could do and say nothing now. It would only add to his father's suffering and provoke a family disgrace.

She moved towards him and touched his collar.

'You both look very splendid. I'm proud of you. We all are.'

Harry climbed carelessly into his saddle and looked down at them with amusement.

'You look more like lovers than respectable people.'

Only then did Blackwood see her start, her eyes spark with alarm. 'Don't be so *vulgar*, Harry!'

Blackwood stooped and kissed her cheek. It was as cold as ever. Then without another glance he mounted his horse and followed Harry away from the house.

Whatever happened after this, things would never be the same at Hawks Hill.

Lieutenant-Colonel Rupert Fynmore handed his hat and riding-crop to a clerk and marched through the outer office and into his own.

It was morning, and although the air was cold and damp the sky remained clear, as if the snow was just a bad memory.

Fynmore glanced briefly at his desk and the carefully arrayed papers which awaited his attention, then, as if for the first time, he looked at Blackwood.

'I hear you arrived back last night?' His eyes moved busily over Blackwood's appearance. 'You could have reported then. I am never too busy to receive one of my officers.' His mouth shot up in his twisted smile. 'Especially one of so gallant acquaintance, what? Delayed, were you?'

Blackwood nodded. 'My half — Mr Blackwood had to retrace his steps and leave some papers with somebody.'

It sounded so peculiar that he flinched under Fynmore's stare. It had been strange, he thought. They had been keeping up a good pace, talking about the African campaign, the squadron, filling in the gaps. Then Harry had reined up his horse and had pointed at a small inn nestled in a curve of the road.

'God, my memory! I was supposed to leave some letters at

a house back there. But for this inn I'd have forgotten completely. You wait there and have a glass. I'll not be long.'

Without waiting for an answer he had turned his horse and cantered back along the road. When he had eventually arrived at the inn about an hour later he had been reticent and apparently unwilling to elaborate on where he had been.

Fynmore snapped, 'No matter. You're here and that's the main thing. Mr Blackwood has told you about the formation of the new companies, right? We have to make a success of it. A step in the right direction. Half the trouble in the past has been the lack of coordination in a squadron. *Send the marines*, orders some admiral or other, and we all tumble into boats and storm ashore, most of us never having worked together before. Monstrous, in my opinion, asking for trouble.'

Blackwood watched him, fascinated. Fynmore seemed to have grown in stature with his new rank, and it was almost impossible to remember him as the cautious, hesitant commander in West Africa.

'I've read your reports, Blackwood. Fine as far as they go. But the medical men are all agreed. Your wound could weaken you again. Can't have that, what?'

Fynmore crossed to a window and raised some papers to his eyes. 'Now let me see. Your own Doctor Sturges says much the same.'

Blackwood stiffened as he saw an envelope pinned to the other papers. He would recognize his stepmother's writing anywhere. He felt trapped, or like a boy at school who is about to be expelled.

Fynmore replaced the papers on his desk and adjusted them until they were in an exact line with the others.

'Still, can't believe everything they say, can we?'

'I'd like to return to duty, sir.'

'Of course.' Fynmore studied him thoughtfully, his sandy hair perfect, his uniform looking as if he had been poured into it.

'I have spoken to the Colonel Commandant. He fully understands the need for experienced officers. The fleet is undermanned and cannot raise enough volunteers for any sudden emergency. The marines, on the other hand, are the *real force*. Like a well-forged weapon which, if properly used, can put a stop to local wars and uprisings before they know what's hit them.' He calmed himself with an effort. 'I got the Colonel Commandant to agree to your secondment on a temporary basis.' He watched his words go home and added smoothly, 'Do your duty, and make good use of your undoubted experience in the field, and I feel sure that this will only be a momentary setback.'

Beyond the room and the thick walls Blackwood heard the measured tramp of feet from the parade-ground, the shouted commands which came from every angle until they merged into a meaningless chorus.

One, probably the sergeant-major's, ebbed and flowed, chased and persuaded above all the rest.

'Advance in column from the left, A Company leading!' There were more shouts and then, '*Stand still, that man!* Wait for the order!'

Fynmore was enjoying this. Watching his disappointment, waiting for him to plead. Secondment on a temporary basis. It was better than nothing. But only just.

'Thank you, sir.'

'Anyway, there's a lot to do before we leave.' He sounded vaguely irritated. 'We are embarking in a troopship the week after next. For Malta.' He squared his shoulders and glared round the office. 'Not like this place, eh? Do some of the recruits good to see what an *old* barracks looks like.'

Blackwood considered it. That was unexpected. An immediate transfer to the Mediterranean. He had imagined that perhaps the new companies had been formed to support the campaign he had left behind in *Satyr*. For although the Navy was having plenty of successes against the remaining strongholds of slavery, the campaign was still dragging on, with fever taking a heavier toll of seamen and marines than anything else.

Fynmore said suddenly, 'I understand Sir Geoffrey Slade is back in England too.'

'Yes, sir. I visited his London house just two days ago.'
There was no need to add that Slade had not been there. His
so-called friendship with Slade must be about the only reason
Fynmore had requested his secondment to the new command.

'Splendid. *He* thinks out every move. I *like* that.'

The door opened two inches and a clerk said nervously,
'The sergeant-major's here, sir.'

'Good. Punctual as usual.' Fynmore glanced around the
office and added, 'Two men for field punishment this morning. I will not have slovenly behaviour and I want everyone to
know it.'

Blackwood followed him through the outer office and into
the pale sunshine.

Fynmore said over his shoulder, 'We are getting some of
the new Minié rifles too. Mine is the first command to have
that honour.'

The sergeant-major stood like a ramrod on the side of the
parade-ground, his stick tucked beneath one arm. In the
sunlight his brass shoulder-scales shone like gold, perfection,
like the rest of his uniform.

His eyes flickered to Blackwood and his mouth opened and
closed like a trap.

'Good to 'ave you back, if I may say so, sir.'

That was all he said, but Blackwood valued his bare
welcome more than a full parade.

He watched the nearest marines marching past, their boots
kicking up the dust, their eyes glazed with the constant
changes of direction, the intricate movements with musket
and bayonet which, if the sergeant-major had his way, would
soon be as familiar as their own feet.

He saw Harry standing by a platoon which was being
instructed in the use of the new Minié rifles. If he remembered the cruel accuracy of these rifles which had taken the
lives of so many of their own men he did not show it. He was
smiling and joking, and even at a distance Blackwood could
sense the relaxed almost carefree atmosphere.

Fynmore said fiercely, 'Deal with *that*, Sergeant-Major.' As the giant strode towards the offending platoon Fynmore muttered, 'Sloppiness will not be tolerated.' He darted Blackwood a quick glance. 'From anybody.'

Harry hurried across the square and saluted.

Fynmore said coldly, 'Those men are raw recruits, Mr Blackwood. You may wish to appear popular in their eyes, but I warn you, they'll not respect you for it. Discipline is what they know and need.'

Harry flushed. 'I'm sorry, sir.'

'Report to the adjutant for extra duties, Mr Blackwood. But first attend to the punishment of two offenders. A dozen lashes each, I believe?'

The sergeant-major grunted. 'Sir.'

'Carry on then.'

Fynmore turned on his heel and strode away, an orderly trotting behind him.

Harry murmured softly, 'Pig.'

Blackwood said, 'You asked for that. *And* you know it.'

Harry grimaced. 'Extra duties too.' He glanced at the procession which had emerged from the guard-house. Two men stripped for punishment, an armed guard and a sergeant with the necessary papers in his hand. He said ruefully, 'I'll be glad to get back to sea.'

Blackwood saw the familiar shape of M'Crystal hurrying across the square.

'Stay out of trouble, Harry. I mean it.'

Harry watched his half-brother shake hands with the big colour-sergeant. What was the difference? The greeting was warm, and yet there was no lowering of the barrier between them. He kicked angrily at a stone.

Never mind. Fynmore would have cause to regret his outbursts. It had been sickening the way Fynmore had lost no time in passing off Philip's ideas to the admiral as his own. By so doing he had gained promotion beyond his dreams, a command which any officer would envy.

He smiled in spite of his resentment and wondered if there were any young women in Malta who might be of interest.

'So you're off again, Philip. Best thing, I suppose.'

Blackwood adjusted his father's pillows and watched him sadly. He had difficulty in forming his words, as if his mouth was frozen. But his voice seemed stronger and his mind had not wandered very much while they had been talking.

'Day after tomorrow, Father. We've not been told much, but it sounds as if they genuinely want an independent unit which can be sent anywhere.'

'Won't be the first time we've had to get the army out of trouble.'

Blackwood smiled. 'There's no war.'

'Will be soon. You mark my words. New weapons, bigger fleets, they're not being made to play with. Only Britain believes in letting things slip. God, these politicians make me sick.' He coughed and snatched a handkerchief from his side before Blackwood could help him. 'Get me a drink, will you?'

Blackwood poured a glass of claret. There was no point in denying him. Oates would fetch it once he had left.

'Don't forget what I told you, my boy. Watch that Fynmore. He'll try to hold you down. You could lose your position, seniority, everything, so keep your eyes on him.'

'I don't know why he asked for me anyway.'

'Then you're a fool. He *needs* you, don't you see that? He's promoted out of his depth. Just like his idiot of a father.' He sipped the wine and was suddenly quiet. Then he said, 'Wish I could be there when you sail. What ship, by the way?'

'The trooper *Liverpool*. She's steam driven, so the passage won't be too uncomfortable.'

His father was getting drowsy. 'I'd like to have seen her. Always a fine sight. Bands playing, people holding up their children as the red coats go past.'

Blackwood looked around the room. His father had always been a strong man. To see him cut down like this was pitiful.

From what the other officers had said, it seemed likely they would not return to England until completing a full commission. This was probably the last time he would see his father alive.

He bent over him and said, 'Send me a letter if you feel like it. Oates will write it if you feel too tired.'

His father glared at him. *'Tired?* I'm not a bloody invalid. This is just a setback, nothing more.'

He thrust out his hand and Blackwood grasped it between his own.

'Take care, Philip. Look after young Harry if you can. The name has to survive in the Corps, always remember that!'

He watched as Blackwood stood back from the bed and gave a fierce smile.

'You'll do, my boy.'

The door opened softly and Blackwood heard her say, 'The doctor's here.'

Blackwood walked towards the door and then paused to look back.

His father said, 'Tell your man Smithett from me. Good marine. Hope for this bloody country yet.'

The door closed as the doctor hurried inside. He barely glanced at Blackwood. He probably felt guilty for his part in the medical reports.

Blackwood forgot him and ran lightly down the stairs where Smithett was filling his bag with gifts from the kitchen.

His stepmother walked with him to the steps and said, 'You despise me, don't you?'

When he looked at her she appeared perfectly composed, but something in her tawny eyes made him hold back what he had intended to say.

'I know about Lord Lapidge, if that is what you mean.'

Her lip quivered slightly. 'Think what you like. Just remember this. But for me Hawks Hill would have been sold up long ago. When I married your father there were so many debts and outstanding claims it was a matter of weeks, not months.' She watched him impassively. 'But all your father thinks about is the Corps. He would never listen when I told him about the estate. I used a great deal of my own money, but I became lonely. You will discover, if your pride allows, that there is no price high enough to buy off loneliness.'

He stared at her, wanting to leave, knowing he could not go just yet.

'What of Harry and Georgina?'

'I did it for them, don't you see that?' She reached out and impetuously seized his arm. 'But you were the one I wanted to *impress*, to share my hopes with. Now it's too late.' Her hand fell to her side and she gave a small smile. 'So be off with you before the roads become dark.'

Blackwood heard the horses being led across the cobbles and noticed that some of the servants and stable-boys had come out to watch him leave. Perhaps to them he was a hero, something of their own, a symbol.

He held out his arms and she came to him without protest.

'Goodbye, Marguerite. Your secret is safe with me. It has to be.'

When he bent to kiss her cheek she put her lips against his and held him for several long seconds.

She exclaimed, 'I shall think of you.' Their eyes met. 'Often.'

Then she was gone and he could taste the salt of a tear on his mouth.

Smithett sat uncomfortably on his horse like a sack of potatoes. He was sorry to be leaving the comforts of Hawks Hill and the admiration of the servants here. But from what he had just witnessed it was not a moment too soon for the captain, he thought.

Not very far from the main coaching road where Blackwood and Smithett would pass, Harry stood by a window in the quiet house and watched the last of the dying sunlight.

His red coatee was draped over a chair, and he held a glass

of brandy balanced in one hand. He was genuinely pleased to
be leaving the country again so soon. He felt different, able to
think out each move, when in those first days in West Africa
he had been almost sick with fear.

He had believed it was Philip's example, but now he was not
so sure. Maybe it went deeper, something which was his alone.

'How do you like it, Harry?'

He turned from his thoughts as he saw the woman in the
opposite doorway. She was very pretty in a doll-like way,
with her hair in neat ringlets and a small, slender figure. She
was wearing a green silk robe which Harry had brought with
him from Freetown. In this quiet, Hampshire house it looked
crude and garish, but she was obviously pleased with it.

'You look lovely.'

'You *mean* that, don't you?'

Harry downed the brandy in a gulp, the sting making him
gasp as it burned through him.

'Of course I do.'

It was hard not to show irritation when she was like this.
He had first met her at a ball in Woolwich while he had been
completing his training. She had made him feel adult and
dashing, but he had never imagined it would come to this. He
was excited, in spite of their difference in ages. He was
nineteen, and she had admitted to being thirty. But she
looked much younger, childlike in her need to be reassured
about everything.

He put his arms around her and felt her stiffen. It had
never quite reached this stage before. Any moment now she
would slap his face or push him away, and then the next time
she might let him go a little bit further.

But there would be no next time. In two days they would
be standing down-channel to show the flag, as Fynmore had
put it.

She protested shakily, '*Please*, Harry.'

But he said nothing and pulled her closer to him. When he
reached around her and touched her neat buttucks she gasped
and almost fell against him.

Harry looked at her eyes, the dampness of her lips.

She said in a small voice, 'I think we'd better stop.'

Without a word Harry picked her up and carried her through the door and slammed it with his foot.

'I'm not stopping.'

He saw her eyes widen with alarm as he dropped her on the bed, and when she tried to pull away from him he gripped the robe and dragged her towards him. The robe was only cheap, he had bargained for it with a street trader. She gave a cry as it parted across one shoulder and then she began to fight him as he tore it further.

Harry barely knew what he was doing. She had been wearing nothing beneath the robe, and as he tore the last fragment aside she tried to cover herself with her hands until he slapped her hard across the cheek.

Then he knelt over her, her protests forgotten as he explored her body and touched her breasts while she lay quite still, her eyes watching his hands as if they belonged to someone else.

She whispered, 'Not like this, please.'

His fingers stroked her nipples and he sensed her anguish giving way to something else.

'One more thing.'

He reached out and turned a bedside photograph on to its face. Fynmore looked younger in the picture, he thought.

Then he thrust her last resistance aside and stifled her pain with his mouth.

When it was over she crawled across the bed, groping after him as he began to pull on his trousers and boots.

She gasped, 'You hurt me. You really did.'

Harry glanced quickly round to make certain he had not left anything. Then he bent over and kissed her, sorry for the red mark on her cheek.

'I'll bring you a better robe when I get back.'

Long after the sound of Harry's horse had been swallowed up in the dusk she lay on the bed, staring at the ceiling, her heart pounding as she relived each frightening, beautiful moment.

Then reluctantly she stood up, her knees like water. She straightened the bed and replaced the photograph on the table.

Only then did she realize what she had done.

# 17

# New Arrivals

Philip Blackwood stepped from the shade of a partially collapsed wall and braced himself for the fierce heat. The sky seemed drained of colour, and the stony ground which surrounded the firing range was white, as if it too had been scorched beyond recognition.

Colour-Sergeant M'Crystal watched him curiously as if to determine his mood.

Eventually he said, 'Second platoon is ready to begin firing practice, sir.'

Blackwood nodded. It was almost too hot to think, let alone speak. And yet in Malta you were rarely out of sight of the Mediterranean. Deep, shimmering blue which made the heat ashore almost unendurable. He had imagined that compared to Africa this would have seemed easy. Yet after their arrival and the excitement of new surroundings, he knew that most of the marines were finding each day longer than the preceeding one.

'How are they shaping up?'

It was ridiculous to ask, he thought. They had been on the island for months, drilling and exercising, performing ceremonial parades and guards as requested by the admiral superintendent or whenever it took Fynmore's fancy. It seemed incredible they had been here so long, had accepted the regular routine and spartan living quarters as if they had known nothing else.

Some had settled down better than others, a few, and Harry was one of these, had grown frustrated and resentful about the total lack of purpose.

M'Crystal said, 'I sometimes think they miss the old muskets, sir. These rifles are *too* accurate.'

It was true. The new Minié rifle had a range of nearly a thousand yards and could outshoot any other infantry weapon. Even the excitement of using it on the range had lost its first glow and it had become just one more time-filling drill.

Blackwood had received several letters from his father, which was unusual. The handwriting was shaky, but his letters were full of news about Hawks Hill, of a new alliance with 'the old enemy' as his father still called France, and a genuine interest in what his two sons were doing in Malta.

M'Crystal asked, 'D'you think we'll be moving out soon, sir?' He waited for Blackwood to face him. 'It's not what some of the new recruits had in mind.'

'Having trouble with them?'

M'Crystal bristled. 'I'd not tolerate that, sir. I've a handful of gallow's-bait I'd like to lose, but even they'll do as they're told or I'll know the reason.'

Blackwood knew that the real cause for M'Crystal's annoyance was a small, tight group of new recruits who had all enlisted together. Liverpool-Irish, they had been in more brawls with the military, seamen and marines from ships in harbour than he would have thought possible. Field punishment, doubling round the square in the blazing heat in full kit and a pack filled with sand until they collapsed had done nothing to break their fighting spirit.

Only Lieutenant-Colonel Fynmore appeared satisfied and content. As the senior officer Royal Marines in Malta he had carte blanche to visit any ship or barracks he chose, and seemed to thrive on the monotony of the routine.

He heard the crack and echo of rifle fire and recalled the times in Africa when so few of the enemy had pinned down his own trained and disciplined men without effort. He found he could go over those days with less anguish, another memory already blurred and out of focus.

'I've heard nothing of a move, Colour-Sergeant. Not yet anyway.'

Each day as he looked at the proud array of warships as they shimmered beneath their awnings in the Grand Harbour he found himself longing to be back in one of them. Maybe all marines were the same. Always wanting the opposite, torn between land and sea.

M'Crystal said softly, 'Colonel's coming, sir.'

Blackwood was tempted to pull out his watch, but knew inwardly that Fynmore's daily punctuality would not have varied by more than a second.

He squinted his eyes against the glare and watched the small procession approaching across the white stones, Fynmore in the lead, very erect in his saddle, one arm down his side as if it was made of wood. The adjutant, First Lieutenant George Speer, and an orderly trotting close behind.

Fynmore halted and stared towards the range. 'Improving,' he remarked.

If we carry on like this the rifles will be worn smooth before they are ever used in action, Blackwood thought.

He said, 'I think we should change the drills, sir.'

'Really?' Fynmore brushed a speck of sand from his sleeve. 'I expect we shall receive orders if and when the Admiralty reveal their intentions.'

Blackwood watched him. There was something unusual about Fynmore today. Not quite so calm as he tried to appear.

'The fact is, Blackwood, I have been asked to attend a reception at the admiral superintendent's residence. I shall let you have a list of officers who should also be present.'

Blackwood sighed. Another reception. They seemed endless.

There were plenty of women present on these occasions. Usually wives of senior officers or officials, they must get equally bored at making small talk with an obedient band of junior lieutenants.

'As a matter of fact, my own wife will be joining me here. The mail-packet arrives at the end of the week and she will be aboard. I should like *you* to arrange for her to be escorted to

my quarters.' He played with his sword-hilt. 'Make her feel
at home.'

The small moment of warmth passed and he snapped, 'Get
someone to chase up those damned buglers. I'll not tolerate
them arriving at Troop like a bunch of silly old women!'

He wheeled his horse about, and followed by the perspiring adjutant clattered towards the Royal Marine Artillery
battery which overlooked the Grand Harbour.

'You heard that, Colour-Sergeant?'

What sort of woman would be married to Fynmore, he
wondered? It was strange he had never brought her to Forton.
He thought suddenly of his stepmother and realized that his
father had not mentioned her at all in his letters.

M'Crystal stamped the details on his memory. 'I'll lay it
on, sir.'

He watched Blackwood walk back into the shade and
shook his head. The captain was the one who needed a
woman, a girl who would take him out of himself. Someone
who cared enough to share his life. He thought of the
captain's young brother. There would be plenty of trouble
with that one if he didn't watch out. Women? He couldn't
get enough of them, even here on Malta. If he brought some
disgrace on the Marines it would put the colonel's head
squarely on the block and things could become distinctly
uncomfortable.

He saw his friend Sergeant Quintin tramping wearily over
the sun-baked ground and grinned. At least he never
changed.

An orchestra played without a break throughout the balmy
evening, and while long fans swayed back and forth above the
heads of the guests, messmen and servants struggled to
supply everyone with drinks.

Blackwood stood near an open balcony and watched the
glittering lights from the anchored men-of-war in the harbour. A complete record of the Royal Navy's progress since

Trafalgar, he thought. Majestic ships of the line, and two or three of the new first-rates which, although similar in appearance, were also equipped with engines and screws as additional power.

Steam gunboats and paddle-frigates, they all symbolized the unchallenged power of the Queen's Navy.

He ran one finger round his collar and felt his shirt sticking to his chest like another skin.

He saw the admiral superintendent and his wife by the stairs greeting their guests, the gold epaulettes and varied uniforms making a fine setting for the ladies' gowns and bared shoulders. Here and there a face stood out. George Speer, the adjutant, head lowered and face set in an interested mask as he listened to the wife of the dockyard superintendent. Poor Speer, he was known to have problems with his own marriage and was probably wondering what had happened at home since the contingent had sailed from Portsmouth all those months ago.

Blackwood saw Fynmore too, his wife standing nearby as the admiral greeted her with one of his set speeches. She was obviously a lot younger than Fynmore, a pretty little thing and outwardly very shy when he had met her at the landing-stage. She was very much in awe of her husband and impressed by the marines he had sent to welcome her and to transport her baggage to the colonel's quarters. In the reflected lights her shoulders looked cool and youthful, he thought. The sort of wife who might do Fynmore's future a lot of good.

Harry pushed through the crowd and stared at the throng with distaste.

'I shall steal away when I get the chance.'

Blackwood watched him with surprise. Harry's disappointment and impatience at the soul-destroying garrison duties had often found other outlets in his zest for women. Usually on these formal occasions he had managed to find someone's wife or daughter who would enjoy his company and some of his daring remarks.

'Don't let the colonel see you.' He smiled. 'Have you met his wife, by the way?'

Harry turned swiftly, his eyes searching. 'Once, yes. Why?'

Blackwood shrugged and signalled to one of the servants with a loaded tray.

'Seems a shy sort of person.'

He twisted round to pick up a glass. He must have had too much to drink without realizing it, but Harry sounded unusually guarded. He even looked guilty.

Blackwood said quietly, 'Well, pull yourself together, man, they're coming over.'

But when he looked round, Harry had been swallowed up in the crowd.

Fynmore said crisply, 'And of course you know my aide, Captain Blackwood.' He watched as Blackwood took her gloved fingers and kissed them lightly. 'My right arm, believe me.'

Blackwood asked, 'Have you settled down after your voyage, Ma'am?'

He saw a small pulse pumping in her throat, the nervous movement of her breasts beneath her silk gown. Like a child at her first party, he thought. But there was something else. An elation, an excitement which she was trying to control.

She said, 'I was grateful for your presence at the harbour, Captain. All that noise and confusion.' She flicked open her fan and waved it below her chin. 'I find this heat very taxing.'

Fynmore was peering round at the others and probably wanted all of them to see his young wife, Blackwood thought.

She said, 'Your brother, is he here?' She put her head on one side. 'You are not much like him.'

Fynmore asked, 'You *know* Lieutenant Blackwood?' He frowned and nodded. 'Yes, I remember vaguely. You met him at Woolwich, you told me.' He smiled, satisfied with his memory.

Blackwood cleared his throat. 'We have the same father, Ma'am, that is all.'

He looked around, his mind grappling with what he had unwittingly discovered. He must have been blind not to see Harry's alarm when Fynmore had announced that his wife was coming to Malta. He had been so wrapped up in his own worries he had even forgotten what the adjutant had said about Fynmore's house in Hampshire. It was suddenly stark and clear, so that even the orchestra seemed to fade as he recalled Harry's casual mention of the letters he had forgotten to deliver to that house near the inn. His reluctance to speak about it afterwards. *The bloody idiot.*

He calmed his thoughts with an effort and said, 'He is somewhere in the building.' He thought that Fynmore was watching him again. 'Shall I fetch him?'

Fynmore chuckled. 'Certainly not. Let the young devil enjoy his freedom, eh? I know he can be an irritation to me, but with instruction he may make a fine officer one day.'

It was the nearest thing to praise he had ever made, and yet Blackwood remained uneasy. Fynmore never said or did anything without a strong reason.

His wife tossed her ringlets as if it was all of little importance.

'I think I shall enjoy my stay here, Captain.'

'I sincerely hope – '

Blackwood stared transfixed as the admiral superintendent released the hand of another guest and turned to reveal the woman at his side.

Fynmore exclaimed, 'In God's name, isn't that the girl we saved, Blackwood?'

Blackwood did not even notice the 'we'. But for Fynmore he would have believed he was going insane or suffering another aftermath to his fever.

He nodded, unable and unwilling to take his eyes from her. 'It is, sir. Miss Seymour.'

Fynmore's wife turned and followed their glances. For a few seconds she showed irritation on her doll-like features, as if she resented the intrusion.

She said, 'Oh, that's not her name, Rupert. She was aboard

the packet too. With her husband, a doctor of some repute, I was told. Much older than she, but of course some of us prefer more experienced husbands.'

Fynmore either ignored or failed to notice her tone.

'Fine looking woman, in spite of everything, Blackwood.'

Blackwood said nothing. Instead of the girl with the shining dark hair and demure gown he saw the one in that squalid hut, cut and bruised, and almost naked to the waist.

*In spite of everything*. In those moments he hated Fynmore and his crude indifference.

He heard himself say, 'If you will excuse me . . .'

He saw their interest sharpen as he made his way among the perspiring, colourful crowd until he was near to the stairway.

If anything she was more beautiful than when he had seen her in London all that time ago. While her husband was speaking to the admiral she stood with and yet apart from them, her eyes downcast as if she was listening to what they were saying.

But Blackwood could remember when he had first seen her aboard *Audacious*, a lifetime ago. She had been the same then, it was her defence.

He heard the admiral say in his booming voice, 'I wish you every success, Doctor Hadley. It is high time that our sick and wounded were treated with greater professional care than in the past.' He chuckled and looked at the girl by his elbow. 'Begging you pardon, Mrs Hadley, but in my early days at sea the work could have been done as well by the ship's butcher!'

Blackwood bunched his fists. She was almost close enough to touch. He must leave now before she saw him and was humiliated by his attention. She and her husband were probably taking passage by another ship very shortly. *He would go right now*.

It was then that she looked up and stared directly into his eyes. As if she had felt him there, had known exactly where he would be.

The admiral pivoted round on his heels, his bushy eyebrows set in a protective frown.

'This is Captain Blackwood. One of our marine officers.'

His eyes said *go away*, but the doctor asked quickly, 'Aren't you the one who . . . ?'

He glanced at his wife and then back at Blackwood as she said quietly, 'He is the one who saved my life.'

The admiral beamed. 'Bless my soul! Then I take back all I said about the marines.' He sensed that he had spoken out of place and added, 'You must join me later, Blackwood. When the masses have departed, what?' He patted his scarlet sleeve. 'Splendid, didn't know about that.'

As the admiral turned to greet another arrival Blackwood found himself tongue-tied and helpless. All he wanted to do was look at her, to hear her voice again, even though there was no hope for more. Instead he was facing her husband, a serious-faced man aged about forty with a studious manner and voice.

'I have heard something of your exploits, er, Captain? My wife's aunt, Lady Slade, mentioned you to me of course. I am really delighted to meet you at long last. I hope to be able to speak with you, away from all this.' He seemed to dismiss the people around him. 'I would find it most interesting.'

She asked in the same level voice, 'Have you been well, Captain Blackwood? I heard of your father's illness, I was very distressed.' Her eyes were steady and yet too bright as she added, 'I never expected to see you here.'

Blackwood looked at her and tried to sound as calm as she had done. It was difficult not to study her from her dark hair to her clasped hands, to seek something lost, or which had never been.

He replied, 'I have been on Malta since my time in hospital, Ma'am. Sometimes I feel I have been here forever.'

Doctor Hadley nodded thoughtfully. 'A man of action, eh? In peacetime you must find life heavy on your hands.'

Blackwood glanced at him and tried not to dislike him. He spoke as if he was conducting an experiment with a patient. But she had married him and so . . .

She said, 'My husband is on a government commission to

look into the methods of after-care in military and naval hospitals.'

The doctor waved a tray aside and asked for a glass of fruit juice. He said absently, 'We shall be staying here at the medical inspector's house while I carry out some tests at the Hospital of St Angelo.'

Blackwood glanced quickly at her as the doctor's fruit drink arrived. She would be on Malta. For a short time perhaps, but *she would be here.*

He tried to sound matter of fact. 'Yes, I see. Most of our sick and injured people go there.'

He saw her hands gripping more tightly together and was suddenly disgusted with himself. She had made her choice and wanted only to forget her ordeal and avoid anyone who might bring it alive again.

He said, 'I should leave now.'

He saw her sudden tension, the appeal in her violet eyes, and felt his heart begin to pound a warning. She did not want him to go.

The doctor said, 'I have just seen the fleet surgeon yonder. I would be obliged if you would remain with my wife until I have spoken with him. He can be very elusive, I'm told, when it comes to inspections within his realm.'

The great hall could have been empty, the music and voices completely stilled.

Blackwood said, 'I have thought about you so much. Just now I imagined I was dreaming, even now I am not sure. You look so lovely . . .' The words were flooding out of him and he could do nothing to contain them. 'You have never been out of my thoughts.'

She held up a fan and clasped it with both hands. 'You must not speak like that! I implore you!' Even as she spoke she studied his face, her eyes tender as she added, 'Do not imagine I had forgotten *you*. But things have changed. You must see that? I cannot bear to see you hurt.'

'Hurt?' He touched her wrist and then held it, feeling her warmth, seeing the response in her eyes. 'I would risk far more than that. Anything.' He lowered his voice, 'May I see you again?'

She glanced away and he saw her breasts moving quickly as she tried to remain calm.

'Do you mean alone?'

'I have to see you. To talk. It may be the last chance.'

She faced him again but her composure was gone.

'This is madness. I do not know what to say, what you expect of me. I am a married woman.' She hesitated, as if aware of what she had just said. It had sounded like a defence, an admission. 'We go on to Cairo after this.'

He gripped her hands in his. 'Please. I will not be a nuisance, I promise.'

She looked up at him and smiled for the first time. 'You could never be that.' Her hands slipped away as she lowered her fan to her waist.

Doctor Hadley rejoined them and said, 'Another job done.' He glanced at each of them in turn. 'You must have a lot of memories to discuss, eh?' But he was humming quietly to himself as if the question was merely put out of politeness.

Blackwood gave a bow. 'I look forward to our meeting at the admiral's table later on.' He released her gloved hand and stepped back. 'Until then.'

He pushed into the crowd and walked halfway across the hall before he knew what he was doing.

She was so right. It was madness. But it was one which left him helpless. Like a ship without a rudder at the mercy of a relentless gale.

He realized he had reached one of the balconies again and stood by the balustrade, drawing deep breaths while he relived each precious second.

In one corner of the hall Fynmore watched Blackwood's behaviour and then said, 'I shall have to keep an eye on him. I'll not have the good name of my command jeopardized. He is one of my trusted officers, and *she's* a married woman. I had a feeling about those two before. It won't damn well do!'

She lowered her eyes and hid a smile. 'Of course not, dearest. If you say so.'

# 18

## *Gesture of Hope*

The Hospital of St Angelo was a quiet, secluded place, in spite of the island's bustle which surrounded it. There were winding, tree-lined paths and a garden which was tended by convalescent soldiers and sailors under the eye of one of the resident nuns. It seemed to have a peaceful effect on the inmates, and as Blackwood walked along one of the paths he found it hard to picture some of them as roistering, hard-drinking servicemen.

She was waiting by a stone bench, a place which they had come to regard as their special meeting-place, even though Blackwood had only visited the hospital twice before.

They sat down in a deep patch of shade and looked directly in front of them as if ashamed of what they were doing.

She said quietly, 'It was good of you to come, Philip.'

The use of his name had come naturally and without reservation, as if they both knew it had been decreed by fate.

Blackwood watched one of the nuns sail past like a ship of the line in her head-dress and pale habit. What did they think about these meetings, he wondered?

He said, 'I wish we could see each other every day. All day.'

He felt her turn, and when he faced her he saw the sadness in her eyes.

'I must tell you. My husband has finished his work here. We sail for Cairo on Wednesday.'

He had been expecting it. But as the days had lengthened

into weeks and he had managed to meet her in spite of all the difficulties, he had somehow put the inevitable aside.

'I had hoped . . .' He took one of her hands and pressed it to his cheek. 'I was wrong to hope, and now I have hurt you.'

She shook her head and smiled. 'That you have not. I have got to know more about myself than I believed possible because of you. I cannot bear the thought of our parting.' Her lip quivered. 'Of losing you.'

When he tried to speak she squeezed his hand. 'No, you must hear me. I married Paul because I had known him for a long while, he was one of my father's protégés when I was still at school. After what happened in Africa, I did not know, did not dare to look for love in any man.' She lifted her eyes and made herself say, 'Now I know. You were really the one. But I could not risk destroying both of us.'

Blackwood thought suddenly of Lady Slade's voice in that quiet London house. *You will end up with a broken heart.*

'I thought that Paul would be different. He is much older than I am and the gap between us seemed more so then in other ways. I needed to lose myself, and to do that I thought I might help him in his work as I had once helped my father.'

The air shook to the sullen rumble of gunfire and she held his hand more tightly while her other hand touched her breast.

He watched her profile, the sudden alarm in her eyes.

'It is all right, Davern.'

He listened to the regular crash of a gun salute and recalled that a new man-of-war was due to arrive from England.

He asked, 'Is he a bad husband to you? If so . . .'

She stared at him and shook her head. 'He is neither bad nor good. He is *interested* in me.'

Blackwood thought of his manner at the admiral superintendent's reception. Cool and *interested*. She was right.

'Anyway.' She played with his hand, her skin warm against his fingers. 'It must not be your concern.' She looked away. 'I wish I had had your courage when I most needed it. I know now you might have understood, have helped me. But I dared not risk it after what you did to save my life.'

She tore her hand away and walked to a low wall and stared at the overlapping white buildings and towers.

Across her shoulder she said huskily, 'You never once asked, did you? You knew they'd raped me, but not once did your eyes ask *what was it like? What did they do to you?*'

She almost fell as he seized her and pulled her against him. 'Oh, how I *wish* I'd died that day!'

Blackwood held her without speaking. He let it pour out of her unchecked, knowing it might help, understanding at last what she had been enduring ever since he had freed her.

And all this time she had lived with her secret, and now that she had told him it was too late.

He raised her chin very gently and brushed some hair from her eyes.

'All I know is that I love you. To lose you now is unthinkable.'

He kept seeing her husband, questioning her, persisting about the details when he should have been helping her forget.

A nun, her hands thrust inside her wide sleeves, hurried along the path and then paused to peer at them.

'Your husband has just come from the admiral's residence, Mrs Hadley.' She bobbed and added, 'Good day to you, Captain Blackwood.'

Blackwood watched her as she vanished around the next bend.

'Bless her. Our guardian angel.'

But she gripped his arm and said fiercely, 'Go now. I have caused enough. I'll not see your reputation in ruins too.'

He held her again and felt her tremble as they came together. It was like hanging to a thread when your life depended on it. A rough word or thoughtless move and it would all change to ashes.

'Listen to me. I *want* you. Do you understand? I cannot face losing you.' He slipped his hand around her waist and pulled her more tightly against his body. 'We are meant for each other. Perhaps we were made to suffer before we could find this love.'

Very carefully and reluctantly he released her, watching her eyes, the way she was looking at him as she fought against her own reactions.

Then she said, 'Please kiss me, Philip.'

He felt her arms wrap around his neck as they touched mouths and then kissed. Blackwood had no idea how long they stayed embraced or if anyone passed by on the path. Her mouth told him without words that it was a gesture of desperate hope and nothing more. A realization of something wonderful which would soon slip away.

She put her hands on his chest and said breathlessly, 'You must go. Please.' She dabbed her cheek with the back of her hand. 'It can do no good.'

Blackwood had to force himself to stand away from her.

'I will write to you. Somehow I shall – '

But she had already turned away and was hurrying after the nun.

Blackwood left the hospital enclosure by a side gate and walked towards the harbour. There were more people than usual on the move, he thought vaguely, probably going to see the ship just arrived from England.

News from home, old friends, orders for the future.

He glanced up at the fortress on the hill where the flag flapped limply in the glare. It was all there waiting for him. Fynmore, Harry, the Corps, routine and duty.

He turned and looked back at the hospital with its domed roof and shady trees. But my life is there, with her, and soon she will be gone.

On the harbour wall he saw the people who had come to watch the display of armed might, and most of all the big three-decker which was moving very slowly towards her anchorage.

She looked much like any of the other large men-of-war, except that she was steering into the wind, her sails loosely furled and her yards manned by some of her company. But the tall thin funnel just abaft her foremast and the tell-tale froth beneath her counter from her screw-propeller showed that she was something different. An admiral's flag fluttered from her mainmast truck, riding above the drifting smoke from the gun salute like a lance pendant.

Blackwood tried to get interested in the ship's reason for coming and where she would go. But it eluded him, and he touched his mouth as if he expected to feel some trace of the girl still there.

They had shared a few precious moments together like conspirators. Could that really be an end to it?

He turned on his heel and strode quickly up the hill towards the battery, his step firm as if to mark his determination.

It was not over, nor would it be.

Harry Blackwood watched warily as Fynmore's wife moved eagerly across the cabin. It was a small, ornate schooner which belonged to a local chandler whom Harry had befriended, the only safe place he had managed to find.

It was unnerving how things had changed. Julia Fynmore was enjoying her power over him and seemed totally reckless about the risks they were taking.

He pulled the small curtains aside and peered across the anchorage. Mostly local craft, but you could never be certain on an overcrowded island like Malta.

She glanced into the adjoining cabin and he heard her give a murmur of satisfaction. She turned and faced him like an excited child.

'It's lovely, Harry. Come here and hold me.'

Harry knew now to his cost there was not much childlike about the colonel's wife.

He put his arms round her and felt her push herself against him. A far cry from the woman he had all but assaulted in Fynmore's house in England.

He said, 'We'll have to be careful, Julia.'

He tried to gauge her reaction, what mad thing she might do if he attempted to finish their affair. She actually enjoyed playing with his emotions.

'Oh, stuff!' She looked up at him and smiled. 'Nobody suspects anything. Rupert's too busy anyway.'

Harry started as the boat tilted slightly and then relaxed again. It was one of those blank-faced deck-hands who lived aboard. Even they might tell someone about their master's furtive visitors.

She began to unbutton his shirt and then kissed his chest.

'Come along, Harry.' She ran her hands over his skin and whispered, 'I can't wait.'

He tried again. '*Please*, Julia.' He saw her mouth pout. 'I'm not supposed to know, let alone tell anyone, but the whole Marine contingent is being taken aboard some of the ships here. God knows what we're going to do or where we're going.'

She shook her ringlets with impatience. 'Oh that. I know all about it. It's because of some silly rumour that the Russians are occupying Turkish territory. As if *that* matters!'

Harry stared at her. It had been only yesterday that he had learned about the new orders. The most surprising part had been that the powerful man-of-war which had dropped anchor in Grand Harbour had been wearing the flag of Admiral Sir James Ashley-Chute. Promoted at long last, and with a brand-new flagship, he was amongst them once more like a small typhoon.

Harry had never thought he would be glad to see the little admiral again. He did not care if the Russians, or even the Chinese, were the cause of the excitement. Anything was better than all the dreary months of inactivity and boredom. And with Fynmore's demanding wife constantly marking down his movements it was a double reprieve.

'Well, it can't be helped, I suppose.' He saw her growing impatience and added, 'But we must be careful all the same.'

He stripped off his shirt and followed her to the adjoining cabin. He hated it, the way it had all changed, the 'games' she invented whenever they had managed to meet.

She turned and looked at him, her slim body swaying to the hull's gentle motion.

'What shall it be, Harry?' Her tongue touched her upper lip. 'You are the pirate and I shall be your prisoner again!'

He pushed her roughly on to the wide bunk and when she pretended to struggle he seized her throat and squeezed it. She had ruined everything, had probably known this would happen from that first meeting when he had been little more than a youth.

He realized that she was choking and that he had almost strangled her in his sudden anger. But to her it was just a part of her game, and when he eventually threw himself on top of her she was more eager than ever to return his demands of her.

The thought of getting away to another place, to rid himself of her clinging attention, gave him new strength, and when they fell apart, exhausted and panting, he even managed to smile.

The flagship's spacious wardroom was packed with attentive officers as Admiral Sir James Ashley-Chute drew near to the end of his address.

On one side of the wardroom, and close to an open gun-port, Philip Blackwood listened to the misshapen little admiral and was fascinated by his vigour and his grasp of the newly arisen crisis in the Black Sea.

The admiral looked much older and if possible was even more bent, and yet showed the enthusiasm and keenness of a junior lieutenant.

Unaware of his half-brother's predicament, Blackwood was also eager to be part of the fleet again, to keep busy until he could find Davern. She had left the island with her husband and would be in Cairo by now. He had thought that the memory of her voice, the touch of her hands in his would make the parting too painful to bear. Strangely, it had given him a strength of purpose, a determination that somehow they would be together again, no matter how formidable the obstacles.

The admiral said crisply, 'The Russians are apparently determined to occupy more and more Turkish territory. The warnings have been all too clear, and if they are prepared to wage war because of their greed, then, gentlemen, so be it.'

He had all their attention now. The slow, unruffled existence of fleet or garrison seemed to fade with the admiral's words, and when Blackwood glanced quickly at some of the others he saw their excitement too. It was infectious, like the little man who dominated the wardroom.

The Navy was to send a small but impressive force into the Black Sea itself. The flag would be in *Tenacious*, the newest of her kind, and armed with one hundred and thirty-one guns. Blackwood had wondered since he had heard of Ashley-Chute's arrival how he had managed to accept the use of coal and all it represented to him. In addition to the flagship there would be three steam-frigates and six gunboats. The lioness and her cubs. They might not win a war but they might discourage the Russians from causing one.

Ashley-Chute's deep-set eyes moved over the assembled captains and senior officers until they came to rest on Fynmore.

He said, 'I expect you will all have noticed a preponderance of scarlet among our ranks.' That brought a few laughs, as he knew it would. 'The marines will be divided among the ships under my flag and if need be will be put ashore in battalion strength. An independent force of infantry, well trained, and better armed . . .' his gaze rested briefly on Blackwood, '. . . than they have been in the past.'

Major Brabazon, Fynmore's second-in-command, whispered, 'He almost sounds as if he likes us!'

But Fynmore's back and shoulders remained like a ramrod, and Brabazon glanced past him and gave a weary shrug.

Blackwood smiled. It was never easy to get the colonel to share a joke at a superior officer's expense. Always careful, never a loose word which might injure his prospects.

He liked Brabazon, a big, comfortable man, a marine's marine who had done more than anyone to mould the recruits and old hands into a single force.

'That will be all for the present, gentlemen.' The admiral

nodded curtly to his flag-lieutenant. 'Flags here will explain about appointments to the various ships and er, barracks.' There was another chuckle. 'Afterwards you will return to your commands and prepare the people for weighing on Thursday.' He made to leave as they all stood up and added, 'Captain Blackwood, come with me.'

Blackwood left his place, surprised at the curt order and aware of the watching eyes. Of Fynmore's suspicion more than anything.

Doors opened and closed behind him and then he was in the admiral's day-cabin, the anchored vessels shimmering in haze beyond the broad stern windows.

Ashley-Chute sat down on a bench seat and crossed his legs before saying, 'You will be aboard *Tenacious*, of course.'

Blackwood took a glass of sherry from the cabin servant and wondered why he was here.

Ashley-Chute sipped his glass and sniffed. 'God, what is the purser thinking of, hmm?' He looked at Blackwood and said calmly, 'I am sorry I could not do more for you. Had your wound been less serious I would have retained you under my command. But had it been worse you would not even be here, so you should be grateful.' He gave what might have been a smile. 'There's going to be a fight. I can smell it. You'll get your chance then, right enough.' He glanced around the gleaming, white-painted cabin with obvious satisfaction. 'I suppose one must make some concessions for progress, eh?'

Blackwood asked, 'Is your son well, sir?'

Ashley-Chute glared. 'I suppose so. He commands one of those stinking gunboats yonder. But it's what he wanted, blast him.'

Then the admiral said abruptly, 'Do you think your new contingent could fight ashore against trained troops? I want the truth now, not some sugary answer just to please me.'

'I'm certain of it, sir. In Africa it was different – '

'Africa was not *so* different, Blackwood. We were used as a means to an end. Perhaps that will be so in the Black Sea. To you the African campaign was a series of actions with no true understanding of the main purpose.' He did not conceal the bitterness in his voice. 'I'm an old man, and it's taken me a long while to understand the dishonesty of politicians.'

Blackwood said, 'Slavery was stamped out, sir.'

'Huh, that would have happened anyway. It was Lagos they wanted, but those politicians had to justify their reasons for taking it.' He spat out the words, 'The seeds of Empire! Bloody rubbish!' He gestured to the decanter. 'Pour some more sherry.'

Then Ashley-Chute said slowly, 'I wanted you to know that I appreciated your part in that campaign. You were the hinge in the door, so to speak, and but for you there could have been a severe setback. As it was, the campaign cost us two thousand officers and men.' He glared at his glass. 'For that stinking coast and all the trouble it will bring us.' He looked up again, his monkey face impassive. 'If you repeat a word of what I said I'll have you boiled in oil.'

'Of course, sir.'

So that was it. The little admiral's way of saying he was sorry that he was the only one who had gained nothing from the whole affair.

'Never try to discover a reason, Blackwood. Just do it. It's always been my way in the past and I have no intention of changing.' He looked around as if to find the right words. 'Not even for the Tsar of bloody Russia!'

Two days later the *Tenacious*, accompanied by her small flotilla of steam vessels, left the Grand Harbour and put to sea. The bands played from the battery and rockets were discharged over the darkening water until the winking lights finally disappeared.

It was a gala occasion, a display of pride and cheerful arrogance for the admiral and his latest command.

It was much the same aboard the flagship, although for different reasons. Colour-Sergeant M'Crystal was grateful to get his worst troublemakers contained where he could watch and control them. Private Frazier cared for his new rifle with something akin to love. He had practised on the range until he could hit a small target at three hundred yards, and could hardly wait to use his rifle in deadly earnest. Corporal Jones, as reliable and conscientious as ever, still nursed the grief for his dead friend, Corporal Bly. It was strange, he thought, that he had never got over it. He knew he was wrong, but he could not find anything to like in the new corporal, and that disturbed him deeply. The Rocke twins settled down again to shipboard life and to the business of tormenting Sergeant Quintin. The adjutant, Lieutenant Speer, grew gaunt with worry as he thought about his wife in England and the affair she had been having when he had last caught her. Lieutenant Harry Blackwood, on the other hand, was twice his old self, always cheerful and easy with his men, with nothing to show of the humiliating strain he had been under.

Lieutenant-Colonel Rupert Fynmore was very satisfied. He was the right age and held the right rank. New horizons stretched in every direction. He had already forgotten how he had dreaded being discharged from the Corps or dropped into some meaningless post which led nowhere. There had never been a general in his family. But now things would change.

It warmed his heart to realize he held the same rank as his late father, the same as Captain Blackwood's father also. He often congratulated himself on his choice of a young wife. She came from a respected military family, and that fact would do no harm at all when the time came.

The network of courier-brigs and fast packets kept the Mediterranean's flag-officers informed of world events, but the mass of seamen and marines remained in ignorance as to what was happening.

While Ashley-Chute's squadron moved eastward on its slow and unhurried cruise, news was received that Russian forces had invaded more Turkish territory, and in self-defence the Sultan had declared war. Later, when *Tenacious* lay at anchor and suffered the indignities of coaling ship, Ashley-Chute was informed that a strong Russian force had sailed from Sebastopol and had totally destroyed a Turkish squadron with great loss of life.

Throughout Ashley-Chute's command there seemed to be little sympathy for the Turks. Russia had, after all, been Britain's ally against them just twenty-six years earlier.

Philip Blackwood had noticed the arrival of several French men-of-war in the Eastern Mediterranean, and their captains had often been aboard to meet Ashley-Chute and presumably to discuss possible strategy.

But daily routine continued, sail and gun drills, coaling ship and washing-down again.

It was an ordinary day too when the flagship's company was piped aft to hear an announcement by the captain.

If Ashley-Chute resembled a monkey, then Captain Montagu Jervis was certainly everything a bulldog should be.

Short but heavily built, he looked older than his years because of his sweeping, 'heavy swell' side-whiskers. He was a stern, even severe captain, but seemed to be quite at ease with his admiral, and Blackwood often wondered what had become of Ackworthy, his original flag-captain.

On this particular morning, as the seamen swarmed aft, Captain Jervis stood with his commander, cap tugged over his eyes, his hands in his pockets until silence had eventually fallen over his ship.

Blackwood waited with the other officers and watched the captain's impressive side-whiskers blowing slightly in the breeze and wondered what was so important.

Jervis said in his hard voice, 'The Russians have shown no sign that they intend to release their hold on Turkish lands, and Her Majesty's Government have consequently ordered us to enter the Black Sea without further delay.'

That was all he said. But it was no longer an ordinary day. Britain was at war.

# 19

## *The Enemy*

Harry Blackwood stared at the shore and grimaced. 'The Turkish Empire? If that is what the rest of it looks like, I think we must be fighting on the wrong side.'

Blackwood glanced at him curiously. His half-brother seemed to be constantly on edge, his original good humour had vanished.

It was true that the first excitement of being part of a war had somewhat disappeared after the squadron had passed through the Bosphorus and into the Black Sea. Nobody was quite sure what he had expected, but with the exception of a few patrols within sight of the Russian coast they had seen and done nothing.

Now, anchored off the Turkish port of Varna at the western end of the enclosed sea, the squadron swung to its anchors and gazed longingly at the low-roofed town.

'Is something wrong, Harry?'

Harry looked at him uncertainly. 'I'm sick of kicking my heels like this. I sometimes wish I'd cut with family tradition and gone for a line regiment. If I have to mount one more guard of honour for the French and Turkish High Command I really will go mad!'

Blackwood tried to put his half-brother's discontent from his mind. When they had last dropped anchor after a fruitless patrol in search of Russian ships there had been sacks of letters waiting for the squadron. Sweethearts and wives, news from home, the vital link with that other world.

There had been one for him posted in Cairo.

He had already written several times to the address she had given him but this was the first real news he had received in reply. It appeared that all his letters had arrived at once, and he was touched that she had taken the trouble to read them all in order and with great care. He was also surprised that it had been so easy to converse by letter. Perhaps he had half expected her to break with him as soon as she had left Malta.

She wrote with warmth and affection, as if they had been lovers instead of brief companions. Blackwood had read her letter so many times it was crumpled from constant handling. Harry, always so confident and assured about his lady friends, would have laughed at him if only he knew.

A midshipman saluted and said, 'Captain's compliments, sir, and would you muster a guard. The admiral is returning aboard directly.'

'Very well. Pipe for Sergeant Quintin, if you please.'

So the admiral was coming back. He had been across in the senior flagship for most of the day, probably giving vent to his own hatred for inaction with his immediate superior.

Harry tightened his sword-belt and stamped his feet on the deck. It had been a close thing that time. He had almost burst out to Philip about the letter he had received from Fynmore's wife in Malta. It had been devoid of love and mystery and had been filled with remorse and fear.

She had apparently met another officer after the squadron had sailed from Grand Harbour, and from the tone of her letter Harry guessed she had not been so successful in gaining the upper hand. She was with child and quite obviously terrified at the possible consequences when Fynmore found out about it.

Harry swallowed hard and stared at the anchored frigates and steam gunboats nearby browsing beneath their usual haze of dusty smoke. She may have had the child already. She had also hinted that she would plead her husband's forgiveness if only for the good of their reputations. If that failed she would do something terrible.

Harry looked forward as the first squad of marines tramped

up a companion ladder and moved to the entry port in readiness for the admiral.

Suppose it all came out about his own attentions to her? Fynmore was already jealous of the Blackwood family, no matter what he pretended. Something like this would ruin everything.

A barge moved from the other flagship's shadow, and with the oars rising and falling like wings turned towards the *Tenacious*.

Sergeant Quintin reported, 'Guard ready for inspection, sir.'

Blackwood watched his half-brother as he carried out a cursory inspection. No shared jokes with his men now. The marines resented his unexplained change. It showed on their stiff faces.

Captain Montagu Jervis strode heavily across the quarter-deck and looked grimly at the barge. He nodded to Blackwood and murmured, 'I hope that Sir James is in good humour. The frigates have reported a coal shortage in the port. It will be a week at least before fresh supplies arrive.' He glared up at the impeccably furled sails of his ship. 'How can you run a modern fleet with stone-age brains in control?'

But when Ashley-Chute's head and shoulders rose over the ship's side he appeared to be in an extremely affable mood.

He touched his hat casually to the guard and waited for the chorus of trilling calls to fall silent. Then to the quarterdeck at large he said cheerfully, 'Prepare for sea, gentlemen. It's *action* this time, so stir yourselves.'

Even Captain Jervis's gruff explanation about the coal supplies did not appear to dampen his humour.

'Well, what did you expect from a bunch of godless heathen, eh, Captain?' He rubbed his hands together and added, 'Just so long as the flagship is ready, hmm?'

With his flag-lieutenant trotting behind him he hurried below the poop towards his quarters.

Later at a hastily called conference Captain Jervis explained the cause of his admiral's excitement.

Just before the outbreak of war with Russia the battery at Odessa had fired on Her Majesty's Ship *Furious*, despite her flag of truce, as she was about to parley over bringing any British subjects away from the port. One of the first operations after the declaration of war had been for the fleet to bombard that same battery and to leave it and many of the harbour installations wrecked and burning.

Now it seemed there was a second large battery which had been sited just to the east of Odessa, which was being used to protect an assortment of Russian men-of-war lying at anchor there.

If a full scale invasion was eventually to be mounted against the Russians, the British and their allies had to hold command of all the sea routes which carried their troops and supplies.

Captain Jervis said in his usual severe manner, 'We will bring those ships to action and destroy them, the battery too if need be.'

It sounded simple enough, and the effect on the ship's company was immediate as the news spread from mess to mess.

As dusk closed over the anchorage *Tenacious*, accompanied by the steam-frigate *Sarpedon*, and the little paddle-gunboat *Rupert*, headed away from the land.

The other vessels watched in frustrated silence as the flagship's company manned the yards and cheered as if they had already won a resounding victory.

Aft in the great cabin Ashley-Chute cocked his head to listen and to share the moment.

During his long career he had been criticized and berated many times, and more than once had been replaced by another officer because of his ideas and tactics. But in each case he had known himself to be right, and when others had doubted he had stood firm. A hard challenge demanded a harder solution. He knew he would never end his days in the peace and security of Admiralty, but he no longer cared. Here was where he belonged. Unfettered by higher authority and with the power of right and justice on his side.

The deck tilted slightly to the thrust of a south-westerly wind and he smiled wryly as he thought of his flag-captain's eagerness to use his mechanical power. That could wait. In his mind's eye he could picture *Tenacious* with all her canvas spread and filling to the wind. There was no finer sight. No wonder the sailors cheered. Ignorant and insubordinate they might be, but they shared his pride in the ship and what she stood for.

They all feared him, and the idea amused him. He recalled Blackwood when they had first met all those years ago in New Zealand. Pale and angry after the savage fight, and determined to defend his dead major's name.

Maybe that was why he had retained Captain Blackwood in *Audacious*. He was the only one he could remember who had ever stood up to him.

His servant tiptoed into the cabin and waited anxiously.

Ashley-Chute waved his hand. 'Some port, I think, Fisher. One of the *special* ones, hmm?'

The servant hurried away, grateful that the sun was still shining over his master's head.


Two days after weighing anchor at Varna the *Tenacious*'s masthead lookout reported land fine on the larboard bow.

They had made very good time, with a strengthening south-westerly under their coat-tails to give them an extra thrust through the water. The frigate and the little gunboat had mercifully avoided any sort of mechanical breakdown, and had even used their sails to maintain station on the flagship.

Admiral Sir James Ashley-Chute appeared on deck within minutes of the cry from the masthead. Blackwood, who had been taking his customary exercise up and down the quarter-deck, moved to the opposite side as the small, monkey-like figure strode to the nettings. Ashley-Chute might pretend that he was calm and unruffled, but Blackwood knew him well enough to see through his pretence.

Captain Jervis said, 'Wind's still rising, sir. I'd like the hands to shorten sail presently. We're in for a full gale, according to the Master, and I must say I agree.'

Ashley-Chute's hands found each other across his buttocks and clasped firmly together as if for support.

'You are the captain. Act as you think fit.' He glanced at the sea and then up at the low, fast-moving clouds. All day the sea had been lively and broken into cruising ranks of jagged whitecaps. Now it looked darker, like the sky. Summer was short in the Black Sea apparently.

Blackwood noticed that the admiral's narrow shoulders were already soaked in spray, and he could almost feel the little man's agitation as he watched the worsening weather.

The admiral remarked curtly, 'Nothing much we can do now anyway. It will be dark in two hours.' Nevertheless, he took a telescope from his flag-lieutenant and steadied it against the ship's slow plunging motion.

Jervis offered helpfully, 'The bay and the Russian battery lie nor'-nor'-west, sir.'

The telescope snapped shut. 'Signal the frigate *Sarpedon* to investigate.'

Blackwood could imagine the relief aboard the black-hulled frigate which had been their constant companion since leaving Malta all that time ago. Free of the admiral's watchful eye, if only for the moment. He saw the signal dash up the *Sarpedon*'s yards and break out to the wind in acknowledgement. Against the threatening clouds the flags looked unusually bright, like painted metal.

Ashley-Chute paced a few steps this way and that.

'Put a reliable officer at the masthead, Captain Jervis.' His deepset eyes settled suddenly on Blackwood. 'Or would *you* do me the honour, sir?'

Blackwood handed his hat to a seaman and unclipped his belt. He had guessed what Ashley-Chute wanted to know. It was not mere curiosity.

'Aye, sir.'.

Ashley-Chute beckoned him over, his manner impatient again.

'The Russians will know what we are about, Blackwood. I need a good eye at the masthead and not merely a sailor's judgement, you catch my meaning?'

Blackwood hurried to the main shrouds and swung himself out on to the weather ratlines. He could feel the wind pushing him playfully against the tarred ropes, the soaking slap of spray against his tunic as he began to climb. It was exhilarating and something he had never really got used to. Up and up, past the fighting top and on to the topmast shrouds, the masts and spars shaking and creaking to the wind's power.

How they had managed in the old days he could never understand. Ordinary men dragged to sea by the hungry press gangs, boys even who were expected to climb aloft in all weathers to fight the hardened canvas, to reef or splice repairs in the drumming rigging, or face the consequences of the lash if they hesitated.

He found a burly seaman squatting on the cross-trees, seemingly oblivious to the pale deck so far below his dangling feet.

If he thought it strange to find a marine coming to join him, and an officer at that, he did not show it.

Blackwood asked, 'Where away?'

The seaman pointed towards the unbroken line of coast, slate-coloured in the failing light.

Blackwood waited for the mast to dip over again and then levelled his telescope on the bearing.

Angry wave crests leapt into focus while an offshore current writhed among them like a giant serpent. He saw the frigate end on, a thick trail of smoke gushing downwind as she forged into the bay, spindrift and spray flying from her bows and paddle-boxes in a wild dance.

He moved the glass very carefully and felt the tarred cordage biting at his skin as the ship plunged into a deep trough. Jervis would have to take in much more sail unless he wanted to lose some of it completely, he thought.

He tensed. There were ships at anchor, their overlapping shadows making them hard to recognize and distinguish.

The lookout called, 'Two, mebbe three men-o'-war, sir, an' a few merchantmen besides!'

He sounded cheerful at the prospect. He had probably already worked out his share of the prize-money if they were lucky.

Part of the coastline flickered briefly, like lightning on a hillside. Blackwood held his breath and counted the seconds. Then he heard the echoing boom of heavy gunfire and watched as several tall waterspouts shot from the water on either side of the frigate. The battery had not been taken by surprise. He saw the spray from the falling columns of water being ripped aside by the wind and pictured the Russian guns already being reloaded and run up for another salvo.

*Boom . . . boom . . .*

The fall of shot was even closer this time, and Blackwood was almost certain that at least one hit had been made on *Sarpedon*'s hull.

A metallic voice echoed from the deck. It was Jervis recalling him with the aid of a speaking-trumpet.

It would soon be dark. Blackwood climbed down the vibrating ratlines and wondered what Ashley-Chute would do. The Russians were in a very strong position. The wind too was in their favour and would soon deny *Tenacious* the sea-room she needed to close the range to any effect.

Ashley-Chute snapped, 'Did you see the battery?'

Blackwood regained his breath. 'I can mark it on the Master's chart, sir. They are heavy weapons.'

They both turned as the booming crash of gunfire sighed over the deck like a storm.

Someone called, '*Sarpedon*'s bin 'it, sir.'

Jervis exclaimed harshly, 'Damn their bloody eyes!'

Then the captain made up his mind. 'Pipe both watches, Mr Norman. Hands aloft and reef tops'ls. Then take in the main-course, lively now!'

Calls shrilled and bare feet pounded across the decks as the flagship's seamen ran to their stations before swarming up the ratlines in a human tide.

Blackwood watched the tiny, foreshortened figures scrambling out on the yards, some above the sea itself, as they began to fist the bulging canvas into submission. If a man fell now he was finished. To hit the sea and drown, or to drop on to the deck, it was all the same to the professional seaman.

Blackwood turned as he heard Fynmore's voice. Immaculate as ever, he was standing with Major Brabazon, the second-in-command, while they watched the bustle aloft.

He guessed that Fynmore hated sharing a cabin with the major, but with so many extra marines aboard, everyone had been made to double up. Blackwood had gone to see Brabazon about gunnery practice but had stumbled on Fynmore instead. It had been embarrassing to see the way he had torn some gold-rimmed glasses from his nose and had rammed them inside his tunic while he had pretended to read his papers unaided.

Ashley-Chute rasped, 'Make to *Sarpedon*. *Discontinue the action and close on the Flag*.'

The signals midshipman called, '*Sarpedon*'s acknowledged, sir.'

Ashley-Chute joined Jervis by the quarterdeck rail. 'Blackwood saw the fall of shot. A stronger battery than I expected. Must be a reason, hmm?'

Jervis watched his seamen sliding down the stays to the deck, their work done for the present. The ship felt sluggish but easier under her reduced sails, and he was relieved.

He answered, 'We shall be in trouble if we tack any closer, sir. We are on a lee shore as it is, and if the wind rises still further . . .' He left the rest unsaid.

The admiral stuck out his jaw. 'I do not intend that − ' He broke off angrily as the signals midshipman called from the shrouds.

'From *Sarpedon*, sir. *Have received two direct hits and am making water. Enemy shipping at anchor* − ' he blinked the spray from his eyes while his assistant, another midshipman, thumbed through his book to ensure that the signal was correct, '− *includes three men-of-war*.'

Jervis snapped, 'Acknowledge.' He bit his lip. '*Sarpedon* will be awash if the sea gets up.'

But Ashley-Chute ignored him. 'Signal her to confirm the size of warships.' He strode impatiently to the opposite side, his body leaning over to the sloping deck.

The soaked and dripping midshipman, who was very aware of the presence of so many superior officers, tried again, 'From *Sarpedon*, sir. *Enemy shipping at anchor. Two frigates and one ship of the line.*'

He gaped down from his perch with astonishment as the admiral shouted, '*Well done*, boy!'

Blackwood felt Harry slide across the spray covered deck to join him. 'I've never heard him praise anyone so junior before!'

Ashley-Chute banged a fist into his palm. 'Don't you *see*, Captain Jervis? The Russians are reported as having no more than fourteen sail of the line in the Black Sea. And one of them is *right here*! Dammit, Jervis, I'll ensure she never gets away. *Never!*'

The flag-lieutenant gave a nervous cough. 'I fear the light is going fast, sir. We shall lose visual contact with *Sarpedon* in minutes.'

Ashley-Chute regarded him coolly. 'I am aware of that.'

Jervis said, 'It is too lively to lower a boat, sir. But I could drift your despatches across to *Sarpedon* and then signal her to return to Varna.'

The admiral looked from one to the other. 'If *Sarpedon* sinks on passage we shall not know if my despatches have reached the admiral commanding at Varna or not. Tell her to lie to and execute repairs to the best of her ability.' He clasped his hands behind him again.

'I have no intention of waiting for support from anybody. There is a ship of the line over yonder, gentlemen, and at first light tomorrow I intend to engage her.' He nodded approvingly as the signals party bent on more hoists of flags and sent them soaring up the yards. 'And you may tell your, er, chief engineer, Captain Jervis, that he had best be ready to put his three hundred and fifty horsepower into motion at the first crowing of the cock, *right?*' He strode aft without waiting to watch the effect of his orders.

Jervis stared worriedly at the listing frigate and the clouds of smoke which appeared to be seeping through her starboard side.

'I never thought I'd live to hear him say *that*.'

Harry said quietly, 'Let's hope he knows what he's doing.'

Fynmore walked over and grasped the nettings to stop himself from falling.

He looked searchingly at the marine lieutenant and said, 'That could be said of many, Mr Blackwood.' He walked away without another glance.

Harry turned his face to the wind and gasped in the cold spray. Fynmore knew something. God Almighty, he *knew*.

Blackwood did not see his anxiety but remained by the nettings and listened to the faint clatter of the frigate's pumps as she fought her lonely battle with her constant enemy.

*And tomorrow it will be our turn.*


Blackwood had never been in a ship of the line when she had cleared for action in deadly earnest. Before it had been a necessary part of training and routine drill, and it was difficult to believe there could be such a difference.

All hands had been roused and piped to breakfast well before daylight, and even that had been different, and he doubted if many of the *Tenacious*'s eleven hundred officers and men had slept very much either. It was like remaking a part of history, or living something which might never occur again.

As the drums had rolled and the pipes had called from deck to deck, Blackwood had felt his own excitement rising to match the occasion. Like his grandfather's old pictures; the Nile, Copenhagen and Trafalgar.

Screens had been taken down and the ship cleared from

bow to stern. *Tenacious* mounted sixteen of the new eight-inch muzzle-loaders, but the bulk of her impressive armament consisted of thirty-two-pounders which had served the Navy for nearly a century. The 'Long Nine', as it was affectionately termed by the British sailor, was still the most reliable for accuracy and effectiveness, or so it was claimed.

When Keene, *Tenacious*'s commander, reported the ship cleared for action, Jervis had gone aft himself to inform the admiral.

The wind had eased and backed during the night, but not enough to lessen the dangers of being on a lee shore.

Blackwood had been with his lieutenants and sergeants since dawn, for with so many extra men it was not easy to place them to full advantage. Aft on poop and quarterdeck and aloft in the three fighting tops, while others were doubled up alongside gun crews with some biting comments from the seamen who manned the batteries on either beam.

Blackwood made his way to the quarterdeck and reported to Fynmore.

Fynmore pursed his lips and squinted above the packed hammocks in the nettings.

'This will not take long, I think.' He did not sound very convinced.

Blackwood took a telescope from the rack and climbed on to a shot garland.

The coast looked hostile and blurred in the grey light. There was drizzle among the pellets of spray and he felt it sting his cheek as he stared at the anchored ships which lay across the larboard bow in an untidy array.

He could see the first-rate quite clearly, a three-decker, she was standing bows-on as she swung to her cable, and he saw her loosely brailed canvas puffing against the yards, and antlike figures creeping about her rigging as they made their own preparations. One of the Russian frigates showed no sign of life, but the other was already shortening her cable and perhaps preparing to weigh if the enemy drew too close.

Weak sunlight glinted on something gold, and Black-wood shifted his glass on to the dome of an isolated church which had appeared between two overlapping hills like a giant sentinel.

Colour-Sergeant M'Crystal said, 'Admiral's on his way, sir.'

He too sounded strange and his Edinburgh dialect more pronounced than usual. Perhaps he was remembering something or feeling the same sense of history.

Ashley-Chute appeared on deck tugging on a pair of freshly laundered gloves. He glanced forward at the groups of men beside their guns and aloft to his flag at the mainmast truck.

He seemed satisfied and sniffed at the keen air as he remarked, 'Fine day for it.' He gave a brief scowl as the hull shivered, as if something heavy had fallen between decks.

Jervis watched him dourly. 'The Chief is warned and standing by, sir. Shall I give the order to raise the funnel and lower the screw?'

The admiral did not reply directly. He was examining his flagship and evidently enjoying what he saw. He took a telescope and looked first at the damaged *Sarpedon*. She had a severe list, and there were black scars on her upper deck to betray the damage which the Russian guns had caused.

Ashley-Chute crossed to another vantage point and studied the enemy. Like Blackwood, he watched the way she lay at anchor, and then gave a snort of disapproval as two additional ensigns broke from her fore and mainmasts, the white flags with their blue crosses strangely peaceful above so much artillery.

He snapped, 'Run up two more ensigns, Jervis. She's the *Rostislav*, by the way. Ran across her in Vigo some years back.'

Jervis had recognized the Russian three-decker from the moment he had come on deck, but knew it would have spoiled the admiral's mood had he told him.

Ashley-Chute said, 'This is what I intend. The shore

battery is obviously sited to protect the main anchorage, in this case the *Rostislav*, hmm?'

Jervis took his eyes from the extra ensigns as they broke stiffly to the wind.

'I suppose so, sir.'

'Be certain of it. So we shall run down on her using the wind to full advantage. Once across her bows we will come about and rake her.' His eyes glinted as he saw it happening in his mind. 'We shall lose the wind-gauge, but no matter. Our Russian friends will not know of our additional power, what you call *progress*, eh? So we shall pass 'twixt the enemy and the shore battery and *steam* sou'-east from the bay.'

Captain Jervis glanced at the commander and then at his admiral.

'Very well, sir.'

It was hard to tell if he was alarmed by the audacity of the plan or by the admiral's sudden reliance on the engine-room.

Ashley-Chute nodded as if to confirm his thoughts.

'Signal *Rupert* to stand by but to stand clear of those guns.' He smiled at Fynmore. 'Not much for your fellows to do today, Colonel. But they may learn something.'

Captain Jervis took a deep breath. 'Carry on, Commander. Load and run out. Mr Irving, alter course two points to larboard, Mr Aldham, pipe the after-guard to the braces and trim the driver, we'll shorten sail again when the range is reduced.'

Like nerves from a human brain, Jervis's officers passed his orders, which were then relayed to each deck. When the last messenger and boatswain's mate had reported to the quarter-deck, Jervis faced the admiral again.

Ashley-Chute took his sword from his flag-lieutenant and clipped it to his belt. It only made him look shorter.

'So be it, Captain Jervis.'

At the shrill of a whistle the gunports opened along the flagship's side, and to a second blast the lines of black muzzles poked out into the poor light. Between decks the gun crews on one side would see their enemy for the first time, even though their admiral's strategy would remain a mystery.

Jervis licked his lips. 'Let her fall off another point, Mr Irving, I do not want the enemy to know our intentions.'

Blackwood watched the anchored ships and saw the Russian three-decker's ports open in response to *Tenacious*'s challenge.

Smoke eddied through a vent and passed swiftly downwind as the engineers fought to keep their boilers under control until the very last moment.

At the top of the main companionway a marine bugler moistened his lips and waited for the order. Blackwood caught his eye and smiled. But the youth did not even see him. He was living each precious second, nursing it for the time when he got home to his parents in Portsmouth.

*Boom . . . Boom . . .*

Blackwood saw the flashes along the dull coastline and waited for the waterspouts to appear. Towering columns of water burst from the sea between *Tenacious* and the Russian, the rigidity of the barrage bringing a chorus of derisive jeers from the waiting gun crews.

Jervis rasped, 'Keep those men silent! Master-at-Arms, I'll flog the next one who disregards my order.'

Blackwood glanced at the powerfully built captain. This day would mean a great deal to him. His ship, his future, even his hopes for a new Navy might depend on it.

The enemy battery crashed out again and more waterspouts towered above the ships before being scattered by the wind.

Jervis said, 'Pass the word to the carronade crew. They may get a chance to engage.'

Ashley-Chute looked at him and said dryly, 'I intend to *rake* her, not step aboard!'

Jervis frowned. 'Pipe the hands to the braces, Mr Norman! Send the topmen aloft and shake out all reefs. The enemy will imagine we've seen our danger and are coming about to beat clear of the bay.'

Men swarmed up the shrouds once more, and as the yards were hauled round and extra helmsmen took their places by the big double-wheel, Jervis shot a glance forward where the boatswain's party waited with tackles and halliards to hoist the long funnel. Below decks, when the order came, another party of men would throw their weight on the lowering gear and lower the shaft and screw into the water.

Ashley-Chute sauntered across the quarterdeck and stood with one foot on a coiled hawser. He glanced up at his flag and the whipping masthead pendant and then said to Blackwood, 'Tell your fellow to sound off, hmm?'

Blackwood raised his hand and dropped it to his side.

All eyes turned to watch as the minute bugler brought his heels together and raised the instrument to his lips.

They were about to become a part of history.

# 20

# A Handful of Rifles

'One of the frigates has weighed, sir!'

Captain Jervis grunted and watched the nearest Russian man-of-war tilt over to the wind, her billowing canvas in violent disarray as she fought clear of her anchorage. She lay on *Tenacious*'s larboard bow some three cables clear, and her captain obviously knew his ship and the bay very well indeed. The frigate tacked hard round until she seemed to be skimming the wave crests with her main-yard, but slowly and deliberately she managed to steer close-hauled between the flagship and her anchored consorts.

Blackwood clung to a stay and watched intently. The frigate captain knew he was in a hopeless position to protect the other vessels in the bay unless he could gain some sea-room. With the wind to his advantage he might even manage to beat well clear and attack the disabled *Sarpedon*. Ashley-Chute would then be forced to discontinue his plan and go to *Sarpedon*'s aid. It would take a lot of time, and by then the enemy might have brought up more artillery or found some additional ships to deter the invaders.

'Man the braces! Hands wear ship.' Jervis's square jaw was set like a crag while his heavy-swell side-whiskers blew forward with the wind. 'Steer nor'-east, Mr Irving.'

With blocks and halliards squealing in protest and the seamen flinging their bodies on to the braces, *Tenacious* began to turn slowly to starboard, so that the enemy frigate seemed to hang across the opposite bow as if held there.

Blackwood saw the Russian ship setting more sails, the

blurred gleam of copper as she rolled over to expose her bilge.

The range was falling away as *Tenacious* and the frigate moved inexorably together. Jervis held the advantage and was using the wind to swing his great ship as if on a pivot so that very soon all his larboard guns would bear on the enemy.

The frigate was almost in line with the anchored *Rostislav*. Forbidden to shout or cheer, some of the British seamen and marines were nudging each other to contain their excitement while gun captains crouched and peered along their sights, hands on trigger lines, waiting for the order to fire.

It was as if someone had drawn an invisible track across the choppy water, Blackwood thought. *Tenacious* was bearing down from the seaward end while the frigate lay somewhere between her and her heavier consort. The other enemy frigate remained firmly at anchor, and even the shore battery held its fire, an unwilling spectator as their aim was blocked by their own vessels.

Ashley-Chute said calmly, 'The *Rostislav* is shortening her cable now.'

Fynmore gave his twisted grin. 'Too late for *him*, sir.'

His smile vanished as a long orange tongue flashed from the frigate's side. Several men on the quarterdeck ducked involuntarily as a ball shrieked overhead and brought down a trailing creeper of halliard from aloft.

'Stand by, the larboard battery!'

Deck above deck the lines of thirty-two-pounders pointed blindly towards the lithe, fast-moving frigate.

'*On the up-roll!*'

Captain Jervis blinked as another ball fanned overhead and punched a hole through the mizzen-topsail.

Blackwood could picture the gundecks, the shadowy shapes of the crews, their eyes gleaming in the light from the open ports. As on the upper deck where at regular intervals the lieutenants stood at their divisions, midshipmen and warrant officers between them like links of a chain.

'*Fire!*'

It was more like hitting a reef than firing a controlled

broadside. The deck bounded beneath their feet, and as the guns hurled themselves inboard on their tackles and the crews leapt forward with sponges and rammers, the smoke erupted over the deck in a solid, choking barrier.

Blackwood wiped his eyes and watched the terrible wave of destruction as it smashed along the frigate's side and rigging like an invisible scythe.

It was awful to see. One moment there was a taut pyramid of sails, a graceful hull leaning as close to the wind as she dared, and in just a few seconds she had been transformed into a wreck. Her foremast and main-topmast plunged over the side in a great mesh of spars and thrashing canvas, while lengths of her gangway and poop were flung high into the air before splashing around her to reveal the extent of the damage.

'Run out!'

Squealing on their trucks the larboard guns were hauled hastily to the ports. The dragging mass of wreckage on the enemy's hull was pulling her round like a cruel sea-anchor, so that eventually her stern would lie exposed to *Tenacious*'s broadside.

Jervis glanced at his admiral. 'Cease firing, sir?'

Ashley-Chute clasped his hands together more firmly. 'No.'

'Fire!'

The range was less than half a cable and Blackwood could hear the iron smashing through the enemy's hull, upending guns and roaring between decks with a hail of splinters and flying timbers.

Jervis called, 'Stand by to alter course.'

As the yards swung round once more and *Tenacious* turned this time towards the land her starboard guns waited impatiently for their chance of action.

The Russian three-decker's anchor broke from the ground, and as sails flapped and then hardened to the wind she began her own fight to escape from the bay which had changed from a haven into a trap.

'Stand by to starboard!'

The careering Russian three-decker would soon be directly across *Tenacious*'s bows. She was almost aback as the wind moaned into her, the same wind which the enemy had relied on for keeping the British attackers well clear and easy meat for the shore battery.

Ashley-Chute snapped, 'No point in any more deception, Captain Jervis.'

Jervis looked at him only briefly. Blackwood saw the glance. Relief that he could use his engine to protect his ship from further risk of running aground. Contempt too for the admiral who had ordered him to continue firing on a sinking, dismasted enemy and cause a terrible and unnecessary slaughter.

'Raise the funnel!'

The working party jerked into life and the tall funnel rose from the deck, its stays humming in the wind. Smoke began to gush from it even as the deck shook and settled down to a steady vibration as the lowered screw started to take effect.

An uneven crash of gunfire cut across the water and Blackwood felt some of the enemy's shots hit *Tenacious*'s hull like muted hammers.

'Starboard battery!' Commander Keene was crouched down as if he alone was sighting every gun. '*Fire!*'

Because she was almost bows-on the Russian ship received less than a quarter of the broadside, but as the sea boiled around her and great columns of water hemmed her in like pillars of ice, she was seen to rock as many of the balls smashed into her. Her sails were pock-marked with holes and lengths of broken cordage blew unchecked in the wind.

Ashley-Chute heard some of the gun crews cheering again and said, 'Let them cheer, Captain, and let those ruffians hear them!'

Grim-faced, Jervis turned away. 'Hands aloft, reef tops'ls! Stand by to come about.' He tried to gauge the engine's beat but it was drowned by the thunder of the guns as another broadside flashed along *Tenacious*'s ports.

The Russian captain had realized what was happening but could do little. Once again his enemy was close enough to prevent the shore battery from helping him in his plight. As *Tenacious*'s canvas was lashed smartly to the yards and the engine brought her further and further round into the wind she stood like a black and white cliff between the Russian and the land. By this time there was so much smoke in the bay that it would have been hard for the gunnery officer ashore to hit anything.

Blackwood ran to the poop ladder and joined Major Brabazon who was pointing down into the water as it lifted against the tumblehome like a tide.

Survivors from the Russian frigate were clinging to broken spars and an upended cutter. Others, torn and bloody, or blackened by powder burns, rolled in the swell like so much grisly flotsam.

Brabazon yelled above the din of gunfire and shouting, 'The frigate broke up, Philip! God, it must have been a terrible end!'

Blackwood winced as a musket-ball slapped into the packed hammocks. Were they that close? And who was brave or foolhardy enough to bother with a musket as the two giants drove towards each other?

Brabazon yelled, 'Look! There's her poop!'

The frigate's battered stern was riding above the water with over a dozen men clinging to its gilded scrollwork like seals on a rock. Others splashed and pleaded for help among the tossing wreckage, and Blackwood thought he saw a woman amongst them, probably the wife of one of the officers.

'*Reload!*'

One of the enemy shots had come through a forward port and yet aft on the quarterdeck they had not even seen it. A gun had been knocked away from the side and two men lay motionless on the planking. As the other guns roared out again Blackwood saw some blood run across the deck and quiver in the sunlight as if it still clung on to life.

Some of the marines growled angrily and thrust their rifles over the nettings and trained them on the swimmers.

Sergeant Quintin snarled, 'Belay that! Save yer 'ate fer later!'

'*Cease firing!*' Jervis stared round fiercely, his eyes red from smoke. 'Tell them to hold their fire, damn you!'

A whistle shrilled somewhere and voices intruded through the din of canvas and creaking spars as the order was repeated to the lower decks.

The masthead lookout, marooned and without hope if his perch was shot from under him, must have been calling for some time but his voice had gone unheard.

Blackwood snatched a telescope from one of the midshipmen and trained it towards the bows. Through the rigging and past the thin funnel and its thrusting smoke until he had found the sea directly ahead. It was like something from a nightmare. As Brabazon had surmised, the enemy frigate must have broken her back under the crushing weight of *Tenacious*'s bombardment and the forepart had plunged to the bottom. Perhaps the shock of hitting the sea bed had torn out her remaining mainmast so that it had risen to the surface again like a missile. Now, as it reared out of the waves it seemed as if the whole ship would follow it. What made it worse were the sodden corpses which still hung in the trails of torn rigging, their drowned mouths wide open as if to scream for vengeance.

Captain Jervis shouted, '*Helm amidships!* Pass the order to stop engine immediately!' He tried to remain calm, not to transmit his anxiety to his immediate subordinates.

There was a sudden and terrible silence as even the enemy stopped firing. The Russian had not understood the reason for *Tenacious*'s unexpected change of course, but used the delay to try and extricate his own ship from her menacing broadside.

The broken mast had fallen back in the water again, its drowned seamen watching intently as the *Tenacious*'s long jib-boom and bowsprit cast a shadow above them. When the mast hit the flagship's bows it was little more than a nudge to the men on her upper deck. She was a new ship, well-found and constructed of the best oak.

'Engine's stopped, sir!'

Jervis clenched his fists until the knuckles shone like bones. 'Raise the screw!'

Ashley-Chute stared at him. 'We'll lose command of her, man!' He looked up at the furled sails, the streaming flags pointing towards the land which was creeping out on either bow like giant jaws.

The broken mast reached the propeller shaft and hit it a smashing blow. This they did feel, and once again as it reeled and plunged beneath the rudder.

A breathless messenger gasped, 'Chief engineer's compliments, sir, an' to tell you the screw is out of action!' His face went even paler as he grasped the meaning of his own message.

Captain Jervis strode quickly to the quarterdeck rail.

'Mr Cuttler! Prepare to anchor!'

Men dashed to the forecastle and Blackwood heard the boatswain yelling at the anchor party to cut all the lashings rather than waste another second.

The admiral's voice was shrill as he shouted, '*Anchor?* Under those damned guns?'

Jervis jerked round. 'Hard over!' He saw the bows swing reluctantly in response to the rudder. The way had all but gone from the ship. She was too close inshore now to beat clear, and without an engine she would soon be hard and fast.

'*Let go!*' He waited only for the great anchor to splash down before he said, 'We've no choice, sir.'

The first lieutenant said quietly, 'The Russian ship is coming about, sir.' He sounded almost apologetic. 'I think she intends to engage us.'

Jervis nodded heavily. 'Very well, Mr Irving. Tell the Chief to do what he can with the shaft and let me know how serious it may be. In the meantime — '

But Ashley-Chute had recovered his composure. 'Colonel

Fynmore, your people will have their chance after all it seems.'

Fynmore seemed to grow in stature. 'Yessir.' He glared at Blackwood. 'Marines stand to, if you please.'

Blackwood beckoned to his half-brother. 'Sharpshooters aloft!'

He saw understanding and determination on Harry's face. Everything had happened so suddenly. Now bad luck or over-confidence had placed them in real danger. As the ship swung to her cable Blackwood could feel the despair transmitting along the gun crews who moments earlier had been cheering their victory.

He saw Jervis speaking with the commander and the sailing master. If the wind changed in their favour, if the screw could be got turning again, if more ships came to their aid . . . There were far too many ifs for any sort of confidence.

Alone and separate from his officers, Ashley-Chute stood and watched the Russian three-decker as she tacked round to begin a slow and careful approach. She would open fire at extreme range to give herself room to claw away if the wind turned her into another victim.

Colour-Sergeant M'Crystal joined Blackwood and said, 'They're all in position, sir. I sent two sections below to reduce casualties.' He watched the oncoming pyramid of tan-coloured sails. 'Don't like it much myself, sir. Sitting target we are.'

Blackwood saw Smithett hurrying towards him with his pistols.

*Sarpedon* was barely capable of staying afloat, and the small gunboat could do little against a powerful first-rate. And there was still one Russian frigate to contend with.

He took the pistols and said, 'So much for the age of steam.'

Admiral Sir James Ashley-Chute folded his arms and studied the oncoming three-decker impassively.

Blackwood stood near him, ready to order a detachment of marines to any part of the flagship where it would be most needed. He wondered if the admiral regretted his hasty action, his eagerness to win a victory without waiting for aid or superior guidance. The Russian *Rostislav* was approaching on almost the same course which *Tenacious* had used in her first sortie. She had brailed up all but her fighting sails, and even without a glass it was possible to see the gleam of metal in her tops as marksmen gathered in readiness for close action.

Ashley-Chute snapped, 'Make to *Sarpedon* and *Rupert*. Attack and harass the enemy.'

Blackwood saw the flag-lieutenant's apprehension as he hurried to the signals party. *Sarpedon* was in no fit state to fight, but she might provide a diversion. Anyway, she and the gunboat were all they had.

The *Rostislav* heeled heavily to the wind, her shape lengthening as she changed tack to cross *Tenacious*'s bows. The range was about half a mile, Blackwood thought. But time was more important than accuracy, and the Russians had all the time they needed.

The flag-lieutenant returned. 'Signal acknowledged, sir.'

The Russian fired a slow and deliberate broadside, the darting orange tongues flashing from bow to stern as gun by gun found its target.

Blackwood felt the hull stagger beneath him as the enemy's shots crashed into it or seared along the side like bolts of lightning.

Voices yelled orders, and men scampered below to assist the boatswain's party and to help those already working at the pumps.

Blackwood saw a marine corporal lift his cheek from his levelled rifle and stare along the deck as if to reassure himself. *Tenacious* was more than a magnificent ship of the line, to him she was home. It was not possible that they could be penned in and destroyed by one arrogant Russian.

Blackwood could see all of it on his face, the shock and the anger, when this corporal had moments before been cheering with the rest of them.

Captain Jervis raised his speaking-trumpet. 'Bow-chasers!'

The forward guns recoiled on their tackles and Blackwood saw two splashes close to the enemy's stern. It was not enough. She was already firing again even as her yards started to change direction in readiness for a different tack.

The shore battery too had reopened fire, and one shot smashed through *Tenacious*'s starboard quarter and exploded in a torrent of iron splinters.

'Sir! *Sarpedon*'s heading for the enemy!' The flag-lieutenant sounded as if he no longer believed anything.

Blackwood ran to the poop ladder and stared abeam. The steam-frigate was not making for the anchored ships or the motionless Russian frigate, but was pointing straight for the *Rostislav*.

Jervis shouted, 'Signal her to stand away, Flags!'

But the admiral's voice stopped the lieutenant in his tracks.

'Belay that!'

He folded his arms again and watched coldly as the *Sarpedon*'s forward guns opened fire. Like *Satyr*, she mounted two massive bow-chasers on her forecastle, but one had obviously been knocked out when she had been straddled by the shore battery.

A great gasp rose from the deck as the shot crashed down by the enemy's bow, the sea cascading over her beakhead and bowsprit in a solid sheet of water.

The Russian captain was already setting his foresail and trying to beat back into more open water. But his gun crews were too engrossed in their work to care for the listing, smoke-blackened *Sarpedon*. Flashes ripped along the gun-ports and *Tenacious* gave a great shiver as iron smashed into the hull and screamed through the rigging.

There was one great crack and the sound of cordage being torn apart, and faces stared wide-eyed as the whole mizzen-mast, complete with spars and furled sails, came staggering through the smoke. It smashed over the side, the trailing shrouds and stays tearing blocks and bolts from the woodwork as if they were nothing, entangling men where they stood and carrying them bodily over the side, their screams lost in the pandemonium and the roar of another enemy salvo.

Smoke billowed from the poop and through open hatchways. Seamen hacked at the treacherous rigging with their axes and tried to shut their ears to the cries from their messmates who were being dragged into the sea or cut apart by the remaining lines.

Jervis yelled, 'Mr Irving!' But the first lieutenant lay dead, a speaking-trumpet still gripped in one hand.

Blackwood looked round for Fynmore but there was no sign of him. Brabazon had already gone below with some marines to help with the dead and wounded there.

More shots crashed and splintered into the side, and a thirty-two-pounder lurched on to its side, pinning down two of its crew, while the others tried to shift the massive gun with handspikes.

Jervis looked at the admiral with desperation.

'We can do nothing, sir! In God's name, we'll lose every man-jack!'

Ashley-Chute tore off a glove and dabbed a cut on his cheek with it.

'Continue firing! That's an order! I'll not strike to a bloody Russian!'

Jervis swung away and then stood stock still, his eyes staring.

Blackwood hurried to his side. He had imagined that the captain had been hit by a splinter.

But Jervis seized his arm and pointed wildly.

'Look at *that*!'

The *Sarpedon* was drifting downwind, signal flags making a small bright pattern above her splintered deck. She must have fired several shots from her big bow-chaser, but in the chaos and horror aboard the flagship it was doubtful if anyone had seen them. One shot must have smashed through the Russian's stern and destroyed the steering gear. She was out of command, her additional canvas already carrying her broadside-on towards *Tenacious*.

Jervis said harshly, '*Sarpedon*'s done it, by God.'

Those last shots must have opened up all the previous night's repairs, for with her engine stopped and her list even more pronounced the *Sarpedon* was little more than a hulk. Blackwood saw the gunboat *Rupert* thrashing towards her, to take her consort in tow or lift off the people – he did not know or care.

Ashley-Chute snapped, 'Captain Blackwood, the Russian will be down upon us very soon. The guns won't bear. You know what to do!'

Blackwood realized that the little admiral was right beside him, his eyes desperate as he watched the enemy getting nearer and nearer. It was no use looking for Fynmore now. There was no time left. Like those other days in New Zealand and Africa.

Blackwood touched his hat. 'Very well, sir.' He tugged out his whistle and blew on it.

Then, as several red-coated figures ran from the line of crouching marines by the nettings, he swung himself on to the main-shrouds and began to climb. Without the mizzen-mast the afterpart of the ship seemed exposed and vulnerable. He climbed faster, and saw Sergeant Quintin peering down from the maintop barricade, his face split into a grin.

'Come to join us, sir?'

Blackwood scrambled over the wooden barrier and glanced at the grim, familiar faces.

'Well, Frazier, now's your chance.'

He saw Harry clambering into the foretop, waved to him as their eyes met across the destruction and death below them.

He said, 'The Russian will foul our cable. She can still fire on us, but our broadside won't bear on her. Make every shot tell. It's up to you now.'

He handed his pistols to Smithett, who had followed him at a more leisurely pace, and picked up a spare rifle.

Once he peered down at the deck and saw the admiral's strange figure below him. Men bustled about him, and wounded were dragged sobbing and screaming to the hatchways, their progress marked by scarlet lines across the deck. In spite of all this, the admiral seemed to stand alone. Whatever happened now he was ruined, and he knew it.

Blackwood thought suddenly of the quiet garden at the Maltese hospital all those months ago. Where was she at this very moment? Would she ever know what had happened to him?

More shots hammered into the hull and he felt the mast sway violently.

Quintin said, ' 'Ere come the buggers! Take aim, me beauties! Glass o' grog for the winner!'

Private Bulford pressed his cheek against the warm wood and curled his finger around the trigger. This might be the day when it all ended, he thought. Even so, it was better than being in prison like his dad.

Private Frazier's mind was empty of everything but for a man he had never met. He was watching him now, a Russian officer, resplendent in epaulettes and frock-coat. *Him first.*

With a shuddering jerk the other ship crossed *Tenacious*'s cable and began to slew into her.

Blackwood pulled the trigger and felt the new rifle kick painfully into his shoulder.

Down there in the enclosed world of smoke and searing flashes men fought and died while the two ships remained locked together. But on the Russian's quarterdeck the captain had already fallen to a shot from *Tenacious*'s maintop, and many of the other officers near him had shared his fate. Russian marksmen fired blindly through the smoke and saw their comrades die as the new pointed bullets cut through their defences and marked them down.

Unnerved by their change of fortune, the Russians tried to work their ship clear. As the *Rostislav* swung drunkenly free of the anchor cable she exposed her quarter and rounded bilge just long enough for Jervis's second lieutenant to point his remaining guns and fire. This time there was no response, and as the Russian drifted down the *Tenacious*'s side she was battered and raked for every yard of the way until blood ran from her scuppers in shining red stripes. There was more smoke too, probably from a burning wad or an upended lantern below decks.

In *Tenacious*'s maintop the marines had risen to their feet to fire down on the enemy's deck. Nobody seemed to miss, and even when a few shots smacked into the barricade they cheered all the louder, like men already driven beyond human help.

A great shudder transmitted itself up the mast and shrouds and a marine yelled, 'God, we're bloody aground!'

But Blackwood felt Quintin grip his hand and wring it until it ached, his normal sense of discipline momentarily lost.

'It's the engine, sir! Gawd, the bloody black gang 'ave got us moving again!' He too was nearly beside himself.

Blackwood grinned and leaned over the barricade to peer at the foremast. He saw Harry looking towards him and then toss him a casual salute.

Up forward axes flashed and cut through the cable, and with her last obstacle thrown aside *Tenacious* forged very slowly ahead.

A few waterspouts burst alongside, but as Blackwood climbed wearily down to the deck he felt the pain of the ship which no amount of cheering could ease.

'*Cease firing!*'

Blackwood saw men being carried to the hatches, some badly wounded, others already dead. The damage was immense, but the engine's steady throb and a growing plume of smoke told the rest of the story.

Jervis studied him grimly and said, 'That was well done, Blackwood. But for your marksmen those Russians would have battered us into submission and then overrun us. It was the closest thing I'd ever wish to see.' He clapped him on the arm and then turned as one of his lieutenants ran to report on casualties and damage.

Major Brabazon met him by the quarterdeck rail and mopped his face with a piece of bunting.

He shook his head. 'Like a bloody slaughter-house on the middle gundeck.' He eyed him curiously. 'You all right, Philip?'

But Blackwood was staring at a small bundle by the poop ladder. It was covered by a White Ensign, but there was no mistaking the outflung, gloved hand and admiral's sword by its side.

Brabazon said quietly, 'They say he just stood there. Never moved the whole time. He was killed instantly.'

Blackwood turned away. Ashley-Chute was no longer part of his life. He had gone and taken so many others with him.

He said, 'He didn't want to live after this.' He glanced at the damage, the terrible stains on the scarred decks. 'I never thought I would, but I shall miss him.'

He was even more surprised to discover that he meant it.

Later, as *Tenacious* moved slowly away from the smoke which had completely hidden the bay like something solid, Captain Jervis sent his men aloft to loose the sails and prepare to tack clear of the land before the damaged shaft broke down again.

Close by, the battered frigate *Sarpedon* clung to the gunboat's towing hawser, unaware that their admiral had died, grateful only they had survived.

Blackwood remained on deck and watched the land fade into a smoky shadow. It had been a very close thing. A lucky shot and a handful of rifles had saved the day, but only just.

He thought a lot about Ashley-Chute and the lessons he had refused to learn. How would he be remembered?

Better to be a dead hero than a live scapegoat.

# The Redoubt

Captain Philip Blackwood stood on a craggy spur of land and looked down at the crowded anchorage of Varna. Ships of every size and class, from stately three-deckers to puffing paddle-steamers, with more coming and going every day. The badly mauled *Tenacious* had left for England and the repair yard several months ago, and now, looking at this great array of allied shipping, it was hard to believe the raid had ever happened, that Ashley-Chute was dead.

Even the role of the marine battalion seemed to have lost its purpose since the death of the little admiral. They had all been landed and encamped at Varna, and while the reports had been wild with excitement about the great Anglo-French force of some sixty-five thousand troops which had smashed through the Russian defences to land on the Crimea itself, Fynmore's command had been held fretting in reserve. The Turkish resistance on the Danube had halted the enemy advance on Constantinople, and with the fleets in the Baltic and the Black Sea harrying their flanks and now actually putting an army on Russian soil, the enemy was on the defensive.

An attempt to capture the vital port of Sebastopol had been repulsed with heavy losses, but undeterred the British had landed elsewhere, had crossed the Alma and had by-passed the Russian stronghold. They had marched south to capture the harbour and town of Balaclava instead. But the casualties were mounting. There had been a steady stream of wounded from the Crimean Expedition, as it was now termed, and their daily arrival made the marines even more aware of their inaction.

Winter was almost upon them, and the optimistic suggestion that 'it would all be over by Christmas' had given way to the prospect of a stalemate until the better weather returned.

Blackwood had received one further letter from Davern. It had been short but intimate. She had heard of Ashley-Chute's death and prayed that Blackwood was safe and well. She had mentioned that her husband had accepted a supervisory appointment with the British Army which, in view of the war and his previous researches, would be of some importance to him.

He had also received a letter from his stepmother. Colonel Blackwood was poorly, his condition worsened by the news from the Crimea. He and his faithful Oates studied the daily reports like retired generals, and Blackwood was saddened to think of his father ending his days in such a manner.

Blackwood turned his back to the sea and began to walk down the track to the camp. He might just as well be at Hawks Hill with his father as here, he thought bitterly. The inaction and lack of direction was having its effect on everyone, Harry most of all. It was almost impossible to get a civil word from him, even on the subject of his father.

A private hurried towards him and saluted smartly.

'Beg pardon, sir, but the colonel's called an officers' conference. Hour's time.'

Blackwood nodded. 'Thank you, Keele.'

What would it be this time? Slackness at drill, or punishment to be awarded to marines who had broken out of camp to sample the doubtful pleasures of Varna?

Later, as he walked with Major Brabazon to the command tent, he said, 'If the men were divided up again amongst the ships they would have work to take them out of themselves, sir.'

Brabazon glanced at him and winked. 'Better than that, Philip. We're under orders. Just between ourselves, we're going across to the Crimea.'

Blackwood looked away to hide his feelings. He had been expecting it, if he was honest, hoping for it. Now that it had happened he felt strangely apprehensive.

Brabazon added cheerfully, 'The sector commander is a Major-General Richmond. Bit of a fire-eater. Must be getting hard for him if he has to call in the Marines!' He sounded confident enough.

Fynmore met his officers and waited for total silence. He was as neat as ever, but his narrow features were strained, as if he had not slept well for some time.

'Gentlemen, the battalion is being embarked this week for the Crimea.' He frowned slightly as several of the junior lieutenants raised a cheer. 'I think that will do, gentlemen!' He waved one hand towards a large map which he had hung on an easel. 'We shall land at Balaclava and await orders. Platoon commanders will ensure that our men are issued with one extra pair of boots, entrenching tools and additional ammunition as will be laid down in my standing orders.'

Blackwood watched him thoughtfully. Apart from matters of duty their paths had barely crossed, hard to believe in an overcrowded encampment. Was it because of the commendation which had been sent to *Tenacious* after her return to Varna? A special mention had been made by the commander-in-chief of the marines' part in the battle's final stages. He had left it in no doubt that but for the prompt action by the marine riflemen in the tops, *Tenacious* might now be an enemy prize and a humiliation to the allies for all time. Fynmore should have been pleased and proud. Unless . . . Always the doubt was there. Where was he when the two ships had come together? Brabazon had never mentioned seeing him, neither had the lieutenant on the middle gundeck.

He looked at Fynmore's curt gestures and wondered what was wrong with him.

Fynmore said, 'I will expect the very highest standards of discipline and determination from all ranks. We shall be with the Army, remember that, and under their overall command.'

He seemed suddenly at a loss, and Blackwood could feel the officers around him growing restless while they waited for him to continue.

Fynmore said vaguely, 'It is upon the Corps, and upon — ' He broke off abruptly and nodded at Brabazon. 'Carry on, please.'

Mystified, the junior officers hurried from the tent, and only Brabazon, Captain Ogilvie of B Company and Blackwood remained.

Fynmore gathered up some papers and let them fall on his trestle-table again.

'Something wrong, sir?' Brabazon watched him anxiously.

'*Wrong?* Why should there be, dammit?' Fynmore glared at him. 'Naturally I'm concerned about the behaviour of my command, but I am relying on you to produce the best results, right?'

'Right.'

Blackwood and the others left the tent.

Ogilvie, a pleasant if unimaginative man, remarked, 'Wife trouble, old chap. Stands out a bloody mile. Always the same when you marry a woman much younger than yourself, what?' He did not see Brabazon's warning glance. 'It needs a man to ride to hounds, that's what I say.' He sauntered towards his company lines, oblivious to Blackwood's feelings and everything else.

Blackwood thought of his father, what his young wife would do if his condition continued to deteriorate.

Brabazon grunted, 'Stupid clod. Sorry about that, Philip.'

Blackwood found that he could smile about it. His father was right, the Corps was a family in itself. It was impossible to keep any secret from anyone.

After an unexplained delay the marines broke camp and accompanied by an Army band marched down to the harbour to board their various ships.

To his surprise Blackwood found the frigate *Satyr* to be one of them. She looked older than the last time he had boarded her, scarred and well-used, but as he climbed aboard he received a further surprise. Tobin was aboard and stepped forward to greet him like an old friend.

'Who knows, Blackwood, we may really achieve something this time, eh?'

Blackwood was warmed and touched by their meeting. For Tobin no longer commanded his beloved *Satyr* but flew a broad-pendant of commodore from her masthead. Blackwood could think of no one who deserved it more.

As the assorted flotilla of vessels moved north-east into the Black Sea the weather worsened and the dust and sweat of Turkey were soon forgotten. There was a bite in the air, and a wind which cut through clothing like cold steel.

As in the rest of the ships the marines in *Satyr* were packed like herrings in a barrel, but they seemed good humoured and glad to be doing something, although M'Crystal still complained bitterly of his Irish trouble-makers even though he never seemed to catch them committing any offence, much to his disgust.

A patrolling brig met them while they were still out of sight of land, and after a brief exchange of signals Tobin ordered a change of course. They would make their final approach by night, Blackwood was told. It would be safer. It did not sound quite so straightforward as Fynmore had indicated.

Blackwood was in his shared cabin when he heard the murmur of voices on deck. He pulled on his greatcoat and hurried up the companion and saw that the deck seemed to be filled with marines and many of the ship's company.

He found Tobin with the captain by the compass, his powerful shape just one more shadow on the crowded deck.

'Shall I order my marines below, sir?'

Tobin was puffing at a massive pipe and shook his head. 'Let 'em watch. It might help later on.'

Blackwood saw the commodore's features light up, and as he turned saw the sky alive with flashes which seemed to stretch from bow to bow.

He heard the sullen boom of artillery fire, and that too was unbroken, like thunder at the height of a storm.

Tobin bit on his pipe. 'Poor devils. It's like this every night, bombardment and artillery duels, shot and shell, they get no rest.' He touched his face as some sleety rain splashed from his cap. 'Then in daylight it starts all over again.'

Blackwood moved among his men, feeling their uneasiness, their surprise at the war's intrusion.

He found the sergeants in a tight bunch by one of the paddle-boxes.

Quintin recognized him in spite of the shadows and said, 'Bit more soldierin', sir?' The others chuckled as if it was a private joke.

Blackwood smiled. 'They need us to show them how it's done.'

He felt someone touch his sleeve and saw Harry's face pale in the reflected flashes.

'Philip, we must talk.'

Blackwood pulled him from the crowd of jostling marines until they shared the warmth of the tall, sparking funnel.

'What is it?'

'It's Colonel Fynmore. His wife wrote to me. She's having a baby, had it by now, I'd think, unless something went wrong.'

The words just tumbled out of him, as if he could no longer bear to carry his secret. 'I think she's told him about it, that I used to . . .' He dropped his eyes and added brokenly, 'Well, you know.'

Blackwood exclaimed, 'But it can't be yours . . .' He nodded slowly. 'But the blame will rub off, I can see that.' He gripped his half-brother's arm, wanting to show anger but feeling only concern for him. 'You idiot, Harry. I should have guessed, I suppose. I was thinking too much of someone else.'

Harry whispered fiercely, 'It might bring disgrace on the whole family, you know what Fynmore's like.'

Blackwood felt his stomach tighten. Suppose Fynmore knew or guessed about Marguerite Blackwood's affair, he would be far more likely to use that against them.

He said, 'I'm glad you told me anyway. Perhaps nothing will happen.' He turned as an extra loud rumble thundered across the black water. It was no time to be worried about things like that. 'Try not to antagonize the colonel.'

Harry made a weak attempt to grin. 'That should be easy.'

He raised his head and ran his fingers through his hair. 'It's been driving me insane, Philip. I feel better now, telling you. My big brother. I think it must run in my side of the family.'

Blackwood started and asked sharply, 'What do you mean by that?'

Harry was still thinking of something else. 'Georgina, didn't Mother tell you? She sent her to Paris to keep her out of trouble with some fellow from the Foot Guards.' He sighed and gulped at the cold air. 'I'm going to turn in.' He hesitated. 'And thanks for putting up with me. I'll not let you down again.'

Blackwood waited by the guardrail until he realized he was half frozen and that the deck had quietly emptied.

It was getting worse, not better, he thought.

The eventual landing at Balaclava was completed almost without incident, and the last marine and piece of equipment was ashore before dawn finally opened up across the black terrain.

An army major met Fynmore and Brabazon while the other officers inspected their men and ensured that nothing had been left aboard ship.

Blackwood stood slightly apart while he waited for the lieutenants to report. In just a matter of hours the marines seemed to have changed in some way. They were on edge, unsettled by the constant murmur of gunfire, the scene of incredible desolation. Shell-scarred houses and fallen rubble, among which small areas of order and planning made a stark contrast. Army huts and tents, guns and limbers, supply waggons and great piles of crates and casks for an unseen army.

But the army was evident here too. Maybe that was the cause of the uneasiness among the marines. The soldiers looked tired out and gaunt, their uniforms stained and often ragged. Many wore beards, something unknown in the Corps. Even the major who was speaking intently with Fynmore and making grand gestures with a walking-stick was a far cry from any parade-ground.

Blackwood looked at his men. Uneven red lines beside the pitted road. Some were staring longingly at the anchored ships, others watched the sky, or tried not to listen to the guns. Each man seemed weighed down by his weapons and equipment. Apart from his Minie rifle and bayonet, every man carried a full knapsack which contained three days' rations, extra clothing, the additional pair of boots, plus blanket, greatcoat and sixty rounds of ammunition and caps which were tightly packed into a black leather pouch. When they finally moved off, each would be carrying nearly seventy pounds in weight on his back.

'A Company ready, sir!'

Sergeant Quintin grimaced as some soldiers shouted, 'Wot 'ave we got 'ere then? *Sea*-soldiers?'

Quintin muttered, 'Sea-soldiers indeed!'

'B Company ready, sir!'

An extra loud explosion shook the earth but the soldiers took no notice. It was a part of their lives.

Fynmore came over and snorted, 'Five miles march to the line. No horses for the officers either, would you believe?'

He glanced at the lines of marines. 'The army have scouts out to guide us. We will head north-west.' He handed his notes to his orderly. 'It will be night again before we can settle down.'

Captain Ogilvie asked mildly, 'May I ask what we are to do, Colonel?'

Fynmore's pale eyes followed Harry Blackwood's figure along the leading platoon. He pulled himself together and snapped, 'The enemy has a strong redoubt in that sector. Open ground. Heavy artillery.' Each phrase was short and terse. 'Lot of casualties.'

Brabazon pulled on his gloves and stamped his boots on the ground.

'What a way to begin. Like a blind man joining the cavalry.'

Nobody laughed.

Blackwood saw M'Crystal with his colour-party, the cased flag carefully laid over his massive shoulder. Sailor one day, infantryman the next.

The lieutenants took their places, the marines shouldered arms, and without further ceremony they marched away from the harbour.

There was little talking along the ranks even when they were marching at ease. It was like nothing Blackwood had ever seen, so he could imagine how much worse it was for the young recruits.

Craggy, broken hills, treeless and hostile, while along the rough, winding track they came across signs of the war they had come to join.

Great puddles which were already crusted with thin ice hid the holes where enemy shells had exploded. Broken and charred waggons, discarded tools and unfilled sandbags marked every yard of the advance. Here and there were little cairns of stones, some marked with a crude cross, others with a man's head-gear or sword. It was probably too hard to dig a grave here, Blackwood thought.

Then there were the wounded. As the guns grew louder and more personal the wounded seemed to grow in numbers. Arm in arm, hopping on sticks, or being carried on stretchers by bearers, they passed the marching marines with barely a glance.

Blackwood quickened his pace to join Harry at the head of the first platoon. He glanced at the men's faces as he strode by. Most were like stone, some looked afraid of what they might see next.

He asked, 'All right, Harry?'

Harry turned his head to stare at a man who lay on his back, his hands upheld like claws. Corporal Jones broke ranks but soon rejoined them as he cried, 'Dead, sir!' The soldier must have died even as he made his own lonely way to a dressing station.

Harry murmured, 'Did you see those soldiers back there? They're still in summer uniforms.' As if to emphasize his remark his feet crunched through some of the wafer-thin ice.

Blackwood had noticed. The marines might complain about their heavy packs, but at least they had greatcoats and blankets.

A runner scampered past. 'Halt the column!'

Fynmore strolled to the head of the marines and tapped the ground with his stick. 'Bloody army,' he muttered.

There was a clatter of hoofs and two field officers, followed by their orderlies, trotted around the next bend.

The senior officer, a grey-haired major-general, reined in his horse and studied the marines for what felt like an eternity.

' 'Tenant-Colonel Fynmore?' He had a thin, incisive voice. 'Your men are two days late.' He did not dismount. 'Arrangements have been made for you to support the line.'

Fynmore stood like a ramrod, his mouth twitching with barely contained fury.

'We were ordered to stand off because of a bombardment, sir.'

The major-general turned to his companion who was smiling hugely.

'D'you here that, Percy? *Bombardment!* Talk about the giddy limit, what?' He touched his hat with his riding crop and then spurred his horse into a gallop.

Brabazon bit on his chin strap and said, '*That* was General Richmond, God help us!'

'Royal Marines, by the right . . .' They were on the march again.

The closer they got to their allotted sector the flatter the ground became. Low hills with tracks and gullies, some man-made, which wound through them like a maze.

The army pickets knew their job well. They seemed able to

smell if a shell was about to crash down on the jagged rocks, even allowed the extra seconds for the marines to get accustomed to the need for instant movement. Down on their faces, then scrambling up again to continue towards the gunfire. Quick, nervous glances to seek out friends, to reassure, to hope.

Then they were crouching and scrabbling along endless zigzag trenches, ducking and waiting as shots crashed into the ground or murmured spitefully overhead.

They came into a cleared, saucer-shaped gun emplacement and somebody gave an ironic cheer as the first of the marines panted past.

Blackwood saw the familiar blue coats around the massive guns, the cheerful grins. It was like a home-coming, in spite of the danger. They were a detachment of the Royal Marine Artillery, and as he looked at their faces he saw a big lieutenant running, arms outstretched, towards him.

Fynmore rasped, 'Fall out the column, Sergeant Quintin. Ten minutes rest, no more.' He glared at the grinning lieutenant. 'And who are you, sir?'

Blackwood shook the man's hand. 'This is Lieutenant Dick Cleveland, sir. Used to be my second-in-command in *Audacious*.' He studied the lieutenant warmly. What a place and a way to meet after all these months and months. 'I see you've changed to the gunners, Dick.'

Cleveland chuckled. 'I thought it would be safer.' He looked round as the ground shook to another shell. 'Wrong again.'

Blackwood looked at his half-brother. How long was the arm of coincidence. It never lost its grip. But for Cleveland breaking his leg after a drunken party at Spithead, Harry would have been sent elsewhere. He might even be at Hawks Hill with their father.

He said, 'Dick is the chap who got you into this mess, Harry.'

Fynmore snapped, 'Enough of this time wasting. Rouse the men.' He tugged out his watch. 'It looks like snow.' He strode back towards Brabazon and the others.

Cleveland pursed his lips. 'I pity you, *sir*.' Then he said, 'This really is odd, meeting you like this.'

'I was thinking the same.' *Audacious*, the summer balls and regattas seemed like part of history.

'No, it's not that.' He had to raise his voice above the din of shouted commands and the clatter of weapons as the marines fell into line again. 'I've been here from the beginning. They couldn't have managed without our battery. But a week or so back we received a lot of new supplies and medical stores at the base camp. You could have knocked me down with a feather, Philip, er, *sir*. Women, out here in the bloody Crimea, well, I ask you.' He put his head on one side and smiled. 'The prettiest one of the lot came straight up to me and asked if I knew *you* of all people!'

The marines shuffled into single line for the next length of trench, but Blackwood could not move.

'Tell me, Dick, for God's sake!'

The lieutenant nodded. 'I should have realized how it was. Her name is Davern something-or-other. You must have marched right past her!'

'Captain Blackwood, sir!'

Sergeant Quintin's boots crunched towards them.

'The colonel wants you to take the lead.'

Blackwood grasped the lieutenant's hands. 'Thank you. Thank you *very much*.'

As the twisting line of marines entered the trench a second lieutenant clambered from a gun pit and joined Cleveland by the track.

'Who was that?'

'That was Blackwood. The best I ever met.' He stared bitterly at a far-off patch of smoke from an explosion. 'Still a captain. He should be in *command* of these bunglers!'

He swung round and thought of the dark haired woman by the harbour. Already they were being called angels of mercy by the wounded and sick from the battle-front. Another great boom of falling shells shook the emplacement and he tried not to think of Blackwood and what was waiting for him.

Two hundred troops had already died there in less than a fortnight.

'Prepare to fire. On the hour, by the hour, right?'

The second lieutenant nodded and hurried away.

The marines repeatedly took shelter as directed by the army scouts and pickets. Breathless and often dazed by the crashing roar of gunfire from both directions, they eventually arrived at their allotted sector. The soldiers had dug holes into the ground and along the side of the trenches and lined them with stout props and timbers. An army captain assured Fynmore that there were also deep caves in the nearest hills where a whole platoon could find shelter and prepare its rations. If they took shelter during each bombardment there was little risk unless someone got buried under falling rocks, he explained. Like the others, the captain looked worn out, his eyes ringed with dark circles to reveal the strain of daily survival.

Blackwood and Brabazon made notes while Ogilvie held up a map for the soldier to complete his explanation. There was a Scottish battalion to the right, a light infantry regiment to the left. He shifted nervously from foot to foot. He was eager to go.

The ground shook once more and some loose stones rolled over the lip of a heavily sandbagged parapet. Far beyond it, pale grey in the dull light, was another hill.

Ogilvie asked brightly, 'And what's directly to our front?'

The soldier glanced at him searchingly then tapped the map with a grimy finger.

'Sloping ground, then that hill. That's where they are. The enemy.'

Fynmore plucked at his lower lip and stared at a flake of snow as it melted on his tunic.

'Carry on, Blackwood. Section by section stand-to. I'll inspect them when you're ready.' He beckoned to his servant and orderly. 'Find my quarters and prepare things.' He walked away with Brabazon, his shoulders squared and straight.

The soldier let out a long breath. 'Thank God.' He waved to one of his sergeants, and at a shouted command the troops began to climb from their defences. 'I never thought . . .' He looked at Blackwood and tried to smile. 'Sorry about this. Can't take much more. Never been so glad to see anyone before.'

He made to leave but Blackwood said, 'If you see a Mrs Hadley at the base camp, she's a doctor's wife . . .' He did not know how to continue.

But the captain nodded firmly, his fear put aside.

'I'll remember. Blackwood. I shall tell her.' Then he was gone.

*Tell her what?* Blackwood winced as the ground quivered and more dust spewed over the sandbags. He remembered what Tobin had said about the nights, the constant bombardment. The defences looked strong enough, but no army gained ground by staying put.

He saw Harry sliding down a bank of shovelled earth and said, 'All ready?'

He nodded. 'They're fine, sir.' He smiled at their sudden formality. 'I've put the old hands among the green ones, although after *Tenacious* I should think most of them know what to expect.' He watched him and added, 'Something wrong?'

Blackwood looked at the dark clouds and felt snow on his face. So light and gentle, like a secret kiss. She was down there now. Just a few miles away. He had walked right past her. What was she doing among all the horror and the suffering?

He said simply, 'If I fall, Harry, tell her for me. Will you do that?'

Harry stared at him, his face shocked. 'You won't! What would I do?' He tried to shrug it off. 'You tell her yourself.'

'When you are quite *ready*, gentlemen.' Fynmore's voice was like the chill air. 'I will inspect the positions.'

Soon it was dark, and as the marines settled into holes and

dug-outs and wrapped themselves in their coats and blankets there was a lull in the firing.

Blackwood made his rounds along the defences and the zigzagging support trenches and visited the sentries who were posted at intervals along the sandbagged parapet.

It was too dark to see their faces, but he recognized many of the voices as each man made his report. Dialects from Yorkshire and Dorset, his own Hampshire, or from Scotland, like M'Crystal, and the harsh accent of the London slums, like Quintin's.

In the stillness he could hear bagpipes from far away and knew M'Crystal would have heard them too. The Scottish soldiers were relaxing. Just for the moment. There was a smell of cooking, the squeak of a ramrod as someone, probably Frazier, lovingly cleaned his rifle.

He felt the searing pain in his eyes as the skies lit up to great vivid flashes. The nightly barrage had begun. Whistles shrilled, and men dived for cover as the air shook and trembled to the onslaught. It came from the hill directly in front of their position. The Russian redoubt.

Blackwood pressed himself against the sandbags and gritted his teeth.

*Crash . . . Crash . . . Crash . . .*

That must be Dick Cleveland's battery firing in retaliation. It went on and on, the air cringing to the din until it was impossible to think clearly.

His grandfather would have been at home here. Would have retold the story better than anyone.

The ground shook again, and pieces of wood flew above the sandbags like shredded paper.

Blackwood continued slowly along the ramparts, touching a shoulder here or murmuring a quick word to another crouching shadow.

He reached a tiny dug-out which had been allotted to him. Smithett was there warming a pot on a small fire, and he had even found some old canvas to hang across the entrance to give an illusion of privacy.

Blackwood lowered himself on to a blanket and held his hands to the flames.

'You're a marvel, Smithett.'

The marine gave a mournful grin and poured some scalding coffee into a mug. He had found it in an adjoining trench which was occupied by a line regiment. Their high and mighty officers would never miss it.

He watched Blackwood's eyelids start to droop as he sipped the coffee. Like most of the old sweats, Smithett had heard all about the girl at the base camp. He could remember that day in Africa when he had helped the captain to carry her from the hut. The hut where they had raped her, where he had cut one of them down with his bayonet.

*Rest easy, Captain.* He listened to the rumble of guns, muffled now as the enemy shifted their sights. *We'll be needin' you tomorrer, I'm thinkin'.* He reached over and caught the mug as Blackwood's head lolled in sleep.

# A Time For Action

Blackwood climbed on to a crudely carved step and raised his head above the parapet. The first day, he thought. He stared directly ahead at the gently curving hill. It looked more brown than grey in the early morning light. No sign of life. He licked his lips and tasted Smithett's coffee. Then he examined the open ground which separated the trench from the distant hill and concealed redoubt. It was hard to look at it without feeling dismayed. A scene of indescribable havoc. The whole area was strewn with remnants of military adornment. Shakos and lance caps, and here and there a once-proud brass helmet. Rusting weapons and the rotting carcasses of slaughtered horses. There was no sign of a dead soldier, which made it worse in some way. As if their disgust had taken them away from where they had been cut down.

On either side of him he heard the marines whispering to one another as they lined the firing-step and aimed their weapons across the deserted battle-field. Looking to right and left Blackwood could see nothing of the army positions but noticed that the marines' sector bulged slightly ahead of the others, a place which might attract the brunt of an enemy attack.

M'Crystal and Quintin had not wasted their time during the night and had been into the Scottish lines to find out what they could. The Russians, it seemed, had nothing to match the British fire power, especially when it came to their rifles. They still attacked en masse, impossible to miss, but hard to stop.

He heard Fitzclarence, one of the newest second lieutenants, speaking with Corporal Jones as he inspected the ready-use ammunition and a stock of grenades which had been provided by the army. Poor Fitzclarence, he was so keen it was painful. The marines called him Girlie behind his back because of his gentle, even frail appearance.

A runner came dashing down the trench and stopped when he saw Blackwood.

'Colonel's respects, sir an' would you join B Company immediately.'

He ran on without waiting for a reply.

Blackwood jumped down and nodded to Fitzclarence. 'I shall be with Captain Ogilvie if you need me.'

B Company was spread out on the extreme left of the sector. It had taken a pounding over the weeks, and much of the defensive parapet had been blown apart. The gaps had been filled with sandbags and huge bundles of lashed sticks which were laid horizontally and called fascines by the military, and which were said to be good protection against small-arms fire.

Captain Ogilvie stood on his firing-step and surveyed the enemy positions without enthusiasm.

'Deuced difficult to see a thing, Philip.' He grinned as Blackwood joined him. 'Colonel just sent word. The army is about to mount a big attack at Inkerman. It's all *I* can do to find the damn place on my map.' He shivered. 'Bloody cold too.'

Blackwood looked across the sandbags. The view was much the same here. There were a few haphazard sap-trenches which snaked away to the left which had been started by the army for some sort of advance position. The sappers had either given up or had been caught in the open during an attack.

'Give me a glass.'

He took the telescope from Ogilvie's orderly and rested it between two sandbags.

The battle-field immediately grew in size and he saw that

it was not totally deserted. Some of the tattered uniforms contained corpses or pieces of them. A Russian trooper lay pinned beneath the carcass of his mount, a sabre still grasped in one hand.

He moved the glass upwards and saw the pale line of the enemy's ramparts. If the army attacked at Inkerman the Russians might be forced to evacuate the redoubt. Perhaps they had already gone?

Blackwood noticed that Ogilvie had one of the new five-shot Adams revolvers which gave its owner a tremendous advantage over the ordinary pistol, which, even when you found time to reload it, would often misfire.

Ogilvie saw his glance and grinned. 'Bought it in London off a Yankee gentleman. Dying to use the thing.'

They both turned as a voice shouted, 'Here they come!'

The word ran along the trench like a fast fuse, and Blackwood marvelled that such a force of the enemy could rise up apparently from out of the ground like a living tide. They must have worked around the foot of the hill, and now advanced on the British lines in a solid mass.

Ogilvie scribbled on his pad and thrust a page into a runner's fist.

'Give it to the colonel, on the double!' He peered along the parapet and shouted, 'Hold your fire!'

Blackwood found that he could watch the advancing Russians without fear. It was like seeing it from a distance, or not being here at all. Long coats, glittering bayonets, here and there a mounted officer. A sea of people, they even rose and fell like waves as they tramped into ditches and over humps of rough ground.

The marines had levelled their rifles and were peering at the enemy, each man within his own thoughts. They could not miss.

Dull bangs and then the whine of shots passing overhead showed that the artillery were awake too. Blackwood watched, sickened, as great gaps were carved through the oncoming mass, gaping, bloody paths which were instantly filled by the press of men behind.

Somewhere a bugle blared, and Blackwood imagined the whole Allied force cocking its head to listen to this small part of the war.

The front of the advancing Russians was about four hundred yards away, and although the British artillery were hampered by the sloping ground and the fear of dropping shells on their own lines, they were doing terrible damage to the closely-packed soldiers.

Ogilvie remarked, 'Must be ten thousand of the buggers.'

Blackwood glanced at him. He sounded completely untroubled.

The sergeants moved behind their sections. 'Easy, lads. Rest your eyes, 'til the order.'

There were several violent explosions from the other sector, and Blackwood guessed that the Scots had come under artillery fire to discourage them from interfering.

*It's us they want.* They probably know we're new in the line. And yet how could that great faceless mass think or plan?

Blackwood steadied his racing thoughts and said, 'I'll leave you now.'

'Quite right too. Don't want our two best eggs in one basket, what?' Ogilvie shook with silent laughter.

'Sir! The trench!' The marine sounded as if he was hysterical.

Blackwood jumped back on to the step and stared with disbelief as the abandoned sap-trench which dwindled away to the left suddenly spewed men over the edge in a wild stampede towards the British line.

*'Shift target! Hundred yards! Take aim!'*

The enemy were already firing as they came, the flashes darting from the ranks and slamming shots into the sandbags. It acted as a signal to the main attacking force, and Blackwood saw the whole mass of them begin to charge, their officers in the lead, leaning forward in their saddles as if afraid they would be overtaken.

*'Fire!'*

Along the trench the marines took aim and pulled their

triggers. Every shot must have found a target, and the pointed bullets probably cut through the leading soldiers to hit the ones close behind.

Ogilvie pulled out his revolver and examined it briefly.

'Must drive 'em back,' he said, as if his remark was addressed to the revolver.

'*Rapid fire!*'

The marines were shooting and reloading as fast as they could, faces grimly intent as they rose to the pock-marked parapet and aimed for the leaders. Horses fell screaming and were overrun by the infantry. Blackwood could hear them yelling, their voices linked into one great roar of sound.

Ogilvie yelled, 'Christ, we're not stopping them!'

There was a terrible crack and Ogilvie's forehead exploded into a gaping red hole.

Blackwood snatched the revolver from his hand and stared wildly at the advancing Russians. Fifty yards, perhaps less. They had no time to reload, but were intent on swamping all resistance by sheer weight of numbers.

Some of the marines were fumbling with their weapons and pouches, others fired before they had found a target. It was all going to be over in seconds.

Blackwood pulled out his sword. There was no other way.

'Fix bayonets!' He hauled himself on to the sandbags and stared along the ramparts. '*Up, marines!*'

There was a hoarse cheer as the marines clambered out of the trench and faced their attackers from behind their bayonets.

Blackwood raised the revolver and squeezed the trigger. He saw a man stagger and fall, an officer turning his horse towards him and spurring it on.

The marines' unexpected challenge made the Russians falter, so that a last ragged volley smashed through the leading ranks before the bayonets lunged, and sabres clanged as both groups hurled themselves together.

The Russian officer had dismounted and was brandishing his sabre to urge his men forward. He was a huge, handsome man, and Blackwood saw him cut down a marine apparently without effort.

But his eyes were on Blackwood, and Ogilvie's senior sergeant leapt forward to join him and gasped, 'Watch that un, sir!'

The sergeant reeled back, a Russian bayonet jammed through his teeth and jaw as he was hurled bodily into the trench.

Blackwood parried the sabre aside. It was like hitting a plough with a broom-handle. He saw the officer's eyes harden as he raised the great sabre for another cut, then the astonishment as he fired Ogilvie's revolver directly into his chest.

The Russian attack waned, and as they began to run back towards their lines the marines knelt down on the rampart to speed their retreat.

There was a wave of wild cheering along the trench, and as a bugle blared the order to cease firing and fall back, Blackwood heard the additional commotion of light cavalry charging from the flank to catch some of the enemy stragglers.

He vaulted down on to the firing-step and stared breathlessly at the men nearest him. A few were down, several either killed or so badly wounded they would fight no more. He glanced at Ogilvie's bloody face and was grateful for his revolver. *Otherwise* . . .

'Stretcher bearers, quickly!'

Blackwood wiped his face and throat and saw blood on his wrist. He was almost afraid to move away from the rampart in case his legs gave way. He felt as if he was shaking all over, as if the old fever had returned.

Smithett was wiping his bayonet on a piece of rag.

He asked, 'They comin' back, sir?'

Blackwood looked at him while his senses recovered.

'I think not. Later, I expect.'

A rumble of gunfire shook the air and shots whined over the trench to burst on the support lines in the rear.

Blackwood took a quick glance across the battle-field and saw that the enemy had disappeared. Swallowed up.

He watched the smoking, blackened holes which marked their advance, the scattered bodies and some crawling wounded. A solitary horse cantered through the carnage to rejoin its army. Blackwood leaned over and saw the officer he had shot sprawled beside a dead marine. The horse would need a new owner.

He heard feet pounding along the trench and saw Harry running towards him.

'You're safe, *thank God*!'

Blackwood climbed from the step. Every muscle ached. He said, 'Ogilvie's dead. I'm not sure about the rest.'

Two marines with a stretcher hurried past and a pain-filled face stared at the officers as the wounded man was carried away.

A lieutenant, hatless, his sword still in his hand, came from the far end of the trench. He stared at Ogilvie's body as if he could not believe it.

Blackwood said, 'Take command here, Mr Frere. I must report to the colonel.'

Together they walked along the trench until they found Fynmore in his command post.

Brabazon looked at them and nodded gravely. 'Rotten about Ogilvie.' It was all he said.

Fynmore had spread his map on an upended crate.

'Just had word from General Richmond. The army is on the move. This sector is the only one under threat.' He looked up, his eyes red from strain. 'That redoubt must be taken.' He nodded firmly. 'No other way.'

The adjutant said, 'The army have already tried, sir, several times.' He seemed to shrink under Fynmore's stare.

'All the more reason!' He returned to his map. 'Anyway, it's an order from Richmond himself, damn him.'

Outside the guns roared and crashed and the sky was hidden in drifting smoke, and yet in spite of it Fynmore's concentration seemed to hold the war at bay.

He said suddenly, 'The Russians were expecting to break the line. We would have had to call for support, and that would have held up the army's advance. In view of the weather, the general might even have postponed it.'

Brabazon said, 'I expect the Russians were surprised at their hot reception.'

'*Exactly*, Major!' Fynmore smiled at him. 'Don't you see? They'll bide their time, sit it out.' He folded his map with delicate care. 'If we let them. They'll not expect an attack so soon, eh?'

The others exchanged glances.

'By us, sir?' Brabazon sounded doubtful.

But Fynmore was thinking ahead. 'Speak to me like that, would he? I'll show him what the Marines can do, blast his eyes!'

They were dismissed.

Outside the dug-out the air quaked from the gunfire, but it was directed on to another sector. There was a lot to do. Bury the dead. Repair the defences. Send the wounded down the line when it was safe to do so.

Brabazon took Blackwood aside and said quietly, 'I'm speaking out of turn. You may know anyway, Philip. But the colonel heard from his wife.'

'Yes.'

'He blames young Harry. He's eaten up with jealousy and anger. Richmond's rudeness didn't help much either. Just thought I'd let you know.'

He walked towards his own company, his face prepared for what he might find.

Blackwood went to his tiny dug-out and squatted on a box. Then he took a pad from Smithett's capacious bag and after a further hesitation began to write.

*My very dear Davern . . . .*

It might be all that he could send. But at least she would know he was thinking of her.

Corporal Jones waited squatting on his haunches while Blackwood yawned and stretched himself awake.

'What's the weather like?'

Blackwood wiped his face with a damp cloth which Smithett had placed beside a mug of coffee and felt the chill in his bones. Beyond the rough curtain it was pitch-black. Another hour before dawn. He shivered.

Jones grunted. 'Snowing, sir.' Even in the frail glimmer from Smithett's candle he looked crumpled and unshaven.

We all look like that. Blackwood glanced round the tiny dug-out and tried not to compare it with a ship's ordered surroundings. A whole day had passed without incident after the Russian attack. Even the artillery had fallen quiet but for an occasional exchange between the two sides. Waiting. Holding their breath.

This was the day. They had gone over it a dozen or more times. It was risky, fatal if anything went wrong before they could cut down the distance from the enemy line. Blackwood patted his pockets and then picked up Ogilvie's fine percussion revolver. If he was to die he would take five of the enemy with him. He smiled grimly at his stupid reasoning.

'Time to go.'

Outside the dug-out the air was like a knife. Every man was wide awake and ready to begin the attack.

He found Fynmore and the adjutant in the command dug-out, the map folded and put away. If they had overlooked anything, it was too late now.

Fynmore looked at him dully. He seemed to have aged terribly in the last few days.

He said, 'If the enemy suspects you are using the sap-trench you must try to draw their fire. Major Brabazon will continue with the attack from the opposite side.' He tugged out his watch but put it away without examining it.

Blackwood nodded. He had hand-picked every man, knew each one of them either by sight or reputation. Curiously enough, the lieutenants were the only inexperienced ones. That too would soon be remedied. Except for Harry.

He looked round and asked, 'I thought Mr Blackwood was with you, sir?'

'He was.' Fynmore examined his pistol and held it to the light of a lantern. 'I've sent him on a special mission.' He looked up and added, 'He volunteered, of course.'

Blackwood stared at him and tried not to think of Brabazon's warning. Not here surely? Not today?

'May I ask what it entails?'

A sergeant peered round the curtain and said softly, 'All ready, sir.' He was whispering.

Fynmore remarked, 'He's gone ahead of your company.' He tried to appear casual. 'Grenade attack.'

Blackwood thought he had misheard. 'But he knows nothing about grenades, sir!'

Fynmore blew out the lantern and watched him through the sudden darkness. 'Good chance to learn then. Being related to you does not make him a special case.'

Blackwood felt strangely calm, even his voice sounded flat, unemotional.

'It's because of your wife, isn't it? You'd go to these lengths just to get your bloody revenge on my brother.'

Fynmore's voice sounded cracked with anger. 'How *dare* you! I'll have you court-martialled for this, stripped in front of the battalion, God help me, I will!'

There were many men waiting for the order to move, to discover if they would live or die, but Blackwood could only see Harry's face when he had told him about Fynmore's wife. Like the day when he had left him at the inn while he had gone to visit her at Fynmore's house.

'That can wait, Colonel. Ogilvie's dead and the major can't manage all on his own.' He turned away. 'What the hell did it matter anyway? She'd have done it whatever you said or did!'

Fynmore almost screamed, 'I've not finished with *you*! Stand still when I'm addressing you! You've gone too far this time — '

Blackwood stepped into the icy wind and felt the snow trying to cool his anger and despair.

'Go to hell, *sir*!'

The marines nearest the command post parted to let him through. Blackwood heard his boots squelching through the slush in the trench and waited for Fynmore to put him under arrest, but nothing happened.

It was a long walk to the other end of the sector, past where Ogilvie had died and on to a tumble-down heap of shattered rampart and torn sandbags, now almost serene beneath their layer of snow.

Two lieutenants, Frere and the willowy Fitzclarence, would be with him, and he saw M'Crystal and Quintin etched against the pale backdrop with the others.

Quintin said harshly, 'All mustered, sir. The packs an' spare gear 'as bin stowed away in a cave. Just weapons an' ammunition.'

The marines were not even wearing greatcoats. Nothing which would hamper their movements.

M'Crystal murmured, 'We heard about Mr Blackwood, sir.' He stared at the drifting flakes. 'He'll be out there by now.'

Blackwood did not answer. There was nothing anyone could do. Harry had Frazier and the new corporal, Fellowes, with him. Two good men. He thought of Harry's smile. No, three good men.

'Let's get on with it then.'

He clambered over the wrecked defences and slithered down a slope, his feet feeling for firm ground as he pictured the little pattern of sap-trenches.

It took all of twenty minutes to find the first trench. The marines flopped into it and began to crawl on their knees, their backs barely covered by the shallow sides.

The snow was a blessing, Blackwood thought. There was an awful stench, and he felt his hands fumble across things which were better unseen.

Once, where the trench was sheltered by some wooden planks, he felt his heart leap as he saw a solitary figure framed against the snow, watching their slow approach.

Quintin swore savagely and pushed the corpse aside with a

musket, and another marine retched as the weapon sank into rotten flesh.

'Pass the word. Absolute silence.'

They would not need telling, but someone might cough or sneeze.

Blackwood raised himself very slowly until his head and shoulders were above the trench. The hill was just to his right, and apparently quite close. He wanted to look back to see how far they had come but dared not move. He could smell burning, or charred wood, and his stomach rebelled as he heard rats squeaking as they did their nightly hunt on the battle-field.

The enemy did not have to rely on trenches here. The redoubt was somewhere on the hill-top, with plenty of natural cover for defending infantrymen.

He looked down and saw his hands on the edge of the trench, the sleeve of his uniform already showing a hint of colour. It would be dawn at any moment.

He wondered if Brabazon with the bulk of the marines was advancing from the other side. If they were all caught in the open they would not even get the chance to run. *Run?* Fynmore would never allow it. He would rather die. Or was he back in his empty command post? Missing, like that day aboard *Tenacious*?

Lieutenant Frere wriggled up beside him and whispered, 'Mr Blackwood's party have three grenades each, sir. I watched them leave. They will throw them all together in some nets which the adjutant found.'

Blackwood bit his lip. Grenades with their unpredictable, hazardous fuses were always a menace to those who handled them. Three in a net would be even more dangerous.

Where were they? Perhaps they had been captured and were tied up somewhere, helplessly waiting for the sound of their attack.

'Can't wait any more!'

He dragged himself out of the trench and gripped Ogilvie's revolver in his left hand. He heard the others preparing to follow him and strained his eyes to measure the last piece of open ground. Less than a hundred yards now. It seemed like ten miiles.

He darted a glance at the first men to join him. Quintin and Jones, Doak and Bulford. As Doak brushed past him he smelled the heady aroma of rum. Bayonets were already fixed, while their shakos and scabbards, and any other useless equipment, were piled in a cave like a memorial.

'Now!'

Blackwood moved away from the trench and, part walking, part trotting, the marines hurried after him, fanning out on either side, the sound of their feet growing as more and more clambered from the trench to follow.

They had been told what to do. Keep the pace down until the last moment. It was a hard order to obey or enforce without making more noise. They were moving quickly already, their eyes wide to pierce the shadows, their bayonets glinting occasionally while the snow eddied around them.

There was a startled cry and a figure seemed to rise straight out of the ground at their feet. Blackwood got a blurred vision of a levelled musket, then saw the man fade into the snow as someone drove him down with a bayonet.

There were more shouts and then the shrill of a whistle. The time had run out.

Blackwood yelled, *'Charge!'*

Then he was running with all his might, seeing nothing but the hill, while he swerved in and out of broken rocks and the remains of some abandoned gun-pits.

Flashes darted through the snow and lit up the nearest faces and pounding feet. Faster, faster.

More shots swept through and past them, and Blackwood heard someone scream and fall.

The firing was increasing from the hill-side and more marines were vanishing in the snow, their cries lost in the din of enemy muskets.

Suddenly there was one great explosion which painted the hill-side livid red, and as Blackwood's eyes throbbed to the sudden glare there was another, even higher, near the redoubt, it had to be.

To the breathless marines it was like a signal, a chance of survival when moments before they had expected to die.

Blackwood slipped and almost fell as he bounded over a fallen tree, heard M'Crystal's powerful voice controlling the charge, containing and driving his men like a shepherd with his sheep.

'*Erin go bragh!*'

The cry was wild like the moment as the Liverpool-Irish marines, the curse of the colour-sergeant's life, charged up the slope, the rest yelling meaningless words as the first group of Russian defenders broke from cover and tried to run for the redoubt. The snow swirled and danced as the figures rushed on, bayonets lunged and clashed, and as some of the Russians paused to fire several of the marines dropped dead or rolled away holding their wounds.

Blackwood saw a soldier running straight towards him, and knocked his musket aside with his sword. More were appearing from a hole in the ground, and he emptied the revolver into the tight group so that they fell back again and blocked the escape of the others.

A marine fell on to his face, and as Blackwood ran past he saw another hesitate and try to grope his way back through the wave of levelled bayonets.

Blackwood yelled, 'Advance, damn you!' He seized the marine by the belt and swung him round. 'Get on!'

He realized it was one of the Rocke twins.

The marine shouted frantically, 'It's me brother, sir! He's down!'

Blackwood forgot him as more shots hammered from the hill-top and the balls whined through the attackers.

A fire had broken out in the redoubt, probably caused by the last grenades. There had been just two explosions.

Blackwood saw a man crawling along the ground towards a discarded musket and slashed him across the shoulder before hurling himself up the last part of the slope. He clawed at buried timber and sandbags and saw Lieutenant Frere, who had managed to reach the enemy rampart before him, wheel round and fall from sight as a musket exploded almost in his face.

It was a scene from hell. Some kind of magazine or store was well ablaze, and against the leaping flames he suddenly saw Harry. The snow was swirling around him, the flakes like droplets of blood in the glow, so that he appeared to be floating.

Beyond him, shining dully through the smoke and snow, was one of the big Russian guns. Harry swung his net slowly round his head and threw it, then as he turned to run he saw Blackwood and waved.

The explosion was deafening, and while the marines flung themselves down and gasped for air in a wave of intense heat, Blackwood heard the nearest gun crash over on to its side.

He got to his feet and groped for his sword.

*'Open fire!'*

The marines dropped to their knees or remained standing while they fired for the first time since they had left their own lines.

Everything was made more confused by the din of exploding ammunition and the crack of rifles. Faces, wild with the fury of battle, loomed through the snow as the first daylight pushed the shadows aside.

Blackwood waved his sword.

*'Again!'*

His cry seemed to hang in the air like something quite apart from him. He saw his sword clattering across the overturned cannon, felt the jarring pain of his body hitting the ground. Voices were muffled as if calling through a blanket, and he tried to get to his feet, to rally them, but his mind rebelled and he fell down again.

Then came the agony, and when he put his hand to his side he felt the wetness and something jagged in his fingers. Someone was crying in terrible pain and he wondered vaguely if it was his own voice he heard.

He saw Harry, his face only inches away as he leaned over him. There was snow on his ruffled hair and he needed to reassure him. He had seen tears on Harry's cheeks, cutting through the grime of that last terrible explosion. But when he tried to raise his arm the pain smashed into him, like a white-hot axe driving into his body.

Beyond Harry there was cheering, *that* he could recognize. A bugle too.

Then just as suddenly there was nothing at all.

Philip Blackwood opened his eyes and kept them fixed on a point above his head. He had expected to see Harry, to tell him everything was all right, and the realization that there was nobody to see and total silence around him made him go stiff with terror.

*I am dead.*

When he tried to move he could feel nothing, and even the air around him seemed misty and warm, when it should have been touched with ice.

He saw a light spreading towards him, watched it fascinated as it played across the pattern of planks above him.

A face looked down and gave a slow nod. The man wore a white coat and there were little red dots on it. Blood.

The realization came through his drugged mind like a bullet.

'Where am I?' How strange he sounded.

The face said, 'Base hospital.' He nodded again. 'Welcome back to the living, Captain.'

He turned away and another face appeared to swim towards him. It was surrounded by a white robe of some kind. He struggled. If he lost her now she would vanish completely.

She rested her hand on his shoulder, her fingers cool against his burning body.

She said, 'I'm here, Philip. I'll never lose you again.'

Blackwood allowed the darkness to close over him once more. Nothing else mattered. They were together.

# Epilogue

Philip Blackwood sat in an old wicker chair, his legs propped on a stool, and stared across the well-tended grass towards the gates of Hawks Hill. It was late afternoon, and he had been sitting here on the familiar stone-flagged terrace as if he was afraid to miss something. How quiet it was, the house and grounds could be empty. Only the far-off chorus of rooks and the sound of cattle in the nearby farm broke the stillness.

Here and there the trees were already tinged with red and gold. It was the start of autumn. It did not seem possible.

He twisted round in the chair and looked up at the house. It was still hard to accept that his father was dead. He should be at that window, waiting by his table to hear the latest news of the Royal Marines wherever they were in action.

As he moved in the chair he felt the tight pain in his side. They said it might never go. It was hardly surprising, he thought bitterly. The Russian shell splinter had destroyed one rib and had left a hole big enough to contain a man's fist.

His father had died even as the ship full of Crimean wounded had dropped anchor in the Downs. In his sleep, his stepmother had told him. As he would have wished. She had kissed him lightly, her lips as cold as he had remembered them. Then she had left Hawks Hill for Paris to join her daughter. She had taken a last look around the house and had spoken with the servants. She showed no emotion or sense of loss. It almost seemed as if she had felt a prisoner here.

She had said gravely, 'It's yours now, Philip. It was what the colonel wanted.' She had brushed aside his protests. 'You

will be well cared for. Make your own life as you want it.'
Then she had gone.

Blackwood saw old Oates wandering through the copse
towards his cottage. Completely lost. A survivor without any
goal in sight. They should have died together. The old
campaigners.

Blackwood felt a prick behind his eyes. Poor Oates, he had
probably known his father better than any of them.

He recalled the moment after his stepmother had left the
house. Oates had waited for Doctor Sturges and a military
surgeon to complete their examination of his wound and had
then carried the colonel's sword into the room. He must have
been guarding it. Saving it for the first Blackwood to return
home.

That had been three months ago. After all the surgical
treatment and pain, the uncertainty and those first steps
along the hospital corridor with the aid of two sticks.

He glanced at the stick by his side, hating it, wondering
what she would say when she saw him. If she came . . . He
felt something like panic. In that one precious letter after
their meeting in Balaclava she had told him that her husband
had decided to end their marriage. He had been offered a
highly important post in India where several military hospitals were to be built under his supervision. It was an amicable
parting. There had been no love, and yet in some strange way
each had needed the other at one moment in their lives.

I will never lose you, my darling, she had written. I shall
love you and take care of you.

But that had been then. The war continued, casualties
mounted. With pain Blackwood had read of the Marines'
exploits and what it had cost. Major Brabazon had lost an arm
during that last mad charge on the redoubt. Colour-Sergeant
M'Crystal, Corporal Jones, the willowy Second Lieutant
Fitzclarence, even the hard man Frazier who had been killed
by one of his own grenades. They and many others had fallen
that day.

And weeks later, while he had been fighting against the

agony of his wound, others had followed. Like their Corps motto, *By Sea and By Land*. The tough campaigner Sergeant Quintin had died at the siege of Sebastopol, and the surviving Rocke twin had walked with fixed bayonet and had attacked a squad of Russians single-handed. Perhaps he had wanted to die after losing his brother. Blackwood wondered if Quintin ever discovered which was which before he too had been killed.

Harry had written him a strangely mature and subdued letter. It had been about Fynmore. With Brabazon in hospital, and most of his experienced officers dead or wounded, Fynmore had been forced to lead the final assault on a hill which overlooked the army's lines.

Harry had written simply. It was the bravest thing I ever saw. Fynmore was terrified and his nerve had cracked long ago, before you captured the redoubt, probably as far back as Africa. But he loved the Corps more than life itself, and he led his men to victory and died doing it. To be so terrified and to do what he did was real courage.

Blackwood had heard since that Fynmore had been mentioned as one of the first recipients of the Queen's new medal when it was eventually struck. Fynmore would have liked that.

He heard steps on the stones and saw Smithett crossing the terrace. *We shall be like my father and Oates*, he thought.

Smithett said, 'Time to get inside, sir. There's a nip in the air.'

In his sober black coat he looked every inch the perfect valet. He was that and far more. Sometimes, as Blackwood sat in the library for a last drink, Smithett would enter, gauge his mood and then bring out his endless tit-bits of memory. About so-and-so in the *Audacious*, or how they had rescued Private Doak from a brothel in Malta.

Blackwood watched the gates. Davern might not even have reached London. She had said in her letter that she would go first to Slade's house. She might have changed her mind. He could not blame her.

'Look, sir.' Smithett took the blanket from Blackwood's legs. 'Me old gran used to say, "A watched pot never boils." She'll come, you see if she don't.'

Blackwood smiled at him. Of course, he had almost forgotten Smithett's close link with both of them. The hut by the river, the smell of death, the look in her eyes as she had fallen against him.

He stared at the copse, the darkening shadows which made the trees look solid and invulnerable. It was all his now, and yet he felt like an interloper, as if at any moment he would see his father striding through the grounds giving orders to Woodstock, the head gardener, as if he were addressing his sergeant-major.

He heard carriage wheels beyond the gates and sighed. 'That bloody doctor again.'

Smithett folded the blanket over his arm, his mournful face giving the hint of a smile.

'Oh, I dunno about that, sir. Now, up we get, nice an' easy like.' He watched Blackwood's sudden anxiety. 'She didn't ferget us arter all, sir.'

Blackwood saw the fine carriage, the one with Slade's crest on the door, sweeping up the drive. Behind him he could hear the housekeeper's harsh voice as she held the servants at bay. Smithett must have spoken with her about this moment. Only he would have thought of it.

Blackwood took a step towards the drive and gasped as the pain shot through him. *Not now. Dear God, not now.*

Smithett snapped, 'Stick, sir!' He thrust it into his hand. 'She's seen more wounded than we have, I s'pect.'

But the stick flew clattering down the steps as Davern alighted from the coach and ran to meet him.

Blackwood felt her arms around his neck and tasted her tears, or were they his own?

Smithett watched for a few seconds and then picked up the stick.

Best leave 'em, he thought. The captain would not need a prop any more.

# *First to Land*

## Douglas Reeman

1899, China. The Mandarins are becoming troublesome again and there are rumours that attacks will soon begin on British trade missions and legations. Captain David Blackwood of the Royal Marines, received a VC in the bloody battle for Benin, Africa but is now being packed off to this apparent backwater.

But there are plenty of troubles in store for Blackwood in the shape of an errant nephew and a beautiful German Countess who insists he personally escort her up river on a small steamer into the heart of the country. China is a sleeping tiger that will soon awake when the Boxer Rebellion erupts into bloody war in 1900. True to their motto, the Royal Marines are the first to land – and the last to leave.

This is the second novel in the Blackwood saga, spanning 150 years in the history of a great seafaring family and the tradition in which they served.

arrow books

# *Dust on the Sea*

## Douglas Reeman

It is 1943, and Captain Mike Blackwood, Royal Marine Commando, is a survivor. Young, toughened and tried in the hellish crucible of Burma, he labours, sometimes faltering, beneath the weight of tradition, the glorious heritage of his family, and the burden of his own self-doubt.

For Blackwood, the horizon is not the lip of the trench seen by men of the Corps in the previous war, but the ramp of a landing craft smashing down into the sea, and the fire of the enemy on a Sicilian beach.

Here, tradition is not enough, and Mike Blackwood must find within himself qualities of leadership which will inspire those Royal Marines who are once again the first to land, and among the first to die.

This is the fourth novel in the Blackwood saga, spanning 150 years in the history of a great seafaring family and the tradition in which they served.

arrow books

# In Danger's Hour

## Douglas Reeman

Aged only 28, Ian Ransome was already a veteran of warfare.
Captain of the fleet minesweeper HMS *Rob Roy*, he daily faced
the ever-present risk of death – from the air or the sea – in
waters strewn with lethal mines.

But the summer of 1944 is on the horizon. As the allies prepare
for D-Day, Ransome must steer *Rob Roy* towards her most
dangerous mission yet: a deadly challenge that will test captain
and crewman alike to the limits of endurance – and beyond . . .

*In Danger's Hour* is the electrifying bestseller by the master
storyteller of the sea, Douglas Reeman. Full of human drama,
suspense and unforgettable battle scenes, it tells the story of the
unsung heroes of the navy's 'little ships' who fought in one of
the most dangerous areas of war.

arrow books

# THE POWER OF
# READING

**Visit the Random House website and get connected with
information on all our books and authors**

**EXTRACTS** from our recently
published books and selected
backlist titles

**COMPETITIONS AND PRIZE
DRAWS** Win signed books,
audiobooks and more

**AUTHOR EVENTS** Find out which
of our authors are on tour and
where you can meet them

**LATEST NEWS** on bestsellers,
awards and new publications

**MINISITES** with exclusive
special features dedicated to
our authors and their titles

**READING GROUPS** Reading
guides, special features and
all the information you need
for your reading group

**LISTEN** to extracts from the
latest audiobook publications

**WATCH** video clips of
interviews and readings with
our authors

**RANDOM HOUSE INFORMATION**
including advice for writers,
job vacancies and all your
general queries answered

**Come home to Random House**
# www.randomhouse.co.uk